John L. Power

The epidemic of 1878, in Mississippi

Report of the yellow fever relief work

John L. Power

The epidemic of 1878, in Mississippi
Report of the yellow fever relief work

ISBN/EAN: 9783742833471

Manufactured in Europe, USA, Canada, Australia, Japa

Cover: Foto ©Andreas Hilbeck / pixelio.de

Manufactured and distributed by brebook publishing software
(www.brebook.com)

John L. Power

The epidemic of 1878, in Mississippi

NOTE.

A copy of this Report is sent free to every person through whom relief funds were received. To others, Fifty Cents per copy—profits, if any, over cost of publication, to go to the Relief Fund.

H. W. Walter

The Epidemic and Relief Work.

Extracts from Annual Report of Grand Secretary.

Jackson, Miss., January 10, 1879.

To the Most Worshipful Grand Lodge of Mississippi :

I beg leave to submit my Tenth Annual Report and Account Current.

*   *   *   *   *   *   *   *   *   *   *

The suddenness and violence with which the yellow fever seized upon the western side of our State, left but little time for preparation to battle with the terrible scourge. Over quarantine lines and into atmosphere odorous of disinfectants, the yellow plague marched at will, leaving terror, destitution and death, in its track. Many of our people, who could do so, fled before its approach, but thousands were unable thus to go to places of safety. For these, relief must be provided as far as human agency could afford it. With business generally suspended, stores closed, and the people of the infected towns shut off from intercourse with the outside world, the situation was such as to excite the gloomiest apprehensions of all who remained within the fever belt. The pestilence begun its work so early and became so general, that three months or more must elapse before our section could be restored to its wonted health, and business resume its accustomed channels. Every day seemed a week, every week a month, and every month a year. Verily, we knew not what a day might bring forth.

When the fever became epidemic at Grenada and Vicksburg, and cases were occurring at other places, I asked permission of our M.·. W.·. Grand Master to draw upon the funds in our treasury for the relief of the afflicted localities. He promptly telegraphed me his approval, and afterwards sent me his written authority to dispense the Grand Lodge funds at will—that he could not rest a moment, nor sleep, in custody of the means of relief when our afflicted brethren were in need of the absolute necessaries of life—that he would rather err, if at all, in liberally helping the needy. Upon this authority, I drew a warrant for five hundred dollars, and had it been necessary

your treasury would to-day be empty. But our brethren, and the people
everywhere claimed the privilege of helping us in our time of need,
and the amazing aggregate of funds that has passed through my
hands, as one of the many agents in the work, shows how promptly,
how nobly, how generously our country, and indeed the world, came
to our assistance. I am sure that our kind friends must have realized
that—

> "No radiant pearl that crested fortune wears,
> Nor gem that twinkling hangs from beauty's ears;
> Not all the bright stars that night's blue arch adorns,
> Nor e'en the rising sun that gilds the vernal morn,
> Shines with such lustre, as does the tear that flows
> Down virtue's manly cheek for others' woes."

On the 21st day of August, while gloomily meditating on the
prospect before us, the little telegraph messenger at Jackson handed
me this dispatch :

GRAND MASTER'S OFFICE,
GRAND LODGE OF LOUISIANA,
New Orleans, August 21, 1878.

To J. L. Power, Grand Secretary, Jackson, Miss.:

The Masons of Louisiana beg to tender their mite of two hundred
dollars to their afflicted brethren of Mississippi. Call on Capital State
Bank, Jackson, who are authorized by Southern Bank to pay it.

EDWIN MARKS, Deputy Grand Master.

Of this I made grateful acknowledgment, and at once sent the following telegram to the country, through the Associated Press :

JACKSON, August 21, 1878.

To the Masonic Fraternity of the United States and Canada :

The Masons of Louisiana have sent an unexpected and unsolicited
contribution of two hundred dollars to their distressed brethren in
Mississippi. We shall be glad to receive and disburse other contributions from the Craft. The distress and destitution at Vicksburg,
Grenada and Canton is appalling. We are in hourly expectation of
the pestilence at Jackson. J. L. POWER, Grand Secretary.

On the same day, by request of Brother W. G. Paxton, Grand
Commander of Knights Templar, I prepared and mailed a circular
appeal to the Templars of the country; and a week later, Brother
John H. McKenzie, Grand Master of Odd Fellows, telegraphed an
appeal for help, requesting that all contributions be sent direct to me,
as Grand Treasurer of that Order in this State. By telegraph, by
express, and by the mails, money came freely—the receipts for a
time varying from one thousand to four thousand dollars per day.

The telegrams and letters herewith submitted show how profoundly
were the sympathy and generosity of the country aroused in our behalf. As I read over these loving messages, even now, tears of gratitude come unbidden. Many others, outside of both Orders, who

were collecting relief funds in different parts of the country, directed
their contributions to me; and His Excellency, the Governor of this
State, transferred to your Grand Secretary the various amounts received
by him, aggregating about seven thousand dollars.

Detailed and classified exhibits of all receipts are herewith submitted :

Exhibit A shows receipts from Masonic sources, aggregating, $47,-
653.04.

Exhibit B shows receipts from Odd Fellows, $16,165.14.

Exhibit C shows receipts from miscellaneous sources, $12,701.24.

Premium on gold, $17.49.

Exhibit D gives a recapitulation of all receipts, making the grand
total of $76,536.91.

It being my wish to publish a detailed report, in pamphlet form,
so as to send a copy to each contributor to the relief fund, I submit
only for record here the summary of funds received :

SUMMARY OF RECEIPTS.

ALABAMA—Masonic	$ 558.64	
Odd Fellows	80.00	
Miscellaneous	140.95—$	724.59
ARIZONA TERRITORY—		
Masonic	50.00—	50.00
ARKANSAS—Odd Fellows	391.85	
Miscellaneous	5.00—	396.85
CALIFORNIA—Masonic	2,330.00—	
Odd Fellows	2,700.00	
Miscellaneous	3,254.00—	8,284.00
COLORADO—Masonic	183.75	
Odd Fellows	75.00	
Miscellaneous	150.00—	408.75
CONNECTICUT—Masonic	1,245.60	
Odd Fellows	300.00—	1,545.60
DAKOTAH TERRITORY—Masonic	100.00	
Odd Fellows	136.00—	236.00
DELAWARE—Odd Fellows	129.50—	129.50
DISTRICT OF COLUMBIA—Masonic	550.00—	550.00
FLORIDA—Masonic	50.00	
Odd Fellows	35.00—	85.00
GEORGIA—Masonic	181.00	
Miscellaneous	17.68—	198.68

ILLINOIS—Masonic	$4,501.14	
Odd Fellows	1,585.00	
Miscellaneous	175.00—	$ 6,261.14
INDIANA—Masonic	727.70	
Odd Fellows	856.00	
Miscellaneous	281.65—	1,865.35
IOWA—Masonic	2,142.45	
Odd Fellows	638.60	
Miscellaneous	18.25—	2,799.30
KANSAS—Masonic	450.00	
Odd Fellows	71.90	
Miscellaneous	51.50—	573.40
KENTUCKY—Masonic	424.00	
Odd Fellows	460.00	
Miscellaneous	12.00—	896.00
LOUISIANA—Masonic	225.00	
Odd Fellows	110.00—	335.00
MAINE—Odd Fellows	160.00	160.00
MARYLAND—Masonic	860.00	
Odd Fellows	285.50—	1,145.50
MASSACHUSETTS—Masonic	410.00	
Miscellaneous	86.50	
Knights of Honor	50.00—	546.50
MICHIGAN—Masonic	2,085.00	
Odd Fellows	1,000.00	
Miscellaneous	1,242.06	
Knights of Honor	100.00 —	4,427.06
MINNESOTA—Masonic	750.00—	750.00
MISSISSIPPI—Masonic	3,136.13	
Odd Fellows	167.65	
Miscellaneous	1,458.58—	4,762.36
MISSOURI—Masonic	2,185.50	
Odd Fellows	35.00—	2,220.50
MONTANA—Masonic	516.00	
Odd Fellows	101.00—	617.00
NEBRASKA—Masonic	763.45	
Odd Fellows	49.80—	813.25
NEW JERSEY—Masonic	1,373.24	
Odd Fellows	388.40	
Miscellaneous	130.00—	1,891.64
NEW BRUNSWICK—Masonic	50.00—	50.00

NEVADA—Masonic	$ 50.00	
Miscellaneous	50.00—$	100.00
NEW YORK—Masonic	9,461.68	
Odd Fellows	1,531.00	
Miscellaneous	1,960.00—	12,952.68
NORTH CAROLINA.—Odd Fellows	56.10	
Miscellaneous	78.00—	134.10
OHIO.—Masonic	2,638.90	
Odd Fellows	2,212.50	
Miscellaneous	10.00—	4,861.40
ONTARIO.—Masonic	500.00—	500.00
PENNSYLVANIA.—Masonic	1,382.05	
Odd Fellows	1,142.84	
Miscellaneous	2.00—	2,526.89
RHODE ISLAND.—Masonic	300.00	
Odd Fellows	200.00—	500.00
SOUTH CAROLINA.—Masonic	411.55—	411.55
TENNESSEE.—Knights of Honor	20.00	
Miscellaneous	1.00—	21.00
TEXAS.—Masonic	1,482.35	
Odd Fellows	152.50	
Miscellaneous	241.70—	1,876.55
UTAH.—Masonic	510.25	
Odd Fellows	100.00—	610.25
VIRGINIA.—Masonic	836.00	
Miscellaneous	1,490.37—	2,326.37
WEST VIRGINIA.—Masonic	931.66	
Odd Fellows	780.25—	1,711.91
WISCONSIN.—Masonic	3,240.00	
Odd Fellows	125.00—	3,365.00
WASHINGTON TERRITORY.—Masonic	55.00—	55.00
WYOMING TERRITORY.—Masonic	10.00—	10.00
UTAH, COLORADO, NEVADA.—Odd Fellows	43.00—	43.00
COLORADO AND SANDWICH ISLANDS.—Odd Fellows	82.75—	82.75
STATES NOT KNOWN.—Odd Fellows	53.00—	53.00
FOREIGN COUNTRIES.—Miscellaneous	1,675.00—	1,675.00

Total Masonic receipts	$47,653.04
Total I. O. O. F. receipts	16,165.14
Total miscellaneous receipts	12,701.24
Premiums on gold	17.49
Total receipts from all sources	$76,536.91

41 States and Territories. 2 British Provinces. Mexico and other foreign countries.

JANUARY 1, 1879.

Exhibit D shows a detailed statement of disbursements, a voucher in every case being herewith filed. The following shows the

DISTRIBUTION OF RELIEF.

Grenada	$ 8,790.00
Holly Springs	8,299.48
Dry Grove	2,565.60
Lake	2,875.00
Greenville	5,082.40
Port Gibson	3,250.00
Vicksburg	13,045.70
Water Valley	3,307.93
Osyka	861.00
Canton	1,350.00
McComb City	1,781.55
Jackson	2,854.65
Sharon	150.00
Yazoo City	600.00
Tchula	110.00
Tallahatchie County	850.00
Tillatoba	500.00
Hernando	500.00
Bolton	1,637.00
Garner	800.00
Crystal Springs	50.00
Senatobia	250.00
Oakland	300.00
Winona	30.00
Byram	50.00
Terry	50.00
Summit	25.00
Edwards	450.00
Near Baldwin's Ferry	50.00
Crystal Springs	50.00
Macon*	500.00
Memphis	175.00
New Orleans	275.00
Natchez Orphan Asylums (Protestant and Catholic)	750.00
Lebanon neighborhood	202.00
Brandon	50.00
Lawrence Station	50.00
Miscellaneous†	319.35
Total	$62,836.66

The judicious distribution of relief was attended with many difficulties. Vicksburg was the only point where our Craft had an organized Relief Committee. I was advised that Bros. Paxton, Fair-

---

* The brethren at Macon had contributed more than six hundred dollars for relief. The recent disastrous fire at Macon, though not destroying their hall, crippled their ability to pay a debt on same—hence $500.00 of their contribution was returned, without any suggestion or solicitation on their part.

† This includes $50.00 for the family of Lieut. Benner, in response to suggestion of Bro. D. C. Creiger, Chairman of Chicago Masonic Relief Committee, who was persistent in his kind remembrance of our State.

child, French, and a few others, had resolved to remain and share the perils of the pestilence as well as the glory of alleviating the sufferings of their fellow-creatures. The Odd Fellows of Vicksburg were also organized with an efficient Committee—Bro. Chas. Lehman as chairman. To these two Committees I forwarded, at various times, amounts aggregating more than ten thousand dollars. A detailed report of the Masonic Committee has been published, and shows the active part taken by our brethren in relieving the general distress in the heroic Hill City.

The following are a few of the many telegrams forwarded and received during the epidemic, and are submitted to show how I endeavored to anticipate the wants of each afflicted place, and how timely was the relief thus distributed:

JACKSON, September 27, 1878.

Col. W. J. L. Holland, Chairman Relief Committee, Holly Springs:

How is your Committee off for funds? Make requisition on me when needed and I will respond promptly. J. L. POWER,
Grand Secretary.

———

HOLLY SPRINGS, September 17, 1878.

To J. L. Power, Grand Secretary:

Five deaths and eleven new cases in the last twenty-four hours. Your last shipment of one thousand dollars to hand. I have no words in which to express the thanks of our suffering people. KINLOCH FALCONER,
for Relief Committee.

———

This telegram had reference to the thousand dollars shipped on the 13th to our lamented Past Grand Master, Harvey W. Walter, who was taken sick the day the package reached Holly Springs. On the 19th, this beloved brother—one of Mississippi's noblest sons—"lawyer, statesman, soldier, patriot, christian"—succumbed to the pestilence, and is seen no more among us.

JACKSON, September 23, 1878.

To Thos. H. Woods, Chairman Relief Committee, Meridian, Miss.:

Desiring to assist your Committee in your noble efforts for relief of Lake, I have had Peoples' Bank requested to pay you one thousand dollars. This is from the Masonic and Odd Fellows' Relief fund. Expend it as to you may seem most judicious for the relief of all at Lake. Can send you more when needed, on your notice. J. L. POWER, Grand Secretary.

REPLY TO ABOVE.

MERIDIAN, September 23, 1878.

J. L. Power, Grand Secretary:

God bless you for your splendid donation. We were greatly depressed, as we had only funds for one more day. So far we have been able to meet every demand from Lake. THOS. H. WOODS, Chairman Ex. Com.

On the 29th I again renewed offers of assistance, and received reply that none was needed. On 7th October, I telegraphed five hundred dollars additional.

The following are responses to telegrams sent Vicksburg :

VICKSBURG, September 13, 1878.

J. L. Power, Grand Secretary :

Will advise should we need any help from you. Thanks.

W. M. ROCKWOOD,
President Howard Association.

VICKSBURG, September 13, 1878.

To J. L. Power, Grand Secretary :

Am out again. We have plenty of funds for the present. Paxton better. WM. A. FAIRCHILD, Secretary and Treasurer.

From Port Gibson :

PORT GIBSON, September, 4, 1878.

To J. L. Power, Grand Secretary :

Many thanks, dear friend and brother, for your kindness in relieving our wants. Your drafts for nine hundred dollars received. Please acknowledge the same to proper sources, and return many thanks. At present, 460 cases and 64 deaths to date. JAS. A. GAGE, Pres. Howard Association.

By the 10th I had forwarded two thousand dollars additional, and received Bro. Gage's prompt acknowledgements.

GRENADA.

I had special difficulty in the distribution of relief to this place. I sent funds to Bro. W. E. Hughes until he was taken sick. On the 6th of September I saw it stated that Bro. Wm. J. Ayres, Noble Grand of the Odd Fellows Lodge, was still on duty. I expressed him five hundred dollars. On the day following, I received a telegram from the Express Agent that the money was received, but that Bro. Ayres had died the day the package left Jackson. Other amounts, sent to the members of Relief Committees, would be acknowledged by their survivors. Eighteen members of Grenada Lodge, No. 31, and eleven other members of the Order, and forty-two members of their families, died in Grenada during the epidemic, leaving seven widows and forty-seven orphans. Fourteen Odd Fellows, and eighteen members of their families, also died of the fever — leaving four widows and twenty orphans to the care of Grenada Lodge, No. 6.

On the 23d of September, I telegraphed the following acknowledgment, through the Associated Press :

JACKSON, MISS., September 23, 1878.

To the Freemasons and Odd Fellows of the United States :

In behalf of our afflicted brethren and their families in our fever-stricken communities, and in behalf of hundreds of others who have been relieved by your timely and generous benefactions, I return you profound thanks for the noble response that you have sent to our appeals for help. I have thereby been enabled to answer promptly every call from the ten places in the State where the fever is prevailing, and, with the funds on hand and now coming, will doubtless be able to meet every demand until the close of the epidemic. Should there be any surplus it will be distributed as judiciously as possible for the benefit of the hundreds of orphans bequeathed by the plague to impoverished communities. In their behalf I would still enlist your generous sympathy. The relief received through me has been dispensed, as far as practicable, through the committees of both orders, without regard to race, color or creed. Such has been the expressed wish of nearly every Lodge and brother contributing. I am now obtaining lists of families having special claims upon our care, so that none may be overlooked in the distribution. I have received to date nearly Fifty Thousand Dollars—nearly all from Masons and Odd Fellows. In due time a full report of this good work, which it has been my privilege to conduct, will be given to the generous contributors and to the public. It will be a testimony to the goodness and the gratitude of the human heart. [Signed.] J. L. POWER,

Grand Secretary of Masons,
Grand Treasurer of Odd Fellows.

Our Masonic brethren, and the Howard Association in New Orleans, and the Howard Associations of Canton, Vicksburg and Port Gibson, had telegraphed their grateful thanks to the country, stating that enough had been received for any probable demand, and that further contributions should cease. I, therefore, felt impelled to do likewise, although against my judgment, for I had reason to believe that other infected points, not so accessible, would need assistance before the close of the epidemic. When I sent out the appeal on the 21st of August, I supposed that the last three pages of my cash book would be sufficient for the entry of the few thousand dollars that might come in response; and when the card of September 23d was issued, I took it for granted that funds would then cease coming. Since that date, however, I have received upwards of twenty-five thousand dollars—the last contribution to hand being on the 3d inst.

THE SPIRIT OF THE GIVING.

The following letters and telegrams are submitted to indicate the spirit and character of the relief received:

GRAND LODGE OF NEW YORK,
GRAND SECRETARY'S OFFICE,
NEW YORK, Sept. 12, 1878.

To R∴ W∴ J. L. Power, Grand Secretary:

In order that it may not be charged against the Fraternity that the funds remitted to the Masonic authorities in the South are expended for the benefit of Freemasons only, the Grand Master directs me to request that you will, if the means at your disposal will permit, consult with the Howard Associations, so that the relief afforded may be as general as possible. The Grand Master makes this request at the instance of brethren who believe that a Mason's charity should be as extensive as the wants of suffering humanity. This sentiment is doubtless as universal with you as with us;

still we must guard against the misapprehensions of our friends, as well as the misrepresentations of the enemies of our ancient and honorable institution.

Fraternally Yours,

JAMES M. AUSTIN, Grand Secretary.

INDIANAPOLIS, Sept. 21, 1878.

J. L. Power, Grand Treasurer I. O. O. F.:

Yours, acknowledging the receipt of my last remittance ($300.00) came duly to hand. Should you need further assistance from our Jurisdiction, do not hesitate to send me a telegram to that effect. Accept our warmest sympathy for your stricken and suffering people.

Fraternally, B. T. FOSTER, Grand Secretary.

GRAND LODGE OF ILLINOIS, I. O. O. F. }
ROCKFORD, Sept. 30, 1878. }

J. L. Power, Grand Treasurer:

DEAR BROTHER.—In your last acknowledgment of $500.00, you stated that you hoped to not need further relief, aside from what was in hand and in transit. If you find that you were mistaken, I hope you will not fail to notify me at your earliest convenience. Illinois wants to render aid as long as there remains a suffering brother in your midst. Hoping that Providence will interpose in staying the hands of the destroyer, and that our brothers, and the citizens of your afflicted State will, ere many days, be again restored to health. I have the honor to be, fraternally yours,

JOHN LAKE, Grand Master.

On the 28th of October, Bro. Lake sent $500 additional.

SAN FRANCISCO, September 18, 1878.

To J. L. Power, Grand Secretary of Masons:

I send you one thousand more, same manner as before. Acknowledge by telegraph, and say whether you want more. We have plenty.

ALEX. G. ABELL, Grand Secretary.

To this I replied:

JACKSON, Miss., September 19, 1878.

To Alex. G. Abell, Grand Secretary, San Francisco, Cal.:

Thanks for your splendid contribution. Our California brethren have done enough. Please don't send any more. Remittances now coming from other places will be ample. Have supplied all pressing calls, and will have something for the widows and orphans when the fever subsides. May you always be able, as you always have been willing, to help the distressed.

J. L. POWER, Grand Secretary.

SAN FRANCISCO, September 18, 1878.

To J. L. Power, Grand Treasurer, I. O. O. F.:

Have telegraphed one thousand dollars to your credit for the relief of Odd Fellows, where most needed, in your State.

W. B. LYON, Grand Secretary.

The receipts from foreign countries include $700.00 from the City of Mexico, through United States Minister Foster; two contributions from the Odd Fellows of Honolulu, Sandwich Islands, and several amounts through the Hon. Wm. M. Evarts, Secretary of State, Washington, at the instance of Hon. O. R. Singleton.

PERSONAL DISTRIBUTION OF RELIEF.

My own reflection, as well as intimations from Grand Master, resulted in the setting apart of about twenty-five thousand dollars for the widows and orphans of our brethren who could not be reached during the epidemic through Relief Committees or otherwise. On this point, the following was issued:

JACKSON, Oct. 15, 1878.

Except about six thousand dollars, received from various sources, all the relief funds received by me have been from Masons and Odd Fellows in nearly every State in the Union. The Masons have contributed about $45,000, and the Odd Fellows about $10,000. I have thus far been able to respond to every call made upon me by fifteen different communities, besides affording personal relief to individuals at different places. Relief has been dispensed without regard to race, color or creed. I am now admonished by those who have the right to advise and instruct me as to the further distribution of relief, that the afflicted families of Masons and Odd Fellows must henceforth be specially looked after. I will not be able, therefore, except in extreme and special cases, to respond to any further calls from general Relief Committees, unless funds for such purpose shall come into my hands. I will thank my brethren in the afflicted towns to report to me such cases as may need immediate relief, giving particulars as to Masons and Odd Fellows who have died, and the necessities of their families.   J. L. POWER,

Grand Secretary of Masons,
Grand Treasurer of Odd Fellows.

In order to carry out more effectually the object thus indicated, I resolved on a personal visit to each of the afflicted localities. Want of time, and the extraordinary labors incident to the work embraced in this Report, prevented the complete carrying out of this programme. The places visited are as follows:

Lake, October 31st; McComb City, November 12th; Bolton, November 26th; Winona, November 29th; Grenada, November 30th; Osyka, December 4th; Holly Springs, December 14th; Water Valley, December 15th. In lieu of a visit to Dry Grove, I requested the Wor. Master and Secretary of Lodge No. 321, to come to Jackson, and after a full conference as to the necessities of families in that neighborhood, handed them nearly eight hundred dollars for distribution.

Of some of the details of this method of distribution, I ask the indulgence of the Grand Lodge while I submit a verbal statement, as it might not be proper to place on record the personal references necessary to explain, and commend this course to your approval. [Here made verbal statement.]

And now, brethren, there is a respectable balance on hand, for the reason that I did not have time to dispose of it. I have set apart

$3,000 00 for Greenville, and have promised a visit to that place immediately after the close of the Grand Lodge. [Visited Greenville February 16th.] I wish also to visit Meridian, Canton and other places, so as to complete the statistics of death and orphanage that I am compiling as an appendix to this Report.

Deducting the $3,000,00 set apart for Greenville, the unexpended balance is $13,700.25, which is derived from the three funds—Masonic, Odd Fellows and Miscellaneous. The two latter funds constituting over a third of the total receipts, and the same proportion being deducted from the total now on hand, the Masonic proportion of the reserve is $9,000.00. As to the distribution of the Odd Fellows' proportion of the fund, the Grand Master of that Order will be consulted; and as to the Miscellaneous portion, there are cases of destitution resulting from the yellow fever where it can be at once and judiciously applied. Should the completion of this work be confided to your Grand Secretary, I would dispose of the Masonic proportion within the next sixty days, upon the following basis, subject to such modification as personal investigation might justify:

Grenada	$1,500.00
Holly Springs	1,000.00
Vicksburg	1,000.00
Meridian	1,000.00
Natchez Protestant Orphan Asylum	1,000.00
Osyka	600.00
Lake	600.00
Canton	500.00
Towns on Mississippi and Tennessee Railroad	500.00
Jackson	400.00
Bovina and vicinity	350.00
Destitute widows and orphans at other places	550.00
Total	$9,000.00

Water Valley, Grenada, Greenville and McComb City, to be further aided from the Odd Fellows' and Miscellanous fund. Our Port Gibson brethren—Masons and Odd Fellows—have respectable relief funds on hand. The Masonic Relief Committee there has recently returned to me a surplus of fifteen hundred dollars of the funds which I had sent the Howard Association, and which was transferred by the Association to Relief Committee. This is included in balance on hand.

The amount suggested for the Protestant Orphan Asylum, at Natchez, will be much needed, as the demands upon such institutions are increased by such terrible afflictions as the one through which we have passed.

Brethren of the Grand Lodge, my work is now submitted for your inspection. As your humble agent in receiving and disbursing so large an amount of money, I have the proud satisfaction of knowing that you will find the facts and figures as submitted sustained by proper vouchers. It is due to myself, it is due to this Grand Body, and especially is it due to the generous and charitable people everywhere, who contributed to the fund, that the manner in which I have discharged the great trust thus suddenly imposed upon me, shall undergo the careful scrutiny of this Grand Lodge. I therefore respectfully ask that a special committee of expert accountants—cashiers of banks, if such are members of this Grand Lodge—shall be appointed to examine and report. I have here thirty-seven packages of vouchers, representing as many communities to which relief has been dispensed—all of which are tabulated—so that while the pile may look formidable, the arrangement is such as to facilitate examination. Should the committee, at the close of their labors, be able to say, "well done, faithful servant," I shall feel amply rewarded for all the labor, anxiety and responsibility of the past few months.

As your agent, in the work of relief, I have had written and said to me enough kind things to satisfy the ambition of almost any man for the good will of his fellows. The moistened eye, the falling tear, the hearty "God bless you!" and "God bless the Masons and Odd Fellows!" have strengthened and encourged me in the prosecution of the work, and have filled me with gratitude for the privilege of being the almoner of the bounties of others. Onerous as has been the duty, I shall regret when it is out of my power to say to the widow or orphan who may apply, *I have no more to give.* To Him who has declared "I will be a husband to the widow and a father to the fatherless," I do most prayerfully commend the bereaved of the Epidemic of 1878.

In closing this report, I desire to return grateful acknowledgement to the railroads, express and telegraph companies, the banks and the public press for zealous co-operation. To the Capital State Bank, at Jackson, I am specially indebted for the facilities afforded in the work of relief. This bank kept open daily, supplying me with currency as needed, and cashing drafts to the amount of sixty thousand dollars, without discount or exchange, in a single instance.

Fraternally submitted,   J. L. POWER,
                                              Grand Secretary.

The foregoing Report was referred to a Special Committee, consisting of Bros. Robert C. Patty, Macon Lodge, No. 40; John S. Jones, Ebenezer Lodge, No. 76; C. L. Lincoln, Columbus Lodge, No. 5; B. T. Kimbrough, Salem Lodge, No. 45; Allen M. Hicks, Dover Lodge, No. 197.

REPORT OF COMMITTEE.

To the Most Worshipful Grand Lodge of Mississippi:

The Special Committee, to whom was referred so much of the R.˙. W.˙. Grand Secretary's Report as relates to the Epidemic and Relief Work, beg leave to report that they entered upon the immediate discharge of the duty assigned, with a view to making report thereon at the present Grand Communication, but now find it impossible, if the examination be made thorough and critical, as desired by the Grand Secretary. They have, therefore, decided to continue their work, and will make report to the Most Worshipful Grand Master, as authorized by the resolution under which the Committee was raised, unless the Grand Lodge shall see proper to order otherwise.

The Committee recommend the adoption of the accompanying resolution in relation to the disbursement of the relief funds remaining in the hands of the Grand Secretary. Respectfully submitted,

ROBERT C. PATTY, Chairman,
for the Committee.

Resolved, That R.˙. W.˙. Grand Secretary, J. L. Power, be and he is hereby authorized and requested to distribute the balance of relief funds now in his hands, in accordance with the suggestions contained in his Annual Report, or in such other manner as to him may seem right and proper.

Adopted.

Since the foregoing was submitted to the Grand Lodge, I have carefully compared the entries in my cash book with the exhibits following, and after correcting sundry errors made in the haste of preparing the report for Grand Lodge, the Exhibits of Receipts are now submitted with great confidence that every contribution through me is fully acknowledged. The disbursement of the balance is being made as fast as practicable, and when vouchers are all in, a final report will be submitted to the Committee as above.

RECEIPTS.

EXHIBIT A.

RECEIPTS FROM MASONIC SOURCES.

ALABAMA.

Aug. 24.	Montgomery Chapter, No. 22, Wm. D. Wadsworth, H. P...$	100 00
Sept. 2.	Helena Lodge, No. 410, Helena, Shelby county, Horace Bowers, Secretary......................................	20 00
5.	D. J. Miller, member of Marshall Lodge, No. 209, Guntersville..	25 00
6.	Per Daniel Sayre, Grand Recorder, Montgomery:	
	Eufaula Commandery, No. 9.............................	26 00
	Cyre Commandery, No. 10..............................	23 00
	Montgomery Commandery, No. 4	21 00
13.	Per Daniel Sayre, Grand Secretary :	
	Athens Lodge, No. 16....................................	25 00
	Forkland Lodge, No. 230................................	20 00
	Tuskegee Commandery, No. 11.........................	7 00
	Benton Lodge, No. 59, Benton, B. Wolff, Secretary.	25 00
16.	Masons of Guntersville, per D. J. Miller...............	46 30
	(See, also, I. O. O. F., and Miscellaneous subscriptions—$150 00 in all—from Bro. Miller.)	
20.	Mobile Commandery, No. 2, and Alabama Commandery, No. 6..	20 00
20.	Selma Commandery, No. 5—this and foregoing through Daniel Sayre, Grand Recorder........................	20 50
27.	Masons of Selma, per Wm. T. Daughtry, Geo. R. Boyd, Committee...	103 84
28.	Reagan Lodge, No. 341, Davistown, Ala., via Oxford, W. E. Bowling, Secretary.............................	15 00
30.	Sir Bernard Jacob, Selma Commandery, No. 5, per Daniel Sayre, Grand Recorder......	15 00
Oct. 7.	Liberty Lodge, No. 65, Liberty Hill, Dallas Co., per Daniel Sayre, Grand Secretary.....................	25 00
10.	Masons of Selma, per W. T. Daughtry and Geo. R. Boyd, Committee......................................	6 00
7.	Fulton Lodge, No. 98, Orrville, Dallas Co., B. T. Garnet, Treasurer.......................................	10 00
	Total from Alabama..$	553 64

ARIZONA TERRITORY.

Sept 20.	Azitan Lodge, Prescott, (used in Vicksburg)............$	50 00

CALIFORNIA.

Sept. 1.	Grand Lodge, per Alex. G. Abell, Grand Secretary, San Francisco, gold...	500 00
5.	Pacific Lodge, No. 136, San Francisco....................	50 00
5.	Magnolia Lodge, No. —, " "	30 00
7.	Excelsior Lodge, No. 128, " " Geo. C. Randall, W. M...	100 00
10.	LaParfait Union Lodge, No. 17, San Francisco.........	50 00
13.	Per Alex. G. Abell, Grand Secretary Grand Lodge, gold...	500 00
19.	Per Alex. G. Abell, Grand Secretary Grand Lodge....	1,000 00
19.	Woodland Chapter, No. 46, Woodland, N. Wycoff, H. P..	100 00

Total from California...$ 2,330 00

Premiums on gold elsewhere aggregated.

COLORADO.

Aug. 26.	Union Lodge, No. 7, Denver....................................	50 00
Sept. 14.	Golden Lodge, No. 1, Golden, Robert D. Haw, Secretary, $50 00; by members, $10 00	60 00
25.	El Paso Lodge, No. 13, per Roger W. Woodbury, Grand Master, Denver..................................	63 75
Oct. 2.	El Paso Lodge, No. 13, per Roger W. Woodbury, Grand Master, (for Masons and their families)......	10 00

Total from Colorado...$ 183 75

CONNECTICUT.

Sept. 12.	Per Jno. W. Stedman, Grand Recorder, Norwich :	
	Palestine Commandery, No. 6, New London..........	53 00
	Hamilton Commandery, No. 5, Bridgeport............	25 00
	Clark Commandery, No. 7, Waterbury.................	100 00
4.	New Haven Commandery, No. 2, New Haven..........	25 00
16.	Columbian Commandery, No. 14, Norwich, Allen Tenny, E. C...	150 00
16.	Grand Lodge, per J. K. Wheeler, Grand Secretary, Hartford..	250 00
21.	Columbian Commandery, No. 14, Norwich, Allen Tenny, E. C...	10 00
27.	Per J. K. Wheeler, Grand Secretary, Hartford.........	386 60
29.	Clinton Commandery, No. 3, per John W. Stedman, Grand Recorder..	21 00
Oct. 6.	Per J. K. Wheeler, Grand Secretary.....................200 00	
28.	New Haven Commandery, No. 2, per John W. Stedman, Grand Recorder.....................................	25 00

Total from Connecticut...$ 1,245 60

DAKOTAH TERRITORY.

Sept. 16. Per Geo. P. Hand, Grand Master, Yankton............$ 100 00

DISTRICT OF COLUMBIA.

Aug. 26. Per Alex. Gardner, Treasurer Relief Committee, Washington,.. 50 00
Sept. 1. Per Alex. Gardner, Treasurer Relief Committee, Washington,.. 250 00
Sept. 7. Per Alex. Gardner, Treasurer Relief Committee, Washington,.. 250 00

Total from District of Columbia.......................$ 550 00

FLORIDA.

Sept. 1. Escambia Lodge, No. 15, Pensacola, per G. E. Wentworth,..$ 50 00

GEORGIA.

Sept. 14. Atlanta Lodge, No. 59, per W. F. Parkhurst, Chairman Board of Relief,.................................... 131 00
" 19. Benevolent Lodge, No. 3, Milledgeville, per Lucius J. Lamar, Sec'y., (for Masons at Vicksburg.)........... 25 00
" 24. Benevolent Lodge, No. 3, Milledgeville, per Lucius J. Lamar, Sec'y., (for Masons at Grenada.)........ ..... 25 00

Total from Georgia...$ 181 00

ILLINOIS.

Aug. 26. Jackson Lodge, No. 53, Shelbyville, $29 00; citizens, $34 00.. .... 63 00
29. Mt. Carmel Lodge, No. 239, Mt. Carmel,............... 20 00
29. Tyrian Lodge, No. 333, Springfield,...................... 20 25
30. Masons of Chicago, per DeWitt C. Creiger,........... 400 00
30. Masons of Galesburg, per Dr. S. L. Lambert, Sec'y., 50 00
Sept. 2. Lexington Lodge, No. 482, per John F. Burrill, Grand Secretary, ... 10 00
2. Freeburg Lodge, No. 418, Freeburg, per W. H. Wilderman, Sec'y.,... 10 00
2. Mrs. Dr. Paul Sears, $10 00; Jacob Knell and lady, $5 00; per R. S. Gordon, W. M. Mt. Carmel Lodge No. 239,.. 15 00
5. Masonic Aid Ass'n., Peoria, per Crosby White, Treas., 150 00

Sept.	8.	Dunlap Lodge, No. 321, Morrison, Frank Clendeniu, Secretary,...	82 00
	9.	Masons of Jacksonville, per Leopold Weill, Treasurer,	75 00
	12.	Greenfield Lodge, No. 129, J. W. Hutchinson, W. M.,	20 00
	16.	Orlin H. Miner, Grand Treas. Grand Lodge, Springfield,...	500 00
	16.	Orlin H. Miner, Grand Treas. Grand Lodge, Springfield,...	500 00
	16.	Marine Lodge, No. 355, Madison county, per Albert H. Judd, W. M.,...................................	20 00
	19.	Sumner Lodge, No. 334, Sumner, M. May, W. M.,...	15 00
	24.	Orlin H. Miner, Grand Treasurer Grand Lodge, Springfield,...	500 00
	24.	Pittsfield Lodge, No. 56, Pittsfield, per O. H. Miner, Grand Treasurer, (for brethren at Greenville,)......	40 00
	24.	Masons of Chicago, per DeWitt C. Creiger,..............	200 00
	24.	Rossville Lodge, No. 527, Rossville, Vermillion county, per Harry Shannon, chairman committee, through Maj. E. G. Wall, for Port Gibson,...........,.	32 50
	29.	Orlin H. Miner, Grand Treasurer Grand Lodge, Springfield,...	500 00
Oct.	2.	Masons of Chicago, per DeWitt C. Creiger,..............	150 00
	3.	Contributions of Lodges, per Orlin H. Miner, Grand Treasurer,..	300 00
	9.	Masons of Chicago, per DeWitt C. Creiger,............	150 00
	14.	Clinton Lodge No. 14, Petersburg, Jas. S. Black, Secretary, (for Masonic relief only,) handed to a Mason's widow, whose husband and two sons had died of fever,............	25 00
	18.	Masonic Relief Committee of Peoria, per Crosby White, Treasurer,...................................	83 65
Nov.	2.	Masons of Chicago, per DeWitt C. Creiger,.............	130 27
	4.	Orlin H. Miner, Grand Treasurer, Springfield,.........	439 47

Total from Illinois...$ 4501 14

INDIANA.

Sept.	2.	Lessing Lodge, No. 460, Evansville, Karl F. Thieme, Secretary,..	25 00
	5.	Horeb Chapter, No. 66, Jeffersonville, per S. S. Johnson, G. H. P.,..	25 00
	9.	Clark Lodge, No. 40, Jeffersonville, F. W. Poindexter, W. M.,..	25 00
	16.	Mt. Vernon Lodge, No 163, Mt. Vernon, Sylvanus Milner, W. M.,...	41 50
	20.	Spencer Chapter, No. 77, Spencer, per John M. Bramwell, Grand Secretary,..............................	40 00
	20.	Sir Knight Collins Blackmer, Lafayette, per John M. Bramwell, Grand Secretary,...	5 00
	20.	Wm. H. Smythe, Grand Secretary, Indianapolis, (sent to Holly Springs direct, at my request,)..............	316 50
	28.	Goshen Lodge, No. 12, and Travel Lodge, No. 306, Goshen, per John B. Walk, W. M. No. 12, and J. A. Carmien, W. M. No. 306,............................	53 25

Sept. 28.	Per Bro. John M. Bramwell, to-wit: Monroe Lodge, No. 22, and Masons of Bloomington,..................	28	55
	Mitamora Lodge, No. 156, Mitamora,..................	31	80
	Greencastle Chapter, No. 22, Greencastle,............	15	00
	Jerusalem Chapter, No. 81, Sullivan,..................	10	00
29.	Sundry Lodges, per W. H. Smythe, Grand Secretary,	63	00
Oct. 4.	Wm. H. Smythe, Grand Secretary, Indianapolis,......	5	00
5.	Kingston Chapter, No. 33, Kingston, Geo. W. Williams, Secretary,.................................	32	00
26.	Washington Chapter, No. 13, Brownstown, D. A. Kochenour, W. M.,................................	11	10

Total from Indiana.. ....$ 727 70

IOWA.

Aug. 30.	Malta Commandery, No. 31, Ottumwa, W. A. Mc-Grew, E. C.,..................................	25	00
30.	Masons of Shenandoah, per J. Swain, ...	15	00
Sept. 2.	Masonic Fraternity of Muscatine, per Wm. B. Langridge, Grand Secretary,...........................	46	00
2.	Masons of Marshalltown, per Geo. Glick, Treasurer Marshall Lodge, No. 108,........................	28	75
4.	St. Bernard Commandery, No. 14, Belle Plains, Jas. Collister, E. C.,.................................	50	00
4.	Masonic Relief Committee, Waterloo, H. W. Jenney, Secretary, through combined efforts of Waterloo Lodge, No. 105; Victory Lodge, No. 296; Tabernacle Chapter, No. 52; Oscalon Commandery, No. 25,	100	00
4.	Appolo Commandery, No. 26, Cedar Rapids, Jas. Morton, E. C.,..................................	50	00
5.	Bluff City Lodge, No. 71, Council Bluff, John T. Oliver, Secretary,..............................	75	00
6.	Mt. Horeb Chapter, No. 46, Belle Plain, $10; a Knight Templar, $1; per W. B. Langridge, Grand Sec'y.,	11	00
6.	Bruce Commandery, No. 34, Red Oak, per C. G. Atwood, E. C.,..................................	50	00
8.	Cyrus Chapter No. 13, Washington, per Comp. W. B. Langridge,..................................	25	00
8.	Davenport Chapter, No. 16,.........................	25	00
6.	Green Lodge, No. 315, Jefferson, Frank Hassett, Sec'y.,	26	80
10.	W. B. Langridge, Grand Secretary Grand Chapter,	68	00
10.	Excalibur Commandery, No. 13, Boone, R. J. Hiatt, Recorder,..................................	35	00
12.	Chapter No. 32, Clinton; No. 35, Decorah; No. 53, Charles City; No. 48, Manchester; No. 74, Clarksville, per W. B. Langridge, Grand Secretary,........	95	00
12.	Commanderies: No. 9, Davenport; Nazareth U. D., Manchester; No. 12, Decorah, per Comp. Langridge,..................................	58	00
12.	Chapters: Hebron, No. 76, Hamburg, $25; Henry, No. 8, $5 25, per Comp. Langridge,..................	30	25
13.	Clinton Chapter, No. 9, Ottumwa,...................	25	00
13.	Trinity Chapter, No. 16, Monticello,................	25	00
13.	Chapter No. 2, Iowa City,..........................	25	00

Sept. 13.	Commandery No. 2, Iowa City,	25 00
13.	Pilgrim Commandery, No. 20, Clarinda, per C. Linderman,	30 00
16.	Masonic fraternity of Waterloo, J. W. Jenny, See'y,	60 15
16.	J. W. Wilson, Grand Master Newton,	400 00
16.	Per W. B. Langridge, Grand See'y, Grand Chapter, viz:	
	Montgomery Chapter, No. 57, Red Oak,	50 00
	Clarinda Chapter, No 29, Clarinda,	20 00
	Potowonot Chapter, No. 28, Fort Madison,	10 00
	Dubuque Chapter, No. 3, Dubuque,	51 50
	Tadmor Chapter, No. 18, Knoxville,	5 00
	Shekinah Chapter, No. 44, Riverton,	25 00
	Corner Stone Chapter, No. 64, Jefferson,	25 00
21.	Per Wm. B. Langridge, Grand Secretary, viz:	
	Oriental Commandery, No. 22, Newton,	26 00
	Baldwin Commandery, No. 11, Cedar Falls,	25 00
	Valley Chapter, No. 20, Cedar Falls,	25 00
	Harmony Chapter, No. 41, Elkader,	15 00
	Osage Chapter, No. 36, Osage,	7 00
23.	From Grand Master J. W. Wilson, Newton,	200 00
24.	Mt. Gerizum Chapter, No. 59, Glenwood, per Comp. Langridge,	10 00
Oct. 4.	Tyrian Chapter, No. 37, Adel,	5 00
26.	Masonic Relief Com., per A. W. DeForest, Desmoines,	45 60
Sept. 13.	Per Wm. B. Langridge, Grand See'y Grand Chapter:	
	Triune Chapter, No. 81, Mo. Valley,	10 00
	Benevolence Chapter, No. 46, Mason City,	25 00
	Jerusalem Chapter, No. 72, Marengo,	25 00
	Marion Chapter, No. 10, Marion,	25 00
	Raboni Chapter, No. 85, Avoca,	16 00
14.	Anchor Chapter, No. 69, Hampton,	15 00
	Lafayette Chapter, No. 61, Bonaparte,	25 00
	Monticello Chapter, No. 42, Monticello,	25 00
	Chariton Chapter, No. 22, Chariton,	10 00
	Sir Kt. J. J. Childs, of Muscatine, (making contributions from here $50 in all,)	3 00
16.	Bloomfield Chapter, No. 25, Bloomfield,	35 00
	Geber Chapter U. D., Monroe,	10 00
	Gate City Chapter, No. 7. Keokuk,	25 00
	Doric Chapter, No. 54, Tama City,	25 00
	Gebal Chapter, No. 12, Newton	15 00

Total from Iowa, ...$ 2142 45

KANSAS.

Aug. 30.	Masonic Fraternity of Leavenworth, per J. V. Ellard, H. P., of Leavenworth Chapter, No. 2	125 00
Sept. 2.	Grand Lodge, per John H. Brown, Grand See'y	100 00
	Kansas City Lodge, No. 220, H. C. Litchfield, See'y,	30 00
7.	Junction City Chapter, No. 17, Geo. F. Trott, See'y..	50 00
10.	Rising Sun Lodge, No. 8, Fort Scott	50 00
20.	Erie Lodge, No. 76, per John H. Brown, Grand Secretary, Wyandotte	20 00
24.	Emporia Chapter, No. 12, Emporia, W. W. Hibben, H. P	50 00

Oct. 21. Solomon City Lodge, No. 105, per John H. Brown,
Grand Secretary... 25 00

Total from Kansas..$ 450 00

KENTUCKY.

Sept. 4. DeKoven Lodge, No. 577, Union County, per Grand
Master Campbell H. Johnson, Henderson............. 16 00
9. Masonic Relief Committee, Louisville, per C. R.
Woodruff, Chairman...................................... 200 00
14. Hopkinsville Lodge, No. 37, Sam'l O. Graves, W. M. 103 00
20. Hamilton Lodge, No. 354, Hamilton, J. P. Johnson,
Secretary.. 5 00
Aug. 30. Henderson Commandery, No. 14, B. G. Witt, E. C.,
subscription by Masons of the town of Henderson, 100 00

Total from Kentucky...$ 424 00

LOUISIANA.

Aug. 21. From Edwin Marks, Deputy Grand Master, the first
contribution received.................................... 200 00
Sept. 2. Aurora Lodge, No. 193, New Iberia, Joe Indest, Sec'y 25 00

Total from Louisiana...$ 225 00

MARYLAND.

Sept. 6. Knights Templar, per Jacob E. Krebs, Grand Commander.. 500 00
24. Knights Templar, per Jacob E. Krebs, Grand Com-
mander.. 360 00

Total from Maryland...$ 860 00

MASSACHUSETTS.

Sept. 7. From Grand Master Chas. A. Welch, Boston........... 100 00
10. John Viall, D. D. G. M. 17th District, 145 Pearl st.,
Boston... 10 00
23. From Grand Master Chas. A. Welch................... 300 00

Total from Massachusetts..................................$ 410 00

MICHIGAN.

Sept. 6.	Zion Lodge, No. 1, Detroit, J. B. H. Bratshaw, Chairman Committee................................	150 00
7.	Wm. P. Innes, Grand Secretary, Grand Rapids........	150 00
9.	Wm. P. Innes, Grand Secretary, Grand Rapids........	200 00
14.	Wm. P. Innes, Grand Secretary, Grand Rapids........	300 00
16.	Wm. P. Innes, Grand Secretary, Grand Rapids........	150 00
17.	Wm. P. Innes, Grand Recorder, Grand Rapids........	325 00
18.	Masons of Michigan, per Wm. P. Innes, Grand Sec'y	280 00
21	Knights Templar, per Wm. P. Innes, Grand Sec'y....	100 00
25.	Knights Templar, per Wm. P. Innes, Grand Sec'y....	400 00
Oct. 3.	Masonic Relief Committee, Detroit, J. B. H. Bratshaw, Chairman............................	30 00

Total from Michigan..............................$ 2,085 00

MINNESOTA.

Sept. 16.	Knights Templar, per A. T. C. Pierson, Gr'd Rec'der	350 00
	Contributions of Lodges, per A. T. C. Pierson, Grand Secretary....................................	100 00
28.	Knights Templar, per A. T. C. Pierson, Gr'd Rec'der	75 00
	Contributions of Lodges, per A. T. C. Pierson, Grand Secretary....................................	225 00

Total from Minnesota..............................$ 750 00

MISSISSIPPI.

Aug. 16.	Grand Lodge, per order Grand Master Chas. T. Murphy.....................................	500 00
26.	Friendship Lodge, No. 127, Como, Panola County....	25 00
29.	Brookhaven Lodge, No. 241..........................	32 00
30.	Aberdeen Lodge, No. 32—for Vicksburg, $75; for Grenada, $75; for Port Gibson, $50..............	200 00
	Mt. Moriah Lodge, No. 86, Black Hawk..............	25 00
Sept. 6.	McComb City Lodge, No. 382........................	25 00
	State Line Lodge, No. 316, L. C. Peaster, Secretary..	25 00
7.	Carrollton Lodge, No. 36. Benj. Roach, Secretary.....	25 00
10.	Masons of Summit, per Geo. T. Gracey..............	41 50
11.	Iuka Lodge, No. 94, $25; private contributions, $19 45	44 45
	J. M. Wesson Lodge, No. 317, $25; members of same, and non-affiliates, $30, per F. B. Hartwell, Sec'y..	55 00
12.	Magnolia Lodge, No. 120, and other Masons, Bay St. Louis, F. W. Elmer, W. M.........................	35 00
	Booneville Lodge, No. 305..........................	100 00
	Claiborne Lodge, No. 110, Geo. P. McLean, Sec'y. ...	10 00
13.	Thos. Hinds Lodge, No. 58, Fayette, Henry Key, Sec'y	100 00
	Coahoma Lodge, No. 104, Geo. R. Alcorn, Secretary	20 00
	Macon Lodge, No. 40, T. T. Patty, Secretary..........	100 40
	Members of Lexington Lodge, No. 24, J. Marlow, Sec'y	23 75

Sept. 13.	Caledonia Lodge, No. 280, A. L. Myers, W. M.........	15 00
16.	Oak Grove Lodge, No. 293, S. G. Martin, Secretary...	20 00
	Members of Tehula Lodge, No. 122, Holmes County, per Jas. T. Meade, G. W. Shackelford, W. M., $10; Jno. Shackelford, $10; A. Marks, $5; W. B. Jones, $5; R. M. Murphy, $5; T. J. Wyatt, $5; S. D. Gwin, $5; P. T. Jones, $2 50; B. Y. Alverson, $2 50	55 00
	Louisville Lodge, No. 75, W. B. Shumaker, Sec'y....	25 00
	Jonesborough Lodge, No. 250, I. W. Park, W. M....	10 00
	Macon Lodge, No. 40, T. T. Patty, Secretary...........	100 00
18.	Ripley Lodge, No. 47, for Vicksburg.....................	10 00
	Greensboro Lodge, No. 49, H. F. Bays, Treasurer......	10 00
	Madison Lodge, No. 73, W. G. Kearney, Secretary...	20 00
	Chapel Lodge, No. 180, E. A. P. Lucas, W. M.........	10 00
19.	Macon Lodge, No. 40, T. T. Patty, Secretary............	150 00
	Pontotoc Lodge, No. 81, M. R. Fontaine, special committee...	27 85
20.	Rienzi Lodge, No. 172, John T. Fowler, Secretary....	25 00
	Fairfield Lodge, No. 304, Ellistown, J. P. Robinson, Secretary...	10 00
21.	Theodocia Lodge, No. 182, Sarepta, J. B. Philips, Sec'y	10 00
	Mt. Moriah Lodge, No. 236, Silver Creek, J. J. Denson, Secretary...	10 00
23.	Woodlawn Lodge, No. 330, Caledonia, A. P. Pressly, Secretary...	15 00
	Pascagoula Lodge, No. 202, per W. Denny & Co., Scranton..	100 00
	Macon Lodge, No. 40, T. T. Patty, Secretary............	74 40
	Marietta Lodge, No. 188, E. H. Tyra, Secretary........	15 00
24.	Double Springs Lodge, No. 251, J. E. Vaughn, Sec'y	20 00
25.	Benj. Franklin Lodge, No. 170, Meadville, T. J. Scott, W. M...	10 00
26.	Sycamore Lodge, No. 385, $25 for Lodge, and $16 for members, per N. J. McMullen...............................	41 00
14.	J. M. Howry Lodge, No. 187, Taylor's Depot, B. F. Archer, Secretary (all the funds in treasury).........	12 00
	Liberty Lodge, No. 37, Wm. B. Raiford, Secretary....	25 00
	Slaughter Lodge, No. 295, Shuqulak, W. D. Clark, Wor. Master..	16 00
	Tabernacle Lodge, No. 340, Pine Valley, J. M. Thornton, Secretary..	15 00
	Macon Lodge, No. 40, T. T. Patty, Secretary............	76 00
	Macon Lodge, No. 40, T. T. Patty, Secretary............	10 00
	Sunflower Lodge, No. 228, McNutt, D. N. Quinn, Wor. Master..	55 00
16.	Abert Lodge, No. 89, Starkville, W. A. Hale, Relief Committee...	27 70
10.	Burnsville Lodge, No. 233, J. K. Moody, Secretary...	17 00
28.	John A. Galbreath Lodge, No. 334, Brandywine Sp'gs	10 00
	Eastern Star Lodge, No. 79, Monticello, $12 80; individual Masons, $22 49; citizens, $35 21, per S. W. Dale, Secretary.......................................	70 80
29.	Cherry Creek Lodge, No. 339, Pontotoc County, W. R. Spencer, Secretary. (This Lodge donated $60, all in its treasury; $30 returned.).....................	30 00
30.	Perkinsville Lodge, No. 331, N. D. Triplett, Sec'y.....	10 00
Oct. 2.	Macon Lodge, No. 40, T. T. Patty, Secretary...........	89 98
	Crooks' Mill Lodge, No. 292, John Russell, W. M......	5 00

Oct.	2.	Jefferson Lodge, No. 146, Scooba, N. A. Chiles, Sec'y	16 30
		Henderson Ray Lodge, No. 297, New Hope.............	15 00
		Canaan Lodge, No. 219, Benton County.................	10 00
		LaGrange Lodge, No. 363, Choctaw County............	10 00
	4.	Union Lodge, No. 106, Mt. Carmel, per Milton Griffith...	75 00
		O. T. Keeler Lodge, No. 358, Olive Branch, A. G. Perry, Wor. Master..	20 00
	5.	Malone Lodge, No. 101, Palo Alto, L. H. Bonds, Sec'y	10 00
	6.	Summerville Lodge, No. 133, Gholson, and citizens, M. Edwards, Wor. Master................................	22 00
		R. E. Lee Lodge, No. 156, Chesterville, Richard Wharton, Secretary, $20; citizens of Chesterville, collected by Lodge, $9...................................	29 00
	7.	Dover Lodge, No. 197, R. W. Shipp, Secretary.........	26 00
	8.	John W. Oliver Lodge, No. 374, W. S. Vaughn, Sec'y	31 00
	9.	Lodi Lodge, No. 134, R. B. Loggins, Secretary.........	10 00
	14.	New Hope Lodge, No. 224.................................	5 00
Oct.	14.	DeMolay Commandery, No. 8, Columbus..................	25 00
	16.	Snowsville Lodge, No. 119, Chester, per E. R. Seward	25 00
	17.	Panola Lodge, No. 66, Batesville, $25; members, $2..	27 00
		Long Creek Lodge, No. 189, Eureka, per J. M. Cox, Secretary, No. 66..	25 00
	23.	Bahala Lodge, No. 173, Beauregard, Benj. King, jr., Secretary...	25 00
Nov.	18.	Plattsburg Lodge, No. 212, Thos. Stevens, Secretary..	5 00
		Pine Lodge, No. 383, Pike Co., C. P. Conerly, Sec'y..	10 00
	25.	Homestead Lodge, No. 168, Deasonville, C. R. Henderson, Secretary...	20 00
	8.	Oak Bowery Lodge, No. 198, Paulding....................	5 00
	11.	Campbellton Lodge, No. 128, Guntown, per W. C. Hines, Secretary..	25 00
Dec.	27.	Concord Lodge, No. 181, Union Church, Simon Lehman, Secretary..	25 00

Total from Mississippi...$ 3,136 13

MISSOURI.

Aug.	21.	Grand Royal Arch Chapter, John W. Luke, Grand Secretary..	200 00
	26.	Mitchell Chapter, No. 89, St. Joseph..................	25 00
		Grand Commandery, Wm. H. Mayo, Grand Recorder	100 00
		Sturgeon Lodge, No. 174, Sturgeon...................	50 00
Sept.	2.	Charity Lodge, No. 331, St. Joseph, D. P. Wallingford, Secretary..	30 00
		Masons of Macon, per John Shepperd, Secretary.......	23 50
	5.	Zaradatha Lodge, No. 189, St. Joseph, per Past Grand Master John Y. Murry, of Miss......................	25 00
	7.	From John D. Vineil, Grand Secretary, St. Louis.....	202 00
	9.	From John D. Vineil, Grand Secretary, St. Louis.....	105 00
	30.	From John W. Luke, Grand Secretary, St. Louis.....	100 00
	14.	From John D. Vineil, Grand Secretary, St. Louis.....	300 00
	16.	From Valley Lodge, No. 413, Dutch Mills, per T. B. Greer, through S. C. Davis & Co., per John W. Luke, Grand Secretary, for Grenada.................	25 00

Sept. 15.	Lodges in St. Louis Co., per John W. Luke, Gr'd Sec'y	100 00
18.	From John D. Vincil, Grand Secretary, St. Louis.....	100 00
23.	Lodges in St. Louis, per John W. Luke, Grand Sec'y	200 00
27.	From John D. Vincil, Grand Secretary, St. Louis.....	600 00

Total from Missouri.............. . ...$ 2,185 50

Also, fiffty dollars contributed by Bro. John W. Luke, Oct. 3, in the purchase of supplies for Holly Springs.

MONTANA.

Sept. 12.	Masons of Helena, per telegraph, no letter advice......	100 00
25.	Cornelius Hedges, Grand Secretary, Helena............	100 00
Oct. 3.	Masons of Virginia City, per J. M. Knight..............	50 00
9.	Gallatin Lodge, No. 6, Bozeman, R. P. Menefee, Sec'y	25 00
	Contribution of R. F. May, accompanying same........	1 50
21.	From same..	25 00
19.	Masons of Montana, per Cornelius Hedges, Gr'd Sec'y	214 50

Total from Montana ....$ 516 00

NEBRASKA.

Sept. 14.	Per Wm. R. Bowen, Grand Recorder:	
	Mt. Olivet Commandery, No. 2....................... ..	23 50
	Carmel Commandery, No. 3............................	5 50
	Moriah Commandery, No. 4............................	25 00
	Zion Commandery, No. 5.............................	25 00
23.	Per Wm. R. Bowen, Grand Secretary, Omaha.........	198 65
24.	Per Wm. R. Bowen, Grand Secretary, Omaha.........	131 15
	Per Wm. R. Bowen, Grand Secretary, Omaha.........	140 00
29.	Per Wm. R. Bowen, Grand Secretary, Omaha.......	95 00
Oct. 12.	Masons of Nebraska, per Wm. R. Bowen, Gr'd Sec'y..	55 50
30.	Masons of Nebraska, per Wm. R. Bowen, Gr'd Sec'y...	25 00
Nov. 18.	Masons of Nebraska, per Wm. R. Bowen, Gr'd Sec'y..	39 15

Total from Nebraska..$ 763 45

NEVADA.

| Oct. 3. | Valley Lodge, No. 9, Dayton, J. L. Campbell, W. M., $40 in gold and $10 in currency........................$ | 50 00 |

NEW BRUNSWICK.

| Oct. 4. | St. John Encampment, No. 48, St. John, T. Nisbet Robertson, Secretary, gold................................$ | 50 00 |

NEW JERSEY.

Sept. 26.	Joseph W. Hough, Grand Secretary, Trenton.........	530	87
Oct. 30.	Masons of New Jersey, per Joseph W. Hough, Grand Secretary..	113	00
14.	Royal Arch Masons, Thos. J. Corson, Grand Secretary..	52	00
14.	Masons of New Jersey, per J. W. Hough, Grand Secretary..	564	87
8.	Royal Arch Masons of New Jersey, per Thos. J. Corson, Grand Secretary..	100	00
10.	Royal Arch Masons of New Jersey, per Thos. J. Corson, Grand Secretary..	13	00
	Total from New Jersey...	$1,373	24

NEW YORK.

Sept. 3.	Excelsior Lodge, No. 195, per J. R. Gilmore, chairman Relief Committee....................................	100	00
3.	Rome Commandery, No. 5, F. E. Mitchell, E. C......	107	00
10.	Through Henry E. Warne, chairman, Syracuse:		
	Central City Chapter, No 70, ...	50	00
	Central City Bodies, A. and A. Rite................	25	00
	Central City Commandery and friends...............	250	00
12.	Gregory Satterlee, Grand Treasurer Grand Lodge, New York..	1,000	00
12.	Sir Knight Cyrus Stewart, Gloversville.................	5	00
	From Townsend Fonday, Grand Commander, Albany:		
	SalemTown Commandery, No. 13....................	100	00
	St. George's Commandery, No. 37, ...	25	00
	Temple Commandery, No. 2......	55	00
12.	Gregory Satterlee, Grand Treasurer Grand Lodge.....	1,000	00
12.	Robert Macoy, Grand Recorder Grand Commandery	25	00
12.	Watertown Commandery, No. 11, Louis C. Greenleaf, E. C..	25	00
12.	DeSoto Commandery, No. 49, Plattsburg, W. S. Gaibord, Recorder..	33	00
12.	Palestine Commandery, No. 18, New York, H. H. Brockway, Gen'o..	70	00
12.	Morton Commandery, No. 4, New York, 127 Hudson St., Wesley B. Church, Recorder.....................	50	00
14.	Through Sir Haynes L. Hart, E. C. Lake Ontario Commandery:		
	Oswego Lodge, No. 127....................................	10	00
	Frontier City Lodge, No. 422............................	10	00
	Aeonian Lodge, No. 679....................................	10	00
	Lake Ontario Commandery, No. 32....................	10	00
16.	Appollo Commandery, No. 15, Troy, per Theo. E. Hazlehurst..	200	00
16.	Gregory Satterlee, Grand Treasurer Grand Lodge.....	500	00
18.	Palestine Commandery, New York, per H. H. Brockway, Gen'o..	33	00
18.	SalemTown Commandery, No. 13, per Townsend Fonday, Grand Commander..............................	75	00

Sept. 18.	Gregory Satterlee, Grand Treasurer Grand Lodge.....	500	00
18.	Robert Macoy, Grand Recorder Knights Templar.....	147	20
18.	Hugh de Paynes Commandery, No. 30, Buffalo, Christopher G. Eox, E. C................	100	00
19.	Genesee Commandery, No. 10, Lockport, per P. D. Walter, Treasurer................	20	00
20.	Dunkirk Commandery, No. 40, R. J. Gross, Recorder	25	00
20.	Malta Commandery, No. 21, Binghampton, F. N. Mabee, E. C..............	50	00
20.	Lake Erie Commandery, No. 20, Buffalo, per Albert Jones, "for general purposes"...........	200	00
20	John Hodge, Lockport...........	50	00
21.	Delaware Commandery, No. 4, Port Jervis, Chas. B. Gray, Treasurer...........	27	58
21.	Gregory Satterlee, Grand Treasurer Grand Lodge.....	750	00
23.	Gregory Satterlee, Grand Treasurer Grand Lodge.....	750	00
24.	Palestine Commandery, No. 18, New York, per H. H. Brockway...........	33	00
24.	Rondout Commandery, No. 52, Grove Webster, Recorder...........	50	00
27.	Gregory Satterlee, Grand Treasurer Grand Lodge.....	750	00
27.	Robert Macoy, Grand Recorder Knights Templar.....	125	00
29.	Robert Macoy, Grand Recorder Knights Templar.....	60	00
Oct. 3.	Masons of 25th District, C. E. Young, D. D. G. M., 209 Main St., Buffalo...........	300	00
3.	A member of Lake Ontario Commandery, No. 2, Oswego, per Haynes L. Hart, E. C...........	2	00
16.	Westchester Commandery, No. 42, Sing Sing, Robert M. Lawrence, E. C...........	20	00
25.	Poughkeepsie Lodge, No. 206, T. W. Davis, W. M., (for Masons and their families)...........	59	50
30.	Otseningo Lodge, No. 435, Binghampton, Horace E. Allen, W. M., "for our own household of faith.".....	15	00
Nov. 7.	Members of Canandaigua Lodge, No. 294, J. J. Stebbins, Secretary...........	56	50
10.	Masons of New York, per Gregory Satterlee, Grand Treasurer...........	1,000	00
Dec. 18.	Masons of New York, per Gregory Satterlee, Grand Treasurer...........	583	65
Jan. 3.	Gregory Satterlee, Grand Treasurer...........	19	25

Total from New York.......................................$ 9,461 68

OHIO.

Sept. 2.	Through appeal of Grand Master W. M. Cunningham, viz:		
	Goodale Lodge, No. 372, Columbus,................	25	00
	Urania Lodge, No. 311, Plain City,................	36	00
	New Lexington Lodge, No. 250, New Lexington,	10	00
	Mt. Zion Lodge, No. 9, Mt. Vernon,................	20	00
	Newark Lodge, No. 97, Newark,................	10	00
	Hebron Lodge, No. 116, Hebron,................	5	00
	Brethren of Goodale Lodge, No. 372,................	14	50
	(The foregoing through Theo. P. Gordon, Grand Treasurer, Columbus.)		

Sept.	2.	Magnolia Lodge, No. 20, H. O. Kane, W. M., ...	105 £0
	2.	John D. Caldwell, Grand Secretary, Cincinnati, ...	200 00
	5.	John D. Caldwell, Grand Secretary, Cincinnati, ...	100 00
	5.	John D. Caldwell, Grand Secretary, Cincinnati, ...	200 00
	5.	Grand Commandery, by W. L. Buechner, Youngstown,	200 00
	6.	Gibulum Lodge of Perfection, Ancient Accepted Scottish Rite, 14° grade, per E. T. Carson, ...	5) 00
	7.	From John D. Caldwell, Grand Secretary, ...	100 00
	7.	From John D. Caldwell, Grand Secretary, ...	100 00
	9.	From John D. Caldwell, Grand Secretary, ...	100 00
	12.	Sam'l. T. Fisk, R. R. Ticket Agent, "a brother in Masonry and Odd Fellowship," $5—one half of which under I. O. O. F. receipts, ...	2 50
	13.	Lodges and Chapter, per Theo. P. Gordon, Grand Treasurer, Columbus:	
		Pickaway Lodge, No. 23, Circleville, ...	25 00
		Mansfield Lodge, No. 35, Mansfield, ...	25 00
		Quaker City Lodge, No. 500, Quaker City, ...	3 00
		Newark Lodge, No. 97, } Newark, ...	85 00
		Ahmian Lodge, No. 492, }	
		Warren Chapter, No. 11, Newark, ...	25 00
		Centre Star Lodge, No. 11, Granville, ...	11 10
		Tuscan Lodge, No. 342, Jefferson, ...	10 00
		Ohio Chapter, No. 12, Columbus, ...	50 00
	14	Through Bro. Theo. P. Gordon, Grand Treasurer:	
		New England Lodge, No. 4, Worthington, ...	39 50
		Greenville Lodge, No. 143, Greenville, ...	46 00
		Spartan Lodge, No. 126, Millersburg, ...	5 00
		H. S. D., for Commonwealth Lodge, No. 409, New York, ...	1 00
		L. D., for Magnolia Lodge, No. 20, Columbus, ...	5 00
		J. E. Goodale, for Goodale Lodge, No. 372, Columbus, ...	2 00
	14.	John D. Caldwell, Grand Secretary, for orphan fund,	200 00
	14.	Same, for general use, ...	100 00
	16.	Same, for orphan fund—not on score of Masonry, but of need, ...	100 00
	18.	From Theo. P. Gordon, Grand Treasurer:	
		Lancaster Lodge, No. 47, Lancaster, ...	101 00
		Mingo Lodge, No. 171, Logan, ...	25 00
		Acacia Lodge, No. 464, Wilkin's Run, Licking co.,	10 50
		Reynoldsburg Lodge, No. 340, Reynoldsburg, ...	5 00
		Lockbourne Lodge, No. 232, Lockbourne, ...	35 00
		Battin Lodge, No. 487, Commercial Point, Pickaway co., ...	5 00
		Sparrow Lodge, No. 400, Sunbury, ...	20 00
		Lithopolis Lodge, No. 169, Lithopolis, ...	5 00
	21.	John D. Caldwell, Grand Secretary, orphan fund, ...	125 00
	25.	John D. Caldwell, Grand Secretary, orphan fund, ...	91 00
	25.	John D. Caldwell, Grand Secretary, orphan fund, ...	100 00
	25.	John D. Caldwell, Grand Secretary, orphan fund, ...	100 60
	27.	Central Lodge, No. 279, Calais, per Theo. P. Gordon, Grand Treasurer, ...	5 00

Total from Ohio..$ 2,638 90

ONTARIO.

Sept. 26. From J. J. Mason, Grand Sec'y., Hamilton, gold,... $ 500 00

PENNSYLVANIA.

Aug. 26.	Melita Lodge, No. 295, Philadelphia,....................	25 00
Sept. 2.	Grand Commandery, per Sam'l. B. Dicks, Grand Commander, Meadville,..	200 00
2.	Masons of Alleghany county, per Jos. Eichbaum, 231 Liberty st., Pittsburg, D. D. G. M., 17th Dist.,......	100 00
2.	St. John's Commandery, No. 4, Philadelphia, Andrew W. Gayley, Recorder, 1909 Pine st.,...................	50 00
2.	Lake Lodge, No. 434, Sandy Lake, per Jas. Yanney, Jr., Secretary,...	10 00
8.	Guyasuta Lodge, No. 513, Temperanceville, per John D. Richards, Chestnut st., 36th Ward, Pittsburg,...	27 00
10.	Western Crawford Lodge, No. 258, Conneautville, E. H. Power, Sec'y,..	18 00
10.	Masons of Alleghany county, per Jos. Eichbaum, D. D. G. M., 17th Dist., 231 Liberty st., Pittsburg,...	100 00
12.	Greensburg Chapter, No. 40, per G. C. Shidle, District Deputy Grand High Priest, 15th District,...........	40 00
13.	Chas. E. Meyer, Grand Recorder Knights Templar,...	200 00
13.	Parker Lodge, No. 521, Parker City, per John Thomson, Grand Secretary,.....................................	50 00
14.	Lodges of Alleghany county, per Jos. Eichbaum, Deputy 17th Dist., Pittsburg,...............................	85 00
14.	Milnor Lodge, No. 287, per Jas. Herdman, Treasurer, 105 Wood st., Pittsburg,...............................	50 00
18.	Alleghany Chapter, No. 217, Alleghany City, per G. C. Shidle, 59 Smithfield st., District Deputy G. H. P., Pittsburg,...	25 00
20.	John Thomson, Grand Sec'y., Philadelphia, ...	124 30
23.	Masons of Alleghany county, per Jos. Eichbaum, D. D. G. M., 17th District, Pittsburg,................	102 75
Oct. 3.	Knights Templar, by C. E. Meyer, Grand Recorder,	75 00
29.	Same, ...	100 00

Total from Pennsylvania...............................$ 1,382 05

RHODE ISLAND.

Sept. 10. Edwin Baker, Grand Secretary Grand Lodge, Providence...$ 300 00

SOUTH CAROLINA.

Sept. 2. Landmark Lodge, No. 76, Charleston, per Chas. Inglesby, Grand Secretary, for Grenada..................... 25 00

3

Sept. 5.	Charles Inglesby, Grand Secretary......................		25	00
8.	Philanthropic Lodge, No. 78, per Chas. Inglesby, for Vicksburg..		10	00
10.	Spartan Lodge, No. 70, per Chas. Inglesby, Gr'd Sec'y		10	00
10.	Union Kilwining Lodge, No. 4, per Chas. Inglesby, Grand Secretary..		52	00
11.	Chas. Inglesby, Grand Secretary..........................		75	00
24.	Chas. Inglesby, Grand Secretary..........................		103	55
Oct. 26.	Chas. Inglesby, Grand Secretary..........................		97	75
Dec. 10.	Chas. Inglesby, Grand Secretary, Charleston...........		13	25
	Total from South Carolina.................................$		411	55

TEXAS.

Sept. 2.	Indianola Lodge, No. 484, F. S. Coffin, W. M..........		10	00
2.	Lathrop Lodge, No. 21, Crocket, B. F. Frymier, W. M., per Geo. H. Bringhurst, Grand Secretary, $28 50 by Lodge, and $17 70 by citizens.............................		46	20
4.	Masonic Relief Committee, San Antonio, R. E. Newton, Chairman...		100	00
14.	Ivanhoe Commandery, No. 8, per Benj. A. Botts, Grand Treasurer, Houston...............................		64	00
16.	Waco Commandery, No. 1, J. E. Elgin, E. C...........		85	00
18.	Murchison Lodge, No. 18, Hallettsville, per Sam Devall, Secretary (citizens of Hallettsville — see Miscellaneous Receipts).....................................		50	00
19.	Masons of Indianola, per H. Runge & Co...............		95	00
21.	St. John's Lodge, No. 51, per E. F. Brown..............		48	00
23.	Warren Lodge, No. 56, Caldwell, John Alexander, W. M..		46	50
23.	Waco Commandery, No. 8, by R. E. Burnham, Chairman Relief Committee, through Benj. A. Botts, Grand Treasurer...		100	00
23.	Whitesboro Lodge, No. 263, A. H. Nichols, Secretary		10	00
27.	Alamita Lodge, No. 200, $10; citizens, $27; per John Ruckman, Helena, from Geo. H. Bringhurst, Grand Secretary..		37	00
30.	Central Relief Committee, Gonzales, Milton Eastland, Secretary and Treasurer, per Benj. A. Botts, Grand Treas'r. (A contribution also sent to Greenville.)		68	50
30.	Farmersville Lodge, No. 214. (No letter advice.).....		15	00
Oct. 16.	Lee Lodge, No. 35, McKinney, $10; and $33 in neighborhood..		43	00
29.	Sir Milton Eastland, Gonzales, through Benj. A. Botts, Grand Treasurer, for Meridian......................		57	00
Nov. 3.	Contributions of sundry Lodges, a Chapter, individual contributions of citizens, and other sources, per Benj. A. Botts, Grand Treasurer.......................		512	15
	(Also, in same package, $14 15 from colored people, Gonzales—see Miscellaneous Receipts.)			
Oct. 6.	Knights Templar, through Benj. A. Botts, Gr'd Treas.		95	00
	Total from Texas.......................................$		1,482	35

UTAH.

Sept.	10.	Chapters and Lodges, per Christopher Diehl, Grand Secretary, Salt Lake,	52 00
	13.	Christopher Diehl, Grand Secretary, Salt Lake,	75 00
	19.	Christopher Diehl, Grand Secretary, Salt Lake,	125 00
	21.	Christopher Diehl, Grand Secretary, Salt Lake,	125 00
	25.	Christopher Diehl, Grand Secretary, Salt Lake,	75 00
Oct.	4.	Christopher Diehl, Grand Secretary, Salt Lake,	58 25

Total from Utah...$ 510 25

VIRGINIA.

Aug.	30.	Liberty Lodge, No. 95, Jno. F. Curtis, W.,M., per R. T. Anspach	20 00
Sept.	2.	Per W. E. Morrison, W. M., Blanford Lodge, No. 3, Petersburg:	
		Prince George Lodge, No. 115, Petersburg,	7 00
		Blanford Lodge, No. 3, Petersburg,	50 00
		Petersburg Lodge, No. 15, Petersburg,	50 00
		Powhatan Starke Lodge, No. 124, Petersburg,	50 00
		Corinthian Lodge, No. 29, Petersburg,	25 00
		Petersburg Royal Arch Chapter, Petersburg,	25 00
	3.	Duquesne Chapter, No. 193, Petersburg,	50 00
	4.	Fairfax Lodge, No. 43, Culpepper, per John A. Hill, Secretary,	37 75
Sept.	5.	Marshall Lodge, No. 39, Lynchburg, per Sam'l. D. Preston, Sec'y., F. Myers, A. Parker Ferguson, Com.,	150 00
	5.	Wm. B. Isaacs, Grand Secretary, for Grenada Masons,	50 00
	10.	Masons in Richmond, per Wm. B. Isaacs, Grand Secretary; for Vicksburg, $50; for Grenada, $50,	100 00
	16.	McDaniel Chapter, No. 29, Lynchburg, J. L. Beck, Secretary,	25 00
	16.	Masons of Richmond, per Wm. B. Isaacs, Grand Secretary, for Vicksburg,	50 00
	19.	From Lodges, per Wm. B. Isaacs, Treasurer Relief Committee,	100 00
	30.	Morotoc Lodge, No. 210, per R. W. Patross, Danville,	46 25

Total from Virginia...$ 836 00

WASHINGTON TERRITORY.

Nov.	16.	Per Aaron Stein, Treasurer Relief Fund, with Wells, Fargo & Co's. Express, San Francisco, $45 in silver and $10 in gold,.................$	55 00

WEST VIRGINIA.

Aug. 30.	Masons of Wheeling, $400; Grand Lodge, $100; per J. H. Williams, Grand Treasurer,	500 00
Sept. 14.	J. H. Williams, Grand Treasurer, Wheeling,	200 00
Oct. 2.	J. H. Williams, Grand Treasurer, Wheeling,	200 00
Nov. 16.	J. H. Williams, Grand Treasurer, Wheeling,	31 66

Total from West Virginia......................................$ 931 66

WISCONSIN.

Sept. 2.	John W. Woodhull, Grand Secretary Grand Lodge, Milwaukee	340 00
6.	John W. Woodhull, Treasurer Masonic Relief Fund.	700 00
9.	John W. Woodhull, Grand Secretary	500 00
16.	John W. Woodhull, Grand Secretary	400 00
27.	John W. Woodhull, Grand Secretary	800 00
Oct. 16.	John W. Woodhull, Grand Secretary	500 00

Total from Wisconsin..................................$ 3,240 00

WYOMING TERRITORY.

Sept. 10.   Masonic Lodge at Laramie City, per W. L. Kidd......$ 10 00

RECAPITULATION OF MASONIC RECEIPTS.

Alabama	$ 553	64
Arizona Territory	50	00
California	2,330	00
Colorado	183	75
Connecticut	1,245	60
Dakotah Territory	100	00
District of Columbia	550	00
Florida	50	00
Georgia	181	00
Illinois	4,501	14
Indiana	727	70
Iowa	2,142	45
Kansas	450	00
Kentucky	424	00
Louisiana	225	00
Maryland	860	00
Massachusetts	410	00
Michigan	2,085	00
Minnesota	750	00
Mississippi	3,136	13
Missouri	2,185	50
Montana	516	00
Nebraska	763	45
Nevada	50	00
New Brunswick	50	00
New Jersey	1,373	24
New York	9,461	68
Ohio	2,638	90
Ontario	500	00
Pennsylvania	1,382	05
Rhode Island	300	00
South Carolina	411	55
Texas	1,482	35
Utah	510	25
Virginia	836	00
West Virginia	931	66
Wisconsin	3,240	00
Washington Territory	55	00
Wyoming Territory	10	00
Total	$ 47,653	04

EXHIBIT B.

RECEIPTS FROM I. O. O. F. SOURCES.

ALABAMA.

Sept. 16. One-half contribution of Masons and Odd Fellows of
Guntersville, through John D. Miller.................$ 30 00

ARKANSAS.

Sept. 14.	H. Ehremberger, Chairman Relief Committee, Little Rock......	150 00	
19.	Fulton Lodge, No. 74, Fulton, W. A. Jett, Secretary	25 00	
20.	Bragg Lodge, No. —, Pine Bluff, telegram to draw for	51 00	
Oct. 12.	Peter Brugman, Grand Secretary, Little Rock..........	140 85	
Nov. 8.	Peter Brugman, Grand Secretary, Little Rock..........	25 00	

Total from Arkansas...$ 391 85

CALIFORNIA.

Sept. 1.	Pacific Lodge, No. —, San Francisco, L. J. Zeigler, Treasurer..	25 00	
1.	Templar Lodge, No. —, San Francisco, L. Washburn, Secretary...	100 00	
5.	California Lodge, No. 1, San Francisco, Geo. E. Dickson, N. G..	100 00	
5.	Parker Lodge, No. 124, San Francisco, gold.............	75 00	
5.	Bay City Lodge, No. 71, gold..............................	50 00	
20.	W. B. Lyon, Grand Secretary, for Bay City Lodge, San Francisco, gold..	1,000 00	
20.	Yerba Buera Lodge, No. —, John Cammel, trustee, gold..	100 00	
20.	Golden Gate Encampment, San Francisco, J. L. Seigler, Treasurer..........................	50 00	
20.	Magnolia Lodge, No. —, San Francisco, J. L. Seigler, Treasurer..	50 00	
Oct. 14.	W. B. Lyon, Grand Secretary, San Francisco...........	1,000 00	
16.	Through Theo. A. Ross, Ass't Gr'd Sec'y, Baltimore,	150 00	

Total from California..$ 2,700 00

COLORADO.

Sept. 14	Union Lodge, No. 1, Denver....................................	50 00
Oct. 16.	Germania Lodge, No. 1, through Theo. A. Ross, Ass't Grand Secretary, Baltimore..............	25 00
	Total from Colorado..$	75 00

CONNECTICUT.

Aug. 29.	Thos. Stirling, Grand Master, Bridgeport...............	100 00
Oct. 23.	Frederick Botsford, Grand Secretary, New Haven...	200 00
	Total from Connecticut...$	300 00

DAKOTAH TERRITORY.

Sept. 6.	Echo Lodge, No. 2, Fort Randall, F. Smitler, Treas'r..	15 00
14.	Humboldt Lodge, No. 5.......................................	25 00
16.	From Grand Secretary, per Grand Master McKenzie	50 00
18.	R. N. Briggs, Grand Secretary, Vermillion.............	10 00
Oct. 16.	Sioux Lodge, No. 14, Standing Rock, per Grand Sec. Briggs.............	36 00
	Total from Dakotah Territory........ .... $	136 00

DELAWARE.

Sept. 23.	Isaac W. Hallall, Grand Secretary,......................	109 50
26.	Isaac W. Hallall, Grand Secretary,......................	20 00
	Total from Delaware...$	129 50

FLORIDA.

Sept. 3.	Mechanic's Lodge, No. 8, Warrington, per Geo. S. Hallmark, G. M.,....................	10 00
14.	Pensacola Lodge, No. 4, R. I. Jordan, Secretary,......	25 00
	Total from Florida ....$	35 00

ILLINOIS.

Sept. 2.	Budah Lodge, No. 75, Budah, John E. Patrick, Sec'y.,	10 00
6.	John Lake, Grand Master, Rockford, ...	500 00
10.	Urania Lodge, No. 243, Jacksonville, J. T. Osborne, Secretary,................................	50 00
	(Same amount for Louisiana, which was forwarded October 16th.)	
13.	Moultrie Lodge, No. 158, Sullivan, per W. A. Cash, Secretary,................................	25 00
16.	John Lake, Grand Master, Rockford,....................	500 00
Oct. 30.	John Lake, Grand Master, Rockford,....................	500 00
	Total from Illinois........ ....$	1,585 00

INDIANA.

Sept. 2.	Mount Vernon Lodge, No—, Lee Wolfe, V. G., Chairman Relief Committee,............................	25 00
2.	Friendship Lodge, No. 4, Rising Sun, S. Heyers, Sec'y,	20 00
4.	B. F. Foster, Grand Secretary..........................	500 00
16.	B. F. Foster, Grand Secretary..........................	300 00
16.	Hope Lodge, No. 83, New Albany, J. B. Banks, Sec'y,	10 00
Oct. 2.	Churubusco Lodge, No. 462, Churubusco, H. C. Preslee, Secretary...	1 00
	Total from Indiana.. ....:.... ....$	856 00

IOWA.

Aug. 29.	Sioux City Lodge, No. 164, Sioux City, C. B. Steadman, Secretary........	25 00
Sept. 2.	Atlantic Lodge, No. 175, Atlantic, Cass co., W. B. Temple, Secretary..............................	30 00
2.	Odd Fellows of Winterset, per A. W. C. Weeks......	33 75
10.	Bedford Lodge, No. 91, Bedford, W. F. Randolph, N. G..	5 00
16.	Lisbon Lodge, No. 162, G. F. Wink, N. G..............	10 00
16.	Odd Fellows of Keokuk, through E. H. Wickersham, P. G. M..	50 00
21.	Carroll Lodge, No. 279, Carroll City, R. E. Coburn, Secretary	40 00
Oct. 16.	Wm. Garrett, Grand Secretary, Burlington..............	81 00
18.	Wm. Garrett, Grand Secretary, Burlington	18 00
Nov. 16.	Wm. Garrett, Grand Secretary, Burlington.....	159 91
27.	Wm. Garrett, Grand Secretary............................	185 94
	Total from Iowa,..$	638 60

KANSAS.

Sept.	2.	Friendship Lodge, No. 5, Atchison, A. R. Platt, Treas,	15 00
	2.	Fort Scott Lodge, No. 22, Fort Scott, H. W. Pond, Secretary......................................	10 00
	7.	Cherryvale Lodge, No. 142, Cherryvale, J. W. Pritchard, Secretary..................................	11 90
	7.	Pawnee Lodge, No. 108, Waterville, A. Kunz, Sec'y.,	15 00
	8.	Schiller Lodge, No. —, Atchison, H. Trulleib, Sec'y.,	20 00

Total from Kansas...$ 71 90

KENTUCKY.

Aug.	29.	Home Lodge, No. 29, Louisville........................	25 00
	29.	Amnon Encampment, Louisville.........................	25 00
	29.	Mercy Encampment, No. 31, Hopkinsville..............	25 00
	29.	Green River Lodge, No. 54, Hopkinsville,...........	35 00
Sept.	20.	Relief Committee of Louisville, per Geo. W. Morris, Grand Treasurer....................	100 00
	23.	Geo. W. Morris, Grand Treasurer, Louisville..........	150 00
Oct.	18.	Geo. W. Morris, Grand Treasurer, Louisville..........	100 00

Total from Kentucky...$ 460 00

LOUISIANA.

Aug.	30.	Keith Lodge, No. 21, Shreveport, by W. T. Dalzell..	50 00
Sept.	16.	Excelsior Lodge, No. 84, Thibadoux, per Past Grand Master Silas T. Grisamore, Secretary.................	10 00
Oct.	12.	Keith Lodge, No. 21, Shreveport, D. Cooper, N. G...	50 00

Total from Louisiana...$ 110 00

MAINE.

Nov. 1.   Joshua Davis, Grand Secretary........................$ 100 00

MARYLAND.

Oct.	12.	Theo. A. Ross, Assistant Grand Secretary, Baltimore, through Grand Master McKenzie, Summit, Miss...	180 00
	29.	John M. Jones, Grand Secretary, Baltimore...........	105 50

Total from Maryland...$ 285 50

MICHIGAN.

Sept. 28.	B. Vernor, Grand Treasurer, Detroit......................	500 00
Oct. 9.	B. Vernor, Grand Treasurer, Detroit......................	500 00
	Total from Michigan..................................$	1,000 00

MISSISSIPPI.

Sept. 7.	Jefferson Lodge, No. 14, Fayette...........................	15 00
10.	Ridgely Lodge, No. 23, Starkville, John A. Jacobs, Secretary..	15 00
18.	Washington Lodge, No. 2, Natchez, by A. Beckman..	54 25
21.	Greenville Lodge, No. 94, sent to Vicksbez for Grenada, used in Vicksburg and charged in disbursements to that place....................................	50 00
Oct. 1.	Ridgley Lodge, No. 23, Starkville, John A. Jacobs, Secretary..	13 40
25.	Fayette Encampment, No. 11, James McClure, Jr., Scribe...	20 00
	Total from Mississippi..$	167 65

MISSOURI.

Sept. 2.	Occidental Lodge, No. 70, Pleasant Hill, individual contributions, through George I. Shepherd, Sec'y...	15 00
12.	M. W. Withers, Lexington, made an Odd Fellow in Natchez and had fever there in 1838.....................	20 00
	Total from Missouri...$	35 00

MONTANA.

Sept. 26.	Golden Star Encampment, No. 2, per Lew Coleman, Grand Secretary..	25 00
26.	Covenant Lodge, No. 6, Deer Lodge, per Lew Coleman, Grand Secretary..	25 00
29.	Cottonwood Lodge, No. 2, per Lew Coleman, Grand Secretary..	50 00
Oct. 28.	August Nogle, Fort Shaw.......................................	1 00
	Total from Montana ....$	101 00

NEBRASKA.

Sept. 13.	Centennial Lodge, No. 59, Fremont, per W. H. Michael	39 80
16.	Wyoming Lodge, No. 29, Factoryville, Cass County, John Murfin	10 00
	Total from Nebraska.....................$	49 80

NEW JERSEY.

Oct. 6.	Live Oak Lodge, No. 105, Orange, Chas. J. Mills, Sec'y	25 00
10.	Howard Lodge, No. 7, Newark, Aaron Matthews, Treasurer	25 00
14.	Lewis Parker, jr., Grand Secretary, Trenton	68 40
18.	Lewis Parker, jr., Grand Secretary, Trenton	150 00
23.	Lewis Parker, jr., Grand Secretary, Trenton	100 00
Sept. 2.	Sumner Lodge, 180, Jersey City, Joseph M. Hough, Secretary	20 00
	Total from New Jersey.....................$	388 40

NEW YORK.

Sept. 28.	C. H. Moses, Chairman Relief Committee, New York	300 00
Oct. 11.	James Godwin, Grand Treasurer, New York	800 00
Nov. 16.	James Godwin, Grand Treasurer, New York	341 00
Dec. 21.	Grand Encampment, Geo. Smith, Grand Treasurer, 200 Bowery	90 00
	Total from New York.....................$	1,531 00

NORTH CAROLINA.

Sept. 25.	From J. J. Letchford, Grand Secretary, Raleigh :	
25.	Neuse Lodge, No. 5, Goldsboro	12 50
25.	Charlotte Lodge, No. 28, Charlotte	5 00
25.	Salem Lodge, No. 36, Salem	5 00
Oct. 3.	J. J. Letchford, Grand Secretary	26 85
12.	J. J. Letchford, Grand Secretary	6 75
	Total from North Carolina.....................$	56 10

OHIO.

Aug. 30.	Belmont City Lodge, No. 221, Martin's Ferry, Theo. Snodgrass, P. G	10 00
Sept. 7.	W. S. Capellar, Grand Master, Cincinnati	500 00
13.	Sam'l T. Fisk, R. R. Ticket Agent, Toledo, "A Brother in Masonry and Odd Fellowship." (See Masonic Receipts for $2 50 also.)	2 50

Sept. 16. Geo. D. Winchell, Grand Treasurer, through Grand
　　　　　　Master McKenzie.. 500 00
Oct. 18. Geo. D. Winchell, Grand Treasurer............. .... 500 00
Jan. 1, 1879. Geo. D. Winchell, Grand Treasurer................ 700 00

　　Total from Ohio..$ 2,212 50

PENNSYLVANIA.

Aug. 30. Fayette City Lodge, No. 511, Geo. K. Wilson, Sec'y.,　10 00
　　 30. Iron City Lodge, No. 182, Pittsburg, C. Blume, Jr.,
　　　　　　Treasurer.. 10 00
Sept. 6. Morris Lodge, No. 936, Prosperity, M. Minton, Sec'y.,　3 00
　　 12. Adoniram Lodge, No. 739, Sharpsville, by J. A. My-
　　　　　　ler, D. D. G. M., Alleghany................................. 5 00
　　 13. Cornplanter Lodge, No. 757, Oil City, by E. H. Wolfe,　2 00
　　 28. Peters Creek Lodge, No. 248, by J. A. Uyler, Dep. G.
　　　　　　M., Alleghany.. .... 5 00
Oct. 1. M. R. Muckle, Grand Treasurer, Philadelphia......... 700 00
　　 24. M. Richards Muckle, Grand Treasurer, Philadelphia,　407 84

　　Total from Pennsylvania.................................$ 1,142 84

RHODE ISLAND.

Sept. 14. Sidney Dean, Grand Master, Providence.................$　200 00

WEST VIRGINIA.

Sept. 5. Wheeling Lodge, No. 9, W. Ellingham, Treasurer...... 25 00
　　 5. Excelsior Lodge, No. 40, Wheeling, Geo. McCulley,
　　　　　　Secretary.. 20 00
　　 5. Franklin Lodge, No. 30, Wheeling, James M. Todd,
　　　　　　Treasurer.. 20 00
　　 8. Evening Star Lodge, No. 54, Mannington, F. R. Stew-
　　　　　　art, Secretary... 10 00
　　 8. Mound City Lodge, No. 13, Moundsville, John L.
　　　　　　Parkman, N. G.. 25 00
　　 10. Magnolia Lodge, No. 42, New Martinsville, Levi
　　　　　　Tucker, Secretary　　　　　　　　　　　　　　　15 00
　　 10. Cameron Lodge, No. 36, Wheeling, O. Moore, Sec'y.,　25 00
　　 11. New Haven Lodge, No. 35, by J. J. Grunstead........ 25 00
　　 11. St. Mary's Lodge, No. 11, St. Mary's, Jas. A. Patter-
　　　　　　son, Secretary... 15 00
　　 12. Huntington Lodge, No. 74, Huntington, Wm. F. Wal-
　　　　　　lace, Secretary... 25 00
　　 12. Cabell Encampment, No. 25, Huntington, Wm. F.
　　　　　　Wallace, Secretary............................... .. .. 5 00
　　 12. Tuscarora Lodge, No. 24, Martinsburg, J. L. Cline,
　　　　　　Secretary.. 20 00

Sept. 12. Friendship Lodge, No. 12, Wheeling, S. G. Frederick, Secretary.. 15 00
12. Odd Fellows at Keiser, per J. J. Koely................. 7 00
13. Monongalia Lodge, No. 10, Morgantown, G. W. Lemans, Secretary.. 10 00
13. Adelphian Lodge, No, 8, Clarksburg, E. W. Davisson, N. G.. 10 00
13. Grafton Lodge, No. 31, Grafton, A. J. Coly, Sec'y., 10 00
13. Eureka Lodge, No. 48, Wheeling, C. J. Hays, Sec'y., 15 00
13. Liberty Lodge, No. 21, Hartford City, Richard Allen, N. G.. 20 00
14. Paw Paw Lodge, No. 78, Paw Paw, Morgan co., D. Thomas, Secretary.. 10 00
14. Marion Lodge, No. 11, Fairmont, A. B. Wilson, Treasurer.. 40 00
14. Concord Lodge, No. 19, Wheeling, T. Zimmer, Sec'y., 20 00
16. American Lodge, No. 76, Scotch Hill, Newburg P. O., Preston co., Allen Morrison, Secretary.............. 5 00
16. Bethany Lodge, No. 7, Degree of Rebecca, Emily Bean, Secretary.. 10 00
16. Mountain Lodge, No. 86, Hinton, Jas. Prince, Sec'y, 10 00
18. St. George Lodge, No. 39, St. George, L. C. Bowman, Secretary.. 15 00
18. Orrel Lodge, No. 20, Newburg, J. Emory Paul, Secretary, p. t.. 10 00
18. Panola Lodge, No. 12, Wheeling, A. M. Harkins, Secretary.. 15 00
18. Palatine Lodge, No. 84, Palatine, James T. Holland, Secretary.. 25 00
19. Putnam Lodge, No. 85, Raymond City, $20, and $15, collected outside of Lodge, A. J. Lowd, Secretary, 35 00
20. Kanawha Lodge, No. 25, Charleston, per J. T. Brodt, Secretary.. 50 00
20. Point Pleasant Lodge, No. 33, Point Pleasant, Adolph Hess, Secretary.. 10 00
20. Clifton Lodge, No. 45, Clifton, Mason co., Jas. Yowell, Secretary.. 10 00
13. Dr. E. A. Hildreth, Odd Fellow, Wheeling, through W. Ellingham, 1400 Main street.......................... 2 00
21. Gratitude Lodge, No. 26, Hedgeville, D. S. Hull, Secretary.. 5 00
23. Hiawatha Lodge, No. 83, Sistersville, Robert Henderson, N. G.. 5 00
24. Wildey Lodge, Mo. 29, Charleston, M. S. Robertson, Secretary,.. 9 75
24. Electic Lodge, No. 67, Farmington, Marion co., J. W. Gribble, Secretary.. 10 00
24. Henrietta Lodge, No. 82, Peytona, Rome co., J. W. Bott, Secretary.. 15 00
24. Olive Branch Lodge, No. 38, Brownstown, J. R. Walker, Secretary.. 5 00
25. Phillipi Lodge, No. 59, Phillipi, C. C. Hoather, Sec'y., 10 00
26. Marshall Lodge, No. 71, Moundsville, Wiley O. Riggs, Secretary,.. 6 00
28. Kate Barclay Lodge, No. 51, Cairo, Ritchie co., E. Earnest, Secretary.. 10 00
28. Volcano Lodge, No. 49, S. J. Chubbuc, Chairman Committee.. 14 25

O:t. 6.	West Columbia Lodge, No. 14, West Columbia, J. Aumiller, Secretary...	10 00
6.	Webster Lodge, No. 5, Webster, H. Walter, Sec'y.,	10 00
7.	Malden Lodge, No. 77, Kanawha, Saline P. O., D. H. Putney, Secretary......	10 00
12.	Mt. Hebron Lodge, No. 48, Bloomery, Hampshire co., J. W. MeBee, Treasurer....................................	20 00
14.	Morning Star Lodge, No. 63, Coalsburg, John Banister, Secretary..............................	10 00
14.	Sharon Lodge, No. 28, Parkersburg, Thos. P. Butcher, Secretary...	20 00
17.	Shinston Lodge, No. 16, Jay F. Ogden, Secretary...	15 00
25.	Melbourne Lodge, No. 69, Middlebourne, Tyler co., J. N. Knight, Secretary...............................	11 25

Total from West Virginia....................................$ 780 25

WISCONSIN.

Sept. 7.	Euclaire Lodge, No. 129, Euclaire, Geo. M. Withers, P. G..	10 00
10.	McDonald Lodge, No. 37, Racine, Jos. Shroeder, Treasurer...	50 00
11.	Wausaw Lodge, No. 215, Wausaw, John Ringle, N. G.	15 00
29.	Racine Lodge, No. 8, Thos. Lewis, Sec'y, per Jos. Shroeder..	50 00

Total from Wisconsin..$ 125 00

TEXAS.

Aug. 29.	Odd Fellows of Houston, per Ike C. Stafford..........	50 00
Oct. 1.	International Lodge, No. 148, Hearne....................	20 00
19.	Encampment, No. 46, Forth Worth, by express—no letter...	29 00
23.	Odd Fellows of Fort Worth, through R. E. Beckham, H. P. Shield, R. Walton, Committee...................	53 50

Total from Texas..$ 152 50

UTAH.

Oct. 16.	Odd Fellow's Relief Association, Silver Reef, Washington county, per Theo. A. Ross, Assist. Grand Secretary, Baltimore..............................	50 00
	Lodges of Utah, by same.	50 00

Total from Utah..$ 100 00

UTAH, COLORADO, NEVADA.

Oct. 14. Per Theo. A. Ross, Assist. Grand Secretary, Baltimore, pro rata contributions from Utah, Colorado, and Nevada.. 48 00

COLORADO, SANDWICH ISLANDS.

Oct. 24. Per Theo. A. Ross, Assist. Secretary, Baltimore, one-half contributions Rocky Mountain Lodge, No. 2, Colorado; Excelsior Lodge, No. 1, Honolulu, Sandwich Islands... 57 75

Nov. 18. Polynesia Encampment, No. 1, Honolulu, Sandwich Islands, per Theo. A. Ross, Assistant Grand Sec'y.. 25 00

Total..$ 82 75

FROM LODGES IN STATES NOT KNOWN.

Sept. 14. Springfield Lodge, No. 7.............................. 28 00
Oct. 10. Black Hawk Lodge, No. 72, Waterloo, Harvey Smith, Secretary... 25 00

Total..$ 53 00

RECAPITULATION OF I. O. O. F. RECEIPTS.

Alabama	$ 30	00
Arkansas	391	85
California	2,700	00
Colorado	75	00
Connecticut	3,00	00
Dakotah Territory	136	00
Delaware	129	50
Florida	35	00
Illinois	1,585	00
Indiana	856	00
Iowa	638	60
Kansas	71	90
Kentucky	460	00
Louisiana	110	00
Maine	100	00
Maryland	285	50
Michigan	1,000	00
Mississippi	167	65
Missouri	35	00
Montana	101	00
Nebraska	49	80
New Jersey	388	40
New York	1,531	00
North Carolina	56	10
Ohio	2,212	50
Pennsylvania	1,142	84
Rhode Island	200	00
West Virginia	780	25
Wisconsin	165	00
Texas	152	50
Utah	100	00
Utah, Colorado, Nevada	43	00
Colorado, Sandwich Islands	82	75
Lodges in States not known	53	00

Total from Odd Fellows..............$ 16,165 14

EXHIBIT C.

MISCELLANEOUS RECEIPTS.

KNIGHTS OF HONOR.

MASSACHUSETTS.

Oct. 3. Boxbury Lodge, No. 205, per A. D. Gill, Treasurer...$		50 00

MICHIGAN.

Sept. 25. Through Jacob Brown, Grand Treasurer, and John A. Webb, Grand Treasurer of Mississippi............	100 00

TENNESSEE.

Sept. 25. Teutonia Lodge, No. 141, Knoxville, per Julius Och, C. M. Baumann, J. H. Madden, Committee, through W. H. Gibbs, Grand Dictator of Mississippi.........	20 00
Total from Knights of Honor.............................$	170 00

ALABAMA.

Sept. 13. Citizens of Forkland, per Daniel Sayre, Grand Sec'y.	60 00
14. Dr. J. C. Francis, Jacksonville............................	5 00
14. D. F. Hoke, Jacksonville......................................	25
16. Citizens of Guntersville, per D. J. Miller, (see collections through same from Masons and Odd Fellows	73 70
28. Elder J. A. Scott, Davistown, per W. E. Bowling.....	2 00
Total from Alabama..$	140 95

4

ARKANSAS.

Oct. 2. Mrs. Alice W. Pettus, Lonoke..................................$ 5 00

CALIFORNIA.

Sept. 6. St. John's Episcopal Church, San Francisco, for sufferers at Canton, through Gov. Stone, gold...........   100 00
9. City of Sacramento and Benevolent Orders, per
Christopher Green, R. A. Carey, and R. G. Weth-
ler, through Gov. Stone....................................   667 00
10. Citizens of Oakland, per Union National Gold Bank,
through Gov. Stone..   700 00
24. Citizens of Maysville, per N. D. Rideout, Mayor,
through Gov. Stone..   387 00
24. Wells, Fargo & Co., San Francisco, through Gov.
Stone...   400 00
Nov. 11. A. C. Henry, Treasurer Citizens' Relief Committee,
Oakland, through Gov. Stone..........................   1,000 00

Total from California...................................$ 3,254 00

COLORADO.

Aug. 30. E. P. Jacobson, Denver.................................   100 00
Sept. 12. L. P. Brown, El Moro, per C. R. Woodward, Cairo...   50 00

Total from Colorado..................................$ 150 00

GEORGIA.

Oct. 6. Proceeds of a Sociable at "Rose Terrace," by Miss
Rosa Yeiser, assisted by Mrs. Louis Raymond........   17 68

ILLINOIS.

Aug. 30. Audobon Shooting Club, Jacksonville, per Geo.
Hayden...   50 00
Sept. 16. Ladies of Belvedere, per John C. Foote, through E.
G. Wall..   165 00
20. Williams & Quigley, Galesburg, being 5 per cent. of
the receipts of their "Little Show.".....................   5 00

Total from Illinois...................................$ 220 00

INDIANA.

Oct. 18.	Light Guards and Governor's Guard, Terre Haute.....	205 65
18.	A. Herz..	66 00
18.	W. H. Wiley, Sup't Public Schools.........	10 00

Total from Indiana.. ....$ 281 65
(Through Thos. A. Anderson, Treasurer Governor's Guard, Terre Haute, to Gov. Stone.)

IOWA.

Aug. 30.	Citizens of Malvern, per F. P. Spencer......	18 25

KANSAS.

Aug. 29.	Citizens of Wilson...	51 50

KENTUCKY.

Sept. 12.	Mrs. Wm. J. Marshall, Henderson............................	10 00
12.	Mrs. Fielding Turner, Henderson............................	2 00

Total from Kentucky..$ 12 00

MASSACHUSETTS.

Oct. 1.	Operatives of Blackinton Woolen Mills, Blackinton, O. A. Archer, Treasurer, through Gov. Stone.........	70 00
Dec. 2.	M. V. B. Bartlett, Natick, through E. Barksdale, Jackson	16 50

Total from Massachusetts.....................................$ 86 50

MICHIGAN.

Sept. 28.	Citizens of Detroit, through Detroit Free Press, for Jackson......	50 00
Oct. 7.	Citizens of East Saginaw, per W. T. Wickware, Treasurer Citizens' Fund, to Governor Stone.............	600 00
19.	Same, through same..	592 06

Total from Michigan.............................. ....$ 1,242 06

MISSISSIPPI.

Aug. 24.	Citizens of McComb City, per N. Greener...............	135 00
Sept. 6.	Yellow Fever Relief Society, State Line, Jesse Byrd, President...	45 00
7.	Collection by ladies of Baldwyn, through Capt. P. M. Savery..	40 55
8.	W. H. Tribette, Terry.....................................	25 00
10.	R. F. McGill, Jackson.....................................	10 00
	Gov. J. M. Stone, Jackson...............................	100 00
	Ladies of Macon, per Geo. G. Dillard, Mayor........	343 00
12.	Citizens of Waynesboro, per Turner & Taylor, through Gov. Stone..	66 00
13.	Aid Society, State Line, per L. C. Peaster...............	25 00
16.	Ladies of Kosciusko, per Miss Mollie Comfort, Mrs. W. D. Sneed, Mrs. A. Judah, Committee............	46 00
21.	Relief Committee of Scranton, per Walter Denny...	100 00
22.	Proceeds of a concert, by the ladies and children of Beauregard, assisted by H. F. Bridewell and family, Port Gibson. Committee: Mrs. Julia Chrisman, Mrs. R. A. Bridewell and Dr. E. A. Rowan	52 00
	D. A. Buic, Franklin co., per Geo. T. Gracy.........,	5 00
26.	Ladies of Baldwyn, per Capt. P. M. Savery............	33 03
28.	Thespian Corps, Liberty, per F. W. Stratton, Treas.,	20 00
30.	Presbyterian Church, Union Church, Jefferson county, per E. E. Smiley—a collection on day of prayer,	19 25
	Congregation of Houston, per S. L. Wilson, ($1 of amount by Mrs. Sallie Shell's infant class).........	37 75
Oct. 6.	Citizens of Caledonia, Lowndes co., per A. L. Myers,	25 00
12.	Rising Star Grange, No. 134, Union Church, Jefferson co., Flora E. Cameron, Secretary..................	30 00
16.	Citizens of Macon, per Thos. J. O'Neill, special committee on relief.......................................	78 00
21.	J. S. Hamilton & Co., Lessees Penitentiary............	100 00
Nov. 8.	Collection at a Prayer Meeting in Brandon in September, per Rev. B. Carradine........................	10 00
14.	Mite Collection at Woodville, by a lady, per Hon. G. F. McGehee..	13 00
18.	S. B. Thomas, Sheriff Hinds county.....................	50 00
27.	S. Gwin, Auditor Public Accounts......................	50 00

Total from Mississippi...$ 1,458 58

NEW JERSEY.

Sept. 24.	Citizens of Phillipsburg, through Gov. Stone..........$	130 00

NEVADA.

Sept. 19.	Citizens of Hamilton, through Vicksburg Bank..... $	50 00

NEW YORK.

Sept. 16. Through E. Richardson, a special subscription in
New York for Bolton:

Treasurer Cotton Exchange	200 00
E. Richardson	50 00
E. S. Jaffray & Co	50 00
Whitfield, Powers & Co	25 00
Peters, Calhoun & Co	25 00
Ware, Murphy & Co	25 00
Woodruff, Morris & Co	25 00
Edwin Bates & Co	25 00
C. L. Robinson, of Bolton	25 00
J. P. Withers, of Bolton	25 00
H. K. & F. B. Thurber & Co	25 00

20. M. C. Richardson, Lockport ... 15 00
Jas. Jackson, Jr. & Son, Lockport ... 25 00
Mrs. Hiram Gardner, Lockport ... 20 00
(Through Augustus Keep, Treasurer Relief Com.)
21. Through John H. Rochester, Treasurer Southern Relief Fund, Rochester:
For Dry Grove ... 200 00
For General Relief ... 200 00
Oct. 3. Henry Slote, Treasurer Ball Committee, Old Volunteer Fire Department, 275 Broadway:
For Lake ... 500 00
For Jackson and vicinity ... 500 00

Total from New York ... $ 1,960 00

NORTH CAROLINA.

Sept. 21. Proceeds of concert by young ladies of Winston, per
Mrs. T. E. Richardson, of Jackson, Miss ... 40 00
Oct. 7. Citizens of Reedsville, per A. J. Ellington, T. J.
Hughes, A. P. Laborbe, Committee ... 22 25
22. Rev. Thos. S. Campbell, Lexington ... 75
Nov. 2. Young Ladies of Emma Seales' Female Academy,
per A. J. Ellington, T. J. Hughes, A. P. Loborbe,
Committee, Reedsville ... 15 00

Total from North Carolina ... $ 78 00

OHIO.

Sept. 13. Ladies' Sewing Society of Universalist Church, London, per Theo. P. Gordon, Columbus ... $ 10 00

PENNSYLVANIA.

Sept. 13. Mr. and Mrs. Craig, Jefferson ... 1 00
Oct. 29. Mr. and Mrs. H. K. Craig, Jefferson ... 1 00

Total from Pennsylvania ... $ 2 00

TENNESSEE.

Oct. 14. From "A Baby," Moffett.. 1 00

TEXAS.

Sept. 17. Citizens of Halletsville, per Sam. Deval, for sufferers
at Canton...... .... 47 60
20. Sunday Schools, Churches and Brass Band of Lam-
passes, by Walter Acker 125 95
Nov. 3. Colored people of Gonzales, for persons of their own
color, per Benj. A. Botts, Houston 14 15
Oct. 3. M. E. Church, Jacksboro, collection through Rev. W.
V. Jones, pastor, to Gov. Stone.......................... 54 00

Total from Texas... .$ 241 70

VIRGINIA.

Sept. 2. Guests and Proprietors of Montgomery White Sulphur Springs, per Jones S. Hamilton, G. Townsend,
G. L. Boney, Committee.............................. 100 00
(Committee also sent $25 to Jackson How'd Ass'n.)
3. Citizens of Petersburg, through Mayor Wm. E. Cameron, and Rev. T. D. Witherspoon, to Gov. Stone... 1,000 00
25. Board of Supervisors, Norfolk County, per Leigh R.
Watts, W. S. Butts, Geo. T. Wallace, Committee,
Portsmouth, to Gov. Stone.............................. 100 00
27. Citizens of Portsmouth, per John H. Hume, Jas. H.
Toomer, L. R. Watts, Finance Committee of Peo-
ples' Meeting, to Gov. Stone.............................. 100 00
27. Citizens of Portsmouth, through J. Thompson Baird,
Mayor, to Gov. Stone................................... 190 37

Total from Virginia ....$ 1,490 37

FOREIGN COUNTRIES.

Oct. 29. Hon. Wm. M. Evarts, Secretary of State, Washing-
ton, from Foreign Relief Fund, for Edwards........ 200 00
Nov. 4. Same, for Jackson....................................... 200 00
9. Same, for Edwards....................................... 200 00
9. Same, for Bolton... 200 00
Sept. 28. American residents in City of Mexico, per Hon. John
W. Foster, U. S. Minister, to Gov. Stone, gold...... 700 00
Dec. 26. Hon. Wm. M. Evarts, Foreign Relief Fund, for Mc-
Comb City.. 175 00

Total from Foreign Countries...........................$ 1,675 00

RECAPITULATION OF RELIEF FROM MISCELLANEOUS SOURCES.

Alabama...$	140 95
Arkansas...	5 00
California...	3,254 00
Colorado..	150 00
Georgia..	17 68
Illinois...	220 00
Indiana..	281 65
Iowa...	18 25
Kansas..	51 50
Kentucky...	12 00
Massachusetts..	86 50
Michigan...	1,242 06
Mississippi...	1,458 58
New Jersey...	130 00
Nevada..	50 00
New York..	1,960 00
North Carolina...	78 00
Ohio...	10 00
Pennsylvania..	2 00
Tennessee..	1 00
Texas..	241 70
Virginia...	1,490 37
Knights of Honor of Massachusetts, Michigan and Tennessee...	170 00
Foreign Countries..	1,675 00
Total..$	12,746 24

ADDITIONAL RECEIPTS.

1879.
Feb. 8. Through Geo. F. Brown, Secretary and Treasurer,
241 State street, Chicago, being the proceeds of an
entertainment by the ladies of the following Chap-
ters of the Eastern Star Order............................$ 158 80
Miriam Chapter, No. 1;
Lady Washington Chapter, No. 28;
Butler Chapter, No. 36;
Queen Esther Chapter, No. 41.

8. Wm. Garrett, Grand Secretary I. O. O. F., Burlington, from Lodges in Iowa................................. 25 62

19. Gregory Satterlee, Grand Treasurer Grand Lodge of
New York, Masonic....................................... 50 00

28. Howard Association, Hazlehurst, balance on hand,
through E. C. Williamson................................ 5 00

28. Lyons Lodge, No. 61, I. O. O. F., Lyons, Iowa, per
J. C. Root, Secretary, for Odd Fellows and their
families... 9 90

Total..$ 249 32

EXHIBIT D.

RELIEF DISBURSEMENTS.

GRENADA.

Aug. 16.	Dr. W. E. Hughes................Voucher No. 1	100	00
23.	Dr. W. E. Hughes 2	100	00
	Odd Fellows Lodge, or Relief Committee.............. 3	30	00
26.	Dr. W. E. Hughes................................ 4	200	00
30.	General Relief Committee....................... 6	500	00
Sept. 6.	W. J. Ayres, N. G., Grenada Lodge, No. 6, I. O. O. F. 7	500	00
3.	Howard Association............................... 8	1,000	00
19.	Mrs. S. H. H., (Masonic)...................... 9	300	00
Oct. 1.	Mrs. W. J. A., I. O. O. F.......................11	200	00
1.	Bro. M.'s three children, (Masonic).................10	100	00
1.	Bro. C.'s children, (Masonic).................12	50	00
1.	Mrs. R., (Masonic)..............................13	50	00
1.	Rev. W. S. McC.................................14	150	00
1.	Mrs. M. C.....................................15	50	00
4.	Bro. J. H. C., (Masonic)........................16	100	00
4.	Mrs. H. M. J., (Masonic).......................17	50	00
4.	Mrs. H. M. J., (Masonic).......................18	50	00
4.	Bro. A. S. W., (Masonic).......................20	150	00
18.	Bro. J. H. Campbell, for relief of Ebenezer neighbor-hood, and of sundry persons in Grenada, (detailed report filed................................21	250	00
Nov. 3.	Grenada Lodge, No. 6, I. O. O. F., (36 orphans, 4 widows)..22	1,140	00
Sept. 27.	Family of Rev. John McC........................23	150	00
Nov. 29.	Mrs. J. K. W. and children.....................24	10	00
30.	Mrs. J. K. W. and children.....................25	25	00
30.	Widow of Bro. W. F. F., Lodge No. 361, (Masonic)..26	50	00
30.	Bro. J. R. F., Lodge No. 361, (Masonic)..........27	10	00
30.	Sir Knight R. A. A., on recommendation of E. C. of No. 15.. 28	100	00
30.	51 orphans and 10 widows, Grenada, No. 31, (Masonic).......................................29	1,825	00
30.	Mrs. S. H. H..................................30	50	00
30.	Grenada Lodge, No. 31, (Masonic)................31	500	00
Jan. 1.	Grenada Lodge, No. 31, (Masonic)................32	500	00
	Grenada Lodge, No. 6, I. O. O. F...............33	500	00
	Total ....$	8,790	00

HOLLY SPRINGS.

Sept. 6.	Col. W. J. L. Holland, Chairman Relief Committee.....................................Voucher No. 1	500 00
9.	Col. W. J. L. Holland, Chairman Relief Com...... 2	500 00
10.	Col. Kinloch Falconer, for Relief Committee........ 3	500 00
13.	Col. H. W. Walter, for Relief Committee............ 4	1,000 00
16.	Col. Kinloch Falconer, for Relief Committee......... 5	1,000 00
20.	Col. Kinloch Falconer, for Relief Committee......... 6	500 00
Oct. 1.	Col. Holland, for Relief Committee..................... 7	1,000 00
25.	Mrs. A. W., whose husband, a Knight Templar, died at Holly Springs................ 8	50 00
3.	Supplies for sick and destitute, purchased in St. Louis........................ 9	491 48
4.	Blankets and clothing, purchased in St. Louis.....10	291 50
Nov. 9.	Capt. J. C. Tucker, services, as per statement........11	100 00
Dec. 14.	Holly Springs Lodge, No. 35, for relief families of Masons....................12	500 00
14.	Widow and five children of Mr. A., (Masonic).......13	75 00
14.	Mrs. A., a destitute widow, husband died of fever..14	25 00
14.	Widow and two children of Bro. K., (Masonic)......15	75 00
14.	Widow and two children of Bro. K., (Masonic)......16	25 00
14.	Widow and mother of a Mason............ 17	50 00
14.	Four children of Mrs. P., who died of fever...........18	100 00
14.	Mrs. M. and two children, husband died of fever...19	25 00
14.	Mrs. M. and two children, husband died of fever...20	25 00
14.	Mrs. S. E. B...........................21	50 00
14.	Mrs. C. and children, (Masonic)....................22	150 00
14.	Mrs. E. J. W...........................23	20 00
14.	Son of Bro. W. S. M., (Masonic)....................24	25 00
14.	Mrs. D., widow of a Mason.........................25	25 00
3.	Bro. L. B. M., (Masonic)...........................26	100 00
20.	Masonic contribution from Indianapolis, direct to Holly Springs, included in my receipts.............27	316 50
20.	Mrs. W. and children.............................28	30 00
Jan. 1.	Relief Fund for Holly Springs Commandery, No. 3, $300; Wilson Chapter, No. 5, $200.................29	500 00
7.	Children of Bro. H. W. W..........................30	250 00
	Total...$	8,299 48

DRY GROVE.

Sept. 16.	R. R. Ledbetter, medicines...............Voucher No. 1	36 90
3.	J. Cohen, 5 gallons whisky....................... 2	16 00
26.	Hofheimer & Bro., champagne, brandy, whisky..... 3	18 60
26.	C. Cosmani, cask of beer......................... 4	19 00
30.	Raymond Relief Committee, for Dry Grove 5	250 00
Oct. 18.	Col. T. S. Dabney, for general relief.................. 6	100 00
Nov. 6.	A. N. Kimball, for 11 days services................ 7	33 00
6.	Morris & Flusser, ice bills from Sept. 20.............. 8	92 00
Sept. 23.	Rev. Dr. Douglas, for general relief................ 9	200 00
27.	Crystal Springs Howard Association, for Dry G've..10	250 00
Oct. 2.	Terry Relief Committee, for Dry Grove.............11	200 00
4.	Crystal Springs Howard Association, for Dry G've..12	500 00
Nov. 9.	Dr. W. E. Herring............ 13	75 00

Dec. 23.	Dr. G. W. West (recommended by W. M. of Dry Grove Lodge, No. 321...........................14	75	00
23.	Three children of Bro. Jas. C., who died 1870; the mother died of fever, 1878.............................15	50	00
23.	Bro. J. W. J., and one child.........................16	80	00
23.	Mrs. C., sister of Bro. J. C. S., who died Sept. 7, '78..17	50	00
23.	Mrs. J. C. W. and five children.....................18	100	00
23.	Mrs. W. D. K. and five children.....................19	100	00
23.	Mrs. O'B. and one child, husband died of fever......20	20	00
23.	Dry Grove Lodge, No. 321, Widows and Orphans' Relief..21	350	00
	Total..$	2,565	60

LAKE.

Sept. 9.	Champagne and whisky....................Voucher No. 1	20	00
23.	Meridian Relief Committee, for Lake................ 2	1,000	00
Oct. 7.	Meridian Relief Committee, for Lake................ 3	500	00
31.	Special car, with relief for Lake.................. 3½	40	00
31.	Bro. W. M. Thornton, for the orphan children of Bros. Lowry, Davison and Crouch.................. 4	250	00
31.	Bro. Thornton, Pres't Aid Ass'n, general relief...... 5	1,000	00
31.	Richardson & Bro., supplies......................... 6	65	00
	Total.................................. ....$	2,875	00

GREENVILLE.

Oct. —.	Greenville Lodge, No. 94, I. O. O. F...Voucher No. 1	13	40
Sept. 21.	Rev. S. Archer, Chairman Relief Committee......... 2	*1,000	00
Oct. 13.	Rev. S. Archer, Chairman Relief Committee......... 3	*1,000	00
Dec. 8.	Mrs. E. S., widow of Mason........................... 4	69	00
Feb. 16, 1879.	For widows and orphans, through Greenville Masonic Lodge................................... 5	2,000	00
16, 1879.	For widows and orphans, through Greenville I. O. O. F. Lodge.............................. 6	1,000	00
	Total...$	5,082	40

* Mostly distributed by Bro. Archer, through Masons and Odd Fellows.

PORT GIBSON.

Aug. 24.	James A. Gage, Pres't How'd Ass'n...Voucher No. 1	200	00
29.	James A. Gage, President Howard Association...... 2	200	00
30.	James A. Gage, President Howard Association...... 3	500	00
Sept. 3.	James A. Gage, President Howard Association...... 4	1,000	00
7.	James A. Gage, President Howard Association...... 5	1,000	00
16.	Bro. Wm. B. Fulkerson, for Masonic Relief......... 6	*1,000	00
19.	Frank H. Foote, Franklin Lodge, No. 5, I. O. O. F... 7	500	00
Oct. 1.	Rev. D. A. P.. 8	100	00
1.	Rev. John G. J.. 9	100	00
8.	Rev. D. H. M...10	150	00
	Total...$	4,750	00
Jan. 2.	Less, returned by Howard Association................	1,500	00
	Total..$	3,250	00

* Five hundred dollars of this was turned over, at my request, to Odd Fellows Lodge. See acknowledgment of Frank H. Foote, dated September 19.

VICKSBURG.

Aug. 21.	W. G. Paxton, chairman Masonic Relief Committee............................Voucher No. 1		300 00
26.	W. G. Paxton, ch'mn Masonic Relief Com...........*1		200 00
29.	W. G. Paxton, ch'mn Masonic Relief Com...........*2		300 00
30.	W. G. Paxton, ch'mn Masonic Relief Com........... 4		500 00
Sept. 2.	W. G. Paxton, ch'mn Masonic Relief Com........... 5		1,395 70
6.	W. G. Paxton, ch'mn Masonic Relief Com........... 6		1,525 00
9.	W. G. Paxton, ch'mn Masonic Relief Com........... 7		1,500 00
18.	Masonic Committee, from Arizona Territory......... 8		50 00
26.	W. G. Paxton, chairman Masonic Relief Com...... 9		1,000 00
Aug. 29.	Chas. Lehman, chairman I. O. O. F. Committee....3†		200 00
Sept. 2.	Chas. Lehman, chairman I. O. O. F. Committee....11		500 00
6.	Chas. Lehman, chairman I. O. O. F. Committee....12		500 00
9.	Chas. Lehman, chairman I. O. O. F. Committee. ..13		500 00
18.	Chas. Lehman, (see voucher No, 8 of Masonic......		50 00
24.	Chas Lehman...................................14		500 00
Oct. 9.	Chas. Lehman 15		500 00
14.	Chas. Lehman...........................16		250 00
Jan. 3.	Chas. Lehman.........................17		700 00
Sept. 17.	Rev. Dr. C. K. Marshall, for ministers and their families.............................18		1,225 00
17.	Rev. Dr. C. K. Marshall, for distribution at his discretion—detailed statements being part of this and preceding voucher.....................19		1000 00
18.	Raymond Relief Committee, to buy cattle for Vicksburg.............................20		300 00
Nov. 18.	Bro. S. F., Mason and Odd Fellow...............21		50 00

Total.......................................$13,045 70

* 1. No receipt filed, but Cash Book and Letter Book show payment.
† 2. No receipt filed, but Cash Book and Letter Book show payment.
‡ 3. No separate receipt filed, but amount included in general acknowledgement of $3,000 00, herewith filed.
NOTE.—Bro. Paxton's Report, herewith filed, confirms the statement as to vouchers No. 1 and 2.

WATER VALLEY.

Sept. 25.	H. W. Freeman, Sec'y Relief Com.....Voucher No. 1		1,000 00
Oct. 5.	A. M. Hardin & Co., St. Louis, supplies.............. 2		22 93
12.	J. W. Hellums, N. G., I. O. O. F., Lodge No. 82... 3		500 00
Dec. 14.	Sir Kt. T. W. W. and, family, Masonic.............. 5		50 00
14.	Comp. J. M. C., of Chapter No. 96, Masonic......... 6		50 00
14.	Widow and daughter of Bro. M. A. R, Masonic.... 7		50 00
14.	Widow and four children of Bro. J. F. C, Masonic. 8		100 00
14.	Widow and child of Bro. J. D. H., Masonic......... 9		50 00
14.	Widow of Bro. A. C, Masonic.....................10		50 00
14.	Four orphan children of Bro. J. D. R., Masonic.....11		100 00
14.	Widow and 4 children of Bro. W. J. M., I. O. O. F.12		100 00
14.	Widow and child of Bro. W. L. B, I. O. O. F.......13		75 00
14.	Mrs. M. A. G., (husband died of fever).............14		25 00
14.	Miss B., Masonic.........................15		30 00
14.	A Widow and 2 children.........................16		25 00
14.	Widow and daughter.........................17		25 00
14.	Bro. R. L. P., I. O. O. F.......................18		50 00

Dec. 19	Mrs. B. and children	19	30 00
23.	Mrs. M. S. M., Masonic	20	50 00
23.	Mrs. M. P., Masonic	21	30 00
23.	Water Valley Lodge, No. 82, I. O. O. F.	22	375 00
24.	Mrs. R. T. and children	23	20 00
24.	Water Valley Lodge, No. 132, Masonic	24	500 00

Total...$3,307 93

OSYKA.

Dec. 4.	Orphan babe of Bro. M. D. B., ...Voucher No. 1		100 00
4.	Miss E. I. D.	2	25 00
4.	Mrs. D. McG. and three children	3	35 00
4.	Mrs. D. M. R. and three children	4	35 00
4.	Mrs. A. C.	5	20 00
4.	Dr. F. and family, (four died of fever in family)...	6	25 00
4.	Mrs. R.	7	20 00
4.	Mrs. M. A. W. and two children	8	35 00
4.	Mrs. B. and family.	9	16 50
4.	Mrs. B. and daughter, and three other children	10	40 00
4.	Mrs. J. A. O.	11	30 00
4.	Mrs. M. R., and three children	12	30 00
4.	Wm. B., (five in family)	13	15 00
4.	Mrs. M. A. McG. and two children	14	35 00
4.	Bro. W. D. D.	15	100 00
4.	L. M. and two orphan children of H. H.	16	35 00
4.	Mrs. A. R and two children	17	30 00
4.	Simon C. for two orphans of H. H.	18	25 00
4.	Seven families, recommended by Bro. Davidson	19	105 00
4.	Orphan son of Bro. Wm. B.	20	30 00
4.	Miss Janie S.	21	50 00
4.	Mrs. L. B. G.	22	25 00

Total...$ 861 00

CANTON.

Sept. 2.	G. W. Thomas, President Howard Association	1	100 00
3.	G. W. Thomas, President Howard Association	2	200 00
11.	G. W. Thomas, President Howard Association	3	250 00
6.	G. W. Thomas, President Howard Association	4	200 00
9.	The L. family, I. O. O. F.	5	50 00
16.	The L. family, I. O. O. F.	6	200 00
16.	The L. family, I. O. O. F.	7	100 00
Oct. 4.	Bro. R. Y. S. and family, Masonic	8	100 00
5.	Mrs. D.	9	50 00
24.	Family of Bro. K.	10	100 00

Total...$ 1,350 00

McCOMB CITY.

Oct. 11.	Mrs. L. E. D., Masonic	1	30 00
12.	Grand Master John H. McKenzie, I. O. O. F., for general relief	2	500 00
12.	Grand Master John H. McKenzie, I. O. O. F., for general relief...	3	180 00

Nov. 12.	McComb City Lodge, No. 385, for general charity..	4	535	00
12.	Drug Store account against Howard Association....	5	171	35
12.	Drug Store account against families of Odd Fellows.	6	40	20
Dec. 4.	Mrs. Mc. N. and three children, I. O. O. F.	7	100	00
11.	Orphans of Bro. S., who died of fever, I. O. O. F...	8	50	00
Jan. 2.	Heber Craft, for widows and orphans	9	175	00

Total..$ 1,781 55

JACKSON.

Sept. 29.	Mrs. D. McC., (afterwards died of fever)	1	50	00
Oct. 7.	Mrs. G., husband and three children died of fever..	2	50	00
14.	Mrs. G., husband and three children died of fever..	3	25	00
14.	Howard Association, special contribution from New York for Jackson	4	500	00
14.	Howard Association, special contributions from Terre Haute, Ind.	5	281	65
14.	Rev. Dr. Watkins, for needy persons	6	10	00
14.	Rev. Dr. Watkins, for Mrs. E. J. C.	7	10	00
28.	Mrs. F. M. B., I. O. O. F.	8	25	00
Nov. 1.	Bro. H. H. S., Masonic	9	50	00
4.	Howard Association, special donation for Jackson..	10	200	00
4.	Bro. W. C. H., Masonic	11	25	00
9.	Rev. Dr. Watkins, for the sick and poor at discretion.	12	200	00
9.	Rev. Dr. Hunter, for sick and poor at discretion...	13	200	00
21.	Mrs. A. J. P. and children, Masonic	14	75	00
21.	Daughters of a Mason	15	50	00
21.	Mrs. D. V. P., mother of an Odd Fellow, deceased.	16	100	00
25.	Burial expenses of Masonic families	17	100	00
25.	Mrs. C. and children	18	10	00
25.	Bro. A. M. and family, Masonic	19	50	00
25.	Mrs. M. K. Y. and family, I. O. O. F	20	50	00
Dec. 23.	Bro. W. W. W. and family, I. O. O. F	21	50	00
7.	Mrs. J. A. C. and children	22	25	00
17.	Mrs. S. and children, Masonic	23	75	00
19	Capitol Lodge, No. 11, I. O. O. F.	24	100	00
12.	Capitol Lodge, No. 11, I. O. O. F., sick and funeral benefits	25	110	00
12.	Choctaw Encampment, No. 3, sick and funeral benefits.	26	67	50
21.	Mrs. M. C., Masonic	27	50	00
21.	Mrs. J. G., Masonic	28	50	00
24.	Mrs. F., Masonic	29	30	00
24.	Children of Bro. B., Masonic	30	50	00
27.	Mrs. G. and children, Masonic	31	50	00
27.	Mrs. A. J. P., Masonic	32	60	00
Jan. 4.	Mrs. B. L. G., Masonic	33	25	00
7.	Mrs. C. and children	34	50	00

Total..$2,854 65

SHARON, MADISON COUNTY.

Sept. 27.	Wm. Benthall	Voucher No. 1	100	00
Oct. 14.	Wm. Benthall	2	50	00

Total..$ 150 00

YAZOO CITY.

Oct. 24.	Geo. M. Powell, Pres't Howard Ass'n., Voucher No. 1		500 00
Jan. 3.	Bro. R. B. M., (Mason and I. O. O. F.)............... 2		100 00

Total.. ....$ 609 00

TCHULA, HOLMES COUNTY.

Nov. 9.	Lucy Tapley, nurse, $60; A. N. Kimball expenses of himself and nurse to Tchula, $50,......Voucher No. 1		110 00

TALLAHATCHIE COUNTY.

Sept. 29.	Bro. W. H. FitzGerald, for gen'l relief, Voucher No 1		500 00
Nov. 4.	Bro. W. H. FitzGerald, for general relief............... 2		250 00
30.	Mrs. C. G. C., recommended by George Washington Lodge, No. 157...................... 3		50 00
Dec. —.	Mrs. C. G. C., recommended by George Washington Lodge, No. 157...................... 4		50 00

Total...$ 850 00

TILLATOBA.

Oct. 11.	J. H. Dame, President Relief Com.....Voucher No. 1		250 00
14.	J. H. Dame, President Relief Committee............ 2		250 00

Total..$ 500 00

HERNANDO.

Oct. 6.	Mayor E. Bullington, for gen'l relief..Voucher No. 1 $		500 00

BOLTON.

Sept. 12.	Mayor E. E. Baldwin.....................Voucher No. 1		500 00
Oct. 16.	Mayor E. E. Baldwin............................. 2		500 00
21.	Morris & Flusser, ice............................. 3		10 00
Nov. 6.	Morris & Flusser, ice............................. 4		10 00
9.	C. D. Williams, President Howard Association...... 5		200 00
30.	Morris & Flusser, ice............................. 6		2 00
26.	Bro. T. C. P., of Bolton Lodge, No. 326............ 7		50 00
26.	Children of Bro. T. A. M......................... 8		75 00
26.	Bro. W. M., of No. 326............................ 9		25 00
26.	Widow of Bro. M. of Lodge No. 326............... 10		75 00
26.	C. D. Williams, President Howard Association... 11		190 00

Total $1,637 00

GARNER.

Oct. 5.	G. L. McSwine, Relief Committee......Voucher No. 1		200 00
14.	G. L. McSwine, Relief Committee.....;............ 2		100 00
19.	C. V. Warren, Treasurer Relief Committee......... 3		500 00

Total.................. ....$ 800 00

CRYSTAL SPRINGS.

Dec. 28. Dr. R. M. Davis............................Voucher No. 1 $ 50 00

SENATOBIA.

Oct. 25. Sam. F. Massey, Acting President Anderson Relief
    Association.....................................Voucher No. 1   250 00

OAKLAND.

Oct. 3. J. M. Moore and J. H. McAfee, relief, Voucher No. 1   200 00
Nov. 9. Oakland Lodge, No. 97, I. O. O. F.........................2   100 00

  Total...$ 300 00

WINONA.

Nov. 29. Mrs. O., (whose husband and child died of yellow
    fever,)..Voucher No. 1   30 00

BYRAM.

Dec. 12. Dr. T. A. Catchings ....Voucher No. 1   50 00

TERRY.

Nov. 9. Dr. D. L. Rawls................................Voucher No. 1   50 00

SUMMIT.

Dec. 4. Bro. C. H. L., recommended by Grand Master
    McKenzie.......................................Voucher No. 1   25 00

EDWARDS.

Oct. 15, Rev. I. J. Daniel.............................Voucher No. 1   50 00
  15. Rev. I. J. Daniel, for general relief.....................2   200 00
Nov. 9. Geo. M. Martz, President Howard Association......3   200 00

  Total...$ 450 00

NEAR BALDWIN'S FERRY.

Dec. 28. Mrs. M. J. L..................................Voucher No. 1 $ 50 00

LAWRENCE.

Dec. 30. Family of Bro. W. D. McG...........Voucher No. 1 $ 50 00

MACON.

Jan. 6. Macon Lodge, No. 40*....................Voucher No. 1 $ 500 00

*This Lodge had sent me, at different times, during the epidemic, $600 00. The disastrous fire at Macon, affecting their ability to pay a debt of $700 00 on their new Hall, I returned $500 00 of their contribution. This was done without any suggestion on the part of the Lodge—the result of personal inquiry as to the damage sustained by the fire.

MEMPHIS.

Oct. 10. W. J. Jones, Chairman I. O. O. F. Relief Committee..Voucher No. 1   25 00
Dec. 31. Mrs. A. J. W.. 2   150 00

Total... $ 175 00

NEW ORLEANS.

Oct. —. Mrs. Mary C. V.......................... ......Voucher No. 1   175 00
26. Families of Revs. Drs. Rice and Trawick............ 2   100 00

Total... $ 275 00

NATCHEZ.

Oct. 23. Protestant Orphan Asylum...............Voucher No. 1   500 00
23. Catholic Orphan Asylums..................................... 2   250 00

Total... $ 750 00

LEBANON NEIGBORHOOD.

Oct. 18. Raymond Relief Committee..............Voucher No. 1   200 00
Nov. 6. Ice.. 2   2 00

Total...$ 202 00

BRANDON.

Dec. 17. Widow and 3 children of Sir Kt. M., Senior Grand
Warden of Grand Commandery at the time of his
death..Voucher No. 1 $ 50 00

MISCELLANEOUS.

Nov. 20. Family of Lt. Benner......................Voucher No. 1   50 00
15. Telegraph bill.. 2   154 35
Jan. 1. Postage, printing, incidentals............................ 3   65 00
Oct. 17. Loan to an Odd Fellow, from Texas.................... 4   25 00
Dec. 9. Rev. S. M. M., who rendered service at various
points.. 5   25 00

Total.......... .... $ 319 35

Subsequent Disbursements elsewhere reported.

REPORT OF RECEIPTS AND DISBURSEMENTS

BY

MASONIC RELIEF COMMITTEE,

VICKSBURG, MISS.

[PUBLISHED PER RESOLUTION OF GRAND LODGE.]

VICKSBURG, Miss., December 27th, 1878.

W. G. Paxton, Chairman of Masonic Relief Committee,

1878.	TO UNIVERSAL BENEVOLENCE,	DR.
Aug. 22.	Louisville Masons, through C. R. Woodruff, P. G. C..$	200 00
22.	Mystic See Lodge, Indianapolis, Ind...................	100 00
22.	J. L. Power, Grand Secretary, Mississippi...............	300 00
23.	Masonic Fraternity, Okolona, Miss........................	50 00
23.	Masonic Relief Board, Houston, Texas..................	50 00
24.	Masonic Fraternity, Sandusky, Ohio....................	40 00
27.	J. L. Power, Grand Secretary, Mississippi.............	200 00
28.	Masonic Fraternity, Rockford, Ills......................	30 00
28.	Garlick & Sizer, Calumet, Ohio..........................	5 00
30.	T. S. Gathright Lodge, No. 33, Oxford, Miss...........	80 50
30.	Masonic Fraternity, Natchez, Miss......................	100 00
30.	Henry Burnett, W. M., Paducah, Ky.......	50 00
30.	Terre Haute Commandery, No. 76, Indiana.............	123 80
30.	Tupelo Lodge, No. 318, Mississippi.....................	25 00
30.	J. L. Power, Grand Secretary, Mississippi.............	500 00
31.	Masonic Fraternity, Portland, Maine....................	300 00
31.	Chas. Lehman, loan to I. O. O. F., refunded...........	100 00
Sept. 6.	J. L. Power, Grand Secretary, Mississippi.............	1,395 70
6.	Mount Pleasant Lodge, No. 216, Ohio....................	7 00
6.	Excelsior Lodge, No. 442, Jackson, Mo..................	50 00
6.	Du Quoin R. A. Chapter, Ills	20 00
6.	Masonic Fraternity, Rockford, Ills......................	30 00
6.	O. S. Beers, W. M., Mobile, Ala	50 00
6.	Naval Lodge, No. 100, Portsmouth, Va..................	20 00
5.	W. B. Isaacs, Grand Secretary, Virginia................	100 00
5.	Emporium Lodge, No. 382, Pennsylvania..............	10 00
5.	Gonzales Commandery, No. 71, Texas..................	75 00
7.	J. L. Power, Grand Secretary, Mississippi.............	1,500 00
7.	Strict Observance Lodge, No. 78, Forsyth, Ga.........	35 00
7.	Masonic Fraternity, St. Joseph.........................	25 00
7.	Seaboard Lodge, No. 56, Portsmouth, Va..............	25 00
7.	Oliver Clifton, P. G. C., Jackson, Miss...........	5 00
12.	F. J. Lewis, K. T. Washington, D. C....................	15 00

5

Sept. 12.	Grand Lodge of Mass., through C. A. Welch, G. M.	100 00
12.	De Molay Commandery, No. 5, Americus, Ga.........	22 25
12.	Del Commandery, No. 44, Port Jervis, Nebraska......	10 00
23.	Knights Templar, Houston Texas....................	27 00
11.	J. L. Power, Grand Secretary, Mississippi...............	1,500 00
11.	Kennesaw Lodge......................	10 00
11.	Amity Lodge..........................	10 00
18.	Masonic Fraternity, Prescott, Arizona......	50 00
18.	Fayette Lodge, No. 707, Washington, Ohio............	85 00
21.	Adelphic Commandery, New York.......................	42 00
21.	Joppa Lodge, No. 315, Bay City, Michigan...........	25 00
21.	Cœur de Lion Commandery, No. 7, Atlanta, Ga.......	47 25
16.	Amount deposited by W. A. Fairchild, P. G. C.......	175 00
Aug. 28.	Freeport Commandery, No. 7, Illinois.................	100 00
28.	Covington R. A. Chapter, Kentucky......	30 00
28.	Centralia Lodge, No. 201, Illinois............................	25 00
29.	Masonic Fraternity, Galveston, Texas................	111 00
29.	Land Mark Lodge, No. 214, Pine Ridge, La...........	10 00
29.	J. L. Power, Grand Secretary, Mississippi...............	300 00
Sept. 28.	Ocean Lodge, Brunswick, Georgia.................	15 00
23.	Mt. Horeb R. A. C., Portsmouth, Va......	10 00
24.	Cincinnati Commandery, K. T............................	50 00
29.	Masonic Fraternity, Rising Sun, Ind....................	10 00
30.	Masonic Board of Trustees. Augusta, Ga........	75 00
30.	Steamer J. W. Cannon, passage money refunded.......	27 00
Nov. 2.	Proceeds sale of horses............................	125 00
7.	Proceeds sale of harness........................	10 00
12.	E. D. Rickley, for K. of P., amount refunded..........	40 00
16.	Howard Association, amount refunded.....	62 15
Sept. 26.	J. L. Power, Grand Secretary...........................	1,000 00
16.	Bro. James Murray, order for groceries and drugs.....	100 00

Total..$9,820 65

CR.

By sundry amounts paid " Relief"...............................$	4,132 32
By sundry amounts paid nurses...............................	1,902 38
By amount paid drugs, Gray & Co................................	138 15
By amount paid Howard Association, order of J. L. Power......	300 00
By amount paid for dry goods, Brown & Bro..............	1 25
By amount paid for dry goods, Schwartz & Marx....................	2 75
By amounts paid for dry goods, Maurice Meyer......................	4 00
By amounts paid for dry goods, Mayer Bros. & Co..............	46 85
By amount paid for dry goods, J. Shlenker & Co...............	35 58
By amounts paid for groceries, W. H. Andrews & Bro..............	402 23
By amounts paid for groceries, O. H. Perry & Co.............	135 79
By amounts paid for groceries, H. H. Kain....................	11 20
By amounts paid for groceries, G. W. Hutchinson, & Co.........	8 15
By amount paid shoe bill, P. H. Gilbert.......	16 00
By amount paid wood bills, North & Co.......................	41 50
By amount paid sundries, Dr. Davis.............................	237 65
By amount paid ice bills, F. M. Lassiter..........................	15 90
By amount paid for clothing, Geo. C. Kress & Co.............	58 25
By amount paid for burials, J. Q. Arnold......................	722 50
By amount paid for bedding, F. Steigleman...................	34 00
By amount paid for one horse, estate of D. W. Booth..............	125 00
By amount paid for liquors, Spengler and Tonella.................	19 30

By amount paid for liquors, Doll & Murphy............................ 1 25
By amount paid for transportation, V. & M. Railroad.............. 142 10
By amount paid for transportation, Mississippi River.............. 61 00
By amount paid for hack hire and drayages......................... 39 00
By amount paid for board bills and nurses........................... 152 00
By amount loaned Odd Fellows.. 109 00
By amount paid for hardware, Lee Richardson & Co.............. 16 15
By amount paid for rent, R. V. Eckman.............................. .15 00
By amount paid for printing, Herald Company...................... 18 40
By amount paid for coal bills, Floweree & Co...................... 30 80
By amount paid for for medical services, E. T. Henry............. 100 00
By amount Murray, orders transferred to Howard Association... 100 00

Total...$ 9,171 45
To gross amount receipts.. 9,820 65
By gross amount disbursements...................................... 9,171 45

Total balance...$ 649 20

W. G. PAXTON,
W∴ M∴ Walnut Hills Lodge, No. 194, Chairman.
T. M. FOLKES,
J∴ W∴ for W∴ M∴ W. H. Stevens Lodge, No. 121.
GEO. CALDER,
W∴ M∴ Vicksburg Lodge, No. 26.
G. G. MANLOVE,
E∴ K∴ for H∴ P∴, Vicksburg R∴ A∴ C∴, No. 3.
WM. FRENCH,
Gen'o Commanding Magnolia Commandery, No. 2.
W. A. FAIRCHILD,
P∴ M∴ Vicksburg Lodge, No. 26, Sec'y and Treas.

REPORT OF RECEIPTS AND DISBURSEMENTS

BY THE

ODD FELLOWS' RELIEF COMMITTEE,

VICKSBURG, MISS.

By contributions received during August, September, November and December, 1878, as follows:

J. L. Power, Grand Treasurer Grand Lodge of Mississippi.......$ 3,000 00
Summit Lodge, Summit, Miss.. 25 00
Geo. D. Winchell, Grand Treasurer, Ohio............................ 500 00
Rising Star Lodge, Evansville, Indiana................................ 10 00
G. P. Theobold, Louisville. Ky....................................... 100 00
Ague Lodge No. 25, through G. L. Moore, Treasurer, Louisville, Kentucky... 10 00
Chosen Friends Lodge, through Wm. Poutch, Secretary.......... 15 00
Watson Lodge No. 32, Mt. Sterling, Ky., through L. W. White, Secretary... 25 00
Meridian Lodge No. 80, Meridian, Miss., through W. L. Sadler.. 10 00
Poughkeepsie Lodge No. 21, New York, through J. D. Neal, Secretary... 32 00

Ottaway Lodge No. 24, Kansas, through S. Dewey, Secretary.... 5 00
F. Altman, Cheyenne, Wyoming Territory....................... 10 00
L. D. Bills, Grand Secretary, Madison, Wis..................... 20 00
Centennial Lodge No. 138, McPherson, Kansas, through L. F.
    Burdette... 5 00
Maple Rapids Lodge No. 224, through A. L. Kross............... 9 85
Relief Committee, St. Louis, Mo............................... 250 00
Ripley Lodge No. 52, Ripley, Miss............................ 25 00
Reno Lodge No. 19, Reno, Nevada, through W. L. Betchel........ 50 00
Adolphe Brandt, Grand Master, Georgia........................ 75 00
Adolphe Brandt, Grand Master, Georgia........................ 40 00
S. B. Hills, Grand Secretary, Wisconsin...................... 35 00
Angerona Lodge No. 289, Pittsburgh, Pa., through Samuel Os-
    born, Secretary....................................... 10 00
Quascagunoenon Lodge No. 39, Newburyport, Mass., through J.
    W. Work... 33 33
Merrimae Encampment, Newburyport, Mass., through Sam'l L.
    Ford.. 25 00
Geo. W. Morris, Treasurer Relief Committee, Louisville, Ky.... 100 00
Magnolia Lodge No. 20, Mound City, Kansas, through Geo. F.
    Dewey... 5 00
North Star Lodge No. 76, Newport, Ky., through Kentucky
    Relief Committee...................................... 25 00
Relief Committee, Newport, Ky................................ 25 00
Union Lodge No. 13, Mobile, Ala., through Can't Get Away
    Club.. 50 00
Manhattan Lodge No 17, Manhattan, Kansas, through Sam'l F.
    Burdett... 10 00
J. T. Menifield Lodge No. 17, Manhattan, Kansas, through Sam'l
    F. Burdett.. 2 00
John Ready Lodge No. 17, Manhattan, Kansas, through Sam'l
    F. Burdett.. 2 00
Oswego Lodge No. 36, Oswego, Kansas.......................... 15 00
Columbus Lodge No. 36, Columbus, Kansas...................... 10 00
J. C. Smith, Grand Scribe, Illinois.......................... 190 00
Tripon Lodge No. 169, Brazos, Texas.......................... 20 00
Metropolitan Lodge No. 27, Leavenworth, Kansas, through
    Thomas Moonlight...................................... 25 00
Old Dominion Lodge No. 5, Portsmouth Va...................... 10 00
J. D. King, Grand Secretary Grand Lodge, Ontario, Canada..... 525 00
J. L. Moores, Grand Treasurer, Grand Lodge, New York......... 28 00

Total...$ 5,361 18
Amount of money expended.................................... 5,298 50

Number of our members and their families relieved............39
Transient members..21
Widows relieved..18
Brothers died.. 3
Transient brothers died...................................... 3

CHAS. LEHMAN, Chairman Committee.

REPORT OF RECEIPTS AND DISBURSEMENTS

BY

GRENADA LODGE, NO. 6, I. O. O. F.,

YELLOW FEVER, 1878.

Amount of contributions received by officers and members of Grenada Lodge, No. 6, I. O. O. F., during the epidemic, as far as can be ascertained from data in possession of the Lodge:

Aug. 20.	Stockman Lodge, No. 19	32	10
19.	Wilkinson Lodge, No. 10	30	00
20.	Ridgely Lodge, No. 23	31	00
20.	Union Lodge, No. 35	25	00
19.	Carrollton Lodge, No. 40	5	00
Sept. 25.	Washington Lodge, No. 2	25	00
Aug. 23.	Iola Lodge, No. 91	5	00
22.	New Albany Lodge, No. —	5	00
26.	French Camps Lodge, No. 62	18	00
23.	DeSoto Lodge, No. 98	10	00
28.	Houston Lodge, No. 25	25	00
21.	Sardis Lodge, No. 13	30	00
19.	Ripley Lodge, No. 19	25	00
21.	Okolona Lodge, No. 37	10	00
22.	Oakland Lodge, No. 97	25	00
22.	Jefferson Lodge, No. 14	30	00
19.	Clinton Lodge, No. 42	10	00
19.	Corinth Lodge, No. 78	25	00
31.	Virginia, Old Dominion Lodge, No. 5	5	00
16.	Tennessee, Memphis Relief Association	250	00
10.	Louisiana, Tangipahoa Lodge, No. 99	15	00
	Kentucky, Hickman Lodge, No. —	25	00
Sept. 20.	Grand Lodge of Missouri	200	00
	J. L. Power, Grand Treasurer	500	00

Total...$ 1,361 10

10 boxes crackers, 12 boxes canned beef, 1 box tea, and 6 pair blankets from Grand Lodge of Missouri.

No. of Brothers sick of the fever during epidemic.....................20
No. of Brothers died of the fever during epidemic.....................14
No. of members of Brothers' families sick during epidemic.....................36
No. of members of Brothers' families died during epidemic.....................18
Total No. of Brothers and their families sick.....................55
Total No. of Brothers and their families died.....................32
Four widows and twenty orphans.

Amount of contributions.. $1,361 10
Amount disbursed.. 855 00

Amount on hand...... .... 506 10

And being distributed as rapidly as the necessities of our brethren and their widows and orphans are made known to the officers of the Lodge.

Members of the I. O. O. F., who died during the epidemic in Grenada, Mississippi :

Wm. J. Ayres, N. G., died September 5, of Grenada Lodge, No. 6.
D. C. Bristol, V. G., died August 23, of Grenada Lodge, No. 6.
J. L. Milton, Treas., died August 14, of Grenada Lodge, No. 6.
A. W. Ayres, P. G., died August 27, of Grenada Lodge, No. 6.
T. P. Barnes, P. G., died August 19, of Grenada Lodge, No. 6.
R. Coffman, P. G., died August 20, of Grenada Lodge, No. 6.
J. E. Saddler, P. G., died August 25, of Grenada Lodge, No. 6.
R. A. Collins, died August 26, of Grenada Lodge, No. 6.
D. M. Moore, died August 11, of Grenada Lodge, No. 6.
Henry Rafalsky, died August 19, of Grenada Lodge, No. 6.
J. C. Gray, under disability, of Grenada Lodge, No. 6.
T. W. Phillips, under disability, of Grenada Lodge, No. 6.
Walter Saddler, member of Vaiden Lodge.
H. T. Haddick, member of Greenville Lodge.
All resident citizens of Grenada.

SAM. LAWRENCE,
N. G. Grenada Lodge, No. 6.

RECEIPTS AND DISBURSEMENTS

BY MASONIC FRATERNITY OF GRENADA.

NOTE.—Most of the funds sent to Grenada during the epidemic were directed to the Howard Association and Citizens' Relief Committee. Although a large number of our brethren remained, there was no organized Masonic Relief Committee. During my visit to Grenada in November, I ascertained that the following contributions had been received by our brethren during the epidemic :

Aug. 14. Citizens of Jackson, per J. L. Power.........................$109 75
   14. Tupelo Lodge, No. 318, Mississippi............................. 25 00
   21. Grand Lodge of Mississippi, per J. L. Power, Grand Secretary.. 200 00
   24. Sardis Lodge, No. 307, per J. A. Rainwater................... 100 00
   24. Masons of Jackson, Tenn., per E. D. Anderson, J. M. McGlathery, Jas. O'Conner............................. 30 00
   24. Morton Lodge, No. 254, per H. O. Pettus..................... 5 00
   26. Grand Lodge, per J. L. Power, Grand Secretary............ 200 00
   26. Patton Lodge, No, 129, per Jas. R. Webb, Secretary...... 10 00
Sept. 10. Ostemaula Lodge, No. 113, Rome, Ga., per H. C. Norton 25 00
Sept. 14. Forth Worth Lodge, No. 148, Forth Worth, Texas, per J. P. Woods, Secretary.. .... 25 00

Total............. ....$729 75

Of this amount $641 50 had been disbursed for relief to November 30th.

J. L. P.

LODGES AND BRETHREN

NOT ELSEWHERE REPORTED

In response to a circular issued, the following contributions are reported as having been sent to afflicted localities. Some of the items are included in my general statement of receipts from Mississippi, pages 26, 42, 52:

Pascagoula Lodge, No. 202, Moss Point:

Aug. 17.	To Grenada, chairman Relief Committee.................:.......$	25 00
Oct. 19.	To Jackson, J. L. Power, Grand Secretary.................	100 00
19.	To Handsboro, C. Taylor, President H. II. A...............	25 00
Nov. 16.	To Handsboro, C. Taylor, President H. H. A...............	100 00
16.	To Biloxi, W. Foster, President Howard Association......	100 00
16.	To Biloxi, Mrs. Lang................................*	36 00
Oct. 21.	Contributions from H. L. H. Chapter to Handsboro........	50 00
21.	Private contributions by Masons to Grenada, Jackson, Handsboro, Biloxi and Ocean Springs.....................	434 25

Irvin Miller, W∴ M∴ Walnut Grove Lodge, No. 242, individual contribution	25 00
Duck Hill Lodge, No. 327—by Lodge $25 00; individual members, $80 00, to Grenada...	105 00
Cornersville Lodge, No. 284—individual contributions—amount not stated..	
Cherry Creek, No. 339—in addition to Lodge contribution, elsewhere acknowledged, Bro. N. B. Berry, sent to Grenada	10 00
Wm. Cothran Lodge, No. 361—By Lodge, for medical attention, $70 00; individual contributions in money and supplies, $45 00..	115 00

Masonic Fraternity of Natchez:

Aug. 25.	Grenada, to A. P. Saunders............................	10 00
29.	Vicksburg, to Wm. A. Fairchild......................	100 00
29.	Port Gibson, to Jas. A. Gage, Pres't H. A.............	125 00

Total from Natchez.................................$	235 00

Sardis Lodge, No. 307:

Aug. 16.	To R. A. Armistead, Grenada..........................	50 00
16.	To R. A. Armistead, Grenada..........................	50 00
	Contributions by members, in August, September and October, sent to Holly Springs, Grenada and Hernando, cash, $173 00; supplies, low estimate, $125 00....................................	$298 00

Total from Sardis Lodge... ....$	398 00
St. Albans Lodge, No. 60—To telegraph operators in New Orleans, $15 00; to N. Greener, President Howard Associations, McComb City, $55 00............................	70 00
Salem Lodge, No. 45, Ashland—Individual contributions: to Holly Springs, $70 00; to Grenada, $40 00...	110 00

Ripley Lodge, No. 47—To Holly Springs, $10 00; to Vicksburg,
$10 00; individual contributions to Holly Springs,
Grenada, Grand Junction, Memphis, estimated at
$200 00.. 220 00
Water Valley Lodge, No. 132—Cash and provisions to Grenada 50 50
Lamar Lodge, No. 148—To Grenada, $10 00; to Moscow, Tenn.,
$10 00.. 20 00
Trinity Lodge, No. 88—Individual contributions, estimated..... 50 00
King Solomon Lodge, No. 333—To Lake, Sept. 10th.............. 25 00
Hazlehurst Lodge, No. 25—Individual members contributed lib-
erally through Howard Association.....................
Cadcretta Lodge, No. 278—Supplies and cash to Grenada........ 25 00
Rising Glory Lodge, No. 215—To Grenada........................ 50 00
Raymond Lodge, No. 21—To local Relief Committee, to pur-
chase supplies for Vicksburg and other places....... 40 00
Summit Lodge, No. 93, I. O. O. F.—To Grenada I. O. O. F.,
Lodge, No. 6, $50 00; to Bro. Lehman, Chairman
I. O. O. F. Relief Committee, Vicksburg, $25 00; 75 00
T. S. Gathright Lodge, No. 33, Oxford—by Lodge, 25 00; indiv-
idual brethren, $55 00—sent to Vicksburg............. 80 00
Macon Lodge, No. 40—($600 00 elsewhere acknowledged)........ 787 28
Evening Star Lodge, No. 70—In addition to supplies, cash....... 20 00
Ebenezer Lodge, No. 76,.. 40 00
Pontotoc Lodge, No. 81... 28 75
Malone Lodge, No. 101... 10 00
Lodi Lodge, No. 134—In addition to $10 00 sent Grand Secre-
tary, by Lodge, individual contributions to Grenada. 15 00
Brethren of China Grove Lodge, No. 298, and members of other
Lodges, and non-affiliates, through said Lodge, cash
$44 00; supplies estimated $250 00.................... 294 00

TOTAL RELIEF TO MISSISSIPPI.

The following is compiled from the best information obtainable:

VICKSBURG.

DEAR SIR: The Howard Association received, in cash, in
round numbers, besides flour, meat, clothing..................$ 184,000 00
City... 19,000 00
Masons, Odd Fellows, Hebrews, Knights of Pythias, Hiber-
nians, Religious Bodies.. 47,000 00

Say in all..$250,000 00
Vicksburg, March 15, 1879.   T. R. ROACH.

HOLLY SPRINGS.

HOLLY SPRINGS, March 15, 1879.

COL. J. L. POWER—*Dear Sir:* In reply to your enquiry of 12th inst., I
would state that the total cash receipts for relief purposes here, as shown
by committee's books, amount to $54,859 42, which includes an item of
$3,955 50, being the face of a county warrant issued under order of the
Board of Supervisors of this county to assist in relieving the indebtedness
of the Committee, and from which (warrants being at a discount) the
Committee realized $3,805 actual cash.

I have endeavored, but ineffectually, to gather some information touching
donations through Benevolent Orders and cannot give you even an approx-
imate estimate. The same difficulty attains as to value of supplies. No
account whatever, was kept of these, though the amount must have run up
into thousands of dollars. Regretting that I cannot give you more definite
information, I am,   Very truly,   ADDISON CRAFT.

PORT GIBSON.

Wm. B. Fulkerson, Treasurer of Howard Association acknowl-
edges total receipts...$ 20,678 27

GREENVILLE.

Rev. Stevenson Archer, Chairman Relief Committee acknowl-
edges total receipts...$31,068 66

JACKSON.

Subscribed by citizens..$ 2.219 70
Received by Howard Association from other States................. 6,964 85
Received by Mayor McGill from other States......................... 5,932 52
Received by other parties for relief, estimated...................... 2,500 00

Total...$17,617 07

CANTON.

Emmet L. Ross, Esq., Secretary Howard Association, reports
  actual cash received..$ 22,222 57
Merchandise, orders..   16 00
                                                                              _____
  Total...   ....$ 22 238 57

MERIDIAN.

Col. J. L. Power—*Dear Sir:* The total amount received at
  Meridian for relief during epidemic is............ ....$ 13,631 55
Expended...................................... .... 12,487 68
                                                                              _____
  Balance on hand..$ 1,143 87

The expenditures include all funds sent and expended by this Society
for Lake ; also five hundred dollars recently sent to Vicksburg.   Our Committee will soon publish a detailed report.   LELAND BARDWELL.
March 18, 1879.   _____

LAKE.

DEAR SIR: The total amount of funds from all sources and
  for all purposes was...$ 4,225 00
March 13, 1879.   W. M. THORNTON.

WATER VALLEY.

The published acknowledgements of funds received by Relief
  Committee, is..$ 5,578 82

GRENADA.

Citizens' Relief Committee acknowledge.............................$ 24,493 43
  No reports from Howard Association or other Relief organ-
  izations.

HERNANDO.

Published acknowledgement of Receipts . ...$ 3,242 20

Total cash contributions to Bolton, Edwards, Osyka, McComb
  City, Dry Grove, Yazoo City, Garner, Senatobia, Oakland,
  Tallahatchie county, and other places, estimated at............$ 35,000 00
Cash distributed by Grand Secretary, not included in amounts
  above acknowledged, estimated..................................... 50,000 00
                                                                              _____
  Total amount of cash received in Mississippi for relief... ......$ 522,632 42
Estimated value of Government supplies, and contributions
  of provisions, medicines, etc., by citizens of Mississippi
  and other States, and donations by railroads in the way
  of disinfectants, free transportation for physicians, nurses,
  etc.. 150,000 00
                                                                              _____
  Grand Total............. ....$ 682,632 42

EXTRACTS

FROM

CORRESPONDENCE,

ACCOMPANYING

CONTRIBUTIONS FROM MASONIC SOURCES.

" Have Love. Not love alone for one, but man as man thy brother call,
And scatter, like the circling sun, thy charities on all."

Nearly two thousand letters and telegrams were received by me during the epidemic. The following extracts are given, as showing the kind and sympathizing spirit of those who so promptly and generously came to our relief:

ALABAMA.

MONTGOMERY, ALA., Oct. 3.—Herein find $20 00, contributed by Liberty Lodge, No. 65. Still sympathizing with you in your great affliction, and sorrowing over the death of so many of our fraternity, and still hoping that the pestilence may soon be stayed by an early frost,

I am, fraternally, DANIEL SAYRE, Grand Secretary.

BENTON, ALA., Sept. 10.—Find contribution of Benton Lodge, No. 59, which please distribute as you may see proper. May God cause the fever soon to cease. Fraternally, B. WOLFE, Secretary.

SELMA, Sept. 24.—We send New York exchange for $103 84, being a third of the funds raised among the Masons of Selma. Expend same in such manner as may best alleviate the suffering of our Masonic brethren and their families. Humbly invoking a speedy interposition of Divine Providence in abating the fearful pestilence,

We remain, fraternally, WM. T. DAUGHTRY,
GEO. R. BOYD,
Committee.

SAN FRANCISCO, Sept. 5.—[Telegram.] Excelsior Lodge has this day placed to your credit, by telegraph, at Agency Bank of California, in New York, one hundred dollars, for benefit of brethren in fever districts.
GEO. C. RANDALL, Master.

CALIFORNIA.

SAN FRANCISCO, Sept. 5.—[Telegram.] I send you one thousand more, same manner as before. Acknowledge by telegraph, and say whether you want more. We have plenty. ALEX. G. ABELL, Grand Secretary.

SAN FRANCISCO, Sept. 9.—We, members of the French Lodge, La Parfaite Union, No. 17, sympathizing with the unfortunates afflicted with yellow fever, and wishing to alleviate, as much as it is in their power, the sufferings resulting from such calamity, have directed the banking house of Lazard Freres, in New York, to hand you fifty dollars, to be used as circumstances may require. By order of the Lodge.

P. G. SABATIC, Master.

SAN FRANCISCO, Nov. 4.—By next express will send you $55 00 (silver $45 00; gold, $10 00;) contributed by the various Lodges of the Fraternity in Washington Territory, for yellow fever sufferers. In addition to this, the Masons of the Territory have sent $100 00 to their suffering brethren in Tennessee. AARON STEIN, Treas. Relief Fund.

COLORADO.

DENVER, COL., Sept. 5.—Your draft for $50 00 contribution of Union Lodge, No. 7, paid. Denver has already sent nearly $2,000 to different afflicted points in the South. Trusting that the scourge may soon be stayed, O. F. WHITTEMORE, Secretary.

DENVER, COL., Sept. 20.—Enclosed find the contribution of El Paso Lodge, No. 13, ($63 75) which please expend for the relief of suffering Masons. ROGER W. WOODBURY, Grand Master.

CONNECTICUT.

NORWICH, CONN., Aug. 31.—Enclosed find check for $25 00, just received from New Haven Commandery. Other contributions will be forwarded the moment received. Personal service is impossible. If that would aid you, the South would swarm with Northern friends with strong arms and warm hearts. Your terrible sufferings are now absorbing our thoughts and conversation; sympathizing heartily with you.

JOHN W. STEDMAN, Grand Recorder.

Other remittances were received from Sir Kt. Stedman, dated Sept. 8, 12, 16, 23, on which latter date he wrote: "A heavy frost is settling down upon us this evening. I pray it may soon reach your stricken region." Oct. 24th, in sending his last remittance, he said: "God be praised for your preservation."

HARTFORD, CONN., Sept. 23.—Your acknowledgement of $250 00 received; also telegram this morning. I enclose you another draft for $386 00, the balance I have on hand, which you can use where it will do the most good among the suffering brethren of your State. This makes $1,686 60 I have forwarded to different places. We hope the cool weather will soon kill out the scourge. J. K. WHEELER, Grand Secretary.

HARTFORD, CONN., Oct. 1.—I send you draft for $200 00 for the orphans. I fear there are many cases where children are left without parents, who will require attention for some time to come. I trust you are not to be afflicted in Jackson. The scourge has been terrible.

J. K. WHEELER, Grand Secretary.

DAKOTAH TERRITORY.

YANKTON, DAKOTAH TERRITORY, Sept. 27.—You may draw for one hundred more, if needed. GEO. H. HAM.
[Answer: Have enough.] Grand Master.

DISTRICT OF COLUMBIA.

WASHINGTON, D. C.—Sept. 2.—On 30th inst., I telegraphed you to draw for $250 00. I am now authorized to have you draw for $250 00 more, making $500 00 in all which we send to Mississippi. We send $250 00 to Louisiana, $250 00 to Tennessee, and expect to make it more. We regret to see that as yet there seems to be no abatement of the scourge.

ALEX. GARDNER, Treasurer.

GEORGIA.

ATLANTA, GA., Sept. 1.—Find $131 contributed among Fraternity to present time. Distribute as may be needed. Be assured of our deepest sympathy and earnest prayers in your behalf,

W. F. PARKHURST, Chairman Relief Board.

Benevolent Lodge, No. 3, Milledgeville, also sent two contributions per Lucius J. Lamar, Secretary.

ILLINOIS.

CHICAGO, Oct. 29.—We hope the fever in your midst has abated, but we cannot hope that the destitution arising from its effects is much if any less. We think there must be many widows and orphans depending upon you for aid. Believe me, Brother Power, the Masons of Chicago have never ceased to remember the distress and misfortunes of their brethren of the the South, and the Committee selected to represent the craft of Chicago in this melancholy matter have ever been sensible of their duty to collect and forward aid as promptly as possible. I enclose you draft for $130 27, balance on hand, which makes total amount sent you $1,030 27. We also sent Brother Frizzell $700. With best wishes, DEWITT C. CREIGER.

SPRINGFIELD, ILL., Sept. 28.—I forward you $300 for benefit of Masonic sufferers from yellow fever. I have your acknowledgements of five previous remittances aggregating $2040. O. H. MINER, Grand Treasurer.

SPRINGFIELD, ILL., Nov. 1.—I send you by express $439 47, being the balance of all contributions to date, received from our Lodges for relief of Masonic sufferers in the South. I presume this will close our remittances for this purpose, as it is understood that the fever is practically at an end, although I have no doubt the suffering and distress resulting from it will long continue. The labor imposed upon you in this connection must have been very great, and well worthy a liberal reward.

O. H. MINER, Grand Treasurer.

MT. CARMEL, ILL., Aug. 24.—Enclosed find $20, contributed by Mt. Carmel Lodge, No. 239. I assure you that your suffering people have our hearty sympathy. R. S. GORDON, W. M.

SPRINGFIELD, ILL., Aug. 24.—I send you $20 25, for relief of yellow fever sufferers where you may see fit to apply it. It is the individual contribution of members of Tyrian Lodge, No. 333. As you doubtless have your hands full will only express the hope that the dreadful scourge may soon cease. FRANK HUDSON, JR., Past Master.

SHELBYVILLE, ILL., Aug 24.—It affords us pleasure to cast in our mite toward alleviating the suffering and destitution caused by the fearful epidemic that is now devastating your State and other sections of the South. Enclosed find draft for $63 00—$29 00 of which was contributed by the brethren of Jackson Lodge, No. 53, and balance by citizens generally.

Accept our sincere sympathies, and hope that the Great Disposer of events may soon remove from your people His afflicting hand and restore them to health and happiness. A. FEAR, Secretary.

CHICAGO, Aug. 27—At what point in Mississippi can the most good be accomplished by coming and bringing relief to yellow fever sufferers? Advise me fully at once. J. C. TUCKER.

SPRINGFIELD, ILL., Aug 28.—I enclose you $10 00, the contribution of Lexington Lodge, No. 482. Though small in amount it shows that the sympathies of the Craft in Illinois are with you in your terrible affliction. JOHN T. BURRILL, Grand Secretary.

MORRISON, ILL., Sept. 5.—Enclosed find $82 00—a donation from the Lodge and individual Mason's, which you are requested to use as your judgment may dictate. We sincerely hope the plague may be speedily stayed. FRANK CLENDENIN, Secretary.

JACKSONVILLE, ILL., Sept. 5.—In sending you the enclosed proportionate sum of $25 00 we trust that a kind Providence may save you and friends from further devastation, and that your country may soon be restored to health and prosperity. LEOPOLD WEIL.

SUMNER, ILL., Sept. 16.—Enclosed find $15 00, the contribution of Sumner Lodge, No. 334, to our afflicted brethren of your State. Place it where it will do most good. M. MAY, W. M.

MARINE, ILL., Sept. 9.—Find herein $20, the contribution of Marine Lodge, No. 355. Hoping that God may restore your people to their accustomed health and prosperity. ALBERT H. JUDD, W. M.

ROSSVILLE, ILL., Sept. 18.—Find Money Order for $32 50, donated by Rossville Lodge, No. 527, for Port Gibson. Hoping the weather may change and thereby abate the fever at an early date, is the earnest prayer of the membership of this Lodge.
HENRY SHANNON, Chairman Committee.

PETERSBURG, ILL., Oct. 11.—Clinton Lodge, No. 18, sends you $25 00, for Masonic sufferers. We had already contributed through our Grand Treasurer. JAS. S. BLACK, Secretary.

NOTE—This special contribution was handed to the widow of a brother who lost her husband and three children by yellow fever.

PEORIA, ILL., Oct. 14.—I enclose you $83 65, the balance of Masonic Relief funds on hand. Distribute where it may be of most benefit to the afflicted. CROSSLEY WHITE, Treasurer.

INDIANA.

INDIANAPOLIS, IND., Sept. 23.—Yours of 20th acknowledging receipt of $45 50 to hand. Enclosed find additional contribution—$56 80. May the good Lord stay the awful scourge.
JOHN M. BRAMWELL, Grand Secretary Grand Chapter.

INDIANAPOLIS, IND., Sept. 18.—As per your suggestion, I have this morning expressed to Colonel Kinloch Falconer, Holly Springs, the sum of $316 50, for relief of yellow fever sufferers. Should you require more please advise me. WM. H. SMYTHE, Grand Secretary.

INDIANAPODIS, IND., Sept. 24.—The morning papers convey the sad intelligence of the death of Col. Kinloch Falconer. I am, therefore, compelled to look to you for receipt of the money sent him. But take your time for it—any time within a month or so will do. Attend to more important matters first. I am well satisfied that your time is fully employed in attending to the wants of the afflicted. God grant that your life may be spared. WM. H. SMYTHE, Grand Secretary.

KINGSTON, IND., Oct. 2.—Enclosed find draft for $32 00, donated by Knightstown Chapter, No. 33. Use it where Masonic charity most demands. We humbly trust that it may be the means of assisting some brother who has been stricken with the scourge that is devastating your country. The amount though small comes from true and sincere brothers, who accompany it with their prayers for the speedy relief our Southern brethren. GEO. WILLIAMS, Secretary.

BROWNSTOWN, IND., Oct. 23.—Enclosed find $11 10, to aid the yellow fever sufferers in your State. Though a little late, we doubt not you can use it to advantage. It is contributed by Washington Lodge, No. 13. D. A. KOCHENOUR, W. M.

IOWA.

SHENANDOAH, IOWA, Aug. 24.—I enclose a draft for $15 00, raised by the Craft at this place. Place it where it will do the most good. You need not acknowledge receipt. J. SWAIN.

NOTE.—We could not refrain from acknowledging so considerate a favor.

MARSHALLTOWN, IOWA, Aug. 28.—Herein find twenty-eight dollars' and seventy-five cents, contributed by brethren here. Place it where it will do most good. GEO. GLICK, Treasurer Marshall Lodge, No. 108.

OTTUMWA, IOWA, Aug. 29.—In response to your call, Malta Commandery, No. 31, donates twenty-five dollars. Trusting that you may soon be relieved from the presence of the dread enemy, and commending you to Him whose coming brought light to those who sit in darkness and in the shadow of death, I am courteously yours, W. A. McGREW, E. C.

CEDAR RAPIDS, IOWA, Aug. 31.—In response to circular of our Grand Commander, I send you fifty dollars, for the benefit of suffering Sir Knights in your stricken State. Our Commandery is not strong, either financially, or numerically, but should there be necessity for further donations, we are ready to respond. JAS. MORTON, E. C., Appollo, No. 26.

BELLE PLAIN, IOWA, Aug. 31.—In response to call of our Grand Commander Van Saun, I enclose draft for $50 00. We deeply sympathize with the afflicted in the South, and hope that you will soon be free from the terrible scourge. JAMES COLLISTER, E. C.

RED OAK, IOWA, Sept. 2.—Enclosed find $50 00, which use for the benefit of suffering Sir Knights, or others, at discretion. Our Commandery has been organized only four months, and financially we are poor, but our hearts open to all that need. Though our mite is small we tender it with our sympathies, trusting and praying that our Southern Sir Knights and all others may soon be relieved from the terrible scourge which is sweeping over your fair land. C. G. ATWOOD, E. C., Bruce Commandery.

WATERLOO, IOWA, Sept. 2.—Herewith find draft for $100 00, the first installment of a fund raised under the auspices of the Masonic fraternity. Apply it where it will be of the most effective service. Our citizens are contributing liberally through the various organizations, both secular and social, in other places and through other agencies, but this sent you is the result of a combined effort of the two Lodges, Chapter and Commandery, by soliciting throughout the city. We hope to be able to make another remittance before the week is ended. Convey to the Sir Knights, Companions and brethren of Mississippi our heartfelt sympathy and earnest prayers for a stay of the pestilence.
H. W. JENNEY, Secretary Masonic Relief Committee.
—On September 13, received another draft for $60 15.

COUNCIL BLUFFS, IOWA, Sept. 3.—I have placed $75 00 in First National Bank, subject to your order, being part of subscription raised here among the brethren. Although the amount is small, we trust it may be the means of doing some good to brethren in distress. We sympathize with you in your affliction, and trust that God in His goodness may stay the ravages of the disease and death is the prayer of your brethren in the North. Will be pleased to hear from you when you can spare the time.
JOHN T. OLIVER, Secretary Bluff City Lodge, No. 71.

CLARINDA, IOWA, Sept. 9.—Enclosed find N. Y. draft for $30 00, contributed by Pilgrim Commandery. We prefer it should go to our Masonic brethren, but you can put it where it will do the most good.
C. LINDERMAN.

MUSCATINE, IOWA, Aug. 29.—Last night the Masonic fraternity held a meeting for the purpose of raising funds for the benefit of the sufferers in the South, in response to your circular of late date. As a result I hand you herewith draft for forty-six dollars. I am sorry it is not more. By order of the Grand Commander, I issued a circular the first of the week calling on the Commanderies to contribute. I hope you will get a liberal assistance from them. There is a wide-spread feeling of sympathy North for your suffering, and prayers are ascending that the term of the pestilence may be shortened. W. B. LANGRIDGE, Grand Secretary.

NOTE.—I received in all seventeen letters from Comp. L., the last one dated Oct. 1st, his total remittances being $1091 75. In his report to his Grand Chapter he said: "I was led to transmit all our contributions to Companion J. L. Power, as from him alone came any appeals to my hands for assistance, and from his location and excellent knowledge of the needs of the afflicted localities, both in that and the neighboring States, I felt assured that our contributions would be well and wisely applied. I have received from him acknowledgments of the receipt of all amounts sent, with expressions of grateful appreciation on behalf of those assisted.

NEWTON, IOWA, Sept. 10.—I, this day, send you by express $400 00, contributed by the brethren of this jurisdiction for the relief of our brothers in the South who are suffering with the yellow fever. As fast as money is received it will be forwarded. May God in His mercy stay this terrible scourge, and may the Grand Architect of the Universe watch over and protect you all in this your time of trial.
J. W. WILSON, Grand Master.

KANSAS.

EMPORIA, KANSAS, Sept. 20.—At the last Convocation of Emporia Chapter, No. 12, it was unanimously ordered that fifty dollars be sent you for relief of our suffering brothers, wherever in your judgment it is most needed. Will remit again from Lodge in a few days. Hoping the terrible scourge will soon cease, W. W. HIBBEN, H. P.

WYANDOTTE, KANSAS, Aug. 21.—At the request of our Grand Master I telegraphed you to draw at sight for $100 00. Should your terrible epidemic continue, we will appeal to our Lodges for further aid. Our people all over the North are hard at work doing all they can to help your people. Keep me advised are from time to time.
JOHN H. BROWN, Grand Secretary.

—Several other substantial favors were received from Brother Brown.

KENTUCKY.

HENDERSON, KY., August 28.—I send you one hundred dollars by express, for the relief of our suffering brethren in your State. This is contributed by the Masons of our town, and we accompany it with our prayers to the G. A. O. T. U., that it may be the means of alleviating the distress and saving the life of some suffering brother. Your people have our fullest sympathy in their distress, and we hope to be able, as occasion demands, to manifest it in a substantial way. May God avert the spread of the dread destroyer, and quickly relieve all those who are within his grasp. B. G. WITT, Em. Com.

LOUISVILLE, Sept. 7.—Your letter and circular of 3d received, and we were deeply moved by the touching contents. Rest assured, dear brother, that our afflicted friends among you have our most earnest sympathies in those your hours and days and weeks of terrible trial and affliction, and that you are constantly remembered in our daily prayers. Enclosed find two hundred dollars. We received a telegram from Holly Springs asking for aid of a general nature, and if any of the sum sent can be used at that point, we would thank you to send it there, giving Col. H. W. Walter information that it is from Louisville Masons. May God grant you immunity from the disease, and spare your life for further usefulness.
C. R. WOODRUFF, for Committee.

HOPKINSVILLE, KY., Sept. 11.—I enclose express receipt for one hundred and three dollars sent you. We wish that it were ten times as much, but feel sure that you will accept it in that spirit which makes strangers in Mississippi and strangers in Kentucky brethren. With deepest fraternal sympathy and affection, SAM'L O. GRAVES,
W. M. Hopkinsville Lodge, No. 37.

HENDERSON, KY., Sept. 2.—I send you sixteen dollars, the contribution of DeKoren Lodge—a small Lodge, and in debt, but remember their suffering brethren of the South to the measure of their ability. I hasten to forward it, with the prayer that God may bless and relieve you.
CAMPBELL H. JOHNSON, Grand Master.

LOUISIANA.

NEW ORLEANS, Aug. 21.—The Masons of Louisiana beg to tender their mite of two hundred dollars to their afflicted brethren of Mississippi. Call on Capitol State Bank, Jackson, who are authorized by Southern Bank to pay it. EDWIN MARKS, Deputy Grand Master.

—This was the first communication received on the subject of relief.

MARYLAND.

BALTIMORE, Sept. 3.—I can assure you our fraters in Mississippi have our deepest sympathy in this the hour of affliction, and we sincerely trust that the Great Ruler of events may speedily remove the terrible scourge from among you. I have expressed you five hundred dollars. I regret that we are unable to send a larger sum at this time, as most of our members had already distributed to other Committees. I shall, however, not relax my efforts.   JACOB E. KREBBS, Grand Com. of Maryland.

--Another kind letter, dated Sept. 18, was received from Grand Commander Krebbs, with three hunered and sixty dollars enclosed.

MASSACHUSETTS.

BOSTON, Sept 17.—I send herewith three hundred dollars contributed by different Masonic brethren for their Southern brethren. Are you still in want of money, and if so to what point had I better send any amount received—to you or elsewhere? I sent to Brother Wheeler, at Memphis just before his death. It could not have reached Memphis till after his death. If sent back I will replace it.   CHARLES A. WELCH, Grand Master.

BOSTON, Sept. 5.—My heart is drawn towards the people of the Southwest who are now suffering from the dreadful scourge of yellow fever, which is destroying so many valuable lives, and to yourself who is doing so noble and characteristic a Masonic work. May the Grand Architect soon avert the terrible pestilence, and send peace and prosperity to your people. I enclose my mite, ten dollars.

JOHN VIALL, D. D. Grand Master, 17th District.

MICHIGAN.

GRAND RAPIDS, MICH., Sept. 3.—As you will see by circular enclosed, we are making an effort to aid our afflicted brothers and Companions in the South. As the result of our beginning I express you to-day one hundred and fifty dollars. Have forwarded same amount to Tennessee and Louisiana. Hope to repeat the good work in a few days more. My dear brother, words seem like idle mockery to those as deeply afflicted as you are in Mississippi, but I assure you our hearts beat in unison with you and yours in this your hour of trial, and that ere long the dark cloud may be lifetd from your plague stricken land is the sincere prayer of you brethren in Michigan.   WM. P. INNES, Grand Secretary.

NOTE.—Nine letters from Brother Innes, contained nineteen hundred and five dollars. On the 15th September he wrote: "Poor Wheeler, of Memphis, I regret to see, is no more, also Rev. Sir Kt. Parsons. They died like Christian Knights. I am sorry to see your Grand Commander Paxton is down." Sept. 21st he wrote; "How truly do we sympathize with you as the news flashed over the wires this morning that such a good and true man as Brother Walter of your State is no more. I learned his sterling worth as a man and Mason while in Buffalo, and desire to mourn his loss with those most near and dear to him."

DETROIT, Sept. 3.—I enclose one hundred and fifty dollars contributed by the Masonic bodies of Detroit, to be used for the sufferers as you may deem best. Hoping, by the mercy of the Supreme Architect of the Universe, that the scourge may be stayed, and that health and prosperity may assume their wonted place among you.   J. B. H. BRATSHAW.

MINNESOTA.

ST. PAUL, Sept. 1st.—The Lord has seen fit to visit your section with a dire scourge, and blessed us with health and prosperity. We propose to do what we can to aid you in your calamity. Herewith find three hundred dollars—first installment contributed by the Craft in this jurisdiction. Our desire is that it may be distributed where it will do the most good.

On Sept. 2d, Bro. Pierson sent three hundred dollars additional, and said: "The Craft in this State are doing what they can, and further remittances will be forwarded as soon as received. We earnestly hope that Providence will permit you and yours to pass this terrible ordeal unscathed, and that you may live to continue to do good in the world."

On Sept. 11th, Bro. P. sent one hundred and fifty dollars more. He said: "I took the liberty of publishing your letter of acknowledgement in the papers. It will have a good effect. No other organization has received acknowledgement of funds contributed. I want to show the people that Masonic contributions are received by those who are best calculated to make proper use."

Sept. 24th, sent three hundred dollars. "Have just learned of the death of Bro. Walter. Does Br. Howry still live?"

Note.—The total amount received from Bro. Pierson is $1,050 00, instead of $750 00, as appears on page 26.

MISSISSIPPI.

A large, sympathetic and substantial correspondence was received from all parts of the State during the epidemic. The cash receipts are acknowledged on pages 26, 27, 28.

MISSOURI.

St. Louis, August 22.—Enclosed find contribution of two hundred dollars from our Grand Chapter. I need not assure you of the intense sympathy felt here for your fellow-citizens. As far as material aid can be available, it is being promptly furnished, but when people are driven to the last appeal, "God help us!" the situation must indeed be fearful.

JOHN W. LUKE, Chairman Ex. Com.

Note.—The several remittances from Bro. Luke will be found on pages 28 and 30. He also rendered prompt and zealous service in the purchase and forwarding of supplies for Holly Springs, at my request.

St. Louis, Sept. 3.—I send you two hundred dollars. Sept. 6.—I send you one hundred and five dollars, and may a merciful God bless the money to the good of the suffering and the needy, and stay the march of the destroyer through your Southern country. Our brethren in St. Louis, and the State, are deeply moved by the unutterable woe that has come upon you, and active measures are being employed to afford material relief. Sept. 10.—I send you three hundred and six dollars. Sept. 24.—I send you five hundred dollars.   JOHN D. VINCIL, Grand Secretary.

St. Joseph, Mo., Aug. 22.—We have read with sorrow the accounts of the ravages of the yellow fever, the suffering and misery of its victims, the destitution of those left helpless by its attacks, and your appeal to Masonic brethren for help. As a small token of sympathy, Mitchell Chapter, No. 89, sends you twenty-five dollars, with the hope that this, together with many larger amounts from other Masonic bodies, may be of much benefit to the afflicted."

St. Louis, Aug. 24.—I send you one hundred dollars for our Grand Commandery. Sorry the condition of our treasury is such we cannot appropriate more. We expect to contribute a like amount to our fraters in Tennessee and Louisiana.   WM. H. MAYO, Grand Recorder.

Sturgeon, Mo., Aug. 24.—Enclosed find fifty dollars, contributed by Sturgeon Lodge, No. 174. The brethren of the South have our deepest sympathy in their dire distress.   S. F. CROSS, Secretary.

ST. JOSEPH, Mo., Aug. 29.—Find twenty-five dollars, donated by Charity Lodge, No. 331. Our Lodge is poor, financially, but if necessary, we can come again shortly.　　　　　　　　D. P. WALLINGFORD, Secretary.

MONTANA.

VIRGINIA CITY, MONTANA, Sept. 22.—Enclosed find fifty dollars, which please use where most needed. We are few in numbers, but our hearts are warm toward our suffering brethren in the South. I trust and pray that the terrible scourge will soon leave your people.

J. M. KNIGHT, for Masons of Virginia City, Montana.

HELENA, MONTANA, Oct. 8.—Have just returned from the annual session of our Grand Lodge. While there, and since, I have received the amount of two hundred and fourteen dollars and fifty cents from our Lodges, to forward for the benefit of yellow fever sufferers. Have sent four hundred dollars to Memphis. Our hearts bleed for you, and we pray devoutly that the delivering angel may come to replace the destroying angel. We wish we could send you some of our frosty nights and pure air. We hope this money may bless the recipients, as it has already the givers.　　　　　　　　CORNELIUS HEDGES, Grand Secretary.

NEBRASKA.

OMAHA, NEBRASKA.—Nine communications from Sir Wm. R. Bowen, Grand Recorder, contained seven hundred and sixty-three dollars and forty-five cents.

NEVADA.

DAYTON, NEVADA, Sept. 16.—In behalf of Valley Lodge, No. 9, I have this day forwarded to your address fifty dollars, to be distributed among your suffering people, as in your judgment their necessities may require. Our heartfelt sympathies are with you in this the hour of great trial and suffering.　　　　　　　　J. L. CAMPBELL, W. M.

NEW BRUNSWICK.

ST. JOHN, N. B., Oct. 15.—Your acknowledgment of 4th came duly to hand. * * Permit me to express my heartfelt sympathy with you in your present affliction, and to join with you in the fervent hope that God in His infinite mercy may ere long remove the shadow of the pestilence from your sunny land.　　　　　　　　T. NISBET ROBERTSON.

NEW JERSEY.

TRENTON, N. J., Sept. 26.—We have this day ordered sent to you the sum of five hundred and thirty dollars and eighty-seven cents, for the relief of those suffering from yellow fever in your State, which you will dispense in your good judgment as needs may be.

JNO. H. HOUGH, Grand Secretary.

TRENTON, N. J., Oct. 1.—I herewith enclose one hundred dollars from Royal Arch Masons of New Jersey. In explanation of small amount sent, I would say that the Companions of our jurisdiction have made their contributions for same purpose to the Grand Lodge fund, which I understand has reached a respectable sum.　　　　THOS. J. CORSON, Grand Secretary.

NEW YORK.

NEW YORK, Sept. 20.—I telegraphed you seven hundred and fifty dollars to-day for the sick and suffering in your State. I do not wish to proclaim it, but we have distributed as follows: Louisiana, three thousand dollars; Mississippi, four thousand, five hundred dollars; Tennessee, four thousand, five hundred dollars—total, twelve thousand dollars.

G. SATTERLEE, Grand Treasurer.

—The total amount received from Bro. Satterlee, is six thousand, eight hundred and fifty-two dollars and ninety cents—pages 30, 31—his last remittance being Jan. 3d, 1879.

ALBANY, N. Y., Sept.—I herewith hand you draft for one hundred and eighty dollars, contributed by Salem Town, St. George and Temple Commanderies. Many of the Templars have contributed to the funds collected in Lodges. I trust that the affliction which has befallen the people of the South may soon be stayed. TOWNSEND FONDAY, Gr. Com.

—In his circular appeal to the Templars of New York, Grand Commander Fonday said: "The terrible pestilence which has attacked our Southern brethren demands prompt assistance, and any relief, to be effectual, must be immediate. 'Do unto others as ye would they should do unto you,' was one of the commands of your Great Captain, and nothing appeals so tenderly to the better feelings of our manhood than to relieve, when in our power, the suffering caused by pestilence and death."

CANANDAIGUA, N. Y., Nov. 4.—Find enclosed a draft for $56 00, contributed by brothers of Canandaigua Lodge for the relief of suffering caused by yellow fever in your vicinity. Apply it where, in your judgment, it is most needed. J. J. STEBBINS, Secretary.

ROME, N. Y., Sept. 3.—In response to your appeal, I enclose draft for one hundred and seven dollars, the contributions of sympathizing brethren of this city, to be used for relief of our distressed brethren, and other citizens, where it will do the most good. F. E. MITCHELL,
E. C. Rome Commandery, No. 45.

BUFFALO, Sept. 19.—Draw on me for two hundred dollars for general purposes. ALBERT JONES, Lake Erie Commandery.

NEW YORK, Sept. 4.—* * * We hope to do more. The people of the North are in sympathy with the people of the South in their troubles. ROBERT MACOY, Grand Recorder.

SYRACUSE, Sept. 6.—Enclosed find three hundred and twenty-five dollars, contributed by: Central City Chapter, fifty dollars; Central City Bodies A. and A. Rite, twenty-five dollars; Central City Commandery of Knights Templar, and their friends, two hundred and fifty dollars. Trusting the same may speedily arrive in good season to assist in relieving the wants of our distressed brethren. HENRY E. WARNE, Chair'n Com.

NEW YORK, Sept. 9.—* * * While we are heavily burdened with calls from widows and sick Sir Knights of our own body, and with a treasury nearly exhausted, we desire to do more, but are unable. I enclose fifty dollars to be used among sick Sir Knights, or the destitute families of such as have laid down the sword for the crown.
WESLEY B. CHURCH. Recorder.

GLOVERSVILLE, N. Y., Sept. 9.—Enclosed find five dollars to be used as you think best for relief of the sufferers by yellow fever. May God bless and second all your efforts. We have raised in our village over nine hundred dollars in all. Courteously, CYRUS STEWART.

PLATTSBURG, N. Y., Sept. 9.—* * * We do heartily sympathize with you and only trust and pray that the scourge may be stayed in its progress, and that our humble efforts to assist you may be of some benefit to your people. W. S. GUIBORD, Recorder DeSoto Com. No. 49.

TROY, Sept. 10.—Our Commandery, Apollo, No. 15, has donated two hundred dollars for the relief of fever sufferers, and have forwarded the same to you in currency. Regretting that our donation is not larger, and hoping that small as it is, it may be the means of relieving some of our dear brothers, and that the ordeal through which you are now passing may soon cease. THEO. E. HASLEHURST, E. C.

BUFFALO, Sept. 10.—Enclosed find one hundred dollars contributed by Hugh de Payens Commandery, No. 30. The whole North seems to be awake to the serious nature of your troubles, and are contributing handsomely for the relief of your people. God grant that the pestilence may soon cease. CHRISTOPHER G. FOX, Commander.

WATERTOWN, Sept. 10.—Enclosed find draft for twenty-five dollars—our mite in aid of the yellow fever sufferers. We prefer, of course, that it should be used in relieving any suffering members of our order, but leave it to your discretion: apply it where it will do the most good. LOUIS C. GREENLEAF, E. C., No. 11.

PORT JERVIS, Sept. 11.—* * * Accept our sincere sympathy in this sad and awful calamity. Our remittance ($27 58) is small, but it may be the means of making some Sir Knights more comfortable. CHAS. B. GRAY, Treasurer Deleware Commandery, No. 14.

DUNKIRK, Sept. 12.—* * * Our whole people are responding nobly to the appeals from the sorely afflicted South. Believe me, dear Sir Knight, your people have our warmest sympathy in this their hour of dire distress. R. J. GROSS, Recorder.

LOCKPORT, N. Y., Sept. 14.—We have published your appeal to the fraternity, and endorsed you as a man and Mason. * * May God in His goodness aid you and bring you out of this severe trial untouched. JOHN HODGE.

OSWEGO, Sept. 14.—On behalf of Malta Commandery, Binghamton, I enclose fifty dollars towards relief of the suffering. * * Allow us to offer you our sincere sympathy to all the afflicted, and may our Great Captain administer to them the consolation which they sorely need in this dark and trying hour. F. N. MABEE, Em. Commander.

RONDOUT, Sept. 19.—In this terrible time of suffering and death to our brethren in your district, be assured that you have our heartfelt sympathy. Words fails us to give expression to our feelings. Please accept the enclosed fifty dollars, and use where it will do most good. Praying that you may be speedily relieved from your great affliction. GROVE WEBSTER, Recorder Commandery, No. 2.

NEW YORK, Sept. 7.—Palestine Commandery, No. 18, desirous of showing their sympathy for your stricken district, beg to enclose seventy dollars, a slight testimony of their enlisted sympathy, and trust you to place it where it will be most useful. That the time of your affliction will soon pass away is our sincere wish. H. H. BROCKWAY, Generalissimo.

BUFFALO, Sept. 28.—I herewith forward you three hundred dollars, freewill contributions of brethren in this district. Trusting that same may help, aid and assist many poor and distressed brethren, their widows and orphans. C. E. YOUNG, D. D. G. M. 25th District.

SING SING, Oct. 12.—Find draft for twenty dollars, from Westchester Commandery, No. 42. Hoping it may do its little part in relieving the sufferings of the afflicted. ROBERT M. LAWRENCE, E. C.

POUGHKEEPSIE, Oct. 21.—Enclosed find fifty-nine dollars and fifty cents, contributed by members of Poughkeepsie Lodge, No. 206, for the relief of their suffering brethren and their families in your jurisdiction. With same, please accept our sympathies. We pray that the plague may soon be stayed. THE. W. DAVIS, D. D. G. M. 9th District.

OHIO.

YOUNGSTOWN, OHIO, Sept. 2.—Enclosed find two hundred dollars, which our Grand Commandery has appropriated for the sufferers in your State. As the Representative of the Grand Commandery of Mississippi near the Grand Commandery of Ohio, I consider it my duty to make an appeal for help to our Grand Commandery at its Annual Conclave last week, and I was requested to remit above amount to you. Hoping that the terrible scourge will soon die away. W. L. BUECHNER, 32°

CINCINNATI, Sept. 4.—I send you fifty dollars contributed by Gibulum Lodge of Perfection 14° grade. We extend to you our deep sympathy in the great affliction that has befallen your jurisdiction. May God in His infinite mercy and goodness keep you from harm, that you may be able to alleviate the sufferings of the afflicted.
E. T. CARSON, 33°, Dep. Ins. Gen. for Ohio.

TOLEDO, OHIO, Sept. 5.—Enclosed find five dollars. May God bless you and spare your life. Your brother in Masonry and Odd Fellowship.
SAM T. FISK.

COLUMBUS, OHIO, Sept. 24.— * * I would like to write you many words of cheer, but I know they are of little avail when you need so much of a more substantial character; but you have my heartfelt sympathy, and my prayer is that this affliction may soon pass from you. Our Lodges have seen published by the Grand Master of Louisiana, that no more funds were needed in that State, and infer from it that all are pretty well supplied; but if such is not the case, please let me know at once, for we still have a little left. May God bless and protect you.
THEO. P. GORDON, Grand Treasurer.

NOTE.—The frequent remittances from Bro. Gordon, will be found on pages 31, 32.

CINCINNATI, Sept. 5.—I send you, of Ohio contributions to Masonic fund for relief, another one hundred dollars. Heartily is given our pittance, as it comes from Masons in good health, with hopes of alleviating something of that unparreled distress that has visited Grenada and Vicksburg. May your unhappy fate have have early alleviation. As long as you need call on us for help. JOHN D. CALDWELL, Grand Secretary.

NOTE.—Brother Caldwell's many remittances are acknowledgd on pages 31, 32. On 10th September he wrote: " I herein enclose two hundred dollars which I hope you will take special care in disposal of, viz: make it a special fund to be applied to the care and comfort of orphans made destitute by the ravaging pestilence. Some of the Cincinnati brothers wish that their portion of the donation be so used as to reach persons—without regard to conection with the Masonic fraternity and without regard to nationality, color, religion or opinion—to relief of humanity. Knowing that numerous orphans have suddenly been exposed to destitution, and in need of some special care, I have thought it best, out of a large fund generally distributed already, to make this independent venture in behalf of the fatherless. If your Relief-Committee will do us the favor to give this direction to the benevolence of the Cincinnati brethren in behalf of neglected and almost forsaken little ones, you will do me a favor, and I may ask that some time some particular report be given of the use that it has been put to. JOHN D. CALDWELL, Grand Secretary.

COLUMBUS, O., Aug. 28.—In answer to your appeal, I herewith enclose a draft for $105 20, as a contribution from a portion of my Lodge to the suffering Masons and their families in your jurisdiction, or elsewhere as you may think best. I hope to be able, within a few days, to send you a still larger amount from the remaining members. We accompany this donation with our warmest sympathy and earnest prayer that the Supreme Architect of the Universe may speedily stay the ravages of the plague. H. O. KANE, W. M., Magnolia Lodge, No. 20.

ONTARIO.

HAMILTON, ONTARIO, Sept. 28.—Have one thousand dollars to divide between Louisiana, Mississippi and Tennessee. Give opinion for division. J. J. MASON, Grand Secretary.

—Five hundred dollars received from Brother Mason.

PENNSYLVANIA.

PITTSBURG, Aug 31.—Find draft for fifty dollars from Duquesne Chapter, No. 193. Let us know when you want more. Our hands and hearts are with you in this trying hour of calamity and sorrow. GETER C. SHIDLE.

—Substantial favors received also 7th and 15th September.

MEADVILLE, Aug. 27.—I send you two hundred dollars by express to-day. SAM'L B. DECK, Grand Commander.

PITTSBURG, Aug. 29.—I enclose one hundred dollars, to be applied in your discretion for the relief of yellow fever sufferers. Hoping your present troubles may soon be at an end. JOSEPH EICHBAUM, District Deputy G. M., 17th Dist.

—Substantial favors also received dated Sept. 6, 8, 11.—Page 33.

PITTSBURG, Sept. 9.—A few days ago our Grand Commander forwarded you two hundred dollars. I send you two hundred dollars more to-day, from the Knights Templar of Pennsylvania, More shall follow soon. We trust in God's mercy that the plague may be stayed in its fury, and that all those afflicted may be speedily healed. The hearts of the Knights Templar of the North are full of sorrow and pain for the sufferings of their fraters of the South. Could human sympathy raise the dead and dying and sick, there would be a grand resurrection at present. CHAS. E. MEYER, Grand Recorder.

—Several other substantial favors were received from Sir Kt. Meyer Nov. 25, he authorized me to draw for one hundred dollars additional which was fraternally declined.

SOUTH CAROLINA.

CHARLESTON, S. C., Aug. 27.—The fraternity of this city desire to aid their suffering brethren in those cities where the yellow fever is prevailing so terribly, and I have invited contributions for that purpose. In response, Landmark Lodge, No. 76, has handed me twenty-five dollars, with request that it be forwarded to the brethren of Grenada. I trust that I shall have the pleasure of forwarding further contributions for our suffering brethren.

CHAS. INGLESBY, Grand Secretary.

—The frequent remittances of Bro. Inglesby, aggregating four hundred and eleven dollars and fifty-five cents, are acknowledged on page 34.

♦ TEXAS.

SAN ANTONIO, Aug. 30.—The fraternity of San Antonio send you by mail one hundred dollars, to be applied by you toward relief of our brethren.   E. R. NORTON, Chairman.

CALDWELL, Sept. 16.—I send you, for Warren Lodge, No. 56, forty-six dollars and fifty cents, for relief of yellow fever sufferers where most needed. Wish we were able to do better.   JOHN ALEXANDER, W. M.

WHITESBORO, Sept. 17.—Enclosed find ten dollars, contribution of Whitesboro Lodge, No. 263. Use where most needed. You need not receipt until fever subsides. Hoping for an early abatement of the fever.

A. H. NICHOLS, Secretary.

HOUSTON, Oct. 31.—I have the pleasure to enclose draft for five hundred and twenty-six dollars and thirty cents, for relief of yellow fever sufferers in your jurisdiction. This amount is made up by donations from a number of Lodges, a Chapter, individual contributions by Masons and citizens, and from various other sources. Of this amount fourteen dollars and fifteen cents is from the colored people of Gonzales, for relief of their own color. Distribute where most needed.

BENJ. A. BOTTS, Grand Treasurer Grand Lodge.

—The several remittances from Bro. Botts, as Treasurer of Grand Lodge and Grand Commandery, are acknowledged on page 34. Also the remittances from Bro. Geo. H. Bringhurst, Grand Secretary.

UTAH.

SALT LAKE CITY, UTAH, Sept. 2.—I forward to your address to-day, fifty-two dollars for the relief of the sufferers in the fever-stricken districts. Please use the money where it will do the most good. * * May God, in his mercy, be with you and the Craft in your State, is the prayer of

Yours fraternally,   CHRISTOPHER DIEHL, Grand Secretary.

—Letter-file shows six communications from Bro. Diehl, enclosing an aggregate of five hundred and ten dollars.

VIRGINIA.

RICHMOND, Sept. 13.—On 10th I telegraphed you to draw for one hundred dollars—for Grenada and Vicksburg. I send you fifty dollars more to-day, for Vicksburg. These contributions are from the Lodges and members in this city, and not from the Grand Lodge. Be assured, my dear brother, if our means were at all commensurate with our sympathy and will, the necessities of our brethren, their widows and orphans would be abundantly provided for.   WM. B. ISAACS, Grand Secretary.

PETERSBURG, Aug. 26.—Masonic brethren send one hundred dollars to-day. More to-morrow. Particulars by mail.

WM. E. MORRISON, W. M. Blanford Lodge, No. 3.

LYNCHBURG, Aug. 24.—Marshall Lodge, No. 39, sends you one hundred and fifty dollars for relief of yellow fever sufferers. We designate you as the medium for its distribution, because you are the representative of our fraternity in Mississippi, and because thereby our contribution may preserve its characteristic as a Masonic charity. In saying this, we would not be understood as meaning that only those generally entitled to Masonic relief, shall exclusively be the recipients. This, in the present condition of things in your State, would be impracticable. We wish you to be our almoner, and leave you untrameled by any directions as to mere details. The sole aim of our Lodge is to do as much as we can to mitigate the distresses which have fallen upon your people, giving preference to those—as far as may be—other things being equal, of our own household.

SAM'L D. PRESTON, F. MYERS, A. PARKER FERGUSON, Committee.

LIBERTY, VA., Aug. 29.—Liberty Lodge, No. 95 sends you twenty dollars, in response to your appeal. Our Lodge is small and treasury depleted, still we hope the many small amounts may in the aggregate give substantial aid to our distressed brethren in your jurisdiction. Our citizens generally, are industriously at work in behalf of the sufferers.

JNO. F. CURTIS, Master.

CULPEPPER, August 31.—Enclosed find $37 75. donated by Fairfax Lodge, No. 43, which distribute as you may think proper for the benefit of yellow fever sufferers. JOHN A. HILL, Secretary.

WASHINGTON TERRITORY.

OLYMPIA, W. T., Oct. 25.—I send you this day, per Wells, Fargo & Co's. express, the sum of fifty-five dollars, being a portion of the funds thus far contributed by our Subordinate Lodges. This is a very small amount, but we trust it will do some good. We have no language adequately to express our deep sympathy for our brethren and the people generally of the Southern portion of the Union, in this most direful visitation, terribly fatal with devastation and death. I enclose you a circular issued by our Grand Master to the brethren of this jurisdiction, appealing to their benevolent hearts, which I have no doubt will meet a generous response.

THOS. M. REED, Grand Secretary.

WEST VIRGINIA.

WHEELING, August 28.—Instruct your Grand Master to draw on me for $500 on account of Masonic relief fund. * * Sept. 13.—I telegraphed you this evening to draw for $200. Have remitted to New Orleans and Memphis; but we think, frm newspaper reports, that assistance is required in the smaller towns within your State, and have thought proper to again send you aid. Use as your judgment may dictate, to accomplish the most good. * * Sept. 13.— * * We still have a little money left. Please advise me where to send it to do the most good. Will be guided by you in this matter. J. H. WILLIAMS, Grand Treasurer.

WISCONSIN.

MILWAUKEE, August 28.—Enclosed is $340, which use at your discretion, regardless of Masonry. Will send more very soon. Our people feel poor, but will do all in their power. * * Sept. 6.—Enclosed is five hundred dollars. Your letter came duly to hand, and shall be published for information of all interested. I pray our Heavenly Father you may escape the plague, and live to continue the noble work you are doing. * * Sept. 11. Enclosed is four hundred dollars to help along the good cause. Hope the dread monster may leave you soon. The papers inform me Paxton is down. I pray God his attack may not be fatal. We ought not to lose such men. * * Sept. 23.—Enclosed find eight hundred dollars for the relief

fund. When through with the terrible job on your hands, a statement of distributions would be acceptable. I may be able to send you more. * *
Oct. 11.—I have the pleasure of enclosing five hundred dollars, to be used at your discretion. Hoping you may live through the terrible war of death which is snatching away so many valuable men and noble brothers,

JOHN W. WOODHULL, Grand Secretary.

—Total receipts from Bro. Woodhull, $3,240.00—see page 36.

FROM THE ODD FELLOWS.

ARKANSAS.

LITTLE ROCK, ARK., Nov. 6.—We have on hand a balance of twenty-five dollars for relief, which you can draw on me for, should you need it for any of our brethren, their widows or orphans.

PETER BRUGMAN, Grand Secretary.

CALIFORNIA.

SAN FRANCISCO, Sept. 17.—Have telegraphed one thousand dollars to your credit for the relief of Odd Fellows where most needed in your State.
October 11.—Have telegraphed you one thousand dollars more additional.

W. B. LYON, Grand Secretary.

SAN FRANCISCO, Oct. 12.— * * Yesterday I requested Bro. Lyon to send you by telegraph transfer one thousand dollars. Am indeed glad it was in our power to respond at once. We have sent same amount to Memphis. It surely is a satisfaction to California that she can aid in relieving the terrible weight of sorrow and grief with which you are loaded. Be assured our hearts are full to overflowing with sympathy for all our distressed brethren. Please keep us advised as time and duties will permit.

E. D. FARNSWORTH, Chairman.

CONNECTICUT.

BRIDGEPORT, CONN., Oct. 3.— * * We deeply appreciate the kindly sentiments with which our efforts to relieve the poor fever-stricken sufferers have been received, and believe it proves there is a potency in associations like ours that is destined to exert a great and good influence in the amicable adjustment of all sectional differences. Hoping that the worst is past, and that it may be many years before another such calamity visits your land. THOS. STIRLING, Grand Master.

BRIDGEPORT, CONN., Oct. 22.—Grand Secretary Botsford has authorized you to make draft on him for two hundred dollars. We are happy to know that we are thus able to respond to your call, and are willing to render further assistance in case you find it necessary to make another appeal.

THOMAS STIRLING, Grand Master.

DAKOTAH TERRITORY.

FORT RANDALL, DAKOTAH TERRITORY, Aug. 29.—Find enclosed fifteen dollars, a small contribution from Echo Lodge, No. 2, for the relief of yellow fever sufferers. Cheerfully would we have doubled and tripled the amount, but our Lodge is small and our means very limited. But we give it with open heart and hand, and in the true spirit of Odd Fellowship. We hope and pray that this terrible scourge has reached its worst, and that we shall soon hear of its speedy and total disappearance. This is the true sentiment of our Lodge, which I am charged to convey to you, and through you to all the afflicted brothers in your State. F. SEMILLER, Treasurer.

VERMILLION, D. T., Sept. 6.—Enclosed find fifty-three dollars, contributed by Lodges in this jurisdiction. Further contributions will be forwarded as soon as received. Trusting it will help to relieve our brothers who are so sorely afflicted, and assuring you and them of our sympathy in their distress. RALPH N. BRIGGS, Grand Secretary.

—Several other contributions, through Bro. Briggs, are acknowledged on page 39.

FLORIDA.

WARRINGTON, FLA., Aug. 29.—At request of Mechanics' Lodge, No. 8, I send you ten dollars, for use as you may direct. We are sorry at not being able to send more, but have not fully recovered from our late epidemic. With the hope that the plague will soon be over.

GEO. S. HALLMARK, Grand Master.

ILLINOIS.

ROCKFORD, ILL., Sept. 12.—In addition to former remittance of five hundred dollars, I enclose draft for five hundred dollars, contributed by our Lodges. Make use of same to best advantage, as your judgment may dictate, in relieving the distress of our Southern brothers. Hoping deliverance is near at hand, and that your suffering people will soon be relieved from the terrors of the fearful scourge, and requesting you to give me prompt information of your necessities. * * * Sept. 30—In your last acknowledgment of five hundred dollars, you stated that you hoped to not need any further relief, aside from what was in hand and in transit. If you find that you were mistaken, I hope you will not fail to notify me. Illinois wants to render aid as long as there remains a suffering brother in your midst. JOHN LAKE, Grand Master.

CHICAGO, Sept. 30.—We are all anxious to know what we can do to aid you. Have done a little, but can do more, and will if you will but advise us of the situation. We are thankful to know that the plague has spent its force, but realize there must be considerable suffering for some time.

J. C. SMITH, Grand Scribe.

INDIANA.

INDIANAPOLIS, Sept. 12.—I send you enclosed three hundred dollars, in addition to the amount already forwarded, making total eight hundred dollars from the Lodges of Indiana. I have forwarded eight hundred dollars to our brethren in New Orleans and other places in Louisiana, to be distributed by Bro. Luther Holmes, Grand Secretary. I have also sent six hundred dollars to the I. O. O. F. Relief Committee for the Brotherhood of Memphis. We send these donations as a free-will offering from the brotherhood of Indiana, trusting they will help to alleviate much suffering, and though they may not re-unite the sundered ties of the households rendered desolate by the scourge, they will nevertheless be reminders that, as Odd Fellows, we have not forgotten the obligations of our Order in this hour of sad calamity that has befallen our Southern cities.

With kind regards, and trusting that a kind Providence may soon stay the march of the destroying angel, I am as ever,

B. T. FOSTER, Grand Secretary.

INDIANAPOLIS, Sept. 21.—Yours acknowledging receipt of my last remittance is to hand. Should you need further assistance from our jurisdiction, do not hesitate to advise me by telegraph. Accept our warmest sympathy for the stricken and suffering.   B. T. FOSTER, Grand Secretary.

IOWA.

SIOUX CITY, IOWA, Sept. 8.—Have telegraphed you to draw on me for twenty-five dollars—donation of Sioux City Lodge, No. 164, so you can have it for distribution at once in this your hour of need. Your people have the heartfelt sympathy of the members of the Order in this city.
                                                C. B. STEDMAN, Secretary.

WINTERSET, IOWA, Aug. 29.—   *   *   We enclose you thirty-three dollars and seventy-five cents, from members of Madison Lodge, No. 136. It is perhaps needless for Odd Fellows to tell each other of their love and sympathy, but such troubles as yours are calculated to "enlist the tenderest of human sympathies," and make our "warm hearts throb for your woes." Hoping a kind Providence may spare our brethren further distress.
                                                A. W. C. WEEKS, for Committee.

CARROLL CITY, IOWA, Sept. 16.—Herein find forty dollars, raised by our Lodge, Carroll, No. 279. Words fail in expressing our sympathy for the unfortunate—those whose families are broken and whose homes are desolate.   R. E. COBURN, Secretary.

BURLINGTON, IOWA, Nov. 12.—Enclosed find draft for one hundred and fifty-nine dollars and ninety-one cents, contributed by Lodges in our jurisdiction. I hope that the worst is over, and that you will receive such aid as will help the widows and orphans left by our deceased brothers.
                                                WILLIAM GARRETT, Grand Secretary.

—The several other remittances from Bro. Garrett are acknowledged on page 40.

KANSAS.

ATCHISON, KANSAS, Aug. 29.—Enclosed find twenty-five dollars, donation of Friendship Lodge, No. 5, to aid the yellow fever sufferers. Hope every Lodge in the United States will send their mite.
                                                A. R. PLATT, Treasurer.

—Four other contributions from Kansas, acknowledged on page 41.

KENTUCKY.

LOUISVILLE, Sept. 24.—Yours of 20th received, and under instructions of our Relief Committee, I send you with this, one hundred and fifty dollars, to be distributed by you to such points as in your judgment it is most needed. We get bad reports here from Greenville, and if they need it most send it to them.   GEO. W. MORRIS, Grand Treasurer.

—Two other remittances of one hundred dollars each received from Bro. Morris.

LOUISIANA.

THIBODAUX, LA., Sept. 10.—   *   *   The fever is now in our town, but so mild that we determined to send you a small sum at any rate, as your wants are greater now than ours will probably be. We have now about forty cases under treatment.   SILAS T. GRISAMORE,
                                                P. G. M., Secretary No. 34.

MAINE.

PORTLAND, MAINE, Oct. 28.—Yours of October 23d to hand. Find draft for one hundred dollars enclosed, a donation from the brotherhood of Maine to the distressed and suffering brothers and their families, as you may deem best.   JOSHUA DAVIS, Grand Secretary.

MARYLAND.

UTAH, COLORADO, NEVADA, CALIFORNIA, SANDWICH ISLAND, BALTIMORE, Oct. 10.—I am in receipt of one hundred and twenty-eight dollars from Odd Fellows in Utah, Colorado and Nevada, and send you forty-three dollars as the proportion for Mississippi. Sept. 14.—I send you two hundred and seventy-five dollars from Odd Fellows in Utah, Colorado, California. Nov. 15.—I have just received from Polynesia Encampment, No. 1, Honolulu, Sandwich Islands, with the "hope that it will not be too late to do good to some Odd Fellow's family," the enclosed twenty-five dollars. Polynesia is a small Encampment, having only 26 members, and the amount is a very generous contribution from the brethren in that distant island. I have heretofore remitted you the contribution of fifty dollars by Excelsior Lodge, No. 1, of Honolula.

THEO. A. ROSS, Assist. Grand Secretary.

MICHIGAN.

DETROIT, MICH., Sept. 24.—Our Lodges have sent me to this time about one thousand dollars. I send you herewith five hundred dollars, and send a like amount to Luther Holmes, at New Orleans. God grant you speedy relief from this dreadful scourge. The sympathies of the world are yours. * * Oct. 4.—I again come to you with the most earnest sympathy, and another five hundred dollars for the relief of our suffering brothers. Prayers are constantly offered imploring that the hand of the destroyer may be stopped, and the news from the suffering district is watched for with the greatest interest, in hopes we may have a favorable change. God bless and keep you. * * Nov. 25.—I sent you one thousand dollars, and Luther Holmes, New Orleans, five hundred dollars, all of which has been acknowledged most handsomely; and I now want your disinterested advice as to where to send the balance. With the sincere and heartfelt wish that the worst is past.

B. VERNOR, Grand Treasurer.

MISSISSIPPI.

STARKVILLE, Miss., Sept. 6.—Enclosed find fifteen dollars, contributed for relief by Ridgely Lodge, No. 23. Our membership is small, but we have sent money to our brethren in several of the afflicted localities.

JNO. A. JACOBS, Secretary.

FAYETTE, Miss., Oct. 21.—Find twenty dollars from Fayette Encampment. Apply it where most needed, and may God assist you in the good work in which you are engaged. JAS. McCLURE, JR., Scribe.

MISSOURI.

KANSAS CITY, Mo., Aug. 27.—Herewith find thirty dollars, contribution of Kansas City Lodge, No. 220, for the benefit of our stricken brethren. Apply it as you may deem best. Would that we could render more substantial assistance in the way of personal help.

H. C. LITCHFIELD, Secretary.

MONTANA.

DEER LODGE, MONTANA, Sept. 14.—Enclosed find twenty-five dollars, donated by Covenant Lodge, No. 6, for the relief of brothers suffering from the yellow fever scourge. Hoping to make further contributions.

LEW COLEMAN, Grand Secretary.

—Other contributions are acknowledged on page 42.

NEBRASKA.

FREMONT, NEBRASKA, Sept. 9.—Enclosed find thirty-nine dollars and eighty cents, appropriated by Centennial Lodge, No. 59, for the benefit of Odd Fellows scourged by the yellow fever. It is sent to you as the brother eminently fitted to disburse it. May the Father of us all help you in your good work, and look in mercy upon the stricken South.

.W. H. MICHAEL.

NEW JERSEY.

TRENTON, N. J., Oct. 5.—I enclose draft for sixty-eight dollars and forty cents for relief of Odd Fellows in your State. * * Oct. 18.—You can draw on me for one hundred and fifty dollars.

LEWIS PARKER, JR., Grand Secretary.

NEW YORK.

NEW YORK, Oct. 8.—Enclosed find eight hundred dollars, for our brethren and their families in your jurisdiction, who may be suffering with yellow fever. Regretting our inability to send you a larger sum, and hoping that it may be the means of doing some good. * * Nov. 9.—Enclosed find check for three hundred and forty-one dollars additional. Rejoicing with you that the pestilence has so nearly passed from your midst, and earnestly hoping that it may be long years ere your State may be so greviously afflicted, I remain, with best wishes for the speedy restoration to prosperity of our beloved Order in your State.

JAMES GODWIN, Grand Treasurer.

NORTH CAROLINA.

RALEIGH, N. C., Sept. 18.— * * Other contributions will follow, which your good judgment will apply where the greatest amount of good may be done. God grant that the scourge may be speedily arrested, and your people restored to their wanted good health.

J. J. LITCHFORD, Grand Secretary.

OHIO.

CINCINNATI, Oct. 11.— * * We are desirous of ascertaining, as early as possible, by what means we can assist you in further relieving the distress of our brethren and their families in your State. Are you in need of supplies of any kind? If you need any, inform us of the kind and amount, and we will send them, or money, if needed. The brethren in Ohio have placed funds in our hands for the express purpose of relieving the distresses of our brethren in the South, and we are anxious to fill our commission—in a way that none shall be overlooked. We trust that the day is not far distant when the wires will flash the information that the fell destroyer has been driven from the land. W. S. CAPELLAR, Grand Master.

—The many letters received from Bro. Capellar show an intense sympathy for our afflicted people. The receipts from him and Grand Treasurer Winchell are acknowledged on pages 43, 44, in addition to which five hundred dollars was sent to Vicksburg and one hundred to Water Valley.

MARTIN'S FERRY, OHIO, Aug. 27.—Your distress signal has penetrated inside the walls of our Lodge. Our heartfelt sympathies are extended to the brothers of your afflicted State. Enclosed find ten dollars, our mite. Would make it ten times as much, but being very short of funds, we do our best. THEO. SNODGRASS, P. G.

CINCINNATI, OHIO, Oct. 16.—Have sent you to-day five hundred dollars, to be used in relieving the wants of our distressed brethren and their families in your State. Permit me to express the hope that the ordeal through which you are passing will soon terminate, and that a kind Providence may again smile upon your stricken people.

GEO. D. WINCHELL, Grand Treasurer.

PENNSYLVANIA.

PHILADELPHIA, PENN., Sept. 30.—At a meeting of the Grand Lodge officers, held this afternoon, the Grand Treasurer was instructed to forward you the sum of seven hundred dollars in aid of the suffering brethren in your jurisdiction.　　　　　SAMUEL HAWORTH, Grand Master.

RHODE ISLAND.

PROVIDENCE, R. I., Sept. 14.—Draw on me at sight for two hundred dollars, to aid suffering brothers and Lodges.　SIDNEY DEAN, Grand Master.

TEXAS.

HOUSTON, TEXAS, Aug. 27.—Accept fifty dollars from the Odd Fellows of Houston.　　　　　I. C. STAFFORD, Grand Representative.

—Other Texas contributions acknowledged on page 46.

WEST VIRGINIA.

In response to the circular appeal of Grand Master Geo. L. Hensel, dated Martinsburg, Aug. 28, the Lodges in this Grand Jurisdiction forwarded their contributions to me direct, instead of through the Grand Officers. Fifty-two Lodges sent contributions, which are acknowledged on pages 44, 45, 46—a total of seven hundred and eighty dollars and twenty-five cents. The letters accompanying same all breathe the tenderest sympathy for our people in their affliction.

WISCONSIN.

RACINE, WIS., Sept. 14.—I enclose you another draft, for fifty dollars, to be expended for the relief of brother Odd Fellows. With our best wishes.
　　　　　THOS. LEWIS, Secretary No. 8.

MISCELLANEOUS CORRESPONDENCE.

In view of the space already occupied with extracts from letters received during the epidemic, the following only are selected from a large correspondence transmitting relief funds, from miscellaneous sources, to the amount of $12,746.24 :

LONOKE, ARK., Sept. 27.—Enclosed find five dollars, my mite for the relief of the sufferers, with the prayer that God will look in mercy upon our suffering land, and bless and strengthen the noble men and women who are so bravely facing danger and death in behalf of the sick and suffering. I am a Mississippian, as you may remember my name.
　　　　　ALICE W. PETTUS.

MARYSVILLE, CAL., Sept. 13.—(to Gov. Stone) : The citizens of our city have contributed for the relief of sufferers by yellow fever in the South the sum of one thousand one hundred and sixty-one dollars, which they desire to divide equally between the States of Mississippi, Louisiana and Tennessee. I therefore enclose you draft for three hundred and eighty-seven dollars. Please accept our donation, and dispose of it wherever you think most needed by the people of your State.　　N. D. RIDEOUT, Mayor.

OAKLAND, CAL., Sept. 24.—I received yours acknowledging receipt of the seven hundred dollars sent through Gov. Stone. The money was contributed by the citizens of Oakland. Please keep me advised of the condition of your people, and if we can assist still further are ready to do so. * * Oct. 28.—I send you one thousand dollars additional.

A. C. HENRY, Treasurer Citizens' Relief Com.

WASHINGTON, Nov. 6.—I have the honor to enclose check for four hundred dollars, being a part of the subscription raised in foreign countries in aid of the sufferers by yellow fever, and forwarded to me for distribution.

WM. M. EVARTS.

—The several remittances from Mr. Evarts are acknowledged on page 54.

TERRE HAUTE, IND., Oct. 14.—(to Gov. Stone): Enclosed find draft for two hundred and eighty-one dollars, to be placed to the credit of some reliable person or association, to be used in alleviating the wants of the yellow fever sufferers in your afflicted State. This is a voluntary contribution by the two military companies of this city and by the persons named in this letter—Light Guards and Governor's Guard two hundred and five dollars and sixty-five cents; A. Herz, sixty-six dollars; W. H. Wiley, Superintendent Public School, ten dollars. If it but relieves the sufferings of those for whom it is used, we shall be happy to think in future that we have contributed our mite to the noblest cause on earth, that of aiding our fellow-men in time of need.

THOS. A. ANDERSON, Treasurer Gov. Guard.

BLACKINTON, MASS., Sept. 25.—(to Gov. Stone): Please find seventy dollars, contributed by the operatives in our mills, for the benefit of the yellow fever sufferers. You have our heartfelt sympathies in your afflictions, and as we cannot well come to you with personal help, the least we can do is to send such means as are at our command.

O. A. ARCHER, Treasurer.

EAST SAGINAW, MICH., Oct. 1.—(to Gov. Stone): Herewith find N. Y. draft for six hundred dollars, sent by the citizens of this city for the benefit of yellow fever sufferers in your State, to be distributed at such points as are most in need. * * * * Oct. 14.—Herein find draft for five hundred and ninety-two dollars and six cents, contributed by our citizens for yellow fever sufferers. With sincere hope of an early abatement of the fever. WM. T. WICKWARE, Treasurer Citizens' Fund.

NEW YORK, Aug. 27.—I reached here yesterday evening from Europe, and am greatly alarmed and distressed at seeing the spread of the yellow fever in the South, and feel that I ought to return, but don't suppose I could, as the railroads all seem to have stopped taking passenger trains. I am glad to see that you at Jackson are taking all precautionary measures, and do hope Jackson may escape the scourge. As I can't now return, I will authorize you to subscribe and draw on Richardson & May for five hundred dollars, in helping the suffering should the pestilence come. I have sent contributions to Vicksburg, Grenada, and Memphis. Should the fever break out in Jackson, telegraph me at St. Nicholas Hotel here, and I will make an effort to raise some money here for your relief. Am anxious to do what I can. E. RICHARDSON.

NEW YORK, Oct. 2.—Our President, Mr. Jas. F. Wenman, to-day wired you to draw on me for one thousand dollars—one half of which is to be used

7

for the benefit of yellow fever sufferers at Jackson, and one-half for same purpose at Lake, it being part of a fund raised here by our organization.

ALONZO SLOTE,

Treasurer Firemen's Ball Committee Old Volunteer Fire Department.

SANTA ROSA, CAL., Sept. 6.—I enclose you a draft for one hundred dollars, to be appropriated to yellow fever sufferers. I wish it embodied in the Masonic contribution, as it is a tribute from me to the memory of my husband. Indeed it is a part of a sum I had deposited to be used for erecting marble over the graves of my dear dead ones, but the necessities of the living seem to me now to present greater claims than the dead. I only wish I were able to send a larger sum to the people for whose sufferings my heart goes out in the deepest sympathy. MARY S. WARE, (of Mississippi.)

—I determined not to collect this generous contribution of this noble daughter of Mississippi unless the demands of the suffering imperatively required it. Toward the close of the epidemic, due apology was made for not using the donation thus heartily tendered.

EASTON, PA., Feb. 14.—(to Gov. Stone): The citizens of Phillipsburg, New Jersey, opposite this place, have raised a fund of one hundred and thirty dollars for the relief of the sufferers by yellow fever. With heartfelt sympathy for the stricken communities of the South in this great affliction, they earnestly pray to the Most High that He will stay the pestilence and say to the Angel of Destruction, it is enough.

WM. HACKETT, President Easton Nat. Bank.

LAMPASAS, TEXAS, Sept. 23.—The great heart of Texas is burthened with sympathy for the plague-stricken districts along the valley of the Mississippi. Our little town asks to contribute its mite to the relief of suffering humanity, and through the aid of the Sunday schools, churches and brass band, the sum of one hundred and twenty-five dollars and ninety-five cents has been collected and placed in my hands, to be forwarded as my judgment might suggest. Knowing the part you have always taken in times of distress and suffering, and as you are in the midst of the great calamity, I enclose the amount named, and ask that you place it where most needed.

WALTER ACKER, (late of Mississippi.)

PETERSBURG, VA., Sept. 8.—(to Gov. Stone, enclosing one thousand dollars): We will never forget the noble Mississippians who battled here for their firesides; and could not efface the debt even if their pecuniary ability were equal to their generous inclination. May God send your cities a speedy deliverance from this fatal scourge, and spare them such visitation hereafter.

"Included in the contribution is the sum of fifty dollars given by the colored workmen in one of our tobacco factories—a cheerful offering from very poor people; also, fifteen dollars from the policemen, who wish to help their brother officers in Vicksburg.

"The papers bring us every day mournful lists of the victims, and I fear with each reading to see the name of some one whom I knew in the old brigade." WM. E. CAMERON, Mayor.

—Mr. Cameron was A. A. and I. General of Davis' Mississippi Brigade. The contribution was distributed to Vicksburg, Port Gibson, Grenada and Canton.

SACRAMENTO, Cal., Sept. 7.—(To Gov. Stone.) On behalf of the city of Sacramento and benevolent orders, we send you six hundred and fifty-seven dollars, to be distributed by you in your State in such manner as in your opinion may do most good to the sufferers by yellow fever.

CHISTOFER GREEN, R. A. CAREY, R. G. WETHLER, Committee.

WINSTON, N. C., Sept. 20.—Enclosed find a postal order for forty dollars, the proceeds of an entertainment given by a few of the young ladies and gentlemen of this town. By applying the small amount where it is most needed, you will confer quite a favor. MRS. T. E. RICHARDSON.

MACON, Miss., Sept. 9.—Messrs. Bush, Redwood & Co. authorize you to check for three hundred and forty-three dollars. We trust you to distribute it where it is most needed in our State. The ladies of Macon have raised this money, and desire our mite to go to the relief of our afflicted people. On the 16th of August I sent to Grenada eighty dollars, raised at my request, by H. L. Jarnagin, Jr., and S. G. Ivy, Esq., in a few hours. I sent it by express, and have never heard from it. I hope it was received and did some good. The colored people here, at their churches last Sunday, raised fifty-one dollars, and sent it to Grenada. The ladies can send sheets, towels, pillow cases, etc., if such things are needed. Let me know and how to send. The colored people wish to know if poultry cannot be transported to Canton, Grenada and other points; if so, they can get up a large quantity. The Masons and Odd Fellows, too, are at work. You will hear from them. GEO. G. DILLARD, Mayor.

CHICAGO, Aug. 28.—(to Hon. E. Barksdale): We are loading to-day, forty thousand rations ordered by the Secretary of War, for Vicksburg. The Illinois Central and our road will transport them by special train to Jackson free of charge. Will you communicate with Raworth, and have him put them to Vicksburg? There will be eight or ten cars. J. C. CLARKE.

NEWTON, Aug. 28.—We will transport them free of charge to Vicksburg, with much pleasure. E. F. RAWORTH, Supt.

NEW YORK, Sept. 1.—I got Chamber of Commerce to-day to send five hundred dollars for Greenville, through Mississippi Valley Bank. Try to communicate with Greenville, and see what we can do. JONES S. HAMILTON.

McCOMB CITY, Miss., Aug. 23.—Enclosed find one hundred and thirty-five dollars, contributed by the railroad employees and citizens of McComb City, for relief where most needed. N. GREENER.

STATE LINE, Miss., Sept. 3.—The citizens of our little piney-woods town have organized a Relief Society, and in their behalf, I send you forty-five dollars, which please disburse for the sufferers. Sept. 10.—I send you twenty-five dollars. L. C. PEASTER, Treasurer.

BALDWYN, Miss., Sept. 5.—Herewith find forty dollars and fifty-five cents, collected from citizens here by a committee of young ladies appointed by the Mayor and Councilmen of the town. True, 'tis but a mite, yet it will be some help, and if necessary our people will respond again. (Thirty-three dollars and five cts. also received Sept. 24.) P. M. SAVERY, Mayor.

SCRANTON, Miss., Sept. 16.—I am directed by the Relief Committee to send you one hundred dollars, to be distributed where you think it is most needed to the yellow fever sufferers. WALTER DENNY.

WASHINGTON, D. C., Oct. 23.—Capt. Odeneal and myself called on Secretary Everts this morning, to appropriate out the foreign relief fund in his hands, $200 00, for use of yellow fever sufferers at Edwards, which he promised, at our suggestion, to remit to your care at once. Several days ago, Col. Hamilton, Gen. McCardle and myself called on Mr. Evarts for an appropriation to Jackson, and obtained his promise to send $800 00, which I hope Mayor McGill has received.   O. R. SINGLETON.

BEAUREGARD, Miss., Sept. 18.—I enclose fifty-two dollars raised at a concert last night by the ladies and children of the town, assisted by Mr. H. F. Bridewell and family of Port Gibson and the string band of Wesson. The announced object of the entertainment was for the benefit of the suffering in Port Gibson. If not needed there, I am instructed by the balance of the committee, Mrs. Julia Chrisman, Mrs. R. A. Bridewell and Dr. E. A. Rowan, to request you to use it where it best relieves the stricken ones. We thank God that in this locality we are still spared the affliction of the plague.   L. O. BRIDEWELL, of Committee.

LIBERTY, Miss., Sept. 24.—By order of the Liberty Thespian Corps I am directed to forward you twenty dollars, to be sent by you where most needed. Our only regret is that we cannot send more. Praying that your noble work will soon stop by the abatement of the fever.
                              T. W. STRATTON, Treasurer.

HOUSTON, Miss., Sept. 27.—You will find enclosed thirty-seven dollars and fifty-six cents, which our congregation contributed for the yellow fever sufferers. One dollar and ten cents of the above amount was given by Mrs. Sallie Sheil's infant class.   S. L. WILSON.

UNION CHURCH, Miss., Sept. 27.—Enclosed find nineteen dollars and twenty-five cents, a collection taken up for the fever sufferers on day of prayer in our congregation (Presbyterian church.) Distribute according to your judgment.   E. E. SMILEY, Deacon.

UNION CHURCH, Miss., Oct. 9.—Enclosed find thirty dollars, donated by Rising Star Grange, to be distributed by you according to your discretion among the yellow fever sufferers.   FLORA E. CAMERON, Secretary.

CALEDONIA, Miss., Oct. 1.—Enclosed I send you twenty-five dollars, the result of a collection taken last evening in our little village in behalf of the yellow fever sufferers. This little mite goes steeped in the tears and prayers of both saint and sinner for the relief of the sufferings of a common humanity.   A. L. MYERS.

WOODVILLE, Miss., Nov. 7.—To you, as the worthy almoner of many charities, I am requested by a lady friend to remit you the enclosed thirteen dollars, the result of a mite collection taken up by her, to be disposed of as your judgment may dictate. With sincere expressions of heartfelt sympathy for our afflicted friends in Jackson we pray for their speedy deliverance.   G. T. McGEHEE.

GRATITUDE.

> "When gratitude o'erflows the swelling heart,
> And breathes in free and uncorrupted praise
> For benefits received; propitious heaven
> Takes such acknowledgements as fragrant incense,
> And doubles all its blessings."

The following extracts are given from many grateful acknowledgements. The personal references to this writer are admitted more to show the general appreciation of the great work, of which he was an humble but zealous agent, than for any praise that he desires to place on record in his own behalf. Though the labor has been arduous, the reward that flows from appreciative and grateful hearts is more highly prized than compensation in any other form. He feels grateful for the sad privilege of being able, through the benefactions of his brethren, to dispense relief to the suffering and the needy :

PORT GIBSON, Sept. 2.—I return many and sincere thanks through you to the noble and generous fraternity you have the honor to represent for the benefit conferred upon me. The check came to hand on time. Perhaps you will receive many notes from those of our faithful preachers who have been in the midst of this dreadful pestilence, and to whom you have sent aid, but perhaps none can or will furnish a coincidence like the following, which I relate to you for your encouragement as a servant of the Lord through whom He does good for His people. * * * I must thank God first, and then your fraternities, and then yourself as the agent through whom the goodness of God has been conveyed to me. * * * Thus we see how God takes care of those who put their trust in Him. He cuts off all our resources, and supplies our wants and necessities from his own fullness. Many, many thanks, for the timely donation.   D. A. PLANCK.

PORT GIBSON, Oct. 3.—With more heartfelt gratitude than I have language to express, I acknowledge the receipt of your draft for one hundred dollars from the Masonic and Odd Fellows' Relief Fund. Very seldom in my long life have I ever received a more needed favor, or one more timely. When I received it, I could but exclaim, "It looks like a special Providence." May the Giver of all good abundantly bless and prosper you, and all others who have so promptly and liberally aided us in our great affliction and extreme want.   J. G. JONES.

PORT GIBSON, Oct. 8.—Permit me in this way to return you my thanks for your letter. When I read it at home there were tears of joy. The remittance, wholly unexpected, will be of great benefit to us in these times of trouble. It is pleasant also to know that others sympathize with us. I am glad that you have been able to do so much good throughout the State. May a kind Providence protect you.   E. H. MOUNGER.

PORT GIBSON, Sept. 19.—Your valued favor, enclosing $500, received to-day. In the name of Franklin Lodge, and of the widows and orphans, I return our hearty and grateful thanks. With it many a silent grief will be stayed, the widowed household made more cheerful. May your blessed work redound to your advantage in this world and the world to come.
FRANK H. FOOTE, Secretary.

WAYNESBORO, April 3.—Many thanks for your kindness. The gratitude of a helpless widow and her needy orphans has nerved me, I hope, to undertake more for the good of the Order than I have done heretofore.

JOHN F. MCCORMICK, Grand Lecturer.

EDWARDS, Oct. 15.—We are grateful for your kindness to the Association, and for the very kind and timely act of personal kindness to myself. In these days of trial and of sorrow, such deeds of Christian benevolence and brotherly affection are like an invigorating cordial to the spirit, worn with watchings and the wrestlings of prayer. May God bless you, and the ancient and honorable fraternity which you represent in this deed of goodness to the sick and suffering. I. J. DANIEL.

MEMPHIS, Dec. 27.—I wish to acknowledge 'to you my heartfelt gratitude for your very kind and generous offering to me, a widowed sister of an adjoining State. I feel, and well know that Masonry is universal, and that Masonic Charity is spread broadcast over our whole country; yet to be so kindly thought of by one who I never had the pleasure of meeting, causes the tears to start, and my heart to overflow with feelings of gratitude and love for you, my good brother, who has sent me this handsome gift. Many, many thanks accept from a grateful but sorrowing heart, and may God bless and care for you and yours, is the wish and prayer of your true and sincere friend and sister, JENNIE S. W——.

CHICAGO, Nov. 28.—Your valued favor, enclosing $50 for benefit of the widow of the late Lieut. Benner, should have been acknowledged sooner, but have just learned the address of the lady, being Mrs. Della Benner, McPherson Barracks, Atlanta, Ga. In behalf of the Chicago committee, I beg to thank you for prompt compliance with its suggestion, and to commend the personal act of adding $25 for the Grand Lodge of Mississippi, nor do we lose sight of the delicacy manifested by you in forwarding this amount to Mrs. Benner through the Chicago committee. * *

DEWITT C. CREIGER.

NEAR PICKENS, Dec. 10.—Many thanks to yourself and the good brothers with whom you are associated, for your kind remembrance of an old man so helpless and dependant as myself. Be assured of my sincere prayer that the blessing of heaven may rest upon you in all your work of good will to the suffering and the destitute. S. M. M.

YAZOO CITY, Oct. 24.—Allow me to tender to you, and through you to the generous donors my sincere thanks for the munificent donation, both as President of the Howard Association, and as a brother and Sir Knight. Seventeen cases under treatment, and seven deaths to date.

GEO. M. POWELL.

GARNER, Oct. 19.—Enclosed find receipt for $500 to hand. Receive the heartfelt thanks of the people of Garner for the much needed contribution.

J. L. COMBS, M. D.

CHARLESTON, MISS., Oct. 21.—The five hundred dollars sent me has just been received. It will be of incalculable benefit to our afflicted people. I had procured everything that was necessary in provisions, medicines and nurses up to this time upon faith the of getting the money. It was as much as we could do to get our sick nursed and the dead buried upon the *promises* of pay. It was exceedingly dangerous service, and employees did not know that any of us who contracted with them would live to see the contracts carried out in good faith. * * W. H. FITZGERALD.

HERNANDO, Oct. 21.—Your remittance of $500 was received per express on 7th inst. It was a God-send to us. * * DONALD MCKENZIE.

SENATOBIA, Oct. 25.—Your remittance of $250 received this morning. It will be judiciously used, and if not expended, returned. Our hopes are high that the worst is over. * * THOS. P. HILL.

NEAR SHARON, Oct. 1.—Your kind letter of September 27th is to hand informing me of aid sent, for which please accept, in behalf of our honored Order, the heartfelt and grateful thanks of three entire families, consisting of sixteen persons, all of whom have been, and are now suffering from the effects of yellow fever. * * W. H. BENTHAL.

JACKSON, Nov. 9.—Yours of this date, enclosing check for two hundred dollars for general distribution is this day to hand. To you, and to the noble brotherhood whose almoner you have been in a season of gloom almost without a parallel, I cheerfully confess myself a debtor. You have pre-eminently followed the lead of the man of Uz, who said, "The cause which I knew not I searched out," and many hearts have been made glad by your thoughtful, timely distribution. For many long years I have aspired to a place among those who *enjoy the luxury* of doing good. May the gushing streams from this fountain flow through your heart forever, and may He who is the witness of a secret charity, say to you "well done." WM. H. WATKINS.

MADISON COUNTY, Oct. 15.— * * I have no words that will adequately express my thanks to you. If you have never been destitute, you can scarcely appreciate my feelings, or realize how much comfort fifty dollars will afford us. I sincerely trust you may never know want. I am deeply and truly grateful for your timely aid. It will supply many wants. * * MRS. ————.

CANTON, Sept. 12.—Please accept our hearty thanks for your constant and substantial remembrances of us. Will keep you advised of our necessities. EMMETT L. ROSS, Secretary.

OSYKA, Dec. 10.—I thought I would write and thank you for your kindness, as I did not do so sufficiently the morning you called. I was taken by surprise, and felt embarrassed. It would be impossible to tell you what relief the money you gave me was to us. God alone knows what would have become of us but for your timely visit. What you gave me was the only money we have had this summer, except $5 Mr. McKenzie sent me. * * My noble young husband died in 1870 from the effects of a wound received in Virginia. In a few weeks after his death my little babe was born, now a manly little fellow of eight years. My dear father was a true and faithful Mason. * * I pray God may forever bless you and yours. He will surely watch over one who has lightened so many sinking hearts.
Very gratefully yours, ————.

OSYKA, Feb. 8.—(From a little boy.)—I am going to write you the first letter I ever wrote in my life, because you have been so kind to me. I started to school the first of January. I had never been before. My teacher says I am a smart boy, for eight years old. Mother has always taught me. Now I will tell you what I did with the money you sent me.

I bought me a good warm suit of clothes, shoes and hat, then I got some books, copy-book, slate and pencil; then I gave the rest to dear mother, and told her to pay her debts; when we had the yellow fever, she had to go in debt. My dear old grandmama is sick all the time. I want to study hard now while I am little, so when I get a big boy I can work for dear mother, grandmother, and my aunties. I am the only boy in the family. My dear papa died a few weeks before I was born. Mother says he was with you in the war. I thank you ever so much for your kindness to me. I am afraid I would not have been able to get to school but for your present. I ask God every night in my prayers to bless you, and I know that he will. I will stop now, for I am afraid you are tired of my letter. If you ever come to Osyka, you must be sure to come and see your little friend.

WILLIE GARNER.

CRYSTAL SPRINGS, Oct. 5.—Yours of 4th, covering checks on New Orleans for five hundred dollars for Dry Grove sufferers, is at hand. The Dry Grove people, or those who may be left of them, ought never to forget the good service you have rendered them in their hour of trial. We are glad in Crystal Springs to be the medium of distribution of the great and noble charities of which you are the trustee, to those at Dry Grove, who are the beneficiaries. We have filled all the requisitions from there to date.
*   *   *

W. C. WILKINSON.

WATER VALLEY, Dec. 24.—Yours to hand, for which please accept the grateful thanks and prayers of two good women. You have made them happy, and my wish is, that you may ever be as happy.

JNO. H. WILSON, SR.

WATER VALLEY, Dec. 25.—Enclosed find receipt of Mrs.———————— for the money which I had the pleasure of handing her this morning. Her tearful thanks fully attested her deep obligations and the timely aid it gave her and her three babes. God bless you in your good work.

F. W. MERRIN.

VICKSBURG, Sept. 23.—Rev. C. K. Marshall, D. D.—Dear Brother: I have received the generous contribution from your hands, and from a word let fall learned that it came from my honored friend Col. J. L. Power, of Jackson. It was as much appreciated as unexpected. Please convey to him my grateful acknowledgments for his thoughtful, generous and *timely* remembrance. May the blessings of our dear Lord dwell richly upon him and the other noble souls who have done so much to relieve the sufferings of our people.

CHAS. B. GALLOWAY.

VICKSBURG, Sept. 21.—Rev. C. K. Marshall, D. D.—Dear Friend and Brother: I am in receipt of the handsome contribution which you inform me is sent by certain friends of humanity and religion for the support of myself and family during this season of distress, when our ordinary source of income is cut off. I beg you to convey to those generous friends my warmest thanks for this munificent donation. May He who said, "inasmuch as he has done it unto the least of these my brethren, ye have done it unto me," reward them abundantly out of His infinite fullness. May our merciful Father shorten these days of chastisement, and enable us to spend the remainder of our days in a more thorough consecration to His service.   Fraternally,   ROBERT PRICE.

VICKSBURG, Nov. 12.—Most gratefully do I acknowledge the receipt by the hands of Dr. Marshall of the relief you were kind enough to send me. Amid sore bereavements, my happy home now desolate and deserted, I thank God that He has given me precious and honored friends, whose ten-

der kindness do so much to soothe the wounded spirit. May the Lord bless you in soul and preserve your useful life. F. M. FEATHERSTON.
—Appropriate acknowledgments are also on file from Rev. Dr. Sansom, and other pastors, white and colored.

HOLLY SPRINGS, Sept. 14.—Money by express received. Many thanks in behalf of our suffering people. Col. Upshaw died yesterday.
KINLOCH FALCONER.

HOLLY SPRINGS, Sept. 12.—Dispatch received. May heaven bless you for your noble labors in behalf of the suffering people of Mississippi.
KINLOCH FALCONER.

HOLLY SPRINGS, Sept. 17.—Five deaths, eleven new cases in last 24 hours. Thousand dollars, last shipment, to hand. I have no words in which to express the thanks of our suffering people.
KINLOCH FALCONER,

HOLLY SPRINGS, Sept. 18.—Ninety-three deaths to date; 220 cases. Thirteen new cases, and nine deaths in last twenty-four hours. You have done nobly by our afflicted people. God bless you.
KINLOCH FALCONER.

HOLLY SPRINGS, Sept. 23.—Col. Falconer dangerously ill, and the situation indeed gloomy. Our best and truest are falling daily. You have done a noble part towards us, and God will bless you for it.
HOLLAND.

HOLLY SPRINGS, Oct. 4.—In reply to your kind telegram of the 1st, will say your generous contributions come to us in timely season. The suffering here is beyond relief to those who have not seen it. Our expenses are very heavy, and demands upon us for clothing, bedding and food are hourly increasing. Friends in every part of the Union have aided us liberally, and thereby saved many valuable lives. Not one has done more for us than yourself. May God bless and protect you is the prayer of
W. J. L. HOLLAND.

HOLLY SPRINGS, Sept. 24.—Poor Kinloch died yesterday afternoon at half-past five o'clock. He spoke so much of you. We blessed you together. Forty new cases yesterday.
HOLLAND.

GOOD SAMARITAN HOSPITAL, CINCINNATI, Oct. 21.—I write you to-day asking you to aid me, if possible. I lost my husband at Holly Springs, with the fever, and sought refuge in this place. I was taken with fever a few days after getting here, and was ill five weeks. Am now recovering my strength a little. I have two little children, and no means at all. My husband was in Grenada, relieving, as far as he could, the suffering there, and thus contracted the disease. He was called to Holly Springs on account of the sickness of our little girl, and died himself in a few days.
* * *

—A grateful acknowledgment is on file for the response which was immediately made to the foregoing application.

GRENADA, Dec. 30.— * * Your recent visit to our suffering town brightened more suffering faces than anything that has yet occurred here.
* * * Jan. 2.—Yours, with five hundred dollars for our widows and orphans came this morning, and will prove a very acceptable New Year's gift. In their name, I thank you, and have no doubt they join me in the wish that you and the reserve fund may never cease.
SAM LAWRENCE, N. G. of No. 6.

GRENADA, Sept. 7.—Bro. Ayres died yesterday. Am in receipt of five hundred dollars from you, and placed same in Odd Fellows' relief hands.
R. A. ARMISTEAD.

GRENADA, Sept. 4.—Your most welcome letter, and your exceedingly welcome offering of one thousand dollars to hand per express. Return our hearty thanks to our kind friends, and assure them their wishes will be respected.   D. W. COAN, Howard Association.

—A large and grateful correspondence is on file from Grenada.

OXFORD, March 10.—The receipts are herewith enclosed. The two widows requested me to return to you their grateful thanks. They were moved with feelings of gratitude, which impressed me of the deep feeling which pervaded their souls.   J. M. HOWRY.

OXFORD, March 17.—God only knows how thankful I feel to you for the timely assistance rendered. It was most unexpected, but none the less thankfully received. May God bless all who are helping the widows and the orphans.   MRS.————————.

—The husband of this lady, after noble service, at Greenville, died there of yellow fever.

BOVINA, Feb. 26.—Enclosed find receipt for the three hundred dollars for our destitute widows and orphans. Accept our grateful thanks for the help thus given us.   WILSON BELL.

FAYETTE, March 19.—Yours received with check for fifty dollars, for which you have the thanks of every brother who signed the petition, to say nothing of the thanks and ascending prayers of the lonely widow.   HENRY KEY, W. M.

SENATOBIA, Feb. 4.— * * We have constantly to thank you for your consideration of our claims and generous responses. Believe us grateful and appreciative.   THOS. P. HILL.

MONTICELLO, March 20.—Thanks for your generous response. It will make the widow's heart glad. Peace be with thee.   G. A. TEUNISSON.

SCRANTON, Jan. 29.—I am in receipt of yours enclosing N. O. draft for $150 00, for Mrs. L. and Mrs. B. The amount is all that I should have asked for had I been consulted. I will apply it in the proportion that you suggest, and I assure you that it will be greatly appreciated, and could not have been bestowed on worthier or more needy persons, particularly in the case of Mrs. L.   M. M. EVANS.

HOLLY SPRINGS, March 3.—Your favor of 1st is received, with N. Y. exchange for $100, which shall be applied to the afflicted and needy colored families referred to in my former letter.   A. M. WEST

JONESBOROUGH, Feb. 28.—Yours, with $75 for our widows and orphans, received. Accept our hearty thanks. You will ever be remembered by the members, widows and orphans of Jonesborough Lodge.   ISAAC W. PARK, W. M.

TUPELO, Feb. 10.—Capt. P. M. Savery has this day handed me N. Y. exchange for one hundred dollars, to be expended in the education of Memory L. Leake, minor son of the late Memory L. Leake (who died of yellow fever at Louisville.) Accept my thanks and heartfelt gratitude for your beneficence. I will endeavor to keep this little fund to itself, and cause it to grow; and at the proper time I will expend it according to the directions contained in your letter to Bro. Savery, which has been shown me.   Fraternally,   H. C. MEDFORD.

ATLANTA, GA., Jan. 25.—Your very kind favor of 21st ult, enclosing one hundred dollars, received this morning, for which you will accept many and sincere thanks from myself and sisters. * * Thanking you again for your kind interest in our behalf.　　　　MATTIE —— ——.

—The father of these ladies died of yellow fever at Vicksburg.

ASHLAND, Jan. 29.—Yours of 27th inst., enclosing check for the children of Bro. J. A. Robinson has come to hand, and I enclose receipt for same. I delivered the check this morning to John H. Morgan, uncle and guardian of the children. He said he could not express this thanks for them, but he would teach the children as they grew up to love and respect the Masons.　　　　B. T. KIMBROUGH.

NEWTON, Feb. 12.—Yours with check for $50 received, for the benefit of Mrs. V—— ——. May God bless and prosper us in our laudable undertakings, and may a double share be given you for your arduous and charitable duties in dispensing the good you have.　　　　GLOVER EARBEE.

NEWTON, Feb. 12.—Accept my most grateful thanks for the donation received through our mutual brother, Mr. Earbee, for I assure you I was needing it, having to depend on my needle for the support of my three children and myself—God, in His Providence having deprived me of my chief support during the epidemic in Meridian. May God ever bless you, and by his mighty hand uphold those who have the heart to dispense charity.　　　　—— ——.

NATCHEZ, Oct. 25.—I received through Mr. DeLap the check for $500, sent by yourself to the Protestant Orphan Asylum of this city. It is difficult for the Board of Managers to express, in adequate terms, their gratitude for the liberality and nobility of spirit which prompted the generous gift. Although we have escaped the pestilence which has desolated so many of the fairest portions of our State, our treasury has been in a very depleted condition, notwithstanding the frequent assistance received from the Masonic fraternity. There are more than forty orphans in the Asylum, and we fear the number will be largely increased by the ravages of fever elsewhere. Permit me, once more, in the name of the Board, to thank you and your brethren of the Orders of Masons and Odd Fellows for this generous assistance.　　　　Very respectfully,
　　　　　　　　　　　MRS. JOHN FLEMING, Treasurer.

NATCHEZ, Feb. 5.—I cannot write you, in sufficiently forcible terms of the feelings of gratitude toward you for your continued acts of kindness. The orphans have great reason to thank God for the day you promised to be their friend. That was no idle promise, no transient feeling of sympathy, called into existence by the sight of those fatherless children, for yours has been the "charity that vaunteth not itself," which, flowing from a sense of duty, and that no labor can ever weary, looks to a future and a better world for its reward. This being the day for the regular monthly meeting of the Board, your letter shall be submitted, and contents suitably acknowledged. In conclusion, may your valuable and useful life be prolonged until these children's children "arise up and call you blessed."
　　　　　　Respectfully,　　　　·　　MARY R. FLEMING.
　　　　　　　　　Treasurer Natchez P. O. Asylum.

* * *Resolved*, That this Board feel themselves under many obligations to Col. J. L. Power for his interest in the Asylum which they represent, as manifested by him whenever an opportunity offers to aid it. Also, *Resolved*, That the handsome donation of one thousand dollars is thankfully received, and highly appreciated, as it will relieve the necessities of the orphans for some months to come, and thereby remove a heavy burden from the ladies who have charge of them.　　　　MRS. JAMES CARRADINE, Secretary.

St. Mary's Asylum, Natchez, Oct. 27.—With hearts overflowing with gratitude we tender our sincere thanks for your more than generous response to our appeal in behalf of our orphans. We are the more indebted on this occasion, coming as it did from one of a different faith, which testifies a disinterested and universal charity, rendering it thereby more pleasing to Almighty God, and highly appreciated by the sisters and orphans. Your kindness on this occasion will never be forgotten; and we can assure you, kind sir, that the prayers of the orphans will not fail to ascend daily to the throne of God for the benefactor who came so nobly to their aid in this their hour of trial.   Sisters of Charity.

Natchez, Feb. 14.—Words are inadequate to express the deep sense of gratitude due you for your noble response to the appeal of the Catholic orphans of Natchez, through the solicitation of our highly esteemed citizen, Col. E. Geo. DeLap. This generous donation, ($200) I will hand to the proper authorities of the two Catholic Asylums. This timely aid is very acceptable, and will greatly assist toward supplying their many wants. That God may shower on you His choicest blessings will be the daily prayer ascending to the throne of agree. May our Heavenly Father bless you for time and eternity,   Mrs. Joseph Arrighi.

Vaiden, Feb. 4. * * Your note of inquiry came yesterday, like a rift in a great cloud. * * Feb. 7.—A thousand thanks for your munificent remittance. It has lightened and cheered my oppressed heart more than mere words can express. I praise God for the great and undeserved mercy He has thus extended me. I must thank Col. B. for sending in my name. I knew nothing of the existence of the Masonic Relief Fund, or if I had would probably have lacked the courage to make my own application. Enclosed please find receipt, and again I thank you in the name of my dead husband. _____.

—The husband of this lady died of yellow fever Oct. 7, contracting the disease whilst ministering to others.

Waynesboro, March 7.—I take pleasure in acknowledging the receipt of twenty-five dollars for Mrs.—————, who is the widow of a Master Mason, and in very destitute circumstances. I am sure that the amount will be sufficient to relieve her considerably, and that she and her little ones will thank Bro. Power and the Masons for their timely assistance. * * * March 20.—I have supplied her immediate wants, and I must say that I experienced a small feeling of envy against you when I saw the gratitude of that poor, lonely, crippled widow with three small children.
          John F. McCormick, Grand Lecturer.

Oxford, Feb. 17.—The eye moistens again this Monday morning, as I again read Miss H's letter and your response. I never felt better in my life, than when I opened your letter and found the draft. I thought you would give $25, and I would go to work to get $50 more here if I could. To-morrow her heart will bound with joy—she will not get my letter till then. How happy one poor soul will be! Your name will be blessed for *this one act* all around the circle of her acquaintance. I named it to two or three here, whose hearts were lighter than before.   J. M. Howry.

Holly Springs, March 12.—I have your favor of 10th, advising of the forwarding remittance of $398 90 to National Park Bank, New York, for account of our Relief Committee, and in thus helping us out of our embarrassment, please accept our renewed thanks for this timely aid—adding, as it does, another item to the long list of favors of which we are your debtor.   Addison Craft.

NATIONAL PARK BANK, NEW YORK, March 12.—It has given us much pleasure to receive this morning your esteemed letter of 8th, from one whose name was so frequently and prominently on our books in connection with the relief funds which we had the satisfaction to transmit for our neighbors and citizens during the prevalence of the epidemic; and we desire to acknowledge our appreciation of your prompt and friendly courtesy in the repayment, from your own fund, of the amount of our duplicate remittance, September 5, 1878, to Holly Springs, for account of Mayor Ely, of this city, $398 90, for which we have, by the same mail, cheque of our friends Messrs. J. & T. Green, as advised by you. We should be glad of an opportunity to personally meet and thank you upon some future occasion of your presence in New York. E. K. WRIGHT, Cashier.

YAZOO CITY, January 2.—Your favor is just received. The familiar envelope was no surprise, for I thought it some circular relating to the Grand Masonic bodies. But the contents were a very great and gratifying surprise, and I rise from my bed to express my thanks. * * I have been minute in giving you an idea of my condition and circumstances, to enable you to judge for yourself with what a sense of relief, with what a burst of gratitude to you, secondarily, and to God primarily, your communication was received. We can now hope to remove the burden of debt without trimming the borders of starvation in order to do so. We may even hope to deploy a few dollars for the purchase of wood, without which we cannot have either health or comfort. From the feeling of helpless want, we are transplanted to the feeling that "now we have all things and abound!" We thank Bro. Power, who so actively illustrates the teachings of Odd Fellowship and Masonry, and of Christianity, which is higher than both; and we thank the God and Father of our Lord Jesus Christ, who has given Bro. Power such a heart. I know, though in a small way, since my means have been small, the blessedness of doing good to others. Then how happy ought you to be who so often do good and do so much— little, no doubt very little, when compared with your desires, yet much, very much, in fact. * * My wife read these letters with eyes burning with tears of gratitude. ————.

BRANDON, April 11.—Enclosed find receipt as requested. Mrs———— and daughter send you a thousand thanks. Without this kindly aid, they would probably have lost their home. Accept thanks and best wishes from your friend truly, ROBERT LOWRY.

VICKSBURG, Feb. 25.—Let me thank you for myself and little girl for the fifty dollars handed me by my friend Dr. Birchett. A greater favor, or one more acceptable, could not have been bestowed at the time, as we were very much in need. ————.

NATCHEZ, March 25.—Your very kind donation was received through Mr. DeLap. I cannot say how grateful I feel for your remembering our family in their distress. * * At present we feel entirely dependant on pa's Masonic brethren, who never forget the widow and the orphan. Again thanking you, I remain, with gratitude. ————.

WEST POINT, Feb. 13.—Yours of recent date was duly received. Your remittance to Bro. J. H. L. G————, for the benefit of his brother's child was a truly appreciated surprise to him and the family connections; and the boy, if he lives, will be taught of the attention and care of his father's beloved Order—the ægis of widows and orphan children. The family are modestly grateful for the true Masonic Charity, and the fraternity and friends of the Order, and of our esteemed deceased brother, will cherish fond and fervent recollections. The record of last year will inspire wonderfully all reasonable men with greater love for and zeal in the Order.

* * *   W. F. FRANKS, W. M.

PORT GIBSON, Jan. 27.— * * I know there was not a member of both Orders who did not fully and gratefully recognize your untiring, constant efforts in behalf of the suffering brethren, widows and orphans, throughout the fever-stricken district, and I assure you there was many a poor widow's heart made glad, and many a child caused to rejoice over the aid thus enabled to be given them through your kindness and labors in their behalf—not alone of those under our special care, but many of the poor without the gates. How noble and grand, how gracious and God-like loomed up the spirit of the Good Samaritan from the hearts of the people throughout the broad land. When dire distress befalls any portion of our common country, it seems to dispel all sectional strife, even political differences are forgotten for the time, and the hearts of the people are permitted to speak untrammeled by prejudice and sectional dislikes, and the true spirit of fellowship and brotherly love prevails. What a wonderful display of sympathy and charity was exhibited, during the prevalence of the fever. Our good friends were ever ready to give for our relief, even more than our actual wants required. For one I shall never forget the constant untiring kindness and sympathy of many dear stranger friends from abroad in our behalf, and we doubt not you have cause to know and acknowledge like favors.   JAS. A. GAGE.

PORT GIBSON, MISS., February 9, 1879.

J. L. POWER, *Grand Secretary, Jackson, Miss.*: DEAR SIR AND BRO.— I have been requested by the Masonic bodies of this town to convey to you their grateful appreciation of your generous remembrance of them during the gloomy period through which our people have just passed, and to assure you of their high sense of your great and noble services rendered not only to our Order but to humanity. As the chosen almoner of Masonic bounty you have dispensed its charities with a discreet but ever open hand, and we cheerfully bear witness to the prompt and disinterested manner in which the trust has been discharged. If we consider the wide field over which your duties extended, the almost universal distress, and the stern necessity for prompt and efficient relief, we can but be amazed at the systematic regularity with which those duties were performed. It only is to seasons of great public calamity that mankind is indebted for its brighter manifestations of moral heroism. To the great calamity which has just passed over us, and left behind so many traces of death and sorrow we all owe a melancholy gratitude for having developed a character so honorable to Masonry and to humanity. Repeating the assurance of the gratitude and admiration of your Masonic brethren, and sincerely wishing you the happiness your services so richly merit, I remain,

Yours fraternally,   WM. B. FULKERSON,
Committee appointed by Washington Lodge No. 8, Clinton Royal Arch Chapter, No. 2, Cœur de Lion Commandery, No. 13.

WATER VALLEY, Feb. 3.—(Resolutions by Water Valley Lodge, No. 82, I. O. O. F.): Whereas, Our town was visited during four months of last year by a fearful epidemic, striking down many and carrying off six of our members, thus entailing upon our Lodge liabilities which it was totally unable to meet; and whereas, Bro. J. L. Power, R. W. Grand Treasurer of Grand Lodge of Mississippi, nobly came to our relief; therefore, Be it resolved, That this Lodge duly appreciates the kindness of Bro.

Power, and the thanks of each and every member are hereby tendered to him. Resolved, further, That the Secretary be instructed to enter this action upon the minutes of the Lodge, and to furnish Bro. Power with a copy of the same.   J. F. DUFF, N. G.

THOS. W. MORGAN, Secretary p. t.   E. H. MIMS, V. G.

GARNER, Nov. 1.—(Extract from report of Relief Committee): Total receipts from J. L. Power, Grand Secretary, $800; from Hon. L. Q. C. Lamar, $25. Resolved, That the earnest and sincere thanks of this committee, and of all the citizens of Garner and surrounding country be most gratefully tendered to Col. J. L. Power, Grand Secretary, Jackson, Miss., and through him to all Lodges of Masons and Odd Fellows for the noble generosity shown us during our great affliction; when, but for the pecuniary assistance thus sent to us, our troubles would have been greatly augmented, and we should have been entirely without means to defray the heavy expenses incurred during the epidemic.

           J. L. COMBS, M. D., President.

GREENVILLE, Feb. 24.—Resolved, That we tender to Bro. J. L. Power, Grand Secretary, our heartfelt thanks for this timely and sorely needed help, and that we recognize and appreciate his unselfish and heroic labors during the epidemic of last summer, realizing the great indebtedness of our afflicted people to the brother whose fraternal appeal opened the great fountain of natural sympathy from which this wonderful benefaction poured upon our land. A true copy from the minutes.

           F. VALLIANT, W. M. Greenville Lodge, No. 206.

THEODORE POHL, Secretary.

GREENVILLE, Feb. 25.—(Resolution by Greenville Lodge, No. 94, I. O. O. F.) Resolved, That the thanks of this Lodge are hereby tendered Bro. J. L. Power, not only for this timely donation, obtained by his intercession from the Odd Fellows of the United States, but also for his noble efforts in behalf of suffering humanity while the pestilence raged.

           CHAS. WHITE, Secretary.

SUMMIT, March 21.—(From Summit Times): Many of our readers who feel an interest in the orphan children of Mrs. Lucie Strohecker—Jennie and Otho—will be delighted to learn that the ubiquitous, ever generous and sympathizing Col. J. L. Power—true to his trust and obligations to his brother Masons, has taken these orphans a good part of their route to their aged grandmother, Mrs. Strohecker, in Charleston, S. C., and provided for their safe conduct the remainder of the way. May Heaven's choicest blessings, flowing responsive to the grateful prayers of widows and orphans, follow him through life and light his pathway through the dark valley of shadows when his good work is finished on earth.

CHARLESTON, S. C., March 13.—The children arrived safely on last Monday morning. To say that we thank you for your generous kindness is to feebly express what I feel for all that your liberal help has done, not only for the orphans, but for the widow. Without your aid I was almost powerless to reach and protect my son's children, and I felt unhappy in being unable to gratify my poor son's often expressed wish that in case of his or his wife's death his children should come to us. * * * When the children have become more settled, and have regularly commenced their life among their new surroundings, they themselves will write. Just now they can only thank you through myself. May God's richest blessings rest on the kind hearts and homes that have spared from their abundance, to the help of the widow and the orphans.   Mrs. H. Strohecker.

Note.—The father of these children died several years ago at Summit. Their mother died of yellow fever at Canton. On being made acquainted with the wishes of their grandmother, funds were sent the W. M. of Canton Lodge to prepare them for the journey. The Chicago, St. Louis & New Orleans R. R. kindly furnished transportation to Grand Junction, and this writer provided for their trip to Charleston from the relief funds in his hands.

From The Clarion, March 12.

"Our associate, Colonel Power, went up the road last Friday morning in charge of four children, made orphans by the yellow fever. Two of them, Hattie and Archie McCallum, are now in Lima, Ohio. They were met at Chicago by members of the Masonic fraternity, who kindly cared for them from Saturday till Monday morning. The other children, Virginia and Otho Strohecker, whose mother died of yellow fever at Canton, are now with their grandmother in Charleston, S. C. They were received and cared for in Atlanta by our former townsman, Mr. H. C. Daniels."

From Water Valley Courier, Dec. 21.

A Generous Work.—Col. J. L. Power of Jackson, who has acted such a noble and faithful part in working up and disbursing funds from the various benevolent orders, as well as general relief fund to the yellow-fever stricken districts of the State, visited our city last week, on business connected with the same good work. In the management of the large funds intrusted to him from the various sources, he succeeded in reserving a very considerable sum of money, which he is now most wisely and prudently disbursing to the most destitute and needy orphans and widows in the districts visited by the epidemic. Col. Power is visiting these localities, and after consultation with leading citizens, and officers of the Masonic and Odd Fellow Lodges he makes such disposition of funds at his disposal as will meet the most pressing wants of the widows and orphans. Such was his mission here and many hearts are made glad indeed by his timely and most welcome visit. Many widows and orphans in Mississippi have cause of deepest gratitude to Col. Power, and the generous givers all over the country, who have placed these funds in his hands, for these timely and noble benefactions. And how grateful we should all feel when we can see these suffering and needy ones afforded aid which we cannot give. Col. Power has only been the faithful instrument for the disbursement of these funds, but he has done it wisely and well, and deserves the especial thanks of all our people. But the kindly spirit in which these funds were donated to our suffering, sick and dying ones, should and does warm all hearts with deepest gratitude, and make us all feel more kindly of our common humanity than we have ever done before.

From Grenada Sentinel, Nov. 16.

While we have no desire to overlook the memory of the worthy dead, we cannot forget that there are living men, some of whom were not so much exposed to the pestilence, who deserve all praise for their noble active services, and among this number we mention the name of J. L. Power, of the Clarion. When we saw that he was receiving and disbursing thousands of dollars weekly, from the Masons and Odd Fellows all over the Union, with no other guarantee of its proper use than his intelligence and honesty, we could but feel proud that on a printer had devolved one of the heaviest obligations and highest compliments developed by the strange fortunes of our suffering humanity. While his heart beat in tenderest sympathy for the sick, the dying and the dead, his head was level enough to know where to appropriate these large sums in behalf of his suffering brethren. It may be thought that we are anticipating results, and so we are, but when his final report is made, it will only elevate his character as a man, a Mason, an Odd Fellow and a christian.

From Holly Springs Reporter, Dec. 19.

Col. J. L. Power, of the CLARION, was in town last week, looking after the destitute, rendering them relief, and gathering facts connected with the plague, for use in the history of the pestilence which he is preparing. He did noble work during the epidemic, and his labors in the cause of suffering humanity have not yet ceased.

HALL OF RISING GLORY LODGE, 215, Osyka, Miss.

To J. L. Power, Grand Secretary Masonic Fraternity of Mississippi: DEAR BROTHER—The Members of this Lodge feeling it a sense of their duty to express in some form their gratitude to you as the good samaritan in their need, after the heavy cloud of affliction had passed, take this simple, but, we trust, lasting method of giving utterance to their feelings.

While we, dear brother, rear no marble column to your honored name, yet within the temple of our hearts have built a shrine of remembrance dear, on which the sacred lights of our Order shall be kept burning in memory of the good dispensed at your hands to the bereaved widow and helpless orphan of our membership, who were cut down by the relentless hand of Death. Like the mighty oak of the forest were they shattered by the blighting bolt, and thus the tender vines of home, left subject to the mercies of every rude blast of sweeping wind of the cold charities of an unfeeling world, 'twas then that an Almighty hand in a mysterious way created in you the great physician to dispense the Balm of Gilead, to heal in part the stricken heart, and give comfort to the mourning soul.

We, a few of the spared monuments of His mighty creation, bless you in our prayers, and do most humbly beseech His Almighty watch and care over you in life to come, as He has during the past year, when like an angel of mercy were you found, ministering to the wants of the afflicted and pouring the oil of joy, and giving words of consolation to those hearts made desolate by the fearful scourge.

> To-day our hearts united raise
> A hymn of joy, a mead of praise;
> A prayer of faith in words, of love,
> To Him who rules, all things above.

Then, dear Brother, receive in simplicity this letter of heartfelt thanks, and may Almighty God ever watch over and preserve you to a long and useful life; and may His richest blessings crown your every effort, is the prayer of your brethren of Rising Glory Lodge, No. 215; therefore be it,

Resolved, That the name of Brother J. L. Power be enrolled upon the books of this Lodge as an honorary member; and, that the W. M. be authorized to procure, and cause to be framed, a photograph of our Brother, for and at the expense of the Lodge.

Resolved, That a copy of the above be entered upon the minutes of this Lodge, and a copy be sent to the Summit Times for publication.

M. HART, Secretary.   W. D. DAVIDSON, W. M.

From THE CLARION.

AN APPRECIATED TRIBUTE.—The associates of Col. J. L. Power have seized the opportunity afforded by his temporary absence to reproduce in the CLARION the following appreciated, and (we who have had the best means of knowing will be excused for adding,) deserved tribute. It is due

8

to him to say that human applause was not his object in performing the deeds that have inspired this tribute. It was a higher one, and is seen in the results which have attended his services to the poor, the lowly, the sorrow-stricken in the hour of affliction. The distinguished authorship of the subjoined communication enhances its value. Though it was published anonymously, we have readily discovered the marks of an eminent jurist who has illustrated in his own successful career that,

"Honor and fame from no condition rise,
Act well your part—there all the honor lies."

Judge Mayers in the Corinth Record.

The distress and affliction in Vicksburg, Grenada, and other places, bring prominently before the country a name already known and associated with so many good works. I allude to Col. J. L. Power, of the CLARION. There are hundreds of men whose names occupy conspicuous places, and the country is loud in their praises, who fall far short of being so useful to their fellows, and who are not guided by so noble a philanthropy as he. It is not amiss to say that he was a poor Irish orphan boy, in Lockport, N. Y., where he worked for a few years at the printing business. He came to Mississippi twenty-odd years ago, married and settled at Jackson. He has been connected with all the benevolent enterprises of the State, and is known everywhere as one of the most reliable, prompt and efficient business men in the State. In a quiet, unpretending way, he is always doing good to his fellow-man. He remained at Jackson, and through his efforts has collected thousands of dollars in all parts of the Union, and has judiciously expended them to the great relief of the afflicted. To see him at work one would suppose "the world was his home, and to do good was his religion." But he acts from well-defined religious principles, and is guided by the true faith of the humble Christian, being a consistent member of the Presbyterian church. He has long been a superintendent the Sabbath School, and attends all the convocations and conventions in that interest, that he may learn how to be more useful. A more unselfish man I never knew. Wherever there is a sorrow to soothe, a tear to dry, a mourning heart to be comforted, a charity to be bestowed, he will be there—

"To do good by stealth and blush to find it fame."

A few years ago I witnessed his reception in the city of Lockport, where he had lived. It was truly an ovation. The officials of the city, editors, bankers, congressmen, ministers, lawyers, and indeed all the prominent men of the city, took pleasure in giving a cordial reception to the former orphan boy, whose conduct among them gave an earnest of his future usefulness and whose career in the far South they had witnessed with such pride and pleasure. I think it but proper to hold up for the encouragement, and for examples to the rising generation, the successful career of such men in their works of true charity and benevolence. Though such rarely receive any reward here below, save the gratitude and love of the recipients of their favors and the respect of the few who know their true history; yet, in the "Sweet Bye and Bye" they will receive "a crown that fadeth not away."

It is not amiss to say that notwithstanding his labors as above stated, he carries on his business with perfect system, and is a most energetic and thorough business man. May God continue to bless him in his good works.

From the Grenada Sentinel.

TWO GREAT INSTITUTIONS.—Though Masonry and Odd Fellowship may differ as to their origin and age, there is one thing nobody will dispute, that they are each a mighty power in the land for good. So powerfully and harmoniously do they work together in the cause of humanity, that they may be called the elder and junior sisters of human charity. While neither of them allow of proselytism, they have, in our yellow fever afflictions of this year, presented to the whole world, the grandest display of charitable brotherhood ever witnessed upon earth. They have each risen in moral grandeur and social power as the necessities of our overwhelming troubles have demanded, for each have poured out their treasure to the suffering brethren of the South with unstinted liberality, and in every case, have cried out in tones that sent a thrill of joy and pride to their smitten brothers of the South: "We have more yet on hand if you need!"

Will not this wonderful display of active benevolence and fraternal love, fill up the ranks of decimated orders in the South with our best young men as soon as the time arrives for quiet, safe intercourse? In fact, will not this mighty outflow of sympathy and relief be read of all men in our whole country, and prepare the way for that mighty chain of fraternal bonds, that in the end, will bind us together as a people in feelings and obligations, stronger than political constitutions and civil compacts?

From the Jackson Comet, February 1, 1879.

LESSON OF THE LATE EPIDEMIC.—We have been deeply interested in the perusal of that part of Colonel Power's report to the Grand Lodge, relating to the contributions to our late yellow fever sufferers by the Masons and Odd Fellows throughout the country. If anybody has allowed any doubts or misgivings to rest upon his mind as to the real benevolence and nobility of purpose which animate these benevolent institutions, it seems to us, that he ought now to dismiss them forever as unworthy of a lodgment among liberal and just thoughts. The record which the Masons and Odd Fellows have made during the dark period of our suffering, is one of moral grandeur, and many, many are the grateful shower of tears which will fall upon and cause it to bloom long in the nursery of thankful hearts. No man can read the account of the transfer of little Horace Walters from New Orleans to San Francisco, under the all-protecting ægis of Masonry, without paying to the noble brotherhood who could perform this tender office so well the tribute of a tear in recognition of their goodness and touching charity. * * * * * * * * * *

The lesson which we draw from this and other princely gifts from our Northern and Western brethren is, that when our people come to understand each other a strong bond of sympathy and fraternity is found to hold them together, and that this bond henceforward to be recognized and strengthened, so that all sections of of our Union may serve as mutually protecting braces for the grand central column.

COLLEGE STATION, TEXAS, April 12.—* * I congratulate you on your benevolent labors. They are more attractive to me than triumph of arms or the prestige gained by parliamentary success. THOS. S. GATHRIGHT.

THE SOLID SOUTH.

BY EMMETT L. ROSS.

Awake! awake, O sluggish Muse!
  If only for a while,
And tune my harp to Homer's lyre—
  Blind bard of Scio's Isle—
That I may sing in fitting words
  Songs of enduring praise
To willing hands and noble hearts
  Who in affliction's days,
Poured out upon our sunny land
  Their stores of love and wealth
That brought surcease to pestilence,
  And wooed back joyous health.

The Solid South pours out her heart this bright, this glad New Year,
And sends a message to all men, all nations far and near;
A message draped with willow leaves, bedewed with holy tears
Of widowed wife and orphaned child, sad youth and tottering years:
A message from her palaces, from cottage, hill and glade,
From council halls, from field and farm, and busy marts of trade ;
A message freighted down with love, with gratitude as great
As ever woke a soul to arms, or bared a breast for State;
A love that throbs in every heart, a gratitude that thrills,
And breaks its bounds like waves that rush to sea from swelling rills.

Some mother bending o'er the tomb that holds her cherished boy,
Some stricken wife beside the grave where rests her girlhood's joy,
Some maiden weeping o'er the mound where troth and lover lie,
Press back their sobs and in their prayers call blessings from on high
Down on the heads, the hearts, the homes of those whose helping hand
Brought succor to our stricken ones and saved our suffering land.
The Southron's hand that erstwhile drew his sabre from its sheath
And dipped its blade in brother's blood to win the patriot's wreath,
Now presses on a throbbing breast in pledge to self and God
That Peace and Love shall ever reign where hostile armies trod.
The fires of hate that lit his soul, nor sword nor gun could quell—
These yield to Love's bewitching wiles, to Love's all-conquering spell:
Deep in his heart is writ the name, the pure unselfish zeal
Of him who dared the Saffron Foe, to conquer woe with weal.
More holy task was never borne than that brave Benner tried ;
No loss more great, no grief more deep, than when brave Benner died ;
No gift in all the bounty sent, more rich, more rare in price,
No words can compensate the boon—our Nations's sacrifice,
Ten million grateful hearts enshrine his memory in their breast,
Ten million tongues his deed extol, invoke his spirit's rest ;
A solid South reveres his name, his valor undefiled—
One common country's love will shield the Martyr's wife and child.

O, Great Jehovah, King of Kings !
  Whose mighty hands control
The fate of worlds, the works of men,
  And Time's unceasing roll—
Let blessings follow in the path
  Of Sorrow's fading tread ;
Let comfort come to those who mourn
  And weep above their dead ;
Pour down unmeasured blessings, Lord,
  Thy choicest and thy best,
To crown our brothers of the North
  And far-off East and West;
Blot out the lines that would divide
  And desecrate our sod,
Bind close our States, give us one Law,
  One Union, and one God.

Canton, Miss., 1879.

TRIBUTES TO THE DEAD.

Friend after friend departs;
 Who has not lost a friend?
There is no union here of hearts,
 That finds not here an end.
Were this frail world our final rest,
Living or dying none were blest.

Thus star by star declines,
 Till all are passed away,
As morning high and higher shines
 To pure and perfect day;
Nor sink those stars in empty night,
But hide themselves in heaven's own light.

HARVEY W. WALTER,

PAST GRAND MASTER, PAST GRAND HIGH PRIEST.

BY BRO. FREDERIC SPEED.

In the stillness of the preceding night a few sparks of electricity flashed over the wires, and all the civilized world read on the morning of the 20th of September last, the brief, but to us who knew and loved him, inexpressibly sad message, "Colonel Walter is amongst the dead of the past twenty-four hours." The noble, brave-hearted man who had, on the breaking out of the great epidemic of 1878, stretched out his hands and bid all the affrighted refugees from fever-stricken points to come to Holly Springs as a place of refuge, lay dead, with his face to the foe. There were some of us whose hearts stood still as we read, and whose eyes filled with tears of anguish, and to whom it was a bitter day as to those in a lonely house from which loved ones had departed. We knew that he was ill, but had refused to believe that any harm could come to *him;* others might die, but surely our dear old friend would pass through the fire, as he had passed over a score of battle fields unscathed. "A thousand shall fall beside thee, and ten thousand at thy right hand, but it shall not come nigh thee," were the words with which we comforted ourselves, when we learned that the dreaded fever had made its appearance at Holly Springs; but alas, we were doomed to experience a bitter disappointment. God's ways are not our ways, and he took whom it seemed to Him best should be taken. Those of us who remain to set up the curtains of our Tabernacle, performing the duty which Freemasonry dictates, submitting, with resignation, to the Supreme Grand High Priest's will, endeavor to place on record our estimate of his worth and to testify our affection for him.

Companion Walter was born in Fairfield county, Ohio, on the 21st day of May, 1819, but a few years later his parents settled at Kalamazoo, Michigan, where his early years were spent. An unfortunate investment consumed his father's entire fortune, and at the age of fourteen our Companion began the battle of life, which he thenceforth fought without parental assistance. Having completed his college course, he came to Mississippi, earning his living by teaching school, while preparing for his admission to the bar. Soon after receiving his license to practice law, in the year 1840, he located at Holly Springs, and from that time his name is inseparably interwoven with the history of his State and county. Prominent in all affairs of a public nature, and a leader upon every occasion, where the public welfare was concerned, he had little or no taste for political life and never sought office; it was the public good and not personal advancement which caused him to spend his time, talents and money, which he did with a liberal hand, whenever occasion required it. In social affairs he was always a welcome and honored guest. In his church, a prominent and useful member. As a jurist, he stood first and foremost in a bar which was famous throughout the land for its learning and eloquence. As a soldier—though opposed to secession—he was amongst the first during the unhappy war between the sections to enter the field, and he did not sheath his sword until the echoes of the last gun had ceased to reverberate. In all the relations of life, brave, true, just, generous, he was always the noble, honorable and kindhearted gentleman, who thought less of himself than of others.

In Masonry, as everywhere else, Companion Walter was distinguished above his fellows. Initiated, passed and raised in Holly Springs Lodge, No. 35, in the year 1842, he rose to be Master in 1845. Present at the first Annual Convocation of the Grand Chapter in 1847, as the representative of Wilson Chapter, No. 5, we find him filling the offices of Principal Sojourner and Captain of the Host in the Chapter for a number of years thereafter, until in 1859 he was elected High Priest. Named as Generalissimo in the dispensation to organize Holly Springs Commandery in 1858, he was afterwards Eminent Commander and continued unto the end an active and zealous Knight Templar.

Companion Walter succeeded to the Grand Mastership on the death of Grand Master Vannatta, in 1844, and for more than thirty-five years was one of the most prominent, active and efficient members of the Grand Lodge. In 1874, he was elected Most Puissant Grand Master of the Grand Council and served in that capacity two years. In 1867 and 1877 he served the Grand Chapter in the capacity of Grand High Priest and was its Representative at the General Grand Chapter in 1877.

In the Ancient and Accepted Scottish Rite, Companion Walter had attained to the Degree of Sublime Prince of the Royal Secret, 32°.

Thus it will be seen how great was the service Companion Walter rendered to Freemasonry, in all its branches, and we are enabled to realize the measure of the calamity it sustained when he was taken from its council chambers. As he said of another, so we can say of him: "His loss would have been to us irreparable, had he not bequeathed to us an invaluable legacy in the example of virtue and piety, which his life so eminently exhibited. I may say with truth, that his knowledge of Masonry was such as to make him the brightest ornament of our Order, while his devoted attachment to its tenets and his daily practice of its precepts had rendered him one of its most exemplary members. As a man and as a Mason, he ever squared his actions by the teachings of Divine Revelation and ever consulted that great Masonic Trestle Board in all his relations with his fellow-man."

Thus, Companions, day by day, as journeying along the rough and rugged paths of life, we pitch our tents and set up the tabernacle of the Lord, we find the company with which we set out growing smaller, and new and strange faces come and stand in their places, but as we draw nigh to the brink of the river, we shall behold upon the other shore the dear friends for whom we grieve, beckoning us to cross over and join them in the eternal spring time of the life beyond the grave.—

"As distant lands beyond the sea,
  When friends go thence, draw nigh;
So Heaven, when friends have thither gone,
  Draws nearer from the sky.

"And as those lands the dearer grow,
  When friends are long away;
So Heaven itself, through loved ones dead,
  Grows nearer, day by day."

EXTRACT FROM ADDRESS BY PAST GRAND MASTER JAS. M. HOWRY AT LODGE OF SORROW.

Our Brother, Past Grand Master Walter, was one of those who favored the hospitable reception of refugees from Memphis, Grenada, Vicksburg and other infected districts, and opposed the quarantine. He saw the mistake he had made, when too late! He hurried his beloved wife and their youngest children off, choosing to remain, together with his three eldest sons, and share the fate of those who remained in the doomed city! The happy family thus separated will never again be re-united this side of the river.

Bro. Walter came to Mississippi in 1840, located in Holly Springs, and by industry and perseverance, soon took position as a successful lawyer. The country was new, fresh and rich, and the field inviting to young men of talent and enterprise, of which Bro. W. availed himself. He married an accomplished and amiable lady, daughter of Col. James Brown, of Oxford, and they reared the three noble boys, already mentioned, to manhood, and the wife and six children, minors, were left to mourn the loss of husband, father and brothers. He was distinguished for his zeal in everything he undertook. He never sought office, though he was voted for by his party friends once for Governor. He bore an active and efficient part in the establishment of the Mississippi Central Railroad, and for the last few years was a Trustee of the State University. He was the friend of education and all enterprises which tended to promote the public good. His Masonic career was a brilliant one. He was admitted a member of Holly Springs Lodge at an early day, and in 1845 was elected Senior Grand Warden of the Grand Lodge of Mississippi. He was made Deputy Grand Master, and he succeeded to the Grand Mastership, by the death of Bro. Vannatta.

He presided over his Lodge, Chapter and Council at Holly Springs, and was elected Grand High Priest, and Most Puissant Grand Master of the Grand Council of the State within the last few years. He assisted in organizing a Commandery of Knights Templar over which he presided, and was a zealous member of the Templar Order. To the day of his death he manifested his devotion to our beloved Order upon all occasions. In the Grand Bodies, he was always placed on important committees, and was recognized as an active, intelligent and useful member, much respected and beloved by his brethren. We could dwell on the life and character of Brother Walter as a man and a Mason, but others claim our attention and we must let this suffice. We will add, however, that the circumstances of his death and burial, and those of his three noble sons, were indescribably sad. They grappled with the monster about three weeks and but a short time intervened between their deaths. The father and one son were buried by the two sons and a servant alone. The two last, FRANK and JAMES, were taken sick and died about the same time, and were carried to their last resting place by two faithful colored men. No wife or mother, brother or sister to follow them—no requiem or funeral obsequies performed by mourning friends! How sad—how solemn the thought!

From Jackson, (Miss.,) Clarion, Sept. 21.]

HARVEY W. WALTER, of Holly Springs, Past Grand Master and Past Grand High Priest of the Masonic Order—lawyer, statesman, soldier, patriot, christian—is no more. He fell at his post in the discharge of the sacred offices of humanity. In all the experience of a long and honorable career, the pole-star of his life was DUTY. Mississippi mourns the loss of one of her noblest sons.

THE MASONIC DEAD OF VICKSBURG AND WARREN COUNTY.

Extract from the Oration of Bro. Frederic Speed, at the Lodge of Sorrow, Okolona, January 15, 1879.

Aye, Sir, another year has passed away like an unbidden guest, and sunk into the gloom and darkness of the past, unregretted ; and we are again assembled round the altar of Masonry to renew the pledges of brotherly love and affection, to extend to each other the hand of fraternal greeting and salutation ; but the season usually consecrated to festive enjoyment is overcast with clouds of funereal darkness, and our hearts are filled with anguish as we resume our labors, for, alas ! death and the dead are with us again, and we mourn grievously the loss of many dear friends, for whose familiar faces which were wont to greet us with smiles, and to cheer and gladden us in the work of building the House of the Lord, we shall henceforth look in vain.

It is well that we should pause in our labors to commune with the spirits of the master workmen who have been called by the voice of the Grand Warden from the labors of the earthly Lodge to refreshment in the Heavenly Temple of our God. It has been tritely said, that, we live only to lose those we love, and to see our friends go away out of our sight, and this is the penalty we pay for living the few brief years which shall swiftly glide under our feet before we, too, shall join the innumerable caravan and cross the dark river of death.

Bruised and bleeding from the many wounds which a heavy calamity has inflicted upon us, we are not yet sufficiently composed to contemplate with calmness the fearful wreck and ruin which death has wrought, or to make choice of words adequate to express our love for those upon whose hearts he has laid his icy fingers, and stilled their beatings forever. Stunned by the magnitude of the blow, we cannot realize that we shall see and hear our friends no more ; that we cannot go to them or they come to us, until we, too, shall take the last sublime degree, and enter through the portals of the tomb into the Grand Lodge, where death is the Tyler, and the Supreme Grand Master of heaven and earth presides.

* * * * * * * * *

If there be any of you to whom the memory of those of whom we shall speak is not dear, I pray you to bear with us while we mourn above this symbol, representing those in which there reposes all that was earthly of many dear friends.

On the 20th day of July last, a powerful steamer stemmed the tide of the the mighty "Father of Waters," as it rushes forward to unite its waters with those of the ocean, carrying a cargo which was destined to destroy thousands of human lives, and to desolate many hearthstones. With each pulsation of her huge engines, death drew nearer and nearer to the doomed cities of the Mississippi Valley, until, on the 23d day of the same month, it landed before the city of Vicksburg, pausing to bury some members of its crew, end to ask aid for others dying from the effects of a fever which baffled the skill of the physician and annihilated all previously formed theories of medical science. From the city hospital, whose doors have always opened to admit the distressed, to which the first victims were carried, the poisoned germs of disease spread in all directions, and a scene of utter woe and desolation began, which baffles all description, even were it our purpose to narrate its history. All who could do so, and who were not detained by the promptings of duty, immediately fled to places of supposed safety. Those who remained prepared themselves as best the could to battle bravely for the lives of friends, the poor and helpless. At once there sprang into being an association composed of as gallant spirits as ever stood where,

> "The cannon mouthings loud
> Heave in wild wreaths the battle shroud
> And gory sabres rise and fall
> Like sheets of flame on midnight's pall,"

or where

> "Death, careering on the gale,
> Sweeps darkly round the bellied sail,
> And frightened waves rush wildly back
> Before the broadside's reeling rack."

All ranks and classes of society volunteered, and brave men vied with each other in the work of ministering to the sick, preparing the dead for the grave, and consoling the bereaved. There were none to

> "Ask the brave soldier who fights by side,
> In the cause of mankind if our creeds agree,"

or to

> "Give up the friend I have valued and tried,
> If he kneel not before the same altar with me."

Class distinction, religious and social prejudices vanished in an instant, and as if by magic the social gulf, heretofore deemed impassable, disappeared. Many of the gallant souls which were enrolled under the banner inscribed with the name of the philanthropist "Howard," went down in the struggle which ensued. God rest them and grant that they may have washed themselves pure from the contaminations and stains contracted in the journey of life by their last supreme act of self-abnegation. To die for their fellows, was indeed a glorious death—for "Greater Love hath no man than this: that he lay down his life for his friends."

Wor. Bro. THURSTON J. THOMPSON was the first Mason to fall in the city of Vicksburg, his death having occurred on the tenth day of August, in the 59th year of his age. Brother Thompson was one of the most useful and zealous members of the fraternity, as the following record shows. It is not known in what Lodge he was initiated, but he affiliated with Bovina Lodge, No. 112, in 1851; and was its Senior Deacon during the years 1852, 1853, and 1850; Senior Warden in 1854, Master in 1855, 1857 and 1858. He dimitted in 1858 and affiliated with Walnut Hills Lodge, No. 194, in 1870; was its Senior Warden in 1874 and 1875; Master in 1876 and 1877, and held the office of Senior Deacon at the time of his death. One of the officers named in the dispensation to organize John Hebron Chapter No. 71, in the year 1859, he continued to fill various stations of importance in Royal Arch Masonry up to the time of his death, when he was Excellent King of Vicksburg Chapter, No. 3. A Royal and Select Master of many years standing, he had filled many offices in the Council and at the time of the incorporation of the Councils into the Chapter, was Secretary of Vicksburg Council, No. 2. Brother Thompson's name appears upon the first return of Magnolia Commandery, No. 2, in 1858, and here, as elsewhere, he proved an eminently useful member, having held various offices in Templar Masonry. But few Masons have such a record, and the bare recital demonstrates in the strongest possible manner how great was the loss sustained by the Fraternity in its first victim claimed by the epidemic of 1878. A man of inflexible honesty, and having an undisguised contempt for all the shams and subterfuges of life; in business, his promise was never known to be broken. Strong willed and uncompromising he was always just and honorable. Warm in his attachment to his friends, he avoided taking many into his confidence, and preferred the society of a few genial spirits to mixing with the multitude. Hence he was seldom found away from his business, and when he was, the Lodge room was generally the attraction, no meeting occurring at which he was not present, when in health. Others may hold, but they cannot fill the place he occupied in our bodies, and many years will probably pass away before we shall find another equally zealous and efficient. God grant that he may have received "the white stone with a new name written," which shall insure perpetual and unspeakable happiness in the Supreme Grand Lodge.

August 20th Bro. J. P. ALLEN fell the 45th in year of his age. Although Brother Allen had not affiliated with any of our bodies, he had not ceased to take in interest in the welfare of the fraternity, and in one of his last conversations with the speaker expressed his regret that he had not availed himself of the privilege of Lodge membership. Brother Allen was a genial and kind hearted man who never permitted himself to speak ill of others. As a journalist he was painstaking and conscientious, and strove to discharge the duties of his calling with justice and fairness to all. He will be remembered kindly by all who were privileged to know him.

September 2d, there died a young but very zealous and promising Brother, CHARLES H. NATHAN, aged 26. Brother Nathan at the time of his death was the Treasurer of William H. Stevens Lodge, No. 121, and of the Royal Arch Chapter. A man of sensitive temperament, who mixed but little with the affairs of the world, preferring his books and scientific investigation, he was cut down just as he was entering upon a career of great usefulness.

Brother J. T. TENNEY, a member of one of the Boston Lodges, stationed at the time at Vicksburg, as one of the Signal Corps observers, died on the 4th day of September. At the breaking out of the epidemic Brother Tenney refused to abandon his post of duty, although permission was granted to him by his superiors to do so. During the two years of his sojourn in Vicksburg he had made many friends who found in him a warm hearted and genial companion, and his aged parent in his distant home was not the only mourner when his noble son yielded up his life.

Brother P. F. WHITEHEAD, M. D., who was not affiliated and probably known as a Mason to but few of his intimates, died on the 5th day of September, was a physician of rare attainments, and stood very high in his profession. Universally respected and greatly esteemed for his sterling qualities as a man and citizen, he died regretted by all classes of the community.

On the 7th of September, Reverend Brother BERNARD H. GOTTHELF, minister of the Hebrew congregation, yielded up his spirit to the God who gave it. Engrossed in the many cares incident to his spiritual charge, Brother Gotthelf had not, although a resident of Vicksburg for the past seven years, affiliated with any of our Lodges, but we had frequent occasion to know that he retained his interest in the Masonic institution, and his sermons testified that he found in its teachings much in common with the ancient creed whose precepts he enjoined upon his hearers. Brother Gotthelf was in his sixtieth year at the time of his death. The greater portion of his life had been devoted to the highest interest of others, and for the space of twenty years he had ministered in spiritual things to one congregation. The unbounded sorrow his death occasioned demonstrated how firm a hold he had upon the affections of his people. And not alone by Hebrews, but by those of all religions was his death deplored, for, by his broad and liberal views, he had won his way into the respect and esteem of all classes of his fellow citizens.

Brother JAMES WARRINGTON, who died September 8th, was Junior Deacon of Vicksburg Lodge, No, No. 26, in 1875, and Senior Deacon in 1876. A man of kindly, generous impulses, he will be missed by a large circle of friends.

Brother J. B. NORRIS, of Chattanooga, Tennessee, a volunteer physician who hastened to relieve the sufferings of the fever stricken people of Vicksburg, offered up his life a sacrifice upon the altar of humanity, on the tenth day of September, aged 32 years. We know but little of the story of this brother's life, but those who came in contact with him as he passed from house to house ministering to the sick and the dying, speak in highest terms of him and the general demonstration of sorrow by the people of Chattanooga, upon the reception of the news of his death, evinces the esteem with which he was regarded by those who knew him best. Though we cannot give his record as a Mason, the last act of his life testified beyond the power of words how deeply imbued he was with the grand Masonic idea of the brotherhood of man. Gladly we weave a wreath of laurel and olive to twine around the memory of the stranger brother, in testimony of our gratitude for the great sacrifice he made in our behalf. In his distant home amongst the mountains he sleeps with his friends and kindred, but the great river, as it winds its way onward to the sea, sings for him a perpetual requiem, and so will it ever be for the brave and the noble upon life's great battle-field.

One of the heroes of the epidemic was Brother CHARLES F. TAFFE, who died on the eleventh day of September, aged 35 years. Brother Taffe, on the breaking out of the epidemic, fitted up a volunteer ambulance and was constantly employed in carrying the destitute sick to the hospital. Writing to his partner in business a few days before his death, he said : " I know I have done wrong in taking this money, (a few hundred dollars of partnership funds,) but I could not stand still and see the poor creatures suffering round me for want of a few dollars, when I had them in my pocket. If I die you can get the money back out of my insurance, and if I live we can work it out all right again." Noble-hearted and brave man, he died as truly for his fellow man as ever did a soldier on the field of battle, or a martyr at the stake. He gave his all—his life—for the poor and the friendless.

Brother GEORGE F. HEFLINGER, aged 30 years, who was Junior Warden of Walnut Hills Lodge, No 494, in 1877, died September seventeenth. Brother Heflinger was a bright and active Mason, an honest and upright man, who loved his friends and delighted to serve them. His presence at our assemblies will be greatly missed, and a void is left, by his death, in a large circle of friends, of which he was the centre.

September 20th, Ill. Bro. WILLIAM ANNER FAIRCHILD, a Sublime Prince of the Royal Secret 32°, who was born in the city of New York, July 14th, 1838, died, aged 41 years. Brother Fairchild was, at the time of his death, the presiding officer of Charles Scott Council Princes of Jerusalem, Prelate Magnolia Commandery, No. 2, Grand Master of the 3d Vail, Vicksburg R. A. Chapter, and Secretary of Vicksburg Lodge, No. 26. He had presided over all the bodies of the York Rite, the Lodge of Perfection, and as Grand Commander of Knights Templar in the State of Mississippi. In all the walks of life Brother Fairchild was an eminently useful man ; in business circles, and in social life he was first and foremost in every good work. Open-hearted and generous to a fault the poor found in him a sympathetic friend, who denied no worthy applicant. No labor was too great, nor burden too heavy for him to bear in the cause of humanity. Brother Fairchild will long survive his funeral in the affections of all who knew him, and none who have fallen before the Southern pestilence will be more sincerely mourned by all classes of the community, amongst whom all the years of his manhood were spent.

Wor. Brother DANIEL A. CAMERON, Past Master of Bovina Lodge, No. 112, and Past High Priest of John Hebron Chapter, No. 71, who died September 28th, though well stricken in years, never ceased to love and revere Masonry. And although he came to his "grave in full age, like a shock of corn cometh in his season," there were few who had known the kind hearted old man did not deplore his loss. The familiar face and cordial greetings of this venerable brother, have been seen and heard for the last time, but we dare to hope that after life's trials and disappointments he has found rest in the "house not made with hands eternal in the Heavens."

A kind friend, a good neighbor and an honest and upright man died when Brother A. ALEXANDER closed his eyes to sleep the sleep of death, on the second day of October, in the 57th year of his age. A Mason of the old school, he was the associate of Stevens and Manlove in the early days of Hill City Lodge, No. 121, and delighted to relate incidents of his Masonic contemporaries of twenty-five years ago, who alas, have nearly all passed away. Many pleasing thoughts are associated with his memory, and there were many who were not of his household who mourned for him.

Brother REYNAULD KALMBACK, who was for many years the Secretary of one of the Lodges in Hermann, Missouri, and who had but recently changed his Lodge membership to William H. Stevens Lodge, No. 121, died on the 8th of October, aged 45 years. An active and an earnest man, he pushed forward every work he undertook with intelligence and determination, and it was through no fault of his that when his sun set, his family were not left with a competency. Several successive years failure of the grape crop in Missouri, in which he had embarked his entire fortune, compelled the abandonment of the vineyards he had planted, and when he returned to Vicksburg it was to begin life's struggle anew. His friends know with what heart and courage he endured adversity, and they were rejoicing that the clouds had began to dissipate, when death stretched forth his icy fingers and laid them upon his heart. Affectionate and kindly in his disposition, he loved his family and friends, and found his chief pleasures in their company. With no enemies and many friends, he passed away honored and respected by all who knew him.

Brother JONES S. WILKINS, of Bovina Lodge, No. 115, died October 9th, aged 33 years. This brother entered with a degree of zeal and unselfish devotion into the work of succoring his fellow citizens, which entitles him to the highest possible praise which we are capable of bestowing, and regardless of danger to himself he sought out the sick and did not relinquish his endeavors until the fatal disease had progressed so far in his own system that he was beyond the reach of medical skill, when his strength failed him and he returned to his home to die. Brave, patient and gentle, he rests in a hero's grave, upon which an oaken wreath, symbol of victory, should ever remain, for he triumphed over the fear of disease and death in going about doing good to the suffering and dying people of his neighborhood.

October 13th, Brother J. WILSON CONKLIN, who was formerly a very active and zealous member of William H. Stevens Lodge, died, aged 44. An amiable and genial man, he had many friends to weep over his bier.

Brother BENJAMIN C. BOOKOUT, who died at his plantation on the Yazoo River on the 17th day of October, aged 40 years, was an active member of William H. Stevens Lodge, No. 121, the Royal Arch Chapter and Magnolia Commandery, and a well known citizen. From his youth, prominently connected with the steamboat lines of the Yazoo Valley he had many sincere friends who respected his sterling integrity, manhood and many good qualities. Generous and charitable in an eminent degree, he had assisted many a poor and forlorn shipwrecked brother through the breakers of life, and there were many prayers breathed when he embarked upon the voyage through the river of death, for his safe arrival in the harbor, where there are no more storms and the weary are at rest.

A kind hearted and amiable old man, who wronged himself more than others, GEORGE W. EDWARDS, died October 23, aged 61. Brother Edwards was a member of one of the New York City Lodges, and died regretted by a large circle of friends and acquaintances who were attracted by his many quaint and humorous ways.

Wor. Brother WILLIAM E. MONETT, M. D., Past Master of Highland

Lodge, No. 113, and a member of the Chapter and Commandery at Vicksburg, who died in his forty-fourth year, was greatly beloved not only by the brethren, but by all who were privileged to know him. As a physician he enjoyed not only the confidence of his patients but also of the members of his profession. Hearty and generous in his nature he had many sincere friends who grieve at his loss and with whom his memory will ever remain fresh and green.

Wor. Bro. John W. Hullum was also a Past Master of Highland Lodge, No. 113; a just and upright man, he enjoyed during a long life the esteem and confidence of all his fellow citizens.

Brother C. V. D. Riddle, of William H. Stevens Lodge, No. 121, died, aged 37 years. Brother Riddle had but recently taken up his residence at Vicksburg, but he had been long enough amongst us to win the confidence and respect of all who had formed his acquaintance.

Bovina Lodge, No. 112, sustained further loss in the death of Brothers S. B. Wall, R. W. Chappell, J. B. Johnson, J. W. Finch, and H. S. Featherston, all of them valuable and useful members of the community in which they resided and true to their Masonic duties and obligations, the brethren will honor the places of their resting, with violets and garlands of flowers.

Thus, sir, the long sad list is completed, and the task assigned, by your kind partiality is finished, but oh! how imperfectly has the duty been performed! Gladly would we have dwelt at greater length upon the virtues and good qualities of the many dear friends of whom we have spoken, and more especially of those of whom we have been compelled to speak but a single sentence, in order to bring this feeble tribute within the limit allowed to us—for it is very pleasant to think and speak kind words in taking a last, long farewell of so many with whom it has been our privilege to toil in life's busy hive. All of them were bound to us by ties which can never be broken, and some were our daily associates and intimate friends, whose memories can never fade so long as life shall last, and who will ever continue to beckon us from the other shore of the river, to cross over and join them in the eternal spring time of the life beyond the grave.

*   *   *   *   *   *   *   *   *   *   *   *

Brethren, in a few more summers we shall cease to hear death repeating into our ears the summons to reap and to bind ; our sheaves, whether they contain chaff or grain, will soon have to be submitted for the inspection of the Master Overseer. But we shall not, cannot die :

> "Immortality o'er sweeps
> All pains, all tears, all time, all fears—and peals
> Like the eternal thunders of the deep,
> Into my ears this truth, thou liv'st forever."

Let us then, standing here in the presence of this coffin, representing those in which the remains of our brethren shall peacefully repose, until the earth and the sea shall give up their dead, renew the solemn obligations of Masonry, not only to the dead, but also to the living. Where, and under what more deeply affecting circumstances, can we find place and opportunity to resolve to maintain, with greater assiduity, the tenets of our profession, than here in this Temple, dedicated to the service of the living God, and in the symbolical presence of this vast array of dead brethren, whose memories we can never cease to cherish. "Our duties to the dead will not cease with these sad ceremonies, though their warfare with the calamities and sorrows, the reverses and disappointments, the wrongs and oppressions of this world are over, the tie which binds us to them is not broken asunder, their causes are still our causes, their memories and reputations we are to watch over and guard with zealous care, and we are to give protection and assistance to any whom they left destitute or unprotected, or who suffering wrong or injury may appeal to us in their names." Thus shall we reap the golden grain, which shall purchase unto ourselves a good reward in the day when we shall meet our brethren again before the great white throne and answer unto them for any neglect to keep not only the letter but the spirit of all our sacred covenants with them.

And now, having renewed our obligations to the dead, let us leave them to sleep on until the great reaper, death, shall be swallowed up in victory; though our voices cannot reach them, nor our feeble tributes bring forth a single response, yet can we say to life's great jailor, the grave,

"Thine for a space are they;
Yet shalt thou yield thy treasures up at last;
Thy gates shall yet give way;
Thy bolts shall fall—Inexorable past."

THE MASONIC DEAD OF GRENADA.

Address of Gen. G. Y. Freeman, Past Master of Grenada Lodge, No. 31, before the Grand Lodge of Sorrow at Okolona, January 15, 1879.

Most Worshipful Grand Master and Brothers:

On behalf of Grenada Lodge, No. 31, it becomes my mournful duty to recount the loss of many of our beloved brothers—but to be able, as I am, to testify to their sterling worth and many virtues, is to me a source of greatest pride and pleasure.

I have no words aptly to portray the true characters, the pleasing attributes and the genuine merit of our noble dead. Now that they have gone from us forever, I can say, if you could have known them just as they lived among us, from the hearts of all here would come a tribute to their memories, more beautiful than any minstrel's lay or speaker's tongue could offer.

The silent "heart worship" of brother for his brother who has gone to "that bourne from whence no traveler returns," gone in honor and in duty, would rear to them a monument "not made with hands," no pile of marble bearing mere empty epitaphs and formal phrases of praise, but a monument whose base is love, whose shaft is respect, whose only inscription is "our loss is their eternal gain."

The occasion affords me no opportunity to even epitomize the lives or Masonic history of the many deceased brethren of whom I would speak. But I would ask you to go back to the time, less than a year ago, when this Grand Body held its regular stated Grand Communication in the little city of Grenada, upon the invitation of Grenada Lodge.

Many now here, there received the fraternal greetings of the members of that Lodge, and mingled with them in the social circles. The mystic links of Masonic fellowship, which had united these brethren, thus thrown together, were warmed by contact and welded into stronger bonds of union. When your labors were ended and your faces turned homeward, no thought of the dire future, no glimpse of the dreadful death angel marred the fresh memories of our recent pleasant intercourse, but we separated with renewed and brightened hopes for the future advancement of our Order, and the welfare of all our brethren. Grenada Lodge gathered new strength and a fresh impetus from its contact with this Grand Body. It began the new Masonic year with every prospect of success and with every hope of prosperity. But in a few short months, what a frightful change! What a calamitous result! There came a dreadful pestilence, a pitiless destroyer, whose mission was as mysterious as his mode of deadly warfare. No place was secure from his approach; the palace of the rich and the hovel of the poor were both the scenes of his fatal work. The strong and the weak, the scoffer and the devotee, the Christian, the ungodly, alike sank down before him in his march of death. The sacred temple of Masonry was no asylum, exempted from the awful "death levy," but from our Lodge were taken the truest and the best—the "light" from the "east," the strength from the "west" and "beauty" from the "south." When this unequal contest began between a mysterious and malignant enemy of unknown power and untold strength on the one side; and humanity, weak and helpless on the other, there were two of our brothers who were very prominent members of the noble profession of medicine, brothers EDWARD W. HUGHES and WILLIAM W. HALL. In the faithful discharge of their duties, they manfully battled with all their skill and energy for the relief of the suffering people around them. When the hour of that fearful pestilence grew darkest, when death seemed poised on every breath, when human skill and all man's efforts to relieve his fellows appeared but the vainest mockeries, and people were fleeing for their lives in terror—these brothers quailed not, but bravely struggled with the deadly foe, when it seemed that no man could face him and live.

When the city of Pompeii was disinterred from the silent tomb, where for 1700 years it lay buried, it is said at its gates and at the post of duty appeared the forms of the Roman sentry. In that awful day, when the raging volcano belched forth, in appalling grandeur, a flaming winding sheet for the doomed city; when the very air was filled with liquid fire, and the streets and gates thronged with terrified inhabitants seeking safety in flight, these guards heroically stood at their posts and bravely met their certain death, because in that agony and peril, no relief came, no permission to escape. But were these disciplined subjects of Imperial Rome, who perished in the performance of their duty as understood by them, any more heroes than those whose names I have mentioned, who fell martyrs to their duty when death seemed inevitable?

Farewell, brave brothers! We can but believe that you who lived so well and died so nobly have been "called off" to fill places of higher trust.

Among the fallen is brother AVERY P. SAUNDERS, one of the most enlightened and zealous Masons I ever met. In his daily pursuits, in social and mental habits, he was a plain, blunt man—unassuming and unostentatious; but his intellect seemed shaped for Masonic investigation, and he roamed in the expansive fields of Masonic lore with all the ease and certainty of an accomplished scholar. His thorough familiarity with the laws, rules and regulations of the Grand and Subordinate Lodges was truly wonderful; his perfect knowledge of the secret work of the Order and his aptness in conferring degrees were equally remarkable. None ever approached the altar of Masonry with assistance from that old man, who did not, as if by magic catch from his very utterance some of his own enthusiasm and zeal. His unpretending avocation as an undertaker in the town made his position one of peculiar peril and importance during this dreadful visitation, but he filled it like a hero, and his courage strengthened as the dangers increased. By his hand were many of our brothers buried, and who knows but during his sad and lonely mission to the burial ground, in the heart of that devoted old Mason and Past Master were murmured over the bodies of his deceased brothers, the funeral services of the Order, which to him were so familiar. Who can tell but in the city of the dead, with its many new made graves, and the air around laden with the poison of death, these mournful words were spoken at each Mason's open grave when the clods fell upon the coffin lid, "Earth to earth, ashes to ashes, dust to dust, and the spirit to the God who gave it."

It happens so that on members of our Order fell the duty of burying all who died, for besides Brother SAUNDERS, there was another whose calling was the same, Brother ROBERT A. COLLINS, a worthy and upright Mason, who also fell a martyr to the fearless discharge of his duty.

The roll of Grenada Lodge shows that in this carnival of death the following worthy members were also swept away: Brothers RALPH COFFMAN, CHARLES M. COFFMAN, WILLIAM M. HANKINS, ROBERT A. IRWIN, JAMES M. KNOX, JOHN L. MILTON, WILLIAM B. MAY, JOHN T. MOORE, THOMAS E. PEACOCK, JACOB POITEVENT, HENRY RAFALSKY, OBEDIAH B. ROLLINS, MYER WILE and WILLIAM WILLIS.

The other Masons and non-affiliates who were "called off" in the great pestilence from Grenada, were Brothers SAXON S. ANGEVINE, WILLIAM T. COLE, WILLIAM C. ESKRIDGE, PETER F. FITZGERALD, JOHN MORROW, HIRAM M. JONES, WILLIAM A. McMILLAN, JOHN S. PAYNE and THOMAS POWELL. Were I to attempt to enumerate the virtues of these brethren, I would but detail for those who knew them no., a part only of what is recorded in the hearts of all who knew them well. In the life and death of each, I find ample ground for such an eulogy as it would be my mournful pleasure to pronounce, did time and occasion allow. They fell victims to the call of duty and humanity. By the bedsides of their kindred, their brethren and their friends, they breathed the deadly poison, and in their efforts to wrest these from the clutch of death, they were slain by that enemy whose fatal grip on others they bravely but vainly strove to break.

Brothers SAUNDERS, ROLLINS and RALPH COFFMAN were Past Masters, and hence members of this Grand Body. Bro. ROLLINS was one of those upright, consistent and devoted Masons who give strength to the institution; always bright himself, he inspired zeal in others. When he fell, Grenada Lodge lost one of its strongest pillars and Masonry one of its surest supporters. Brother RALPH COFFMAN was a "worthy, true and well-tried" Mason, whose Masonic history for nearly forty years leaves its shining example in the records of Grenada Lodge. He was fast growing old, but had reared about him a family full of promise, full of usefulness, full of loveliness, and in whose bosom he was reaping the beautiful harvest of the seeds he had sown. Before his death, in anguish he had seen the partner of all his joys and his sorrows, his tender loving wife, his only son, the inheritor of his name, and his two fair and faultless daughters borne away forever from his stricken home, so lately the scene of perfect happiness to all and where now he remained like a solitary tree in a weary desert, with no kindred bough to break the piercing blast, nor leaf to shelter from the burning sun. Arising from his sick bed when, because of his own extreme illness, the full extent of his bereavement had been concealed from him, he went to seek his loved ones, but finding that all had gone, crushed and broken hearted, he sat down in his lonely home and wept, and still wept, till a merciful God freed his soul that the broken circle might be re-united in the spirit land. And it would seem a kind providence so ordained that the very weight of his sorrows brought him a reward in his dying hour—when he felt that his imprisoned spirit was to be freed to join the dear ones gone before.

It is some consolation to us to know and feel that most of our brothers met death without that pang which usually adds to its terrors and which comes from the parting from those we love; but here the strong arm of death seemed often tempered with mercy, for whilst it severed many and left cruel heart-wounds among those pursuing the weary path of life, that journey beyond the grave, upon which our deceased brethren entered, but carried them to those who had gone before and whom they longed to join. They were mercifully spared what the poet so fitly describes:

> "What is the worst of woes that wait on age,
> What stamps the wrinkle deeper on the brow,
> To view each loved one blotted from life's page,
> To be alone on earth, as I am now."

There is one of our number who fell upon another field of usefulness and duty, and whose name I would especially mention, Bro. WILLIAM WILLIS. Though residing in Memphis for several years past, he had never severed his connection with Grenada Lodge, and by that Lodge was always esteemed an active, worthy and honored member.

It is a grand sight to see life unhesitatingly offered up when duty or the ties of blood demand—but 'tis beautiful and holy when the sacrifice is made upon the altar of pure and unselfish philanthropy. It is a divine precept that "love is the fulfilling of the law," and it is written "greater love hath no man than this, that a man lay down his life for his friends." When the shadow of death covered the city of Memphis, and the great pestilence began its deadly work, there was no call of duty nor tie of blood which bound *him* to the fate of that stricken city, but with the heroism of one who receives the death stroke in his own heart, that some loved one may live, he died—died of his love for his fellow-man. It is said Brother Willis at one time ruled in the East in the same Lodge room where once presided the illustrious Washington. Of these two Past Masters, who will say that the self-sacrificing death of the one was not as creditable and as beautiful as the splendid career of the other? When justice writes the epitaphs of those who fell in the great epidemic of 1878, none will be grander than that of William Willis.

There was a hero Mason who, when the first cry of distress was heard from stricken Grenada, came from another State to devote himself to the relief of its stricken people. There, at the post of self-imposed duty, in the fiercest and most trying period of the pestilence, he labored until the foe he had so nobly battled against, struck him down in the midst of his work, and the immortal soul of BUTLER P. ANDERSON took its flight, amid the tears and lamentations of the living, to join the spirits, lately gone before, of those for whom while living, he had so nobly striven. His "praise is hymned by loftier harps than mine." Yet in this memorial service for our deceased brethren in Mississippi, partly in whose behalf he came—in whose behalf he died, I would speak his name with reverence. His own Grand Lodge has appropriately perpetuated his virtues and paid fit tribute to his memory, but no where should he be mentioned with more love and gratitude than in the Grand Lodge of Mississippi, in whose jurisdiction he acted the hero and died a martyr.

Our brothers have gone! No more to mingle with us around the sacred altar of Masonry! No more shall we greet them at the south, the west or the east gate; no more shall we gather with them in the temple; no more shall we hear their words of wisdom, of affection, of caution. Our Lodge room is darkened, many of its shining lights have been removed. The "habiliments of woe" which hang around its walls are less mournful than the heart of the Mason who enters and knew well in the life those whose deaths we deplore.

In the "Ark" they have been "wafted safely o'er this tempestuous sea of trouble." By the "Anchor" they have "moored" in that peaceful harbor where the wicked cease from troubling and the weary are at rest."

9

TRIBUTES TO THE DEAD OF GRENADA.

THE TELEGRAPH HERO—WYATT M. REDDING.

Click, click,
Like the beat of a death-watch, sharp and quick,
From hearts that are stifled and lips that are dumb,
With the lightning's speed and the lightning's thrill,
The dark words go and come :
Click, click, and a pulse is still—
There's a form to shroud, and a grave to fill;
For the Yellow Death is upon the air,
And the city lies in the clutch of despair.

Not less a hero than he whose plume
Goes blood stained down in the conflict's gloom,
Not less a martyr than those who slake
A blood-thirst, bound to the burning stake,
Is he who stands at the last defense
Against the shock of the pestilence.

Click, click,
His heart is strong and his fingers quick ;
'Tis a fearful work of hand and brain,
Each click is a groan, each word is a pain !
But he falters not in his fight with death,
Even under his wings as he breathes his breath.

The shrouded city before him lies,
And the dead drop down 'neath the burning skies,
Never a smile, or a word to cheer,
Brightens his eye or falls on his ear,
All is dreary, and all is dumb,
Save the hourly wail from the stricken home.

Click, click,
'Tis the only hope where the dead are thick,
Where the living strewn by the plague's hot breath,
Are sown with the ripening seeds of death,
Still, the hero boy at his key-board stands,
With his stout young heart and his busy hands,
And many a far-off city feels
The thrill of the wire, and its mute appeals.
And hands are stretched from the east and west,
Their upward palms, with a blessing blest,
As it comes to those who meet their doom
Like scorched leaves struck by the hot smoon.

Click, click,
Like the beat of the death-watch, sharp and quick,
'Tis the last note struck, 'tis the first wild touch
He gives the key, as he feels the vague
And creeping chill of the deadly plague
Ere it burns with the strength of its fever clutch;
He falters, falls, and his work is done,
And the fiend has marked his victim won.
Not long he dallies with those who fall
Beneath the curse of his yellow thrall;
O, city ! beneath his merciless sway,
Mourn, mourn, for your hero dies to-day."

William Ward, in Macon, (Miss.,) Sun.

THE PHYSICIANS OF GRENADA.

At a meeting of the Medical Society of Grenada county, held in Grenada, on Wednesday, Jan. 1st, the following preamble and resolutions were unanimously adopted:

WHEREAS, During the terrible epidemic of last summer and fall, our Association lost its President, P. F. FitzGerald, M. D., and three other of its members, E. W. Hughes, M. D., W. W. Hall, M. D., and R. S. Ringgold, M. D. They were men of whom any State might be proud—any profession would feel honored and any people lament. They were of the purest and best in our ranks; inspired by a spirit of sublime heroism, met calmly and fearlessly the doom of martyrs, in the discharge of duty. Their deeds are enshrined in the hearts of their people and point the lesson, that man's first duty, his highest privilege, his noblest choice is to labor, and if need be, die in the service of his fellow man. They stood unflinchingly between the suffering and death, calmly resisting his stroke, faithful to the end and earnest in their efforts to stay the work of the dread destroyer. As citizens, they were respected and valued for their pure morals and social virtues.

As an expression of our sorrow and profound sense of affliction at this untimely and irreparable loss, be it

Resolved, That in the noble and heroic death of our associates, Drs. Hughes, Hall, Ringgold and FitzGerald, we have lost four of our most useful and efficient members, and the country equally in physicians and citizens.

Resolved, That we will remember them with increasing fondness, and never cease to link their names, their deeds and their virtues with this Association and the medical annals of the State.

Resolved, That we extend our hearty condolence and deepest sympathy to the family of our departed associates and friends and commend to them the soothing mercies and comforting influences of an all-wise Creator.

Resolved, That a copy of these resolutions be sent to the families of our lamented friends, and also spread upon the minutes of our Association, and a copy be furnished to our city papers for publication.

WM. MCSWINE, WM. POWELL, G. W. TRIMBLE.

JUDGE THOMAS WALTON.

From Grenada Sentinel.

Amongst all of our citizens who *voluntarily* staid to confront the plague, not one had less reason to stay, or could have found better inducements to have gone than Judge Walton. There was not a soul to whom he was connected by blood in the town. His friendships here were few, and not very strong, for we have heard it stated that he was not a very social man in his habits, or tastes. He had no property here to look after, and had just bought him a comfortable residence in Greenwood, to which he was making arrangements to move, as a peaceful, fixed home for his future years. Besides these, a fine span of horses and a handsome buggy, with ample funds at his command, awaited only his decision, and would soon have been beyond the poisonous breath of the pestilence. We learn that he had even prepared to go, and had everything in readiness for his departure, when something called him from the hotel up town.

Here the character of Judge Walton changes, so far as we have presented it. The scene that met his eyes, at once attracted his attention and called into active play all the slumbering energies of his restless nature, and all the silent sympathies of his very soul. The people were fleeing in every direction without future aim or purpose. Some were calling out in public bids of an exorbitant price, for vehicles with which to send away their helpless, frightened families. Everything betokened confusion and fear.

Surveying, for a moment the disorderly scene, he remarked to another good man (whose name we have not forgotten) that it will never do to leave these people in this reckless condition. His purpose was taken, and placing away the traps of his departure, from that hour with wonderful discretion, unflagging energy, and intrepid courage he devoted himself to the relief of the people, until the hot breath of the fever was burning his own cheeks. With the assistance of others, a relief committee was organized, of which he was a leading member, and matters began to have a more even aspect, if such an expression is allowable at any stage of affairs during the terrible days of the pestilential visitation. Never, even amid the thunders of battle, did this man's heroic intrepidity shine out in such clear force and power. We have learned, that so long as he was up, the work of the committee went smoothly on, bringing order out of confusion, and system out of derangement. His kindness and fellow-feelings were on the constant lookout for words of consolation to the feeble and faint-hearted, and deeds of charity to the sick and afflicted. His presence was everywhere in the town, consoling, addressing, commanding as his convictions of duty suggested, and the exigency of the hour demanded. His duties were mostly outdoors but promiscuous and arduous. Thus he continued until he fell a splendid triumph to the great destroyer. Just before the fatal moment of dissolution, with his mind perfectly calm, he wheeled over upon his back, straightened out his feet, with arms close to his side, and hands erect, he braced himself for the last throe of expiring nature, and with eyes wide open and looking fixedly above, he surrendered to God the spirit that made the most intrepid man in the hour of extreme danger we ever knew.

Whatever may have been the mistakes of his past life, (if such they were) there are none so unforgiving that would not freely place them under the martyr's crown he so richly deserves, and cheerfully say, that amongst the greatest sacrifices of the pestilence in 1878, will ever live the name and memory of JUDGE THOMAS WALTON.

JUDGE J. C. GRAY.

At a meeting of the Sénatobia Bar and officers of Court held on Saturday the 16th day of November, 1878, G. D. Shands was called to the chair, and J. P. McCrackin and C. A. Lewers appointed Secretaries by the chairman. In a terse and elegant manner the chairman stated the object of the meeting to be to express the feeling of this Bar and officers of Court, upon the death of our late lamented Chancellor, the Hon. J. C. Gray. Upon suggestion the chairman appointed as a committee to draft suitable resolutions, John E. Mathews, C. L. McClendon and Eugene Johnson.

Said committee reported as follows:

In the wide-spread grief and affliction that prevails throughout our plague-stricken section, there is no loss that so nearly touches our hearts as that occasioned by the death of the late Hon. J. C. Gray. His place cannot easily be supplied in the walks of life. Dignified and firm, he was yet affable and kind. Possessing great learning and ability in his profession, catching legal points with the greatest facility and readiness, he was yet patient and attentive to argument, anxious even to detect if there might not be some error in the conclusions at which he has arrived. As a Judge, able and pure, he inspired with the most profound respect and reverence all who practiced in his Court. As a man, gentle, frank and noble, he awakened in all who knew him the warmest friendship, the deepest love. The holding of one Court in our county made every member of this Bar, the Sheriff who opened his Court, the clerk who wrote his minutes, the landlady with whom he lodged,—indeed all who came in contact with him, his *warm personal friends*, and we all looked forward to meeting with him at his successive Courts with the greatest pleasure. There was a personal attraction about him which few men possess and which cannot be described. We offer the following:

Resolved, 1st., That in the death of the late Honorable J. C. Gray, the State of Mississippi at large, and especially this Chancery District has suffered an irreparable loss; one that will long be felt and grieved, not only by the members of the legal profession, but by the good and true in every sphere of life.

Resolved, 2nd., That as a body and as individuals, we hereby express our sincere and heartfelt grief at his untimely death, and offer our condolence to the few surviving members of his grief stricken family.

Resolved, 3rd., That the chairman of this meeting take the proper steps to have these resolutions and proceedings spread upon the minutes of the Chancery Court.

EUGENE JOHNSON, JNO. E. MATHEWS, C. L. McCLENDON.

MILTON, PEACOCK AND GERARD.

From Grenada Sentinel, November 16.

We were pleased to see the respect paid to the memory of the former Mayor and Alderman, who expired in the late epidemic, Dr. John L. Milton, Messrs. T. E. Peacock and A. Gerard.

Dr. Jno. Milton, the Mayor, was widely and personally known for many miles around Grenada, where he had lived for thirty years and upwards. A dentist by profession, he studied it both as a science and as an art, and had arrived to a degree of excellence in it, that entitled him to rank with the best and most successful practitioners of the State. A man of public spirit, he took a lively interest in passing events that effected the welfare of the county or State, and once during the war served with credit in our State Legislature. He was twice elected Mayor of Grenada, and the last time, the office was conferred on him without distinction of party, a compliment which he appreciated by devotion to the duties of his office. As ex-officio Magistrate, he was familiar with the statutes of the State, and administered the law with an impartial hand. When the fever broke out, he aroused his energies to the necessities of the hour, and worked with redoubled energies for the amelioration of our sanitary condition, until he was stricken down by the plague. He remained amongst the frightened few that were left to face the pestilence, exercising the utmost stretch of his authority, the entire resources of his mind, and his whole stock of experience in behalf of his suffering fellow-citizens. Starding high in the confidence of the Masons and Odd Fellows, he was a marked man in their council chambers, and was ever heeded with profound respect. Long a member of the Methodist church, his character for consistent piety and church loyalty was never questioned. His domestic relations were surrounded by all the charms of confidence and love, while a large circle of many friends ever stood ready to administer to his comfort and happiness wherever occasion presented.

Thomas E. Peacock was raised in this county, and inherited many noble qualities that distinguished him, from an honored ancestry. Since the war, he has lived with his family in Grenada, actively and successfully engaged in the business of a merchant of the firm of Peacock & Powell. Quick to perceive and quick to act, the advantages or disadvantages of a business proposition were readily decided. Honest in trading and indulgent in feelings, his personal influence did much to make the house of Peacock & Powell one of the strongest in Grenada. Respected among his rival associates for intelligence and integrity, his opinions in business circles were never without weight, while his example was in many respects regarded as a model. Having laid the foundation of a competent fortune, he established himself here as his life-long home, where in the midst of an active business, the charms of domestic life, the respect of his fellow-citizens, he passed his days, until he died in the prime of manhood of the terrible fever. Warm in his feelings and decided in his opinions, his position upon questions of public interest was never a matter of doubt. As a member of the Methodist church, his pew was not only regularly filled, but in the claims of Christian charity, his heart and his purse were freely exercised.

Mr. Gerard was a Frenchman by birth, and although he never forgot the sunny hills and the pleasant fields of his own native land, he was in spirit, in duty and in deeds an American citizen of the most liberal stamp. Grenada, for many years, had been his home, where he raised a large and interesting family and set before them an example of private and public worth, which they may well regard as a legacy of inestimable value. Quiet and sincere, he pursued the even tenor of his ways, attracting the respect of all ranks of life by his fidelity to the principles of industry, honesty and truth. Ready ever to respond to the call of duty he shouldered the musket of a Confederate guard, the more peaceable business of an alderman's life and the sorrowful duties of yellow fever help, with the same equanimity of temper. In the relations of domestic life, Mr. Gerard was a good husband, a kind father and a true friend.

Such in brief, were three good and useful citizens that long exercised the influence of their good characters upon the public interest of our town, and long will they live in the memory of those whom the pestilence spared as high specimens of personal integrity and liberal feelings.

COL. KINLOCH FALCONER,

DIED OF YELLOW FEVER AT HOLLY SPRINGS, SEPTEMBER 23, 1878.

From THE CLARION, Sept. 25.

It is hard to realize that these sad words have to be written. Two weeks ago Col. Falconer left us in good health to attend a sick father at his home in Holly Springs. He reached the bedside of his parent barely in time to bid him a last adieu. Soon his brother, the gentle, generous and brave Howard Falconer, was taken ill with the prevailing epidemic and was called to his last account. The angel of death next claimed the unselfish and devoted subject of this notice for a victim, and he, too, has been struck down with the robes of a high office upon him, in the meridian of life and the bloom of his useful manhood. Again has Mississippi been called to weep at the grave of one of her best and truest sons. It will be a pleasing thought to his friends that in the trying scenes of the last days of his life, he was resigned to the will of his Heavenly Father whose mercy and goodness disrobe even the pestilence of its terrors. In a letter written to a friend in this city on the 17th inst., two days before he was seized with the illness that terminated his life, he thus, as if anticipating the fatal result, expressed the Christian's resignation and faith : "Oh! the scenes here are beyond human power to describe. I realize that there is One alone who can save. My prayer is made to Him and my hope is in Him."

From Starkville Citizen.

In 1857, the editor of the Oktibbeha Citizen was editor of the Marshall Democrat in Holly Springs. Kinloch's father was the editor of the Holly Springs Herald. Howard, an older brother of Kinloch's were both boys and did the work in their father's office. It affords us a melancholy pleasure to be able to embalm his memory in the columns of the Citizen, and make a brief mention of his short and brilliant career. We became acquainted with him in his early boyhood, when his smiling face would once a week illuminate the Democrat, as carrier boy of the Herald. The Falconers were a talented family, and left their mark on all they touched. But this brief notice is devoted to Kinloch.

As soon as Kinloch was old enough, he became an apprentice in his father's office, where he was inducted into all the mysteries of printing to be learned in a country newspaper office. He was by turns devil, carrier, roller boy, typo and pressman. He became a thorough printer in all branches and was known eventually as one of the fastest compositors and best office managers in the State. But his general education was not neglected during his apprenticeship. When he could be spared from the office he attended the fine schools for which Holly Springs has always been noted. In 1858 he entered the Junior class of the University of Mississippi, and graduated as a second honor man in the class of 1860, and afterward became associate editor with his father of the Southern Herald, and studied law.

At the breaking out of the war, he enlisted as a private in a Holly Springs company, commanded by the gallant Captain Thos. W. Harris. He was the Private Secretary of Gen. Bragg, and afterwards Bragg's Adjutant General. In December, 1862, at the age of twenty-two, at the request of Gen. Bragg, he was appointed by the Secretary of War to duty with the staff of the Army of Tennessee, with the rank of Major. He soon became the best known of the officers of that staff. Everybody knew and honored him, from the private soldier to the Commanding General. Thoroughly efficient and strict in the discharge of his official duties, he was at the same time affable, kind and easy of access to all. In the latter part of the year 1865, he became a partner of Hon. John W. C. Watson in the practice of law; and in the summer of 1866 he received his diploma from the law school of the University. But his first love, the newspaper, had an irresistible attraction for him, and in August, 1867, he became associated with his brother-in-law, Columbus Barrett, as editor of the Holly Springs Reporter. The Reporter immediately took position among the leading papers in the State, and Col. Falconer added largely to its reputation and popularity. In 1868, was nominated as the Democratic candidate for Lieut. Governor, on the ticket with Gov. Humphreys, and he was triumphantly elected. But the same votes which elected him defeated the new Constitution under which the Anti-Johnson Republicans were seeking to reconstruct the State, and the State was continued in the hands of the military."

At the time of his death he held the office of Secretary of State, having been elected on the Democratic ticket in 1875. Leaving his office in Jackson, where there was no yellow fever, he went to Holly Springs, his native place, right into the jaws of death, to comfort his dying father and sick brother, and when both had died, he himself was smitten with the plague, paid the penalty of his sublime devotion to filial affection and noble humanity. Thus has passed away in the zenith of splendid manhood, one of Mississippi's grandest sons, doubly a hero, heroic in war's carnage, grandly heroic in the carnival pestilence. Peace to thy ashes! Rest in Heaven through the long ages of eternity to thy great soul!

From Holly Springs South, Nov. 6th.

KINLOCH FALCONER.—Summoned to Holly Springs by the sickness of his venerable and beloved father, on whose decease he took the place of Col. Walter made vacant by his death, he entered at once upon his. labors of love. But his labors were brief, for he was soon stricken down, when he went to his rest. He was lately Secretary of State of Mississippi, and we doubt whether in office, or out, the State had within its limits a man of superior talents or of higher promise. There was no office within the gift of our people of which he was not worthy or to which he might not with confidence aspire. A brave soldier, a true gentleman, a man of general knowledge and varied attainments, he was at the time of his death fast becoming the idol of the State, which suffers greatly in his loss, and which mourns him from its northern limits to the gulf. Holly Springs was his home, where his father and brother resided. And the county of Marshall may well be chief mourner at his honored and lamented grave. Some of us fled to live, but we have returned to mourn.

COL. W. J. L. HOLLAND.

Holly Springs, October 25, 1878.—Col. J. W. L. Holland, late Chairman of the Relief Committee, departed this life at 2:30 A. M., this morning, aged thirty-six years, six months and twenty days.

Another name is added to the noble army of martyrs, another is given to the bright catalogue of those who have sacrificed themselves to the cause of philanthrophy; another grave is made in which lies the peer of the best among so many that were the most honored and most useful citizens of Holly Springs. The people of that place were so confident that their location and the purity of their atmosphere rendered them safe, that they did not establish quarantine. When refugees from Memphis and Greenville brought yellow fever there, some uneasiness, and anxiety existed, but the patients had either died or were convalescent, and all apprehension had ceased. But the fatal seed was germinating while the citizens were thus lulled into a sense of security, and on the first day of September the whole city was thrown into consternation by the discovery that forty-six cases had almost simultaneously been developed. Of those forty-six cases only three survive. All the people of the town who could do so, fled, panic-stricken, except the heroic few who determined to remain and aid the helpless as long as they might be able, in the terrible crisis. Of that devoted band one after another went down, until Col. Holland stood alone, the only male white citizen in the place who had not been attacked. Physicians and nurses from abroad hurried to the rescue, and money and supplies were lavishly bestowed, but the scourge knew no abatement until the material was exhausted. During all these fearful weeks, from the first of September, Col. Holland labored in his ministration of mercy. He saw his gallant comrades, the Walters, Falconers, and Fants, fall around him until all were gone. Spared to see the work he had undertaken well nigh finished, the fever at last laid him prostrate, and, though tenderly nursed and cared for by loving friends who had come in from their places of refuge in other States, that they might personally minister to him in his sickness, their efforts did not avail, and his noble spirit passed away just when the last flutter of the wings of the destroyer was heard.

Col. Holland had no relative in the ill-fated town to claim his service; he had no property interests there which his presence might protect. Humanity alone prompted his action. When the fever began its ravages in Grenada, he volunteered to go there with supplies, and he gave up his own rooms to refugees from that place who came sick to Holly Springs. With great administrative ability he organized and conducted the difficult business of the Citizens' Relief Committee, of which he was President, and his coolness and firmness and system have been of incalculable benefit in a crisis where those qualities are not generally found. Through his dispatches to the press he kept the beleaguered town in communication with the world; and many an absent one, on the rack of anxiety and suspense, was indebted to his considerate kindness for tidings from loved ones.

Amid the accumulating horrors of the days which so wearily followed each other, his generous purpose did not falter. In the constant peril which shadowed every step, his high courage did not fail. He died as he had lived, and was good and brave to the last. As the Confederacy had no soldier more gallant, so this trying battle with pestilence had no volunteer more unselfish, none more devoted, none more true. How much he will be missed! His tall figure and handsome face, his genial humor and kindly disposition, his fine intellect and rare social qualities, will be remembered by all. Holly Springs has furnished its quota to the roll of honored names of those who risked their lives, and in so many cases lost them, in the effort to help others.

"The earth hath bubbles as the water hath;" but she hath also creatures of heroic mould who make our human nature glorious.   H. C.

From Holly Springs Reporter, Nov. 21.

The death of our associate and dear friend, W. J. L. Holland, who fell at his post, ministering to the wants of the sick and dying in the recent epidemic, creates a void in our heart, and in the heart of this community, that cannot be filled. In his death the State has lost a chivalrous and patriotic son, the press an able, energetic and zealous member, and the community in which he lived a jewel above price. An intimate business and social acquaintance of ten years, justifies us in saying that in all the nobler attributes which go to make up the true man, he had few peers, and though we should live three-score years longer, we would hardly look upon his like again. Mr. Holland was the most unselfish man we ever knew. His heart was like an "ample shield, could take in all and room enough for more." When charity was demanded of him, his "bounty was as boundless as the sea," his sympathy as deep.

His services to the stricken and dying in this community, can never be forgotten. He outlived two Relief Committees, and for a time he was the only member of the committee able to do duty, left standing alone "like a beacon upon the waste or a rock in the broad ocean." But he proved himself equal to the emergency and performed the work of several men till re-enforced by other noble and willing hands. Just as the clouds of the pestilence were lifting from the town and the hearts of our stricken people were beginning to brighten up with the hope of an early deliverance from the deadly plague, he was attacked, and though he received every attention that experienced physicians and loving friends could bestow, he lingered but a few days,

"When the weary springs of life stood still,"

and all that was left of the brave and noble Holland was consigned to the dust. Rest his soul in peace!

From Holly Springs South, Nov. 6.

COL. W. J. L. HOLLAND.—The press of the State teems with eulogies of our contemporary of the Holly Springs Reporter, who was taken sick at the very close of the epidemic, and who has gone down to an honored and lamented grave. We had expected to the very last to have the opportunity of returning and thanking him, as one of the survivors of the plague, for the zealous and brave work he had done in behalf of suffering humanity. But it has been ordered otherwise, and he now sleeps with our many loved and lost. We believe he would have survived, but for the unfortunate accident of being thrown from a buggy and injured while doing his work of mercy. It is said by medical men that slight injuries and causes, which produce derangement of the vital forces are seized by an epidemic and converted into its own channel. The injury suffered, though not serious under ordinary circumstances, was sufficient to lay him up exhausted with his labors, and was the immediate cause of a fever, which assumed the epidemic form. He was one of the most active and successful newspaper men with whom we have been acquainted, and his loss is sadly mourned, especially at home, where he was best known. His energy and determination saved our town from being plundered, and contributed largely to the means and appliances for the saving of the lives that remain. His memory will be cherished with affection by every survivor of the Holly Springs epidemic.

From THE CLARION, Oct. 30.

The insatiate destroyer which has struck down the truest and best of our land, has had another sacrificial offering in the death recorded in the above funeral notice. W. J. L. Holland was a conspicuous member of the Mississippi press; and was worthy of his calling. He was active, useful and public-spirited in his profession. His form was a model of manly beauty and strength, and was a fitting tenement for his brave and gentle spirit. When the dreadful destroyer made its appearance in the community where he lived and was loved, with the soul of a hero he confronted it and went about doing good regardless of self, as if it was a life business with him. He wrote of his comrades with tears; committed their dust to its native dust with tender hands; and then returned to his work of danger and of love to alleviate the suffering of others. For this high purpose he tore himself from the pleasures of life and its bright promises. His sympathetic heart was touched by every wail of distress and echoed back its notes. He will be sadly missed from the ranks of the fraternity of which he was an ornament. He will be sadly missed at the annual reunion of its members, for his genial nature shed light and warmth wherever he moved. Even when the pestilence raged, his presence " was like moonlight on a troubled sea, brightening the storm it could not calm." Farewell, brave and generous friend. No monument of marble is needed to perpetuate your memory. It will live in the good deeds which you laid down your life in doing.

WILLIAM M. ROCKWOOD.

Vicksburg, Sept. 28.—(Telegram to Cincinnati Gazette.)

William M. Rockwood, President of the Howard Association, died this morning—died like the Christian hero that he was, with a brave heart. His life was one long series of good works and charitable deeds. No enterprise for the public good was complete without him. He was President of the Young's Men's Christian Association, ex-Chief of the Fire Department, and a leading pillar of the Presbyterian Church. He was a most untiring worker, and whatever his hands found to do was well done. So when the epidemic broke out, and the Howards organized, the direction of affairs was, by consent, intrusted to his hands. No position was more worthily filled or duty more faithfully discharged. Night and day he stood at his post and performed the arduous duties of his office, while men wondered at his endurance. The poor looked up to him as a savior, and the rich honored him for his manly deeds. His death-bed scene was most affecting, and invested with an interest that was almost national. The doors of his bed chambers were thrown open, and his friends summoned to take the last farewell. Although his sight had left him, his memory was clear, and the name of every friend brought to his lips a tender message of adieu. There were no dry eyes near his bedside but his own. He never faltered, but shook every man by the hand with a calm resignation and a quiet joy, such as only a consciousness of an unblemished life can give. He had no fear of death, and his last thought was of the Howards. "I am going to meet my friends in Heaven; keep the good work up, friends;" and so with a smile on his lips and joy in his heart, William Rockwood glided peacefully to his eternal home. His funeral was a sight to be remembered. White and black, rich and poor, Jew and Gentile, scoffer and infidel, all flocked to do honor to the noble dead. The cortege was nearly a mile long, every available vehicle was called into requisition, and many rode on horseback; others walked, and all along the line stood men with hats reverently doffed, and women in every attitude of grief, and poor invalids, whose welfare had been his only care in life, crawled to their doors and windows, wept a mournful requiem as the sad procession moved by. He will need no epitaph to record his virtues. His memory will live in the hearts of the people, and find there its fittest tribute.

Remarks of Rev. C. B. Galloway, at Memorial Service.

"God gives us love;
Something to love, He lends us."

And so short was the loan of our dear and honored brother, the pure and pious WILLIAM M. ROCKWOOD. As we recall his many virtues, his gentleness of heart; his tenderness of sympathy, his integrity of purpose, his beautiful simplicity of character, his earnestness of zeal, his consistency of life and heroic courage in the discharge of duty, we wonder in sorrow at the strange Providence that so early severed the tie that bound our hearts together. Broad in his views and evangelical above all narrow denominationalism, he was among the earliest advocates and most zealous supporters of the Young Men's Christian Association. So conspicuous was his fervent piety and world-wide his Christian love for humanity, that he was, by one common consent, called to be our President and entrusted with the general management of our noble evangelical organization. We never had for one moment to regret our choice. He rather bound us to him with tenderer ties. There he displayed all the wealth of his sanctified affection. No duty imposed upon him, however difficult its performance, was ever shirked or relegated to others. Duty was the inspiring watchword of his consecrated life. Whether to offer a word of exhortation, conduct a meeting for prayer, or sing a song of salvation, he was ever ready. He was modest without timidity; pious without ostentation; courageous without unholy ambition. As an Association, we have lost a brother and chief officer whose name will ever be spoken with reverence, whose virtues will be enshrined in our hearts, and whose memory will ever be as fresh and green as the magnolias of our Southern land. The salvation of our young men, for which our Association came into being, was the burden of his heart and the subject of his daily prayer. But he has gone, and his works do follow him. The chair made vacant will be hallowed because he has occupied it. Heaven grant that the mantle of this ascended Elijah may fall upon the shoulders of a worthy Elisha.

In the Pantheon of illustrious dead, who have yielded up their lives as a glorious martyrdom to duty during the late, sad, wasting pestilence, no grander, purer figure has a place than WILLIAM M. ROCKWOOD. Let him tenderly rest under the smiling heavens of our Sunny South. And may the flowers bloom brightly and the winds sigh gently and the birds sing sweetly over his peaceful grave.

From Address by Rev. Dr. Price, at Memorial Services.

I have selected this subject and pursued this train of remark, because it seems to me that the most conspicuous, and the most characteristic, and the most honorable trait in the life of WILLIAM M. ROCKWOOD, was that it was spent in unselfish work, both in the engagement of private life, in his relations as a citizen, and in his still higher obligations as a Christian and an officer in the church of Christ. I think all who knew him were struck with this feature of his character. He was an *earnest worker*. He *served* his generation by the will of God. Give him a duty to perform, and no man would perform it with greater zeal and conscientiousness. He had lived in this city so long, and had been so conspicuously identified with every good cause, that the justice of this characterization will at once be recognized by all who have resided here for any considerable time; while to those who did not know him personally, the briefest review of his history will suffice to indicate the estimation in which he was held, and the extent to which he was trusted, as well as the weight of the responsibilities and duties which he was required to sustain and did sustain.

He was a native of Nashville, Tenn., and was born in the year 1838. His parents were Walter Rockwood and Elizabeth Ann Swett, sister of the late Daniel Swett, both being persons of exemplary piety. He made a public profession of religion when a boy, and was admitted to the membership of the First Presbyterian Church of Nashville, under the ministry of the Rev. Dr. Edgar. He came to Vicksburg in the year 1852, and was taken into the family of his venerable relative, Mr. Swett. It was no small advantage to a lad coming into a strange place, to be brought under the influence of such a man, so conscientious, so upright, so laborious, so public-spirited, so pious, and so devoted to the advancement of the cause of Christ. WM. ROCKWOOD appreciated Mr. Swett's character, and entertained the profoundest veneration and love for him. It is not improbable that some of those moral excellencies which justify and call for this memorial service, were due to that venerable man's influence. Little did we suppose, when in the early summer we laid him away beneath the green sod, we should so soon be called to perform this sad office for his beloved nephew, and that only a few weeks later, she who had been a loving wife to the one, and a second mother to the other, should rejoin their sainted spirits in the skies. Sadly have we been bereaved. "The Lord gave and the Lord hath taken away, blessed be the name of the Lord." We doubt not that they are now side by side amid the choir of the redeemed, singing those praises in which they so much delighted, and in which their voices blended so harmoniously on earth.

DR. P. F. WHITEHEAD.

Correspondence Louisville Courier-Journal.

VICKSBURG, Sept. 5.—This is the darkest day we have had yet. Dr. Whitehead is dead. He was a Kentuckian, and Kentucky may well be proud of her son, and mingle her tears with ours; for she has none left that are nobler than he. He was the very type of a perfect man, strong as a lion, gentle as a woman, handsome as a god. Among his professional brethren he was the acknowledged head, yet none were more modest than he. Nature had placed the stamp of nobility upon his brow, and he who ran might read it. When the fever broke out he might well have gone as others did. His practice was confined to a class of people who have the means to go North every summer, and who had gone this time; but he stood by his people in the hour of their need, and he died in the cause of humanity. His name will add lustre to the diadem of glory already made brilliant by the names of Booth, Barber, Bursley and Doll. Vicksburg will long remember him, and Kentucky will be untrue to herself if high on the roll of her distinguished sons she fails to engrave the name of P. F. Whitehead.

Courier-Journal Editorial.

He cannot be forgotten. But his name should not be left to the fond memory of tradition alone. In our State cemetery at Frankfort another shaft should be reared to commemorate the deeds of those brave sons of Kentucky who have fallen in the battle with pestilence. On this shaft should be inscribed the name of the brave and devoted WHITEHEAD, and around it should be gathered the names of all those who have fallen in this Summer's terrible war, battling at the front to save the stricken and the doomed, or standing valiantly at the posts to which they were assigned by duty, unswerved by the dreadful devastation surrounding them.

HOWARD FALCONER.

From Holly Springs South, Nov. 6.—Died at Holly Springs, Sept. 28, 1878, in the 43d year of his age.

While Col. Walter, on the outbreak of the epidemic, was the first to take general direction, and prepare for the emergency, HOWARD FALCONER was the first to volunteer as nurse for the sick. Indeed he had sent word to

Grenada that he would go there as soon as needed, as did his heroic compeer, Butler Anderson. And but for the sickness of this place first brought from there, he would have done so. The first case of fever here was that of Mr. Downs, who came from Grenada, and that case he was the first to visit and nurse. He was soon joined by Mr. Frank Walter, and they together nursed Mr. Downs until his death; and also his companion refugee, Mr. Martin, until his recovery. It was some weeks after before either Mr. FALCONER or Mr. Walter were taken sick. They might still have fled and been saved. But their labors knew no relaxation, and they were together freshly and daily exposed. The father of Mr. FALCONER, the venerable Thomas Falconer, having been taken down, his attentions were unremitting, and his renewed exposure was long continued. He was one of nature's noblemen, and a man of that native generosity and excellence of character which never shrinks from a duty in the utmost peril. Whatever we could say of any other man must in justice be said of him. We had no more able or reliable man of our bar, which, for its number, was the peer of any State of the Union. He was a man of great industry, energy and acute discernment. He was a thoroughly furnished lawyer. We doubt whether the loss of any other member of the bar of Holly Springs could be more felt by our people. We had but begun to learn his eminent worth and talents, when, in the prime of his manhood and the midst of his usefulness, he was taken away. Alas! how shall we express our emotions of grief, when so many, and so good men are swept from our midst. In the presence of so dire distress, our tears of anguish dry up as before a burning conflagration. God rest his soul.

––––––

COL. E. W. UPSHAW.

From Holly Springs South, Nov. 6.—Died at Holly Springs, August 13, 1878.

This old and talented and excellent citizen, who, on all occasions, even before the epidemic, was a ministering angel around the couch of the distressed or sick and dying, and who, with his self-denying nature, threw himself into the midst of danger, when the call was loudest for his valuable services in ministering to the sick of the epidemic, has also fallen. A braver, better nature or a bigger heart never throbbed in a man's bosom. None ever knew him but to love him. He was a true friend and a true man in the highest sense. We mourn him as a brother gone to his reward. If there are good men in heaven he is among them. Col. UPSHAW was for several years connected with the press of Mississippi, and is widely known throughout the State. He married the daughter of Gen. A. B. Bradford, one of the foremost men of the State and Major of the regiment, which, under Jefferson Davis, so distinguished itself in the battle of Buena Vista. Having lost his wife several years since, he was a widower at the time of his death. He was a man of culture, information and considerable intellectual power. And having lately resumed the practice of the profession of law, he was rapidly rising to a position of honor and profit. It would be difficult if not unjust to say that any man had a better heart than he. And few there who were his superiors as men of intellectual power. He rests in peace.

––––––

BAR MEETING.

At a meeting of the Holly Springs Bar, held in the office of Maj. Wm. M. Strickland, on the 20th day of December, A. D. 1878, the following report was made by the Committee on Resolutions:

Your committee who were appointed to prepare and present a suitable and appropriate expression of the sentiments of the Bar, for adoption at this meeting respectfully submit the following report:

This is a most sad and solemn occasion. While this Bar has repeatedly been called in times past to mourn the loss of distinguished and beloved members, yet at no period in its history has it met under circumstances so painful, so sorrowful, so lamentable, as the present. Even the dread calamity of civil war was not so rapacious in its demands, nor so terrible in its havoc upon our ranks. H. W. WALTER, JAMES FORT, HOWARD FALCONER, KINLOCH FALCONER, A. F. MOORE, FRANK C. WALTER, R. L. WATSON, E. W. UPSHAW and A. W. GOODRICH, were the victims from among us who fell before the direful pestilence of 1878, a sacred holocaust to our common humanity. It is said that a man may die for his *friend*, and this is regarded as the very acme of human love; but these brethren, or most of them, died that others might live, whether friend, or foe, or stranger. They gave themselves as free-will offerings upon the ever blessed altar of brotherly kindness and charity, that charity which thinketh no evil, but suffereth long and is kind, and seeketh not his own. "Greater love hath no man than this." · While they were learned in the law, able in debate, eminent in their profession, and possessed of all those high moral and social qualities which made them everywhere honored and beloved, and rendered them influential and valuable citizens; their crowning glory was their total abnegation of self when the wail of suffering and the cry for help came; and they are now enrolled among

* * * The few immortal names
That were not born to die.

But they are gone from us, they will pass in and out among us no more forever. Surely ours is no common grief. Therefore,

Resolved, That no words can adequately express our deep sense of the calamity which has befallen our State, our county, and our city, and especially our profession everywhere, in the death of these distinguished and lamented brethren, whom we loved while living, and whose memories we will cherish as a sacred trust so long as hearts beat and consciousness endures; and not only we, but the whole community sorrows over their newly made graves.

Resolved, That our tenderest condolence and profoundest sympathy are hereby tendered to the respective families and friends of our said deceased brethren, whose loss is utterly beyond all human estimate or computation, and can only be recompensed in the great hereafter, by Him who, speaking through His Holy Apostle tells us that "these light afflictions which are but for a moment, work out for us a far more exceeding and eternal weight of glory." And we desire here, speaking for this Bar and for that great profession of which we are members, to express our steadfast faith in that christianity whose precepts bring us such comfort and consolation in the hour of trouble.

Resolved, That a copy of this report and resolutions be presented to the Circuit and Chancery Courts of this county, the Federal Court at Oxford, and the Supreme Court at Jackson, with the request that they may be entered upon the minutes of said Courts respectively; and that a copy be also sent by the Secretary of this meeting to the respective families of said deceased brethren.

Resolved, That the Holly Springs South and Reporter, and the press throughout the State be respectfully requested to publish the proceedings of this meeting.

WM. M. STRICKLAND, Chairman,
R. S. STITH,
JAS. H. WATSON,
JAS. T. FANT,
LAURENCE JOHNSON,
Committee.

On motion the report was received and the resolutions unanimously adopted, and Gen. W. S. Featherston was elected to present the same to the Supreme Court of the State, and Judge R. S. Stith to the Federal Court. The meeting then adjourned *sine die,*

W. S. FEATHERSTON, Chairman.

ARTHUR FANT, Secretary.

Remarks by Gen. Featherston in presenting the Resolutions to Supreme Court.

Fully concurring in all that is so truthfully said, and so well expressed in the resolutions, I feel called on to add but little to them. Indeed, sirs, when my mind recurs to the mournful, crushing and heart-rending events of the pestilence of 1878, I am rendered incapable of doing justice to its victims.

The events were such as to shake the throne of reason, to tax the soul to its utmost powers of endurance, and to unfold to man the full extent to which he may, in the providence of God, be made acquainted with the sufferings and sorrows of his fellow creatures.

To notice in detail, the life and character of each one of the nine, whose names appear in the resolutions, would furnish matter for a volume, and could not be attempted in a short address.

War, pestilence and famine are the three great rods of correction which our divine Master holds over rebellious man; and within but little more than one decade the two first have fallen heavily on our people.

During the late war, our State was called to mourn the loss of thousands of its purest, noblest, and best citizens, and brightest intellects, whose lives were sacrificed on the altar of their country for the common good. Our conquered territory was curtained with the dark drapery of death, and covered with devastation and woe. How sad and sorrowful were our people then; but alas! they had not quaffed the cup of sorrow to its dregs; they had not learned the extent to which the human soul may be taxed, and had not been made acquainted with human suffering and human sorrow, in all their fullness and overwhelming power. They were to be taught this lesson by the pestilence of 1878.

Our professional brethren, whose memories we now commemorate, had all save those who were prevented by youth and old age, passed through the dangers, hardships and privations, of the late war, with untarnished reputations, as citizen soldiers.

They returned from the battle's storm to the peaceful walks of civil life, to surrender their lives in a better, a nobler and a more exalting warfare. Their mission in the former was to destroy, in the latter to save life.

They died in fighting the battle of suffering, sickening, dying men and women, in ministering to their wants, alleviating their pain, in smoothing the pillow of death and giving comforting assurances to their departing spirits.

Noble martyrs to the cause of suffering humanity. They died in illustrating a doctrine impressed upon man by the revealed word of God, and daily practiced by our Saviour, in his pilgrimage on earth.   *   *   *   *

The subjects of these remarks in their fall, exalted the character of man. In the language of the resolutions, "theirs are numbered among the few names that can never die." "There are deeds that should not pass away, and names that must not wither." Four of them, Fort, Goodrich, Moore and Watson fell early in the attack made by the insatiate archer. They were on our picket line and received the first shots of the advancing foe, as he threw his cohorts around an ungarrisoned and unprotected city. The other five, Walter and Walter, Falconer and Falconer, and Upshaw, had passed through the heat of the battle, and were cut down by the random shots of the retreating enemy. Sad fate for noble soldiers: but they died in the discharge of the noblest duty man ever performed for his fellowman.

In their profession our brethren were learned, able and honorable. In all the relations of life, they sustained unsullied reputations, and won the good opinions of mankind. They were wise in counsel, heroic in action, pure in conduct, elevated in sentiment and feeling; and last though by no means least, they were nearly all followers of our divine Master.

One of the number and the junior of all, said when appealed to, to flee to a place of safety, "no, I will stay, and if I die, let my epitaph be, "Duty."—Frank C. Walter.

Sirs, it is gratifying to us, who belong to the legal profession to know that in this instance, as in every other in the past history of the world, in every great and good work, which has for its object the amelioration of the condition of man, lawyers have held position in the front rank of the army of progress and reform, in numbers equal to those of any other vocation known to civilized life.

It has been truthfully said, that the wealth of a State consists not in its dollars and cents, but in its good men. Mississippi has just cause, then, to mourn the loss of the subjects of these remarks. Sirs, who supposed, twelve months ago, when the eloquent and impetuous Walter and the calm and philosophical Howard Falconer were addressing this Court on grave question of law, that their voices were then being heard for the last time within this Hall. "Man cometh forth like a flower and is cut down; he fleeth also as a shadow and continueth not."

THE PHYSICIANS OF VICKSBURG.

From the Vicksburg Herald, January 26.

The undersigned resident physicians of Vicksburg, publish the following
ADDRESS:

On the 10th of August, 1878, the announcement was made that a case of yellow fever had occurred in our city. For several days transportation from town was taxed to its utmost capacity. It had been so long since any of us had witnessed a severe epidemic, the terror was not half so great as it should have been. Hundreds of families able to leave staid, and the few of them yet remaining know what it is to feel utter desolation.

Within a week we knew that the Angel of Death with his army had camped among us. Then it was the Howard Association of Vicksburg went to work, being composed of some of the choicest spirits that ever labored in the cause of humanity. They sacrificed to the great cause such noble specimens of Christian manhood as Bursley and Harrison, Fairchild and Rockwood. But for this grand institution and the full-handed response to their call for charity which came from ever portion of our beloved land, showing us in very deed to be one people, with one interest from sea to sea, from lakes to gulf, we would have heard the cry for bread added to those scenes of misery and distress with which we were made but too familiar.

This great Association made yet a more extraordinary call, when it asked physicians and nurses to come and help us. That charitable persons with money are willing to give it in the cause of suffering humanity, is not astonishing; but that men and women can be found bold enough voluntarily to encounter the storm of death, that for two long months raged in every part of our city, is wonderful, it staggers belief. And we doubt if any other country on the wide earth can produce its parallel.

In obedience to this call came about thirty doctors, and numerous nurses, many of them never having had yellow fever. Of these Drs. Sappington, Barber, Norris, Blickfeldt, Roach, Happoldt, Blackman. Potts and Glass died. In our county, Drs. Leach, Nesmith, Birdsong, and Monette were taken off.

Dr. A. R. Green, a colored man, did good work for many days, and was then numbered with the dead.

[NOTE.—Dr. Barber located here so short a time before the epidemic, that we felt toward him as we did toward the visiting physician, and therefore name him with them.]

'Twas not a spirit of recklessness that prompted them to come, nor was it the hope of gain, or the interest of science, that nerved them to the task which they must have known was one of extreme danger. But it was that same lofty sentiment, that determination to do all in their power to ameliorate the sufferings of their fellow-men which has immortalized Florence Nightingale. They came, they worked like men struggling for the right. Seven visiting Physicians and a large number of nurses died, away from friends, home, and loved ones. They died, were buried, and are forgotten. No poet laureate sang their praises, no monumental marble tells their story.

> But if one soldier dies,
> Doing Charity,
> 'Tis lauded to the skies
> For its rarity.

The physicians of Vicksburg should ever hold the visiting Physicians in the kindest recollection, and never forget that they came to us in the darkest hour of the blackest season ever witnessed in our city. They came like good Samaritans, dividing our work and cheering us in our despair.

As this dark cloud of pestilence advanced upon us, what a time it was for self-inspection, cogitation and determination with the Resident Physician. We knew that the great labor of an epidemic falls upon the Doctors; we knew, too, how weak our weapons were against this fell destroyer. We knew, moreover, the meagre compensation we would receive for such heavy work, day and night, until tired nature could endure no more. And yet, we all, whose health and business would permit, determined to stay and fight this invisible enemy to the last.

The boldness of the Physicians is not appreciated. The people think it our *duty* to battle with disease, whether it comes as the sneaking chill, or the army of an epidemic. The people are mistaken; we have no contract with them, our engagements are with our patients only. Nor does any moral obligation rest more heavily upon us than on any other educated class of society.

We will particularly notice the deaths of Dr. Z. T. Woodruff, D. W. Booth, P. F. Whitehead, and J. R. Hicks. Reverently and tenderly we record their names. Ours to love and regret, but for a commonwealth to mourn. Drs. Woodruff and Hicks died from home. They were advised by us to leave this malarious country, and seek for health in a mountainous region, little dreaming that we would never see them alive again. Had that thought occurred to us, we would not have urged their leaving so hurriedly, and would have shaken the parting hand more warmly, and our " God bless you" would have borne a tear upon its crest.

Drs. Booth and Whitehead were in magnificent health, two as fine specimens, mental and physical, of the genus homo as could be found. Unlike the knights of old, they wore no linked armor to ward off the arrows of this twin brother of death. They were armed alone with undaunted courage and faith in the power of medicine, which has proven so short, so weak so often. They fell with their harness on, trying to relieve their suffering race, and to establish that the science of physic is mighty, and must prevail over disease. How often, when the storm raged most furiously, and our patrons were dying in spite of our best efforts, we would involuntarily exclaim, "Would that Booth or Whitehead were here! He would give us words of comfort; he would tell us what to do; he would cheer our sinking patient; he would make him hope again."

To all our friends who have gone before us—let us hope to a better land—we would say most sincerely, we have missed you on the street, we have missed you at the bed-side, we have missed you everywhere.

> And when the festive board is again spread,
> We will miss our loved dead,
> And will quaff in deepest silence,
> The fullest draft to their remembrance.

C. J. MITCHELL, M. D.,   E. T. HENRY, M. D.,
J. R. BARNET, M. D.,   E. G. BANKS, M. D.,
J. M. HUNT, M. D.,   T. G. BIRCHETT, M. D.,
S. D. ROBBINS, M. D.,   W. T. BALFOUR, M. D.,
R. O'LEARY, M. D.

TO THE DEAD OF HOLLY SPRINGS.

A TRIBUTE BY HON. THOS. S. GATHRIGHT.

CENTRAL, TEXAS, Oct. 22.

EDITORS CLARION : A deep feeling of relief came upon me this morning, when I read in the Galveston News that there had been heavy frost in Mississippi from Osyka northward. Oh! the night of death that has fallen upon our glorious old State! The noblest sons of a common mother now sleep beneath her soil—heroes in a struggle where there is no glamor, no music, no shouting of contending hosts, no dreams of glory to animate, and no vision of rewards to inspire. They fell in a quiet hand-to-hand contest with death in its most hideous form, encouraged only by a sense of duty to their suffering fellow men, confronted by the black spectre that carried the wand of death, and with shadowy strokes beckoned whom it would to the grave. On every field of Mexico, Mississippi made her name illustrious by the deeds of her sons. In the late war, the regiments of Mississippi won for her imperishable renown. H. W. WALTER leaves a name to his poor wife and children which when tried in the alembic of glory, shall be more beautiful and fragrant than the name of Cæsar. Kinloch Falconer, the Christian gentleman and soldier, the scholar and patriot, has crowned his beautiful life with a deserved immortality. Brass and stone cannot survive the deeds these men have done, but in grateful recognition of the rich treasure that the character of such men bequeaths to prosperity, Holly Springs should erect a shaft of purest white, and inscribe upon it the names of WALTER and FALCONER, and the names of many heroes and heroines, that the world does not know. They were there and they grappled in secret and alone with the same monster, animated by the same spirit of benevolence and devotion that nerved Walter, Falconer and Holland, to meet duty in the presence of death. Life is not the greatest boon; a glorious death is man's highest achievement. To be true to humanity in times of prosperity and general tranquility is well, but it does not require any great gifts or graces; but to be true in the face of difficulties and death, is the test of greatness. No applause can reach "the dull cold ear of death," and no thanks from grateful hearts can penetrate the gloom of the grave. It may be that in the chambers of that still house in the ground—in the streets of that shadowy city, strains of melody from the shore beyond may touch the sensibilities and wake up and renew the manhood and womanhood of martyrs who fell in the cause of suffering humanity.

I have felt, day after day, that no end could be more coveted, no advent to the spirit world could be more auspicious than that which is found by the bedside of suffering, and in clasping the hand and making firm the footsteps of those who are going into the cold river. As I have read the telegraphic columns of my daily paper with feelings of this sort, I have almost envied the issue of lives so glorious.

I labored in Mississippi as I can never labor elsewhere; I spent all the flower of my manhood there: I guided the steps of thousands of her children, and suffered too upon her borders, and thought I loved her and her people; but I never knew my feelings until I saw the black cloud, charged with death hanging over her fair land, and heard the loud wail of her stricken cities and villages, and even the cry of mercy as the shadow of death fell upon the country.

God is just, and overrules all things. He will recompense the people of Mississippi for all she has suffered in the loss of her sons and daughters and in the terrible laceration of every sensibility of their nature. Where the darkest night brooded longest, where suffering lingered latest; where the dark, death fiend stalked most boldly, there will sunshine and melody and the genius of religion and truth come and invoke happiness and prosperity from out of misfortune, and the people shall all see that it is well. But for such reflections the stroke of Providence lately laid upon our people would be intolerable.

Since writing the above, I have seen dispatches announcing the death of COMPTON and HOLLAND. Holly Springs is indeed well stricken. It was enough to lose Walter and Falconer. Now come COMPTON and HOLLAND. The one a man of learning, of great breadth of culture, of enlarged views of science, and a heart that never erred in its impulses. His errors were of judgment. In the course of his public life, he was the recipient of applause and of censure. No man who knew him ever doubted his broad and catholic generosity, though he may have condemned his political life.

The other, Col. HOLLAND, a gifted and cultivated gentlemen, proved years before his death that he was a hero, and the conclusion of his life is one that may well be enrolled upon the annals of martyrdom. HOLLAND and COMPTON! At their graves chivalry and humanity may meet and weep. In them was what valor and beauty worshipped, and more than that, what poor, wrecked and weeping humanity could love and trust. The last of the martyrs, the noblest of men, the best of friends!

My heart is full to overflowing and bleeds for every household where the scourge set his deadly foot. For the poor orphans and disconsolate mourning ones, all over Mississippi, I pray God daily.

Bright skies are coming; the beautiful frost and snow will herald the good days of the happy future.

I am so thankful that THE CLARION was spared, and know it will join in the general joy for such manifest good will and brotherhood as the plague of 1878 evolved.   WILLIAM.

DR. J. F. SAMPLE.

From CLARION, Oct. 23.

We record with profound regret the death of Dr. J. F. Sample, of Tunica county, who volunteered to assist at Memphis, and was assigned to duty by the Howards of that city. He was a good citizen and his name deserves to be written high on the roll of the "Heroes of Humanity."

BUTLER P. ANDERSON.

From Grenada Sentinel, Oct. 5.

There are many persons, both at home and abroad all over this great country, whose names, if our people knew them, they would have reason ever to hold in profound respect. But, there is one among the many, which it seems to us, the people of Grenada should remember and honor until it is as familiar and beloved as were the tutalar divinities in the households of ancient Rome—we mean none other than BUTLER P. ANDERSON. To fly to the rescue of friends and kindred, is obeying the laws of the human heart; to risk life to save a country, is inspired by the voice of innate patriotism. Both of these things are common among men, and have their rewards in favors and honors that elevate the survivor sometimes to rank and fortune, and if he die, crowns his fame with a community's gratitude or a nation's tears.

In the case of Butler Anderson, all such incentives were wanting. He came to help strangers, few of whose faces he had ever seen; he came to work for a people without the obligation of contract, promise or reward; he came to risk his life in battling with a disease that had baffled medical skill for ages; he knew the inequality of the struggle, for he had been in it before, amongst his own people and friends. Under such circumstances, how deep must have been his sympathies, how earnest his wishes, how strong his convictions of duty; in a word, how deep and broad his philanthrophy. When he left his little children with a kiss for the last time as it proved, and bade his devoted wife a tearful good-bye to behold her once more at his dying side, his heart must have quivered with emotion, like the straining timbers of a ship lashed by the fury of a storm. These unseen, but bleeding wounds of the heart, he suffered for our people crying for help when there were few to save.

We will not undertake to describe his labors here. They were many and arduous, and even painful in a high degree, as we have learned that he carried his right arm in a sling for many days, on which glistened a large and furious carbuncle. Wherever the greatest suffering, wherever the most danger, there this kind but intrepid man could be found, doing all that a calm judgment and a tried experience could prompt for alleviation of the one and aversion of the other. After four weeks incessant, daily toil, and often sleepless nights, he fell a victim to the destroyer he had come to combat, a sacrifice to the humanity which inspired him. In one of the rooms of the Chamberlain House, surrounded by every attention that the circumstances would justify, he expired. This was not all he gave us. Mrs. Anderson, broken-hearted and almost alone, started with the sorrowful tidings to her little ones at home in Memphis, but ere she reached the spot consecrated by so many tender memories, she was stricken with the epidemic, and died amongst the good people of Hernando, thus, indirectly falling in the same cause which her Christian-minded husband had so earnestly espoused.

Good people of Grenada, we have written this in no spirit of meaningless panegyric. We refer his praise to other and more brilliant pens than ours. Our purpose was simply to show you the great sacrifice that this benefactor made in our behalf, that we might call your attention to another fact of equal, if not greater magnitude. Where are those little, helpless orphans, and whose are they? are questions which every right-minded man and woman of our town will answer at some future day, in a response that will bring consolation to the hearts of the bereaved children, and honor to the name of every surviving son and daughter of Grenada. To do otherwise, a liberal and enlightened country, which, from every quarter, has sent multiplied thousands to our relief when we cried for help, would hold us in abhorrence, and finally, write the epitaph of our heartless people, "Died of Ingratitude."

REV. DUNCAN C. GREEN.

From the Grenada Sentinel.

In the list of Christian heroes who fell before the ravages of yellow fever during the past summer, we notice the name of Rev. Duncan Green, son of our venerable Bishop, Right Rev. Wm. M. Green. Placing his young and interesting family beyond the lines of infection, he remained with his church and people, administering the consolations of religion and the assistance of friendship, until he laid down his young life in the cause of his Divine Master. Few young clergymen had a brighter future for usefulness and happiness. Surrounded by all the sweets of domestic peace, with education, books and refined society, life had many charms for him, outside the pale of the church to which he had consecrated his services. With all these endearments, when the dark wing of the destroying pestilence overshadowed the little and thriving town of Greenville, with the courage of a Christian hero, he entered upon the untried but terrible field of labor before him, and in a few days yielded up his own life, a sacrifice to humanity and Christian duty. To his sorrowing family and especially his aged Christian father, we extend our warmest sympathies.

PROF. WILLIAM CLARK,

President of Franklin Female College, Holly Springs, died of yellow fever at Tuscumbia, Ala., Sept. 13, 1878. He was born in Lunenburg, Vermont, Oct. 2, 1825, and was the sixth son of Judge Spencer and Elizabeth Clark. He graduated with honor at Amherst College, and the following year, (1852) came to the South and first located in Memphis, Tenn., but soon made his home in Mississippi. In 1855 he married Miss Mary Barton, daughter of the late Roger Barton, and their union was blessed with six children, four of whom survived; and never was there a more tender and affectionate husband and father.

WILLIAM A. FAIRCHILD.

From the Clarion, Sept. 21.

Our dispatches from Vicksburg contain the sad announcement of the death, on yesterday, of this prominent and useful citizen. He was truly one of the heroes of the Heroic Hill City. He was in the very prime of life, and blessed with all the surroundings that make life desirable. As Secretary and Treasurer of the Masonic Relief Committee, as a friend and as a nurse, he labored day and night in alleviating the distress that surrounded him on every hand. But the plague had marked him, too, as one of its victims, and none will be more mourned in the city where he fell. Mr. Fairchild was widely known as an insurance agent, and was still more widely known as a zealous and intelligent Mason, having recently filled the position of Grand Commander. Well may the Templars of the State, and of the Union, drape their swords and banners, for no truer Knight has ever donned or doffed the armour of their chivalrous and magnanimous fraternity. Verily, "greater love hath no man than this: that a man lay down his life for his friends."

DEATH OF YOUNG MEN IN JACKSON.

From Clarion, October 23.

Near one-half the whites who have died in our city within the past few weeks are young men who will be missed from society, and especially by the families of which they were, in several instances, the sole dependence for support. Since our last issue the names of WILLIAM L. PARKER and HARVEY PIERCE are added to the list. Mr. Parker, after several years of faithful service, was promoted to the position of deputy postmaster, and had been in charge of the office here for two months. Mr. Pierce has been for a number of years one of the most popular salesmen in the house of Robinson & Stevens, and was in sole charge of the interests of that firm

With deep regret do we chronicle the fall of such useful members of our community.

WILLIAM McCALLUM.

Died in this city, of yellow fever, September 27th, WILLIAM McCALLUM' a native of Jackson, in the twentieth year of his age. For the last five years he had been a compositor in the CLARION office, in which he learned his trade, and grew from boyhood to the early manhood when he was stricken down. There is something peculiarly sad to us in his death. Long association had produced a more than ordinary attachment for him. When the alarm of fever was created here, by the first death on the 31st of August, though he had never had the disease, he was one of the number to pledge the conductors of this journal that come what might, he, who had stood by them so long and faithfully, would still remain. He was true to his word. When he was overtaken by the disease, he was at his post. Of all our acquaintances he was one of the last we would have supposed liable to the disease. He was a model of manly strength, sanguine, hopeful and resolute. He was the only support of a widowed mother, sister and brother. May God in his mercy temper the winds of adversity to the bereaved household whose light and hope have been suddenly extinguished.

TRIBUTE TO MEMBERS OF THE PRESS.

From Correspondence of Jas. A. Stevens, Esq., of Columbus, in THE CLARION.

Then, there was the gallant and generous HOLLAND—the acknowledged "Prince" of that happy crowd—tall and graceful, with his bright, steady eye, the snuff-colored frock coat that fit him so well, and always with some passing kind words for the obscurer members of the gang. You remember his convivial powers—his wonderful memory of names and faces—and that vein of unaffected kindness that threaded all he did and said and looked. Never a man who will be so missed from the annual reunions as Colonel Holland.

And there was KINLOCH FALCONER—how natural it seemed to link his presence and Holland's at a Press Convention! They were peers in social fascination, equally brave, accomplished and popular, and it looks now almost right and natural that they should go down to their graves together with an act that finished off and rounded up the beauty of their brief careers. Did you ever notice how much Falconer's expression resembled that of the younger Winthrop of the colonial days, whose picture art has preserved, and whose beautiful and courageous character Bancroft has immortalized? Holland and Falconer! Heroic spirits, ye sleep well!

And WILLIE ADAMS, we cannot forget him, with his sombre brow, but generous heart and modest worth. Only those who knew him well ever imagined the many dry pleasantries that welled from his mind, keeping up an almost constant ripple of merriment wherever he went. But for his single infirmity—that of so many noble natures, alas!—he might have almost attained the influence and force of his celebrated father.

There was J. P. ALLEN, of Vicksburg—not at Holly Springs, but the acknowledged "mine host" at his home last year, and how gratefully he is remembered there! He literally made himself sick in his efforts to have the occasion of the editors' visit a pleasant one, taking upon his own shoulders the place of a "committee of one," and seeing to every thing—every hour of our stay, betraying the warm-hearted gentleman he was. I remember the last time we conversed together, was during the steamboat excursion down the Mississippi. He looked sadly worn and worried, and told me, to an expression of surprise on my part, that he was doing too much drudgery in the craft, but could not help himself. Mr. Allen was a graceful poet, and as a writer of humor had no equal in the State, since Dr. Woods and Henry Moss left us. Peace to his gentle memory.

How, too, we will miss those other heroes of the plague, O. V. SHEARER add the jolly UPSHAW.

"The old, old fashion Death!" dear CLARION, is a curious, an awful, yet a familiar one to us all! For,

"Men may come, and men may go,
But he goes on forever!"—

and after a little while, perhaps, he will be tapping at the door of others of the Mississippi Press Association.

MASONIC DEAD OF CLAIBORNE COUNTY.

Worshipful Master:

I cannot allow this Lodge of Sorrow, where such eloquent tributes have been paid to the memory of Masons elsewhere, to close without something being said with reference to the Masons of Claiborne who died during the recent epidemic. I make no pretensions, sir, to eloquence. I i speaking of them I cannot hope to interest this Lodge as those who have preceded me have done. My only apology for speaking of them at all is that I knew them and I loved them.

There were eight Masons who died in Claiborne during the prevalence of the yellow fever. Three of these: J. D. FAIRLY, THOMAS E. JONES and J. I. BROMLEY, were members of John A. Galbreath Lodge, at Brandywine—all good and useful men. Jas. I. Bromley was a physician and died like a true soldier at the post of duty. Thomas E. Jones was a young man, only about twenty-five years of age. He left a place of safety to go and nurse a family who had the disease; he took it and died. Were this life the end, then we might pity this brother dying thus, as he was entering on the enjoyment of a vigorous manhood; we might weep for him passing thus early out of life, a sacrifice to humanity, did we not, with the eye of faith, behold him entering that other life, upon whose threshold he was met, I doubt not, by the Lord of life, with a crown of glory in his hand.

DR. HENRY C. SNODGRASS was a member of and Past Master in Mississippi Lodge, No. 56, at Rodney. I can say but little of him, of my own knowledge, my acquaintance with him being very limited, but I have heard him spoken of as an elegant and accomplished gentleman, and an able and successful practitioner. Of his devotion to Masonry, his rank of Past Master gives evidence; that he was devoted to his profession, his death bears testimony; and what higher eulogy could be passed on any man than this: "He died in the discharge of duty."

REV. J. J. HARPER and REV. D. A. J. PARKER were members of Claiborne Lodge, No. 110, at Rocky Springs. They were also ministers in the Methodist Episcopal Church, South, good men and good Masons; for such death had no terrors; after useful lives they died in the assured hope of a glorious immortality.

Past Master C. H. BARROTT, of Washington Lodge, No. 3, at Port Gibson, whose name, together with the date of his death, appears suspended here on a card, was a man whose devotion to Masonry was sincere and ardent, whose attachment to the fraternity underwent no ordinary trial; he was a member of the Roman Catholic Church; he was informed that he must either abandon Masonry or his Church; he refused to give up his Masonry, saying that Masonry was good religion for him, and in this I agree with him; Masonry is good enough religion for me, and those who do not regard Masonry as in some sort a religion, have, in my judgment, a very inadequate conception of our institution. I admit that, in a sectarian sense, it is not a religion. With sects and sectaries it has naught to do. It meddles with no man's creed; but it is religion for all that. It is that universal religion, that world-wide religion, taught by the martyrs and prophets and sages of all ages and in every clime, and which is summed up by that apostle of common sense, St. James, in this wise: "Pure religion and undefiled before God and the Father is this: to visit the fatherless and widows in their affliction, and to keep oneself unspotted from the world." If we assiduously practice this, not neglecting to cultivate those Masonic virtues which enlarge the heart and make it a fit temple for the indwelling of a Deity, such as brotherly love and toleration, kindness and charity toward our fellows, no matter of what creed, then I do not for one moment doubt that we shall all meet at last around God's great altar in the Grand Lodge above, no matter with what ceremonies we may worship him here; no, nor even under what name. The religion of Masonry is the religion of love, the God of Masonry is the God of Love. In that God, Bro. Barrott was a sincere believer. Of that religion Bro. Barrott was an earnest and zealous disciple.

> "No farther seek his merits to disclose,
> Nor draw his frailties from their dread abode;
> There they alike in trembling hope repose,
> The bosom of his Father and his God."

Bro. HENRY S. WHEELESS, of Washington Lodge, No. 3, is the only one remaining for me to speak of, and I can scarce do this without tears. He was a young man and a young Mason. He was possessed of many qualities, such as were calculated to endear him to us, and in his death both our Lodge and the community at large sustained a heavy loss. He was honest in purpose, abstemious in habit, attentive to business. Brave, high-minded, generous to a fault, he detested all that savored of meanness or littleness. I shall only mention one incident in his life: At one time when the fever was at its worst in the town there was a scarcity of ice; none was to be had for love or money; oh, the heart-sinking that announcement produced; those who have never been in the midst of a fever epidemic cannot realize the horror of it; how every little piece of ice is treasured up; how much more precious than gold it becomes. I was at that time nursing a little boy, the son of a poor widow. He was in a critical condition indeed; already that restless, nervous tossing which precedes the comatose state, sooner or later to end in death had set in; I was in despair. Henry Wheeless had a little ice; he had been guarding it with zealous care, as two of his own family were then down with the fever; I would not have dreamed of asking him for any; money would not have induced him to part with it; he came voluntarily and offered to divide with me; it was a very small quantity, it is true, but it was enough; it saved the boy's life. This is a small matter; but ah! Worshipful Master, are not the small, the trivial things of this world the mighty matters of eternity? Do we not all remember, sir, that when Christ sat over against the treasury, watching those who put in their gifts, it was the widow's mite which attracted His notice, and elicited that memorable comment that goes rolling down the ages for the eternal instruction of the generations of mankind: "She has given far more than all!" And who knows, sir, but that when that lump of ice, small though it was, comes to be weighed in the scales of Omnipotence, it may outbalance all our good deeds?

There is a class of Masons who have died during this epidemic, of whom I would gladly speak, but I cannot, for I know not their names. They met Death in the discharge of duty. Perhaps they fill unmarked graves. Perhaps they died without even a friend to take note of their departure. For them the lyre of song thrills not; they are mentioned in no poet's lays; as to their deeds the voice of the orator is silent, the only memory remaining of them the short line, in our Worthy Grand Secretary's list, which gives their names and the number of their Lodge—in many instances perhaps, not even that; but what matters it that their names and deeds pass unnoted, unremembered, unrecorded here, they will be noted one day, they will be recorded; written not on the perishable paper on which our records are, not even in accordance with the wish of the Hebrew poet—with an iron pen in the rock forever, but in a far more indestructible, far more indelible, far more imperishable form than this—written with the finger of God himself, in letters of living light, over his eternal adamantine throne, there to be read by the eyes of the glorified throughout the endless ages.

COAHOMA LODGE, NO. 104.

Extract from Oration by Bro. H. P. Reid, at Lodge of Sorrow, December 15, 1878:

It can be said to the honor of our deceased brother, GEORGE RANDOLPH ALCORN, who departed this life on the seventeenth day of October, 1878, in the forty-second year of his age, that he, as a Master Mason, was often tried and ever found to be true to the sacred vows and obligations which he took upon himself when he was clothed with that proud insignia of honor—the white apron.

Raised to the sublime degree of Master Mason in Coahoma Lodge No. 104, in the year 1869, he was, at the annual election of that year, made Secretary of said Lodge, and the jewel of his office ever shone bright and lustrous, by reason of duty well performed, from that time to the hour in which the sickle of death reaped him down.

He served his country as an officer, in times both of peace and war, and as a civil officer he was courteous, prompt and rapid in the discharge of his duties, and no one ever came in contact with him as such but felt that the trust he held was well reposed. He filled several high and responsible positions, but upon the robes of the several offices he left not a single stain.

LAKE LODGE, NO. 298.

The pestilence that desolated so many homes during the summer of 1878, seemed to scourge with more than ordinary severity the devoted little village of Lake, and not only was nearly every household made to mourn the stilling of well-known footsteps, and the hushing of cherished voices, but also, we as a Lodge gave back to earth many worthy and well beloved brothers. In the East the Master calls no more from refreshment to labor, but we trust that his vanished spirit hath found eternal refreshment above. In the West the sound of the Warden's gavel was silenced; the Senior Deacon forever ceased to welcome visitors to our Lodge; from a hand stiffened in death the key to our treasures fell; the Tyler's sword was no longer raised aloft to guard our portals; and, with these five officers, two worthy members joined in the sleep of death. The names of our dead are: GEO. C. McCALLUM, W. M., WM. H. EVANS, S. W., LEE SCOTT, S. D., and P. M., JOHN H. CROSBY, Treasurer, JAMES N. COUCH, Tyler, and ROBERT DAVIDSON, GEO. F. LOWRY, members.

To their worth and integrity as Masons we can cheerfully and proudly testify; and while we mourn their loss, it is a consolation to us to know that with a sublimity of self-sacrifice and a moral courage that cannot be too highly praised, they practiced that charity which our Order teaches, and fell fighting as soldiers of love and mercy, when in our midst pestilence walked in darkness and destruction wasted at noon-day.

H. C. ROBINSON LODGE, NO. 379.

WEST POINT, Miss., January 31, 1879.

Among our dead of last year, and the epidemic, we lost a once very dear member of our Lodge and community here—DR. A. S. GERDINE, a sketch of whose life I now furnish, on the call you made for items.

A. S. Gerdine, was born in Lowndes county, Miss., June 22, 1848; raised and educated in his native State; entered the war when a mere youth and served through to its close; graduated in medicine at the Louisiana Medical University in 1868; practiced his profession among his old friends until 1875, when he settled in Areola, Washington county, Miss.; married Miss Sallie B. West, of Washington county, in August, 1877, who, through a Providential dispensation, departed this life in June, 1878, leaving an infant son ten days old. Dr. G. left the bounds of his practice, during the prevalence of the yellow fever, and treated successfully the disease in an adjoining practice, his first patient being the family of the resident physician; after a partial abatement in the fever he returned with his friend and neighbor Dr. Gaddis, and together they quarantined themselves, so as not to expose their friends or families; at Dr. Gaddis' he was attacked and died of black vomit on the 23d of September, 1878, and was interred alone in the garden of Dr. Gaddis, who was taken down at a neighbor's across on the other side of Deer Creek, and buried in his, Williams' garden. Both of said physicians were members of H. C. Robinson Lodge, No. 379, located at Areola, Washington county, Miss.

Bro. Gerdine was a man and a Mason in reality. I had the honor and pleasure of conferring all the Degrees upon him from that of Entered Apprentice to Royal and Select Master. He was made a Mason in 1869, and received the Chapter degrees in 1870, served as Master of Canon Lodge No. 159, and High Priest of West Point Chapter, No. 95, prior to his moving to the Bottom. He was bright in both bodies, but pre-eminently so in the Chapter, and was esteemed and beloved by the fraternity, and hosts of friends here and in the swamp. WM. M. FRANKS.

Brethren Who Died at Meridian and Lauderdale.

(SKETCHES KINDLY FURNISHED BY PAST GRAND MASTER WM. S. PATTON.)

Patton Lodge, No. 120, has to mourn the loss of Brothers A. A. CURRIE and J. B. LYLES, whose seats are vacant, caused by the ravages of yellow fever. Both died on the 25th day of October, 1878. Brother Lyles at his post of duty as a physician at Lauderdale. Brother Currie resided at Meridian and was a member of the Relief Committee, which duty he strictly attended to until he was stricken down. Although taken from us ere their sun had attained its meridian height, yet the memory of them and their past Masonic lives well up before us as beacon lights which will never be erased from our memories. Men of genial and kind feelings, warm and personal attachments, noble and tender impulses. Their sun has gone down whilst it was day time, and the last sleep has overtaken them at the meridian of life. The grim monster laid his icy touch upon their hearts, and soon, ere friends could realize that the vital spark had flown, all that was mortal was laid away in the cold and speechless grave to await the dawn of the resurrection morn. Such is the chronicle of the closed lives of Brothers Currie and Lyles who have lately passed beyond the shore of time, and entered on the conditions of immortality while in the prime of manhood. May their many mourning friends soon become reconciled to the calamity which hovered about them for many days, and may the shadow resting on each suffering heart soon give place to a day of sunshine and uninterrupted bliss, and may they have that peace of mind that cometh from a perfect God.

Bro. Currie was a native of Kemper county, Miss., commanded a company in the 13th Mississippi Regiment during the war; was made a Mason in Patton Lodge, No. 129; a Royal Arch Mason, in Patton Chapter, No. 52; a Royal and Select Master in W. S. Patton Council, No. 24.

Bro. Lyles was born in Alabama; moved to Mississippi when quite young; was made a Mason in Patton Lodge, No. 129.

Bro. John Ethridge, one of the first victims of yellow fever, died on the 27th day of September, 1878. At the time he was quarantining the city. Bro. Ethridge was made a Mason in Marion Lodge, No. 62; moved to Meridian soon after the close of the war, in which he was engaged for four years. He affiliated with Lauderdale Lodge, No. 308, and remained a consistent member until his death. He leaves an affectionate wife and a large family of children and numerous friends to mourn his death. It is to be hoped that their loss is his eternal gain.

Bro. Robert J. Moseley was made a Mason in Marion Lodge, No. 62; Royal Arch Mason in Meridian Chapter, No. 25, and received the Orders of Knights Templar in Cyrene Commandery, No. 9. Bro. Mosely had held the office of Sheriff of Lauderdale county for several years, amassed considerable of this world's goods, but like many others, his liberality and generous disposition was the cause of many losses to him. He remained in Meridian during the fever. Kept his house open until he was stricken down, and after nine days suffering died on the 9th day of October, 1878. He was a native of Kemper county, Miss., aged about 49 years. Generous, true to his friends and liberal to a fault. His body has been consigned to mother earth; we trust his immortal soul has winged its way into the presence of the Grand Master above and with Him ever to dwell.

Bro. John Ward, made a Mason in Livingston Lodge, No. 41, Alabama. He was a dimitted Mason at the time of his death. Born in Ireland, and like the greater portion of that noble people, was generous to a fault. Bro. Ward was a peaceable, quiet citizen, beloved by all who knew him, and his death which occurred on the 8th day of October, 1878, was received with sorrow by many, and especially the poor and needy who have shared his generosity in times past. Peace be to him; we can cheerfully leave him in the hands of Him that doeth all things well.

Bro. J. C. Peters was a dimitted Mason; was made in Marion Lodge, No. 62; dimitted and moved to Meridian; pursued his occupation as machinist and house painter. He was peaceable, quiet citizen, meddling with the business of no one. He remained in the city during the epidemic, and near the close of the disease, and on the 14th day of November, 1878, sickened, and in a few days passed to that bourne from which there is no return. His age about 50 years.

Bro. W. T. McLean was thrown on his own honesty and industry in early youth. His untiring energy and perseverance soon gained him friends, and step by step he soon rose to distinction as a man of business. A native of Alabama; made a Mason in one of the Lodges in the city of Mobile. In 1863 he moved to Meridian; he and his partner were engaged in a merchant flouring and meal mill. Although an entire stranger, he soon gained the confidence of the citizens and surrounding country. Brother McLean did not for a moment neglect his duty as a Mason. Soon after his arrival he placed his dimit in Lauderdale Lodge, No. 307; punctual in his attendance; and the second year after his affiliation was elected Worshipful Master, which station he filled with credit and honor to himself and pleasure to the members. Brother McLean was an Alderman of the city; he was one of the efficient members of the Relief Committee; stood to his post as a faithful sentinel during the epidemic, visiting the sick, feeding the hungry, and always ready and willing to aid and assist those not able to help themselves. Thus he labored day and night, until overcome by toil and fatigue he fell a martyr to the dreadful scourge. He is gone—gone to that undiscovered country from whence none ever returns. Though taken in the meridian of life, in the midst of his usefulness, he did not live in vain. His deeds as a man and a Mason, will shine with that freshness which time cannot impair, and such brightness as passing years cannot dim. We can truly say:

> "Farewell, dear brother, thou'rt gone from our sight,
> God speed thee to Heaven, lost star of the night."

BRO. WM. V. RANEY, a native of Georgia, settled in Lauderdale county, Miss., at an early date. Served the county as Sheriff, and also as Chancery Clerk, commanded a company of cavalry during a portion of the war. Was made a Mason in Marion Lodge, No. 62, some thirty years ago. About the year 1850 moved in the vicinage of Lauderdale Springs, and affiliated with Patton Lodge, No. 129. Soon after the organization of Patton R. A. Chapter, No. 52, he received the Chapter degrees. At the surrender, like many others, he was left pennyless; moved to Meridian, but still retained his membership in Patton Lodge, though not feeling able to pay his Lodge and Chapter dues and support a large family, the Lodge still claimed him as a worthy member. He was a consistent member of the Methodist church, a strong advocate for temperance, and withal an honest, good citizen. He was 69 years old at his death, which occurred on the last days of November, 1878. He leaves an affectionate wife, several children and numerous relatives and friends to mourn his loss, which it is to be hoped, has proven his eternal gain in the Supreme Grand Lodge on high, where God, the Grand Architect of the Universe alone presides. Peace to his remains.

GREENVILLE LODGE NO. 94, I. O. O. F.

Tribute Adopted at Meeting of Lodge November 12, 1878.

The storm of death which swept over our city during the months of September and October, struck our Lodge with terrific force: and our beloved brothers,

WILLIAM MARSHALL,	A. B TRIGG,	WILLIAM J. MANLEY,
Noble Grand,	GEORGE W. ELLIOTT,	JOHN MANIFOLD,
LYMAN STOWELL,	EDWARD P. BYRNE,	JOHN H. NELSON,
HENRY FREUNDT,	THOMAS M'LEAN,	HENRY MUNK,
WILLIAM L. PORTER,	WILLIAM EHLERS,	

fell before its fury. Falling, as they did, at a time when the funeral honors of our Order could not be paid to them, nor any evidence of our fraternal esteem exhibited in the customary manner, it is meet and proper that we should now pay tribute to their worth, and assure their surviving friends and families of our appreciation of our lamented dead; therefore,

Resolved, That by the death of these brethren our Lodge has sustained an irreparable loss, and the community been deprived of some of its best and worthiest citizens. To their bereaved families we tender our heartfelt sympathy, and assure the widows and orphans of our dear brothers that our fraternal regard for them will not perish with the dust of the departed, but will live with the memory of the noble men who have gone from our circle. Our mourning hearts meet theirs in brotherly regret for our mutual loss; and we pray God to shield and shelter them from the further storms and sorrows of life.

> They need no tears who lived a noble life,
> We will not weep for them who died so well,
> But we will gather 'round the hearth and tell
> The story of their strife.
> Such homage suits them well;
> Better than funeral pomp or passing bell.

Resolved, That these resolutions be spread upon the minutes of the Lodge, and that the Secretary have them published in the Greenville Times and Local and Advertiser, and forward copies to families of the deceased brothers.
E. BOURGES,
E. STAFFORD,
S. R. DUNN, JR., Committee.

TRIBUTES TO KNIGHTS TEMPLAR.

HOLLY SPRINGS COMMANDERY, NO. 4.

At the regular conclave of Holly Springs Commandery, No. 4, Knights Templar, held at their asylum January 27, 1879, the following resolutions were offered and adopted :

Whereas, During and subsequent to the epidemic which recently visited this community, the following officers and members of Holly Springs Commandery, No. 4, were summoned to the asylum above, viz : SIR H. W. WALTER, P. G. G.; SIR E. W. UPSHAW, P. E. C.; SIR HOWARD FALCONER, Prelate; SIR P. A. WILLIS, Recorder; SIR THOMAS A. FALCONER, SIR U. H. ROSS, SIR HUGH WINBORN and SIR R. W. McCLAIN, members.

Therefore, Be it resolved,by this Commandery, That in this sad visitation of an allwise Providence, we have sustained an irreparable loss and the Order is deprived of the wise and valued counsels of valiant and courteous Sir Knights who were among its brightest ornaments.

Resolved, That we tender to the respective families of the lamented deceased our profound sympathies, and these resolutions be spread upon the minutes of this Commandery and a copy be sent to the families of the deceased and published in the Holly Springs papers. Also that we wear the usual badge of mourning for thirty days.

ST. CYR COMMANDERY, NO. 6.

Died, in Water Valley, Miss., on the 28th of September, 1878, of yellow fever, frater SIR KNIGHT J. O. HENDRICKS.

At a regular conclave of St. Cyr Commandery, No. 6, held at their Asylum, in Water Valley, Nov. 14, the following resolutions were adopted :

Whereas, It has pleased the Supreme Ruler of the universe to call from his labors here below, our beloved *frater,* Sir Knight J. O. Hendricks, to his eternal rest above. Therefore,

Resolved, That we, his *fraters,* deeply deplore his loss, and will ever cherish his memory. Yet believing that God doeth all things well, we bow in humble submission to his dispensation.

Resolved, That St. Cyr Commandery extend to his widow and orphans its sympathy, and mingle its tears with theirs.

Resolved, That we wear the usual badge of mourning for thirty days, and that a copy of these resolutions be furnished the family of our deceased *frater,* and that the city papers be requested to publish the same.

MEMORIAL SERVICES.

From the Holly Springs South, January 8.

In the summer of 1876 the young men of Holly Springs organized the Autrey Rifles, a volunteer military company, named after the gallant Col. James Autrey, who entered the Confederate army from this city and was killed at the battle of Murfreesboro. This company, under the captaincy of Maj. Geo. M. Govan, has always been in a state of great efficiency, handsomely uniformed and thoroughly drilled. Though its numbers were not very large, the epidemic of last summer struck from its rolls nine names ; that is, three honorary members, A. Fox Moore, W. J. L. Holland and Frank Ganter ; and six from its ranks, Howard Falconer, Frank C. Walter, Glenn Fant, Samuel Bonner, Winfield J. Featherston and Joseph Lebolt. This list, it is certain, could not well have been surpassed for personal worth, purity of character and public spirit, and therefore it was meet and proper that they should have had paid to their memories the tribute of the memorial services which were held in the Presbyterian Church of this city last Sabbath afternoon. These services were conducted by two of our city pastors, the Rev. Mr. Miller, of the Baptist, and Rev. Mr. Craig, of the Presbyterian Church. The survivors of the company turned out on the occasion in full uniform, and the Church was filled to overflowing by citizens, all anxious to manifest the esteem in which the memories of the deceased were held, and their sense of the public loss which had been sustained in their death. The sermons were appropriate, impressive and solemn, and the eulogies in good taste and well merited. After the benediction, the company marching to the music of our well-trained city band, repaired to the cemetery, and there over the graves of their lamented dead, fired the usual military salute of musketry.

> "When musing on our famous gone,
> We doubly feel ourselves alone."

RISING GLORY LODGE, NO. 215.

This Masonic Lodge, at Osyka, adopted appropriate tributes to the memory of Bro. MARTIN D. BOND, Senior Warden, who died of yellow fever October 4, 1878—"A brother in whose bosom always glowed the great principles of Masonry and Charity, and who, by his upright and honest walk through life, endeared himself to the brethren." Also tribute to the memory of Bro. ISAIAH CERF, Treasurer, who died of yellow fever, October 8, 1878—"a true and worthy member, a faithful officer, the widows and orphans a helping benefactor, his family a kind and devoted husband and father, and society a worthy citizen."

BOVINA LODGE, NO. 112.

WHEREAS, Divine Providence has in His wisdom seen proper to remove from our midst Brother J. B. JOHNSON, while acting Secretary of this Lodge, and R. W. CHAPPELL, Tyler, and Past Master D. A. CAMERON, S. WALL, J. W. FINCH, J. S. WILKINS, and J. H. FEATHERSTON, members; and,

WHEREAS, As we are bound together by an indissoluble tie as Masons, it is right and proper at all times to pay a just tribute of respect to the memory of deceased brethren; therefore,

Resolved, That in the death of Brothers Johnson and Chappell, the Lodge has lost efficient officers, and in the death of Brothers Cameron, Wall, Finch, Wilkins and Featherston, the Lodge has lost valued members, and in the death of all of them, the community has lost their association, and the example of many virtues, Bovina Lodge a vacuum that will not be easily filled.

Resolved, That we bow in meek submission to the will of Him who has control of the Grand Lodge of the Universe, believing that He doeth all all things according to His will and purpose.

Resolved, That we sincerely sympathise with the relatives and friends of our deceased brethren, and hereby tender to them our heartfelt condolence.

Resolved, That the members of this Lodge wear the usual badge of mourning for the space of thirty days, that the foregoing resolutions be spread upon the minutes, and a copy of the same be transmitted to families of the deceased.

Memorial Tribute Adopted December 12, 1878.

To the W. M., Wardens and Members of Greenville Lodge No. 206, A. F. A. M.:

BROTHERS—The roll of the Craftsmen has been called, and to the names of W. A. HAYCRAFT, P. M., EDWARD P. BYRNE, P. M., NEWMAN J. NELSON, P. Treas., JOHN H. NELSON, LYMAN STOWELL, WILLIAM J. MANLEY, DUNCAN C. GREEN No. 28, A. B. TRIGG, JOHN MANIFOLD, GEORGE W. ELLIOTT, E. STEINBERG, P. M., No. 23, THOMAS PAGE, M. J. MORZINSKI, the response has been: "Died on the field of honor."

Yes, they have gone—the veteran in the ripeness of his age and experience, the Masters who ruled and governed the Lodge with honor and love, and the young Craftsmen with whom it was our delight to mingle. They have gone in the full ear, in the ripened grain, and in the green leaf. But they died with their loins girt and their hearts firm in the self-sought labor at which the summons found them. To them duty was inspiration. They believed that—

> Whether on the scaffold high,
> Or in the battle's van,
> The fittest place for man to die
> Is where he dies for man!

They trod the rugged road of duty with heroic step, and went down to death as to a bride. They met it face to face and flinched not. Not for them do we mourn, but for ourselves and for the loved ones who have passed under the rod of this great bereavement. Our brothers lived in the enjoyment of the highest esteem of their fellow-men, and died amid the universal regrets of the community. May we so live, that dying, we may be as sincerely mourned.

C. M. CURELL,
W. R. TRIGG,
J. C. HEARD,

JULIUS LANDAU,
JACOB HIRSCH,
FRANK VALIANT,
Committee.

FACTS, FIGURES AND INCIDENTS.

COMPILED FROM VARIOUS SOURCES.

——◦◦°◉°◦◦——

GRENADA.

From Dr. Cochran's Report to the Sixth Annual Convention of the American Public Health Association at Richmond, November 19, 1878.

The town of Grenada stands on an elevated plateau on the south bank of the Yalobusha river.

The natural drainage of the town is excellent, and every rain washes the streets and gutters clean.

It is said that many of the back yards were very filthy, and that the privy vaults, which for the most part are simply pits or wells dug in the ground and walled up with boards or bricks, and easily pervious to water, are very rarely emptied. The famous sewer about which so much has been said in the newspapers is not a sewer at all, but a wet weather brook which meanders diagonally across the town, of which it is the principal drain. During dry weather it dries up completely throughout its whole extent, and during a heavy rain it runs like a milltail, and often overflows its banks. It is open to the air and the sun from its source to its mouth, a distance of about a mile, except that, about the middle of its course, it is walled up and covered over with wooden boards for a distance of something like a hundred and fifty yards.

The first fourth of this covered portion passes diagonally across one of the streets. The next fourth passes diagonally under a livery stable. There is then a short open portion through the back of the stable. It then passes diagonally under a stone-house, and thence diagonally through a street. It is impossible that any part of this drain should become very filthy, or noxious except that part of it which is covered over, and I cannot believe that even this part of it could become so loaded with filth as to constitute an important factor in the generation of any sort of sickness. A considerable part of the wooden walls and cover of portion of the drain had decayed and the cover was falling in, so that it was obliged to be repaired. In making the repairs the decaying timber was removed, and the filth that had accumulated in the bottom was dug out and thrown upon the street. Something like fifty yards were perhaps renovated in this way, and the excavated material thus exposed to fester in the sun and exhale its impurities into the atmosphere, to be wafted about by the winds, is said to have been extremely offensive.

Whatever bad influence these emanations may have exerted in other ways, I am satisfied that they had nothing in the world to do with the generation of the yellow fever poison which spread desolation through the community a month later, for this work was done in June, and the fever did not make its appearance until the last of July, and the health of the place, until a few days before the outbreak of the epidemic, had remained good. The population of Grenada before the outbreak of the fever numbered about 2500, of whom about 1300 were whites and about 1200 blacks and mulattoes. After the stampede there remained about 325 whites and about 1000 blacks. Of the whites who remained, and who were not protected by a previous attack, only five escaped the fever.

The total number of cases count up 1040. The total of deaths is 336; white deaths about 230; black deaths about 90. The first acknowledged case, although it was not at the time acknowledged to be such, occurred with the person of Mrs. Capt. Fields, formerly of Okolona, Miss., who lived on the corner of First street, at the depot. The history of the Field family will be given in detail presently.

The second case was Mr. R. A. Young, clerk of Bryant & Davis, who kept a variety store, dry goods, groceries, etc., on First street, in which he spent most of his time during the day. He was also the proprietor of a liquor saloon, or bar room, which he visited of evenings. He was taken on the 3d of August, had black vomit; suppression of urine—in short, a malignant case of yellow fever—and died on the 7th of August. No exposure to infection could be traced in this case. It was pronounced by the attending physician to be bilious fever and jaundice, but was subsequently admitted by them to have been yellow fever. From these two cases the fever spread like a conflagration over the town.

The cases in the Fields family consisted of fourteen persons, as follows, namely: Mrs. Field herself was taken sick on the 20th of July, and died on the 31st of the same month. She had black vomit, skin very yellow, and the body after death was very much discolored, swelled up rapidly and became very offensive. Her disease was named by the attending physicians malarial congestive fever. She died on Monday night, was put in a metallic case on Tuesday afternoon, and was buried from the Presbyterian church on Wednesday. The funeral was largely attended, and there being some leak in the casket, the body smelt so bad as to attract general remark, and to cause great nausea to many who were near it in the church, and several subsequent cases were ascribed to this fact. She was treated by Drs. Hughes and Hall, both of whom died during the epidemic, who at the time pronounced the case to be one of congestive malarial fever, but afterwards they were satisfied it was yellow fever.

Mr. Gray Fields came from Grand Junction to attend his mother's funeral. He remained two or three days, and returned to Grand Junction. Subsequent history unknown.

Thomas Fields was with his mother during her sickness. A few days after her death he went into the country, where he got sick. He was brought back to town sick, and died on the 13th of August.

Harry Fields was with his mother during her sickness, was attacked on the 8th or 9th of August and died on the 11th.

Waddel Fields was with his mother during her sickness, went into the country soon after her death, did not return and did not have the fever.

Mrs. Sheppard, Mrs. Fields' daughter, was with her mother during her sickness, went into the country soon after her death, was brought back sick on the 1st of September, and recovered.

Mattie Fields lived at Okolona with her sister Catty, wife of Mr. Abernethy of that place, came to her mother's funeral and returned as soon as the funeral was over. She died near Okolona in five days after she started back. Mrs. Abernethy also came to attend her mother's funeral, went back home to Okolona and escaped. Lemuel Sheppard, Mrs. Fields' grandson, went into the country soon after her death and escaped. Katy Sheppard also went into the country, but contracted the fever and died about the middle of September.

The report goes to show that out of a family of thirteen, of whom several were but slightly exposed, there were ten cases, 'seven deaths, three recoveries and three escapes. Dr. Cochran continues:

"So much of interest centers about this family, and it proved so prolific a focus of infection, that it would have been gratifying to be able to account, in a definite and circumstantial way, for the origin of the disease in the first case. But this I was unable to do. Mrs. Fields lived about two squares from the railroad depot, and about the same distance from the nearest part of the so-called sewer. Her house was in a good sanitary condition. She had been, about a week before she was taken sick, to the depot, one morning before breakfast, to put her daughter Mattie on the train to go to Okolona. It is not known whether she went into the cars or not, but as the train stayed twenty minutes for breakfast, it is believed that she did. About this time several cars loaded with various freight for Memphis were stopped there and disinfected for the Memphis quarantine. I was not able to obtain any other presumption of exposure than this. In the immediate neighborhood of Mrs. Fields' residence, and among all the families who had visited her, there occurred, in rapid succession, a large number of cases."

Here follows a long list of cases, and the statement that the disease made its appearance in several families who had not visited any case of yellow fever, and who had been subjected to no known source of infection except that they had attended Mrs. Fields' funeral, and had remarked the bad smell of the body in the church. Here again follows a long list of cases, and Dr. Cochran continues: "I have related these cases in some detail so as to show how almost every white person who was exposed to the fever in the sick rooms and by contact with the sick was attacked within a few days. It is said that only five white persons of those who remained in the stricken city escaped infection. The local physicians were very unwilling to admit that the earlier cases were yellow fever. Notwithstanding the rapid occurrence of new cases and deaths it was not until the 11th of August, nine days after the death of Mrs. Fields, that the physicians announced to the community that the disease which had so mysteriously entered the town, was the Southern epidemic. Immediately the whole population was seized with panic, and everybody who was able to get away, fled as speedily as possible. They fled into the adjacent country and to distant cities, and carried the seeds of the pestilence with them to bear disastrous fruits, as at Holly Springs, Grand Junction, etc. About one thousand of them went into camps, located three miles from town, and although some of them occasionally visited town, the camps escaped infection. A considerable number of negroes went out to the camps in the beginning of the epidemic, but most of them returned before it was over. As a rule, the negroes took the disease later in the season than the whites, and the south-western quarter of the town, which is almost wholly inhabited by blacks, was last to be invaded. The disease among them was of a much milder character than the whites, and their percentages of mortality very much smaller. Nothing can show the tremendous energy of the epidemic more than the simple statement that during its prevalence there was only a single death from any other cause than the yellow fever."

The following is as complete a list as can be obtained of deaths from yellow fever, in Grenada and vicinity:

GRENADA DEATH ROLL.

Mrs. Field,	Thomas Powell,	Miss Kate Clarke,	Cally Davis,
Harry Field,	Rev H. T. Haddick,	M. Conley,	Mrs. I. S. Parker,
Thomas Field,	Dr. W. W. Hall,	Price Carl,	Miss J. Satterfield,
Mattie Field,	Mrs. W. W. Hall,	Ella Carl,	M. Friedman, N. O.
Katie Sheppard,	Rev. J. G. Hall,	German Carpenter,	Mrs. Smith,

Mrs. Wilson, Mrs. J. G. Hall, Dr. J. R. Wilkings, I. K. Wood, Mrs. Davi.son, Mrs. J. C. Stokes, Mrs. R. A. Irwin, Rev. J. M'Campbell Mrs. Ir'ne Bakewell John Stokes, Robert A. Young, Samuel Marshall, Mrs. Doak, James Stokes, Mrs. R. A. Young, Mr. Cary, Miss Lula Doak, Judge J. C. Gray, Miss Lula Kendrick, A. P. Sanders, W. T. Beauchamp, Mrs. J. C. Gray, Bob Mayhew, Charles Weigert, J. W. Beauchamp, J. N. Gray, S. S. Angevine, Mrs. W. A. Below, Mrs. McMillan, Ed. Gray, Miss M. Angevine, Frank Holly, Mr. McMillan, Mrs. Ingram, Jacob Poitevent, Rev. J.K. Armstrong Mrs. L. French, Eugene Ingram, Mrs. J. Poitevent, Mrs. E. E. Vinson, T. E. Peacock, Miss Flo'ee Ingram, Miss. M. Poitevent, Chas. Newell, Miss M'me Peacock, Prof. Welsh, Wyatt M. Redding, J. A. Williams, Mr. Dejarnett, Mrs. Sidney Welsh, Tom F. Marshall, Tom Phillips, Sallie Dejarnett, M. Wile, Miss Sallie Leedy, Mrs. Wolfe,old lady George Cromwell, Mr. Strang, Mrs. Kettle & child, W. T. Cole, John Cromwell, Emanuel Wile, Charlie Hall, Mrs. W. T. Cole, Miss Maria Mole, W. C. Eskridge and Alex. Rafalsky, Clayton Davis, George W. Lake, child, Mrs. J. A. Morrison, Miss Mary Hughes, Mrs. Geo. W. Lake, Walter Eskridge, Dr. Gillespie, Mrs. Gillespie, Miss Annie Lake, Fox Eskridge, R. A. Irwin, Mattie Postell, Delia Lake, Mrs. W. B. May, J. M. Knox, Dr. Ringgold, Mrs. Sadler, Dr. W. B. May, Samuel Kendall, Colman Armstrong, Miss Rosa Sadler, Dr. Hankins, Sammie Marshall, Miss Helen Lacock, Walter Sadler, Mrs. Hankins, John P. Eason, Johnnie Doak, Jos. E. Sadler, Miss Fannie Peebles G. W. Campbell, John Mitchell, Amos Sadler, Henry Rafalsky, Frank Mitchell, Mr. Lehman, Robert Sadler. O. B. Rollins, Dr. Wolfolk, Mr. Applegate, A. W. Ayres, Marshall Rollins, Fred Fenner, Abb Garner, W. I. Ayers, Ben. Gage, R. S. Bowles, B. P Anderson, Miss Jennie Ayers, Dr. Gage's 2 chid'n, Mrs. Scanlin, Herman Heshburg, Miss Lizzie Ayers, B. M. Doak, Mrs. Dr. Ringgold, C. Housman,Sardis, Dr. E. W. Hughes, Mrs. Hooks, Mrs. McDonald, E. F. Thompson, Mrs. E. W. Hughes, David Hooks, Lunwig Hummel, Sallie Barnes, Mrs. Hughes. James Burke, Cawein's child, George Collins, Mrs. J. E. Hughes, Mrs. Scanlin's child Mr. Shaw, Isaac Williams, R. Coffman, Wm. Chandler. Mrs. Bailey. Mrs. W. E. Long, Mrs. R. Coffman, R. A. Collins, Charles Yates, W. '. Shankle, Charles Coffman, Tom Irby, Mary Lacock, R. D. Crowder, Mrs. Chas. Coffman, Dave Moore, G. T. Coon, E. G. Eli, Miss Kate Coffman, Mr. Rivers, Mrs. Sallie Telfair, Mrs. Eliza Eli, H. S. Derrick, Dr. J. L. Milton, Sam. Flippin, Wm. Latham, Mr. H. S. Derrick, John Morrow, Mrs. Flippin & ch'd, Mack Wright, Miss M. Huffington, Barry Rose, Willie Beck, Martha Hosbin, Miss S. Huffington, F. K. Hall, Sallie Miller, Ida Rosser, Miss M. Huffington, Hugh Graham, Mrs. Alex. Turner, Dr. P. F. Fitzgerald Miss. M. Huffington, H.B.Sherman's inf't O. P. Sander, Mollie Sanders, Miss M. Lacock, Robert Stevenson, Mrs. O. P. Sanders, Mrs. Spencer, Miss Alice Lacock, Harry Hart, John Wright's child Mrs. Mollie Rush, Miss Addie Bishop, T. P. Barnes, Mrs. Nowell, Joseph Nowell, Miss Belle Bishop, John Thomas, Mary Mitchell, James Mitchell, Eugene Bishop. H. M. Jones, Charles Mitchell, Hattie Rosser, Mrs. J. M. Bishop, R. Williams, Sr., Mr. Boatright, Mrs. Beasly, Mrs. E. Shankle, John T. Moore, James Meador, Henry Burt, Mrs. Pete Kirby, Jos. A. Morrison, Miss K. Burt, Robert Shankle, Pete Kirby, A. Gerard, James Morris, Belle Morris, Wm. Shankle, Mrs. Alice Signiago, W. Whitley, —— Brady, Robert Shankle, Judge Tom Walton, Miss Whitley, Mrs. Brady, Mrs. McLean, Thomas Kendall, Ed. McLane, Miss Lawrence, Miss. Lula McLean, Samuel Flippin, Dr. Trotter's child, Miss MarthaHarbin, D. C. Bristol, Hugh R. Davis, John Gelchrest, Miss Sallie Harbin. Miss Emma Bristol, S. L. Downs, Patrick Hart, ——266.

COLORED PEOPLE.

Alice McSwine, Dan Young, Mrs. Luke Barnett, Henry Ratliffe, Susan Sims, John Byron, · Harriet Gause, Grace Braceford, Walker Brantly, William Bates, Alice Johnson, Maggie Bowles, Calvin Davis, Henry Halliday, Alex. Davis' child, Billy Bowles,

Ike Drane,	Henry Yan,	Monroe Rosseau,	Man unknown,
Emiline Tullilove,	Martha Gillam,	Tom Madison's ch'd	Miley Golden,
Peter Jones,	Frank Buffaloe,	Rev. Alex. Phillips,	Rhoda Harris,
—— Moon,	Moon's wife,	Wm. Ross, Jr.,	York Smith,
William Carter,	child of Patterson,	Rev. T. E. Miller,	Layard Reede,
Sarah Walker,	Sarah W. Shiece,	Thos. Mitchell,	Dancy Wiles,
Silpha Mller,	Bray Lindsey,	Henry Vance,	—— Jackson,
Lizzie Walters,	Peter Jones child,	R. Seerbank's child	Man unknown,
Mary Davis,	Emiline Davis.	Eliza Walker,	Charlie Brusan,
Jane Beale,	Huston Harper,	Lydia Evans,	Mary Duncan,
Lizzie Smith,	Eliza Phillips,	Caroline Statham,	Isalia White,
Man unknown,	Era Phillips,	Lucy Minter,	H. White's child,
Winston Simmons,	Laura Harris,	Lizzie Austin,	Amanda Drane,
Nicholas Jackson,	Paul Carpenters,	Amanda Jackson,	Eliza Coleman,
Martha S okes,	Luke Patterson,	Millie Stepney,	D. A. Willixms' ch'd
Like Barnett,	Becky Hardwick,	Furguson's child,	
Albert Gause,	Tom Brown,	Henry Crowder,	——82.

INCIDENTS OF THE GRENADA PLAGUE.

Cor. St. Louis Globe-Democrat.

Far up the town is a store where provisions are distributed to all, rich and poor, black and white. The negroes never fail to show up for their rations, but can not be found when a grave is to be dug or a corpse to be removed. They will not move unless paid a five dollar bill for each errand. The relief committee at Grenada have disbanded, owing to some of the members having left the town, while the balance are prostrate with the fever. There are only three of original inhabitants now left in the place who are not prostrate. They are R. A. Armstead, the Southern Express agent, Samuel Heber, and a boy waiter in the Chamberlain House.

Armistead, the express agent, has been attacked with the fever.

*　　*　　*　　*　　*　　*　　*　　*

Mr. Heaberg carried a telegraph dispatch to a Mrs. Marshall, who had lost her husband and three children by the dire disease. She was found lying on her bed, completely exhausted both in physical and mental strength. The sight of this poor woman lying in her bed, moaning for husband and children, all dead in a week's time, brought tears to the eyes of her three visitors. The telegraph message came from absent friends, and breathed words of sympathy, love and encouragement. She thanked the telegrapher, and, in response to the question, "Can I do anything for you, Mrs. Marshall?" said : "No, but God bless you for your kindness; only God can help me now." Opposite Mrs. Marshall lay Tom Marshall, the telegraph operator, who is a brother-in-law of Mrs. Marshall. He was found lying at the very point of death. Three of his little children had died within the last ten days, and now he was almost gone. On another bed lay his wife, not sick with the fever, but broken-hearted and dying from the loss of her little ones.

OUR FIRST VISIT TO GRENADA.

Grenada Sentinel, Nov. 12.

During the prevalence of the epidemic in Grenada, we ventured a time or two from the heights that overlook the town on the west, to look upon the scene below and draw upon our imagination to supply that which the organs of vision did not furnish, and thus view one of the most unequal struggles of the nineteenth century, the contest between a few hundred weak but good men and women, some of whom deserve a hero's fame and others a martyr's crown, and the destroying pestilence. Not, however, until several days ago did we venture within the immediate sphere where the battle between life and death was fought and lost. As we approached the square, many things reminded us of the terrors and desolation of the last two months, and we were right glad to shake off the gathering gloom, as we met the cordial welcome of sorrowing friends, a few of whom remain to tell of incidents and scenes seldom witnessed anywhere on earth, but never here before. Long excluded from association without, they were truly glad to see faces, familiar in the past, once more kindling with the smiles of friendship, and to hear voices, to them many weeks silent, once more attuned to sympathy and love. To see our friends who had stood the heat and burden of those long, oppressive days looking so well, touched our heart with feelings of gratitude to the kind Providence which had so graciously protected them. May their lives in future be sweetened by recollections of duty nobly done, and sacrifices nobly offered.

Despite our efforts to the contrary, our mind would wander from the living to the dead, from the real of the present to the shadows of the past. The comparatively deserted streets, the closed doors, and the vacant houses, each had a tale to tell of suffering and of sorrow, of despair and death. In some cases, the occupants of these silent tenements, whom we had known so long and loved so well, seemed to linger a moment e'er the cordial welcome came as in days of yore. But, no voice came, no form appeared, but the bitter fact came up, that they now slept on yonder hill, in the quiet city of the dead. Silently we bade adieu to the living and wended our way filled with sad speculations upon the vanities of human life.

From Oration by Dr. John Brownrigg, of Columbus, before State Medical Association.

On Sunday, the 9th day of last August, in the stillness and beauty of a summer day, it was announced in Grenada that yellow fever was epidemic. The fearful whisper caused mothers to clasp their children in their arms and fathers to prepare rapidly for flight. The members of this Association well remember the hospitality of its citizens, and the elegant reception given us by the ladies of the place. Many of the ladies we met that evening are the brides of the pestilence. All is changed; the besom of destruction has swept over the place and this generation will not recover from its saddening effects. The plague destroyed social organization and the mechanism of civilization as if they had been living beings. Law and police, the board of health and the relief committee, were all stopped by death. There are human fiends lurking in the heart of every community, and where pestilence kills the good, these human hyenas come to the front to prey upon the carcass of society. They fired upon the doctors as they drove through the darkness, and one narrowly escaped being shot. The birds took to the forests, dogs and cats left their homes and disappeared. The grass grew in the streets, except the one leading to the burial ground. There was no business except in coffins and at the drug store. The telegraph operators and the druggists stood their ground, corpses rotted in the sun on the platform at the depot, but the boy operator stifled the odor with a handkerchief soaked in carbolic acid solution and kept his finger on the instrument. The cars swept swiftly by. The railroad which had brought death now brought bread to feed the dying and coffins to bury the dead. The boy operator moved the heart of Christendom with his simple words, describing the sufferings of the people, and succor came at last. The physicians were nearly all dead, and there ceased to be any system of order or responsibility. Then that wonderful Association, called the Howards, and the physicians came, and hope revived in the hearts of the stricken people. The influence for good of a few brave men, at such a time is not limited to the narrow sphere of their personal services. The panic-stricken people behold their calm and fearless faces, and

> A beam of comfort, like the moon through clouds,
> Gilds the black horror, and directs their way.

Helpless women and children, trembling in the agony of despair, cling to them as their deliverers. They are like rocks in the tempest-tossed ocean to which ship-wrecked mariners can cling, or the beacon-light to the vessel which has lost her reckoning and drifts at the mercy of the waves.

It requires more moral courage to brave the dangers of the pestilence than those of the battle-field. The soldier who falls in battle inhales with his last breath the sweet air of heaven, and often the last sounds that die upon his ear are the victorious shouts of his companions, as his life-blood flows upon the green sward of his native land, for which he dies. Those who fight the pestilence must inhale its sickening breath. Its physiognomy is hideous and disgusting. It drives its poisonous fangs into mother's breasts and tears with its yellow talons the quivering flesh of infants. With its fiery tongue it licks on maidens' cheeks its treacherous blush, and quickly stains their corpses with its black wings dipped in putrid gore. Sometimes, in the fearful stillness of night, it sobs. Its sounds are like those from the bottomless pit. Weeping and wailing, and the wild laugh of its maniacs, are its music. Its victims hide themselves to die like wild beasts. The man who goes to fight the pestilence must take his life in his hand and put his trust in God. To our brothers the "cry of humanity was the bugle call to action." True martyrs of our faith, they walked calmly through the valley of the shadow of death, extending a helping hand to their suffering and dying companions, and at last yielded their pure spirits to the God who gave them. Animated by a lofty sense of professional honor and duty, their hearts touched with sublime pity, they offered themselves a sacrifice on the altar of love for their fellow-men. From distant lands and from our own country, the knights-errant of our order, animated like Godfrey and Richard, by the true spirit of chivalry, came to contend with this great enemy of the human race. Lima, Peru, and Marseilles, France, were represented, and brave men also from among those who had been our enemies, came to aid our people in their distress, and some of these are among our honored dead.

GREENVILLE.

REV. STEVENSON ARCHER'S SEPTEMBER ACCOUNT TO REV. STUART ROB-
BINSON.

Dr. Robinson: God has been merciful to me and raised me from the yellow fever bed, and I am again at work. He folded me in his arms as I passed through the scorching ordeal. But a fearful havoc has been made among the citizens of our beautiful little town. About seven hundred people remained out of two thousand five hundred, to face the grim destroyer. Of this number nearly five hundred have been prostrated, and of these two hundred and twenty are dead. Among them are Mayor A. B. Trigg, all the council but one, a colored man, the city marshal, and the Rev. Duncan Green. The doctors were all prostrated but two, and the Methodist minister. Whole families have been swept away, and until the past week we have scarcely well ones enough to hand the sick a drink of water occasionally. For ten days we were shut up to this horrible sorrow and suffering, but now we have fifty nurses from New Orleans and Vicksburg, and from both points little boats were sent with provisions and medicines, and four physicians. Dr. Williams, from Baton Rouge, came in our hour of greatest trial and staid ten days. Drs. Archer, of Point Coupee, and Slaughter and Walker, of New Orleans, and Fawcett, of Concordia, are now with us. From abroad generous donations have reached us, and so far as man can smooth the case it is being done. I faced it for twenty days, night and day, from the hut of the pauper to the luxurious apartments of the rich, from the den of the woman of the town to the couch of the holy matron, and I never conceived of such suffering, such ghastly sorrow. I had to succumb then, and for eight days took my turn scorching and tossing, but again am at work. May God ever keep your days from such and your people shielded. I followed the first patient to the grave; of the attendants at the funeral but two now live. Twenty of us formed a Howard Association in the beginning; of that but three now live. I write because to you I first lifted the cry of sorrow, and from you had the first response. Your son and brother in Christ.

STEVENSON ARCHER, Greenville, Miss.

Population before epidemic, about 2800; during epidemic, about 1300. Total cases about 1100. Total deaths 299, of whom 195 were white, 101 colored, 3 Chinese. Adult males 162; adult females 90; male children 23; female children, 21. First death, August 23; last death, November 28.

LIST OF DEATHS.

Aug. 23d—Mobray, 4 years, Aug. 25th—Dave Woodruff, col, Aug. 30th—Perry boy—Aug. 31st—Pat Finnegan.

Sept. 2d—Wm. Marshall, E. J. Byrne, young man, John Simpson, Mat Fox, man, D. E. Brooks, Mrs. D. Morris, Rebecca Morgan. col., Unknown man, col.

Sept. 3d—Pryor, girl child, Fred Perry, boy, Jonas Houston, col., Maria, cook at Newman's......Sept. 4th—C. Bathke, Mrs. Fanny Brooks, Mrs. Jae. Perry, J. A. Chiasa, Mrs. Shorey's child girl, 5 years, Sow Lee, Chinaman, Mark Kyle.

Sept. 5th—Ed McKenzie, col., daughter of R B. Scott, 8 years. Josephine Fox, 5 years, Mrs. Thos. Mowbry, Mrs. Jones. wife Elder Jones, col., Lyman Stowell. H. Putnam, boy, W. A. Haycraft, Mrs. D. Shanahan, country.

Sept. 6th—Mrs. M. Morris, Elijah Gray, col., Jerry Strather, col, Philip Barnett, Miss Willie Scott, Milton Jones, painter, a young man, Caroline Zeigler, col.

Sept. 7th—Col. C. E. Morgan. Eliza Belfield, col., Perry, boy, Mrs. Cox, Capitola Harris, col., Jas. Perry, Wm. Telfer, Emma Duvall.

Sept. 8—Chas. Huntley, Jas. Young, col., Julius Ratchlitz, Maj. Alexander. col., Beontine White, colored girl, Mrs. Nellie Guy, col., J. Walker, boy, in country, Richard McCullough, Jas. Corney, Chas. Irving, col., Winnie Smith, col., Griffin Guy, col., Mrs. Young.

Sept. 9th—Dave Harris, col., Edward Caffall. Mrs. Geo. Sanford, Mrs. J. S. Ballard, Burden Bahn, col., Mrs. F. P. Smith, Geo. Stream.

Sept. 10th—Mrs. Shorey, Geo. Bird, Miss K. A. Ballard, Henry Harris, col., Fred. Pryor, Chas. Shows, col., Boynton Houston, col., Dr. Stafford, Aleck, butcher, Lulu Ware. col.

Sept. 11th—Willie Caffall, Mrs. Julia Pogle, Unknown blacksmith, Louisa Maskey, Lizzie Johnson, col., Mrs. T. P. Perry, Abe Smith, Emma Hawkins, col., Eva Wetherbee. Elliott Dodge, John Bannion, col., Wm. Brown, col., Geo. Dorman, Steve Sutton.

Sept. 12th—Louis Caffall, Louis Radjesky, Mrs. Beck, Mrs. Fleischer, Mrs. Trammel. Theo. Habicht,.

Sept. 13th—Mrs. L. P. Wetherbee, Mrs. B. Hassberg. Walter Quick, E. Steinberg, Wash Walker, col., Mrs. Platt, Ehler, boy, H. B. Putnam, Mrs. Ehler, Dr. V. F. P. Alexander, Robt. Cooper, Jas. McCann.

Sept. 14th—Raphael Marshall, Jas. Minzies......Sept. 15th—Rev. Duncan Green, Walter B. Butler, Thos. McLean, Frank Wagner, J. Radjesky, Long Hon, Chinaman, Jake Husk, col., Bennie Diggs, Wm. Taylor, Henrietta Rogers, col., Toll Underwood, col., Chas. Bigelow, col.

Sept. 16th—Ella Jones, child, col., Mrs. Ballard, Chas. Boswick, J. H. Buckner, Jas. Davidson, Stephen Green, Jas. Connell, Mary Jones, col., Kyle, Mrs. F. Pryor, Mrs. Henrietta Bathke, Joe Badwick, Jackson Hays, col., Bigelow child, Mrs. Habicht, Henry Laurens. Gus. Forrester.

Sept. 17th—Frank Gallagher, Johnnie Ballard, baby. D. E. Young, col., Mrs. M. Sievers, Anna Platt, Unknown man, Gus. Coughler, Geo. Brown, col., Helen Finlay, Frank P. Smith.

Sept. 18th—Henry Freundt, Willie Harris. colored boy. Mrs. L. Polle, Wm. Ehlers, W. L. Porter, John S. Ballard, Willie B. White, Nellie Warden, John Ralph, Margaret Williams, col., N. J. Nelson, M. Morris, W. P. Kretschmar

Leonard Phillips, Abe Wall, W. J. Manly, T. P. Perry, Tom Sylvester, Mary Jarves, col.. Caroline Marks, col., Chas. Williams, Unknown man, col., Fanny Diggs, Calvin Kelter, col.

Sept. 19—Lou Hamun, Dan. Shanahan, Elvira Blackburn, col., Mrs. J. S. Barnhurst, Dave Morris, Ben Sands, man, col., Micheal Duffy, Alex Moray, col.

Sept. 20th—Albert Wheeler, Mrs. T. B. Shaw, Mrs. Small,' John Simphondorfer, L. Wiesenfeldt.

Sept. 21st—Thomas Miggins, John Barnhurst, Julius Lockman, Geo. Trammel......Sept. 22d—Jas. McLean, Margaret French, col., J. Kintsler, A. B. Trigg, Jacob Watts, col., Eliza J. Clark, Arthur R. Yerger, Anna Berry, girl, Adolphe Fletcher, boy, L. P. Wetherbee, Amelia Kinstler, girl, Helen Bailey, babe, col., Lorenzo Griffin, col., Harry Vaughn.

Sept. 24th—Emma Pernel, col., Chas. Griffin, col., —— Perry, child, Anderson Greathouse, col., Mrs. L. M. Funoy, col., Fanny Kelly.

Sept. 25th—J. Gossett, Garrett Scott, Steven Stewart, col., A. Fleischer, Mrs. G. W. Elliott, John Manifold, Abe Hamburger, boy.....Sept. 26th— — Pryor, child, Bertha Morris girl, col., Forest Barr, C. F. Meisner, Racheal Radgesky, girl, Mrs. A. Ward.

Sept. 27th—Alec Grant, col., Dick Cheatham, col., Nancy J. Smith, col., Jas Gregory, col., Gus. McAlister......Sept. 28th—L. E. Morgan, G. W. Claiborne, colored child, Pat. Byrnes, Racheal Amburg, col., Infant child of W. J. French, Sophia Youcum, Geo. Brazier, W. Tilley, Jr., T. B. Speaks.

Sept. 29th—Mrs. L. Weisenfeldt, John H. Nelson, Eliza Kress, Helena Shaw, girl......Sept. 30th—Wes. Wetherbee, J. H. Saunders, col., Marshall Woodson, col., Henry Thornton, col., Mrs. L. M. Mary White, col.

Oct. 1st—L. M. Langley, Mrs. Mitchell, J. H. Saunder's child, col., Minnie Kleiber, Mrs. Stafford, Mary A. Cook......Oct. 2d—Rev. T. Page, Lena Herman, girl, Jake Byers, Louisa Clarke, Dr. McCall.

Oct. 3d—Alex Johnson, col., Milton Kelter, col......Oct. 4th—M. W. Johnson Cedar Manager, col., Walter S. Berry, child, Rosa Edingburg, col., Mrs. Mattie James, Monroe Fletcher, col.

Oct. 5th—Nancy Keene, col., King Hinds, col., G. W. Elliott, Thomas McMorris, col., Dan. Johnson, col......Oct. 6th—Dr. Archer......Oct. 7th—Mary Ann Barr, girl, col., Mable Wetherbee, girl, Infant child of Dave Morris......Oct. 8th —Mrs. E. C. Greenfield, Perry Ellis, Infant child of E. Johnson, col.

Oct. 10—Oscar Smith, col......Oct. 11—Wm. Myers, Geo. R. Clark......Oct. 12— Fred. Johnson, boy......Oct. 15—John Cottrell, Tom Johnson, boy; Infant of John Rice, col.. Infant of Dan. Wilson, col......Oct. 19—Phillis Carter, col......Oct. 20 --Emma Childs......Oct. 21—Loyd Talbot, col., Margaret Freeman, col......Oct 22 —Ah Ways, Chinaman..... Oct. 24—Adaline Geinelle.

Nov. 11—Sam Hammond......Nov. 13—Katie Brown, Mary Brown, col......Oct. 14—Gid Austin, col., James Jennings, col......Oct. 15—Mrs. Sam Brown, A. W. Shadd, col......Oct. 28—Mrs. Mather.

Deaths in the Country.—Henry Monk, Henry Lemler, Blanche Snowberger, child, —— Morzinski. child, M. J. Morzinski, Mrs. Marcella Hartman, Jack Winter, C. K. McAlister, Wat Brashear. Mrs. Wm. Montgomery, Shirley Winter, child, D. L. Stone, Dr. A. S. Gerdine, Dr. Oden, Dr. Gaddis, Mr. Kleiber, Mrs. C. A. Winter, Pat. McCune, Mrs. Felix McLean, Mrs. C. McAlister, Wm. Montgomery.

HOLLY SPRINGS.

Population when epidemic commenced, 3500; during epidemic 1500; of whom about 300 were white and 1200 colored. Total deaths, adult males: 130; adult females, 70; colored adult males, 48; colored adult females, 29; white children, 15; colored children, 12. Total deaths, 304. Total cases, about 1440. Mortality among whites, 71.66 per cent; among colored. 7.41 per cent.

Aug. 25—E. L. Downs and Miss Lake, from Grenada......August 31—A. W. Goodrich......Sept. 1—At. Wiltshire, from Grenada......Sept. 2—Wm. Mackin, from Memphis......Sept. 3—Isaac Tandler and James Chisin.

Sept. 4—A. F. Brown's child, H. A. McCroskey, Frank Gauter and Robert McLain.

Sept. 5—James Fort, Mrs. James Nutall, B. P. Oliver, Bateman's child, Mrs. Stephen Knapp, Wm. Hogan and Mrs. E. A. Thomas.

Sept. 6—Gus Smith, Herman Snider's child, B. D. Nabers, A. F. Moore, Mrs.

Leak, W. R. Todd, John Chenoweth, Sam Abernathy and Sam Crockett.

Sep. 7—B. S. Crump, Dr. Charles Bonner, James Walker, Chas. Glassy, James Nuttall, Sam Bonner and R. L. Watson......Sept. 6—Miss Julia Waite, Bateman's child and Mrs. Blank.

Sept. 9—R. G. Campbell, Thomas A. Falconer, George Wing, Virginia Lynch and U. H. Ross.

Sept. 10—Wm. Crump, Mrs. J. R. Dougherty, Miss Cornelia Record, Hal. Johnson, Clem. Read, Victor Smith, W. J. Marett, Mrs. S. H. Pryor, Willie Wooten, Charles Chenoweth, E. T. Brinkley's child, Alex. Seyple, J. C. Potter, R. W. Fort and A. A. Armstrong.

Sept. 11—Clarissa Davis, Father Operti, Charles Schneider, Winfield S. Featherston, Jr., Mrs. Richard Daniel and Richard Daniel.

Sept. 12—Minerva Lynch, Miss Read, Henry Epps and Scott Epps.

Sept. 13—Mr. Brannon, Lizzie Lane, (colored,) E. T. Brinkley's child, E. W. Upshaw, Mrs. John Potter, Mrs. R. Hastings, Sam Kimball and Dinah Ingram, (colored.)......Sept. 14—Mariah Anderson, (colored.)

Sept. 15—George Kimball, Ben Casey, Pat McGuire, George Johnson, (colored,) and Em. Jones, (colored.)

Sept. 16—Laura Demmy, Lewis Thompson, Mr. Dunn, James M. Kean, Lotta Ingraham, (colored,) O. J. Quiggins' child, and Mrs. George Kimball.

Sept. 17—Mrs. E. D. Miller, Caroline Washington, (colored,) Ben. Boyd, (colored,) Mrs. R. L. Watson, Peter Webber, Miss Mary Stewart and Mrs. W. S. Featherston.

Sept. 18—Mrs. John Foreman, J. W. Webber, J. H. Stone, Mrs. Martin Knable and Jane McGary.

Sept. 19—Stephen Knapp, Mrs. Louis Thompson, child of Rebecca Lea, (colored,) Wm. Collins, (colored,) and Col H. W. Walter.

Sept. 20—E. T. Brinkley, Capt. Jno. Fennell, Dr. Manning, Miss Lizzie Butler and Howard Falconer.

Sept. 21—Hugh Winburn and Julia Stojowski......Sept. 22—Sister Stanislas, Avent Walter, John Larouche, Eugene Leidy, Jr., Charles Harris, (colored,) Jim Fowler, (colored,) Molly Cox's child, (colored,) Henry Harris, (colored,) Mary Gholson and Henry Carter, (colored.)

Sept. 23—Miss Liza Allen, Albert Rollins, (colored,) Henry Morton, (colored,) Mrs. Stone, Kinloch Falconer, Miss Darthula Allen, Miss Nancy Allen and Dr. F. M. Fennell.

Sept. 24—Thomas Henderson's child, Margaret Glassey, Mrs. Gaitley's son, Willie Castello, Dr. J. W. Fennell and Amelia Maughan.

Sept. 25—Dan Phillips, (colored,) Jacob Berry, (colored,) John Power, Miss Annie Stewart and Mrs. Hutchinson.

Sept. 26—Mrs. Harrington, Wm. Yancy's child, Jim Wells, Dr. Lewis, Mrs. Yancy, James R. L. Hunt, Frank Walter, Mrs. Jeff. McGowan, Jimmie Walter, Gordon Allen, Sister Stella, P. Hebdon and J. M. Lumkin.

Sept. 27—Mr. Johnson, Glenn Fant, John Banks John Hastings, Mr. Gholston, at depot, Mrs. Kate O'Gray, Jim Wells' wife, Mrs. Archie Straws and Cowan Roxy.

Sept. 28—Thos. Wade, Mrs. McGhery, Alex. Hohenwart, Austin Saunders, Mrs. Crown McGuire, Miss Lucy Fort, Sister Margarette, Martin Thomas, Molly Virginia, Eli Walker, Guy Allen, colored child, and Miss Georgie Featherston.

Sept. 29—C. H. Walker, Dr. W. O. McKinney, Mrs. McDermott, unknown white lady, unknown person, Dan Oliver, Wm. Washington, (colored,) L. P. Parish, Jno. German, Jno. Pearson, Eli Chew, (colored,) and Lucinda Simms, (colored.)

Sept. 30—Strauss' infant, Herr's infant, Rufus Howard, (colored,) Doctor Raymond, (colored,) Henry Elliott, (colored,) Flora Anderson, (colored,) Smith Baker, Randall Moore, (colored,) and Miss Christina Carlson.

Oct. 1—Mrs. C. J. Herr, Mrs. Parish, A. C. Henderson, Mike Tiernan, Haywood McKissack, Henry Cowan and Joseph Herr.

Oct. 2—Sister Corinthia, Peter Stineman, Maughans' child, H. J. McKeugh, Amanda Sutton, (colored,) Martin Knable, Jane Hill, (colored,) Webber's child, Augustus Bowman, Martha Walker, Mrs. Julia Roberts and Col. A. J. Hess, of Philadelphia.

Oct. 3—Selden Fant, Daniel Gray, (colored,) Mrs. B. A. Myers, Jim Wells' child, (colored,) and Hal Johnson's child, (colored,) Thos. Gilbert, (colored.)

Oct. 4—Mr. Daily, E. H. Crump, Miss Lizzie Malci and James Henry......Oct. 5—Sister Victoria, Millie Bradford's child, (colored,) Mr. Miller, Lucius Boxley, (colored,) Henry Edmundson, (colored,) John Hawkins, (colored,) and Mr. Diller.

Oct. 6—Miss Allen and G. Strather, (colored)......Oct. 7—Jake Malei, and Dow Craft's wife, (colored.)......Oct. 8—Allen Brogden, (colored.)......Oct. 9—James G. Adams, James McHugh and George Parks.

Oct. 10—Child of Chas. Harris, Paton Edmondson, (colored,) and Mrs. Haley. ......Oct. 11—Jeff McGowan, (colored,) and Sister Lorentia......Oct. 12—Ida McGowan, (colored,) Mrs. James Miller, and G. Thomas.......Oct. 13—Jacob Krouse and Alsey Lea, (colored.)

Oct. 14—Mrs. Lane, Millie Shotwell, (colored,) Willie Price, (colored,) and Edward Brim.

Oct. 15—Wife of Paton Edmundson, (colored,) and son of Shokesburg......Oct. 16—John Ellis, (colored,) and Joshua Watson......Oct. 17—Child of Paton Edmundson, (colored,) and Charity Gains, (colored.)

Oct. 18—Joel Lackey, Dennis Lane and Ed. Willis......Oct. 19—James Calvin, Burton Connington and Willis Edwards......Oct. 20—Rachel Cochran, (colored,) Henry Vandive and Polly Martin.

Oct. 21—Robert King, Squire Yowell, Lula Lessner and Mr. Mooney......Oct. 22—Peter Goalar's son, Alf. Rogers, (colored,) Mrs. Compton, Amelia Martin, (colored,) and Thos. Dressler.

Oct. 23—Harried Moseley, (colored.)......Oct. 24—Dr. Compton, Josephine Martin, (colored,) John Kimbrough and John Tiernan......Oct. 25—W. J. L. Holland, Mrs. Dr. McKinney, Mrs. Peter Gheelan and Dennis Gaitwood, (colored.)

Oct. 26—Mrs. Gutheries and Mrs. Byers......Oct. 28—Mrs. Sam Collin, (colored......Oct. 29—Miss Cora McWilliams......Oct. 30—Tede Nelms......Nov. 1—R. A. McWilliams' twins.

Nov. 2—Thomas Hebdon, and Henry Armstead's child......Nov. 5—Robert Adams and Eugene Cochran......Nov. 14—W. T. Barry's child......Nov. 15—James Donohue......Nov. 18—J. E. Tobin.

A GARDEN OF DEATH.

HOLLY SPRINGS, MISS., Sept. 17.—The writer of this, and those who so heroically stand by his side, have endured every vicissitude of war, but all acknowledge that they have never seen any such dangers as threaten us every moment. The orphans who crowd around us every morning and tell us they are left alone, or the faithful nurses who come bearing keys of the homes entirely swept of every soul that lived there, and asking us to take charge, and the dying messages brought to our ears, are enough to remind us that we are in the midst of the very garden of death. One day we meet our friend and do all we can in the good work; and the next we hear that he has fallen and appeals for our aid.

To-day I saw a great strong man burst into tears, and say: "Oh, God! I had rather have died than to have lived and witnessed such scenes." But with all this gloom and sadness around us, we feel that we must do our duty, let the consequences be what they may. I really believe were it not for messages of sympathy, and the offers of aid we receive from our mournful friends far away, we would die—all of us—from wretchedness and despondency. We of the little band who live here have associated with us the noblest set of strangers that ever came to the relief of their fellowman. There are a number of these, some whose names have already been given, but not one more devoted to our cause, or more faithful at his post than D. Flannery, the superintendent of the telegraph company, who has come here and remained with us, doing immense work, and no one has ever yet heard him complain. He leaves us to-morrow, to our deep sorrow and regret, but a faithful successor takes his desk in the person of W. T. Harrison, of New Orleans, who has heroically volunteered to share our fate.

Chicago is represented by Capt. J. C. Tucker, who has as bravely and as faithfully stood by us as a man could.

The death list to date reaches the startling figures of ninety-five, and not three weeks has passed since the plague began its work of death in our midst.   HOLLAND.

HOLLY SPRINGS, MISS., Sept. 27.—There are about four hundred people for the fever to feed upon, and quite as many in their beds. All the time we have underestimated the magnitude of this plague. Entire families, some of them numbering eight or ten, are down with the disease. Among the physicians, ten have been stricken down, four of these have died. Five druggists have gone down, three have died. Of the ministers who have fallen, two are dead. In the post-office, two out of three are in the cemetery. Several of the nurses have taken it and some have not recovered. In almost every way the fever has manifested a mortality simply appalling. Three days ago thirty new cases and twelve deaths were reported, and the following forty-five new cases and ten deaths; while yesterday there were twenty-three cases and eleven deaths. To-day the number of new cases is eighteen and the deaths twelve. After having recruited five different times the relief committee yesterday numbered only one.

HOLLAND.

The following is an extract of a letter from the wife of the pastor of the Presbyterian Church, at Holly Springs, Miss.:

We seem here to dwell in "the valley of the shadow of death." Mr. Craig has been sick for twenty-seven days. He can never be any nearer the grave until he is laid in it. He does not remember anything that occurred for two weeks, and I have had to tell him little by little of the long list of loved ones and lost ones. I have had quite a hospital. Miss C. is down in one room and Mr. S. in the parlor. I have no one to help me; can get no one. The two nurses are busy with the sick. * * * I know you all do feel for us, but you 'can never know all the painful story, the terrible physical sufferings; these mournful, unattended burials; the sad stillness of death and desolation that prevails. Oh, it is beyond the power of words to describe. * * * Some (a great many) have died in unutterable agony and wild delirium; others have gone down step by step into the Jordan, leaving sweet echoes as they passed out of sight. Dr. Frank Fennell died in the country, almost neglected. Dr. Wm. Fennell attended him and with one other person buried him in the night. To-day Dr. Wm. Fennell was brought to town and buried. General Featherston is better. He moved to the country; his son Winfield died, and then Mrs. Featherston; both were coffined and buried at two o'clock at night by strange hands. . . . You can perhaps imagine how lonely I am when I tell you that I am the only lady between your house and Mr. N's, one way, and Dr. D's and the Mc. place on the other (fully a mile). I seldom see a white face except the doctor's. Sometimes I sit out on the front porch and cry—so much that is sad around me and my utter powerlessness to help over whelms me. Oh, may God have mercy upon us all. He has laid His hands on our idols; may we worship and serve Him alone. . . I live in a kind of dream, a fearful dream, and can not think or write coherently. There is something peculiarly near and vivid in the sympathy of Christian friends, and I never so valued their prayers as now. You do not know how I feel as I lie down at night, breathing the very air in which this "pestilence walketh in darkness." It may please the Lord to spare me. I know I am His, living or dying.

FROM TELEGRAMS BY COLONEL HOLLAND.

ROOMS RELIEF COMMITTEE, HOLLY SPRINGS, October 18, 1879.

Mr. J. C. Young, Danville, Ky.:

* * * * * * * * *

Since the inception of the disease there has been the most indescribable confusion in every department. This was occasioned by the heads of every department being stricken first. For instance: The Nurse Department lost Colonel Walter first, Colonel Falconer next, and their successor was so completely exhausted by his labors I had to look after it for several days myself. His clerks, one by one, left, till seven have gone down. In the drug store three were stricken down, and two of these from New Orleans. In the post office all stricken, two died, two convalescent. In the express office two had fever, one died. In the Commissary Department all went down. In the Medical Department eleven physicians fell, four died, and one of the convalescents will never get well. Of ministers here five fell, two died. Of messengers for Relief Committee not one could stand; all went, half died. Of nurses two out of seven had it, several died. Of teamsters all save one, and since this was written he has fallen; several died. Of the Relief Committee I am all left of the first body, the second also. It has been recruited seven times, and still there are only three who have not had the fever—two of these of New Orleans, who are acclimated. I would not make this sad recital, but I feel well satisfied the outside world does not appreciate our situation. We have a safe full of keys and valuables belonging to families that have all been swept away. In one house here there were twenty-seven inmates; all had the fever, eight died, and at no time were there less than ten in bed. The nurses fell there like the rest; one fainted after she had been in the sick room only an hour, and at once took the fever; she is from New Orleans, and is an old yellow fever nurse. In other families there are none left, save, perhaps, some little lonely orphan, whose tears would melt a heart of stone. We have so many orphans to look after, who are left in an unprotected state and without anything. They throng to these rooms daily, and recite stories of real truth that would startle any one. The Sisters of Bethlehem have exhibited a heroism simply grand and beautiful. They came into the hospital and watched with sleepless care the stricken patients, as if it were a pleasure; none too poor, too black, too repulsive for them to attend with special pleasure, and speak words of cheer and comfort, that made the patients feel like they were at home and under a sister's care. One by one the loveliest and the best fell, till all went down save one—Sister Laurentia. She stood like a monument of womanly graces, brightening us all by her brilliant eyes and cheerful talk. Finally this good woman followed the rest, and now she sleeps by the side of five others in our cemetery. In all this revel of disease and death it has been our pleasure to witness some of the grandest examples of manly and womanly virtue I have ever expected to see. If my time was my own, I should like to speak of some of these, but when we meet I shall tell you of some of them.

In the hurry of writing this poor letter, I forgot to thank you for your kind invitation to visit your city after I could be spared from here. I do feel deeply grateful, and no place I would more like to visit, no people I would like more to see than yours. But I felt I had been spared, and that my services were needed in other infected places after my work was done here, so I offered myself to Jackson, Miss. But there is at present no one to take my place here, and I shall stay until some one does. We have but three or four citizens here on duty; balance strangers. With high esteem, Sir, I am sincerely your friend, W. J. L. HOLLAND.

HOLLY SPRINGS, MISS., Sept. 11, 1878.—Some eight hundred people here—whites, three hundred; colored, five hundred, besides hundreds in the country who have fled their homes without anything. Many of them are falling victims to the insatiable disease. Such appeals as they bring to us would melt a heart of stone. I might tell of some of these, but the crowded state of the wires forbids. The requiems to the dying are sung by the honest watch-dog, whose master or mistress is being borne away to the silent city of the dead.

The outside world can not imagine what is going on here. I would like to tell, but no words can express it. The widow and orphan appeal to us hourly for comfort. To-night a young woman lately married, was brought to the office weeping bitterly. She said, "Please send this telegram to my friends. My husband is dead. What shall I do?"

Scores of instances hourly occur to remind us that some extraordinary calamity is in our once happy and prosperous little town, bringing grief to every home.

September 21st, Frank Walter and his brother James, who have so faithfully and efficiently filled their places, surrendered to the terrible monster. Hardly had the news reached our ears before it was announced that Dr. Sheldon, representing the Can't-Get-Away Club of Mobile, and who had charge of the hospital here, was a victim. The physicians with one accord give to this man the post of honor, as he has turned out more convalescents than any one of them. Many bright and shining lights may go down in this great struggle, but not one of a more brilliant character than Dr. Sheldon. Like Dr. Manning whose heaven-lit blue eyes seemed to reflect the depth and purity of a great and good soul within, Sheldon was mourned by us all. His convalescents were numbered by the score, and they all speak of how tenderly the little doctor nursed and cared for them. The situation is growing worse.

The hospital is full, and it looks as if every man must go down. The godlike Sisters, in their mission of mercy, have paid in their conduct a beautiful tribute to Christian fortitude. There are thirteen of them, belonging to Bethlehem Academy, the Catholic school here, and ten have fallen. First the good Father O'Berti died like a true Christian minister. Father Lancey, his successor, goes his daily rounds with a smile on his face which we love to see.

Every messenger and clerk around this office have fallen. Every clerk has gone, and each morning as I take my place there are tales of sorrow told me. Wish I could paint them for your readers. Hourly scenes occur which I long to tell about. Such a calamity never befel a people. All we do is done to help and cheer. When the mails are opened and the noble men around me look up with tearful eyes, I look away and wish I could stay this fearful scourge. Holly Springs has reason to congratulate herself; for in all parts of the United States the good people have responded to her calls. How shall we thank them?

*　　　*　　　*　　　*　　　*　·　　*　　　*

Already we have spoken of Colonel Walter, but we little dreamed he would be suddenly taken from us. If we could weep, we would weep. If we could mourn, we would mourn. If we could tell the woe and heartache, there would be tears, there would be all that sorrow and distress could ask. But the silence of the tomb pervades the hearts of our little band. The best have gone down, and we have asked others to take their places. In not one instance have we seen the one that would refuse to take his place whenever we assigned him. This is no time for compliments; but when the day comes, the public shall know who has stood by us.

We said we had no tears, but there is a time when they flow, and that is when we read the telegrams, the letters from friends far away. Tell them they give us heart and make us stronger, better, and brighter, but for this we would feel heartsick and weary, and our suffering people tender their prayerful thanks for the kind and generous assistance their friends in all parts of the Union have shown.

HIS LAST DISPATCH.

HOLLY SPRINGS, MISS., October 19.—To-day there have been six new cases and one death. Your correspondent happens to be among the new cases, after struggling with Yellow Jack since the beginning of the epidemic. He desires through you and in the name of this people to express the lasting gratitude to our friends in every part of the Union, who have so generously and nobly contributed to us in so many ways.

W. J. L. HOLLAND.

Colonel Holland died October 23d, and in his dying moments was nursed by her whom he expected to marry.

DRY GROVE.

Sketch Prepared for this Report by Rev. W. K. Douglass, D. D.

Dry Grove, a mere cross-roads hamlet, lies twenty-two miles southwest from Jackson, being ten miles west of the New Orleans Railroad, and eighteen miles south of the Vicksburg and Meridian. It is not itself upon any thoroughfare, but its peculiarly remote and secluded situation had become a proverb. At the breaking out of the epidemic its immediate center comprised two stores, a postoffice, wagon shop, blacksmith, shoemaker, public gin and mill, physician's office, Masonic Lodge and school house, and an Episcopalian Church. Calling this a village, its western limit was the residence of Dan. Williams, Esq., the neighborhood Justice, and its eastern, the Training School for the education of candidates for the University of the Episcopal Church under the charge of the Rector of that Church. It was vacation at that institution, though three of the students were present, all of whom fell victims to the disease. It is estimated that within the above limits were gathered, white and colored, not more than one hundred souls. The surrounding country is thickly studded with small plantations, chiefly cultivated by their proprietors, who, according to their location, trade at Dry Grove, Terry, Crystal Springs, and Edwards. There were two physicians, Drs. West and Dickson, practising in partnership. Another physician, Dr. Mitchell, lived two miles north, whose time had been chiefly given to his plantation, gin and mills, but who gave his services with praiseworthy self-devotion during the epidemic. Dr. E. Crum and Dr. Herring, practising each about four miles distant, also went in and out doing what they could.

Everything in the situation seemed to indicate more than ordinary security from contagion. The neighborhood had been sought by persons desiring to escape from threatened railroad towns, and applications for places for refuge were received by the people of Dry Grove at the very time when the pestilence, walking in its own darkness, was laying its hands on its victims.

The middle of August, the pond supplying the public mill with water, was drained and deepened. The character of the deposits dragged out upon the adjacent soil, gave serious apprehensions of malarial poisoning. Hence, when on the first of September, Dr. Dickson, whose residence was nearest, Jack Stubbs, Howard Callendar, brothers-in-law and partners in the wagon shop, Mr. Callandar's daughter, F. Cherry, a student of the Divinity School, Miss Horton, and a number of colored people, were taken ill, no grave fears were excited.

Dr. Dickson went to his father's house, some miles distant, and was in a few days apparently restored. The Callendar family did not call in a physician, but as their case excited universal sympathy, night and day watches from the neighbors were in constant attendance. When, in a few days, the fatal termination of Stubbs's case became probable, the result was popularly attributed to imprudent exposure and want of medical advice, at the outset, rather than to any fatal character of the disorder. At noon, on Saturday, September 7, Stubbs died. Mr. Callendar and his daughter on the 8th, all having had black vomit. A number of cases immediately followed, but there were no further deaths until the 12th, when young

Cherry was taken. Deaths followed daily. The case of this young boy, far from home among strangers, excited unusual attention, and being among the first, he was nursed and tended with unremitting care and but an hour before his death supposed convalescent. In two weeks the physician who attended him, and all who had been with him in his illness, were laid in the silent earth at his side. All indeed, save one, the writer of this sketch.

A variety of circumstances combined to cause much individual suffering. There was, after the first days, always "lack of woman's nursing," though no "lack of woman's tears." For a time it was impossible to receive and distribute the relief so generously, indeed lavishly, sent from friends. The scattered dwellings of the people, with the insufficient means of transportation, the claims of dear 'dying ones at home, interfered with those neighborly offices which all were more than ready to perform. A single instance, among many, may give an idea of the destitution. The writer called at a house where he found all the inmates, four in number, three of whom died, in bed. Two professional nurses were there, but not a particle of food nor any, even the most necessary, conveniences of a sick room. He was himself riding a mule, every vehicle being in use, but what arms and pockets could hold was soon brought. His own case, with many advantages over others for assistance, may also strengthen the impression which can never reach the reality. As one after another the dead had been borne forth from my house, the attendants had been sent to more needed households. Two who had been offered that night, had thus been sent, and my wife and myself were alone with a single hired nurse, a colored woman from New Orleans. The last stroke of that "insatiate archer" fell at two o'clock, and I arose myself and dressed for the first time and watched by the silent dead until morning. The expected help not having come, I walked out from that dwelling which I had once thought never to leave alive, in search of some one to bury the dead. I passed up the deserted street in vain. At last I saw a man on horseback, and called to him. He said: "I have come for ice for my wife who is very low, but I can send it by a negro and I will make the coffin if I can find any lumber." I replied that I would strip the ceiling from a room. He then said: "I have a shed at home which I can tear down, and I will use that." We went to the church 'yard, where I found the negroes we had employed to dig graves, and selected a spot. Our church yard was filled, and I marked the grave outside. I returned to my home, sent the nurse to one who was soon to follow, and watched through the day alone. In the evening the coffin came and with it Dr. Mitchell and Mr. Caston, my faithful assistant, whose hands had been full with the duties thrown upon him by my illness. But for these, I must have placed the dead in the coffin with my own hands. As it was, it was necessary for me to drive the little wagon used as a hearse. The dogs seeing the house deserted, followed, and made the funeral procession. I repeated the glorious words of the burial service, and Mr. Caston, before the grave was closed, went to his bed after three weeks of faithful service for the Lord Christ, to receive so early his crown of martyrdom.

That very day, the Howard Association of Crystal Springs, sent two of their number, Judge Holt, a man of rare experience in epidemics, and Dr. Jones, to establish a depot of supplies. This reduced our chaos to order and relieved some sources of suffering.

It was no fault of our people that so great confusion had existed. At that time there was not in the neighborhood of Dry Grove a man who was not ill himself or bound to the bedside of the sick of his own household. Those who could labor did their duty with a steady courage, worthy of the desperate battle-field on which they fought. Our physicians, West and Dickson, remained bravely at their posts. The latter was himself one of the victims. From the neighborhood around, Drs. Mitchell, Crum, Deason, Herring and Jones, the three last were severely attacked but recovcred. The family of Col. T. S. Dabney, three miles distant, came at a time when such help was most welcome and nursed until one of their number took the fever herself. Geo. C. French and Wm. T. Caston, Divinity students, labored until they fell victims to the unrelenting destroyer. Ular Flewellen, J. E. Johnston, young Allie Mitchell, Harry Carson, are among the survivors who can be mentioned with praise.

The original source of contagion still remains an inscrutable mystery. Many remarks have been in circulation, all of which have been diligently scrutinized and their falsity ascertained. But whatever view may be taken of the origin there can be no question that the unexampled fatality must be attributed to local causes. The "germs" fell into good soil and bore their fatal fruit.

The scenes of suffering cannot be described; they can only be indicated by statistics. One household, the Coker family, ten in number, were all ill at once. Eight of these died within a week. The Morgan family, four in number, were all taken at once—three died. At the Episcopal parsonage all were sick at the same time, and but one recovered.

The undersigned desires to say for himself that with a most profoundly grateful heart and a deep sense of the benefits conferred upon his people, he finds it impossible to make acknowledgment in words. He must be either much more, or much less, than man not to have felt in his heart the extremity of human misery. He does not attempt even to himself to vindicate the ways of Divine Providence; that is presumption. But he can truly say that he finds his confidence in humanity strengthened, his conviction of the power of a Christian faith deepened as he sees the old martyr spirit not yet dead among the disciples of Christ.

W. K. DOUGLASS.

CASES AND DEATHS AT DRY GROVE.

Jack Stubbs, died Sept. 7.
Hiram Callendar, died Sept. 8.
Lulie Callendar, died Sept. 8.
Frank Cherry, died Sept. 12.
Dan. Williams, Esq., died Sept. 14.
Mrs. Phoebe Stubbs, died Sept. 15.
Miss Nellie Horton, died Sept. 18.
Walter Williams, died Sept. 18.
Mrs. Octavia Williams, died Sept. 18.
Rev. Wm. K. Douglass, recovered.
Hugh Stewart, P. M., died Sept. 24.
Geo. C. French, died Sept. 22.
Mrs. Sarah Douglas, died Sept. 26.
Miss Netta Douglas, died Sept. 23.
Henry M. Williams, died Sept. 25.
Mrs. James Coker, died Sept. 24.
Mrs. J. H. Flewellen, died Sept. 26.
Sarah Flewellen, died Sept. 26.
Mrs. Elizabeth Clowers, died Sept. 27.
Miss Mary Coker, died Sept. 27.
Miss Jennie Coker, died Sept. 27.
Miss Bettie Caston, died Sept. 27.
Zella Flewellen, died Sept. 29.
Jimmie Stewart, died Sept. 29.
Arthur Stewart, died Sept. 29.
Henry Coker, recovered.
Nettie Coker, recovered.
Mrs. J. E. Johnston, recovered.
Nettie Stewart, died Oct. 1.
Miss Edith Caston, died Oct. 2.
Charles Caston, died Oct. 3.

W. Thomas Caston, died Oct. 3.
Miss Jane Flewellen, died Oct. 3.
Wiggins Caston, died Oct. 4.
Ular Flewellen, recovered.
James H. Stewart, died Oct. 8.
Geo. Dixon, M. D., Oct. 9.
W. B. Herring, M. D., recovered.
W. M. Denson, M. D., recovered.
George Morgan, died Oct. 10.
Charles Morgan, died Oct. 12.
Mrs. Elizabeth Morgan, died Oct. 12.
Miss Mary Morgan, recovered.
Mr. Calvin Griffin, died Oct. 13.
Mr. Thomas Wall, died Oct. 13.
Mrs. Mary Johnson, died Oct. 14.
Mrs. Smedes, recovered.
Ethel Douglass, recovered.
Miss Leona Rogers, recovered.
Miss E. C. Moncure, recovered.
Two children of Augusta Terry, date of their death unknown.
Maggie Johnson, died Oct. 15.
Miss Kyle, died Oct. 20.
Mr. W. D. Kyle, died Oct. 25.
Mrs. Amanda Johnson, Oct. 25.
Mrs. Cooke, Howard nurse, died Oct. 25.
Susie McCowen, recovered.
Mr. Calvin Williams, died Oct. 30.
Miss Judith West, recovered.

Total cases, 60; total deaths, 46.

There were a large number of negroes ill from the first, of whom not more than one or two died, and it is doubtful whether these were yellow fever at all.

PORT GIBSON.

Population about 1100. Frst case, August 3d. Total cases in town and country, about 1500; total deaths in town and country, about 275.

DEATHS IN PORT GIBSON AND ADJACENT COUNTRY.

C. L. Barrot,
Mrs. Paul Barrot,
Paul Barrot,
Miss Sallie Burnet,
Rev. S. R. Ber 'ron,
John Broughton,
Jimmie Broughton,
Mrs. J. C. Bertron,
Dr. Brumley,
John Crowley,
Wm. Daugherty,
Andy Dempsy,
May Daugherty,
Mary Daugherty,
Willie Day,
Joseph Day,
Charlie Day,
Miss A. Disheroon,
William Disheroon,
Lindsey R. Evans,
Mrs. R. L. Evans,
Mr. Faust,
Mrs. Faust,
Maj. J. D. Fairly,
Butler Fife.
Wm. Fife, (child)
Eliza Fife,
Wm. Fife,
W. R. Gordon, (son
of R. F. Gordon,)
Miss Lizzie Green,
Miss Gayoza Green,
E mma Griffing,
W. A. Green (daugh-
ter)
Wm. Guess, (child)
Estelle Greer,
Joseph Green,

Mrs. Mary Greer,
Malcomb Gilehurst,
Levenia Greer,
Eugenia Greer,
Simon Harris,
Rev. Geo. Hall,
Mrs. Huber,
Mrs. T. C. Healey
and two children,
T. S. Hawkins (in-
fant,)
Tomie Hawkins,
Eva Humphreys, (D.
B. H.)
Ben Humphreys, (G.
W. H.)
Mrs. D. B. Hum-
phreys,
Jacob Haeley,
John Henderson,
Mrs. John Ingram
and child,
T. E. Jones,
Eliza Jones,
Miss Fannie John-
son,
Dorsey Kilcrease,
Thomas Kelley,
Thos. Kava-
naugh,
Mrs. S. M. Kirk-
bride,
And. J. Louder,
Samuel Little,
Geo. Leisher,
Frank Leisher,
Mrs. Sam'l Mackcy,

John Leisher,
E. E. Leisher, (in-
fant.)
Mrs. Mary M. Lynch
Janie Leonard,
Johnie Lee,
Tyre Lilly,
Billy McCann,
R. H. McClinton,
Miss Jennie Mason,
W. H. Martin,
Dr. Wm. Moore,
Ella Moore,
Duncan Moore,
James Murphey,
Simpson McClure,
Mrs. L, T. Newman,
Bernard Newman,
Sidney Newman,
Corinne Newman.
Patrick Nolan,
James Nance, Jr.,
Mike O'Day,
Katie O'Connell,
Mrs. Dan O'Connell
Bertron Purnell,
Mrs. R. S. Patton,
R. S. Patton, Jr.,
Joseph Price,
Robert J. Price,
Mrs. Eliza Price,
J. A. Price,
—— Price,
Mrs. John Peoples,
Aug. Sammelson,
Mrs. H. J. Simonson
Mrs. Dr. J. G. Strow-
bridge,

Chas. Shreve, Sr.,
Chas. Shreve, Jr.,
Mrs. Chas. Shreve,
Dr. J. G. Strow-
bridge,
T. N. Stewart,
Geo. Scharff,
Mrs. Geo. Scharff,
Dr. H. C. Snodgrass
A. K. Shafer, Jr.,
Dr. W. D. Sprott,
Philip Sylvester,
Adolph Thaler,
Mrs. Adolph Thaler
Rodolph Thaler,
Tobias Thaler,
John Thaler,
Judge Jno. B. Trash-
er,
Mrs. T. C. Trevel-
lian,
Casey Thomas,
Mrs. Tucker,
Fritz. Ungerer,
Gen. J. D. Vertner,
(infant)
Miss Mary Wheeless
Capt. H. S. Wheeless
John Woods,
Charlie Weeks,
Jimie Weeks,
N. S. Walker, (in-
fant)
Dr. Thomas Young,
Mrs. Dr. Thomas
Young,
Maj. Hasie (child)

Total number of colored deaths, 95.

Total number of cases treated in the county, not less than 1,200.

The above list of deaths is made up with the assistance of Howard officers Gage, Englesing, Fulkerson, and J. L. Foote, undertaker. It is not claimed that it is a full list of deaths in the county, from the fact that to obtain a full and complete list is impossible. Many white and colored people have died from this fever of which I have no official information thus far. The Howards have extended their helping hand to every corner of the county that could be reached. Local pickets alone kept them from covering the whole ground.   R. F. GORDON,

Oct. 31st, 1878.   Health Officer, Port Gibson, Miss.

LAKE.

Population about 350. Total cases, 330. Total deaths, 80.

DEATHS AT LAKE.

W. E. Crowson, Mrs. W. E. Crowson, Frank Tate, Lee C. Scott, George Jones' col., Ann Bragg, col., Randall Flowers, col., W. H. Evers, H. Y. McFarland, Dr.

J. J. Tate, L. B. Wilkins. John Clay, W. J. Crosby, Rob't Davidson, Semp. Tate, Matthew Young, Mrs. W. S. Hoskins, Rev. Wm. Banks, col., John Bragg's child, col., Mrs. Martha Lowry, Geo. F. Lowry, J. S. Yarborough, Mrs. Thos. Ray, Mamie Evers, Mrs. J. P. Snead, John Couch, Mrs. J. S. Yarborough, Carrie Evers, Chas. McFarland, Miss Lula Lowry, Mrs. Evers, Mary McFarland, S. D. Kennedey, J. N. Couch, John H. Crosby, Jesse Long, Sarah Burge, col., Mrs. Hugh McFarland, P. Saunders, Mrs. G. C McCallum, Mrs. M. P. Saunders, Miss Fannie Saunders, Mrs. S. D. Kennedy, Sarah Ann January, Miss Tate, Mrs. Evers' babe, Mrs. Shackelford, of Meridian.

Sept. 28—Windom Moody, col......Oct. 1—Ella Burge......Oct. 2—Mary Mc-Callum, Mrs. Kittie Scott, Chas. Banks, col., Oscar Long, Rob't Hoskins.

Oct. 3—Willie Weaver......Oct. 4—Lyda Adams, L. Ritter, nurse, Mrs. R. A. Ray......Oct. 5—Mrs. Rachael Burge, Adolphus Long.

Oct. 6—John R. Weaver, Raney McGroarty, W. J. Adams......Oct. 5—Kate McCallum......Oct. 10—Richard Burge, Henry Clay Atkins, col.

Oct. 11—Mrs. Jas. Stewart, Charley McCallum, Mrs. Stewart's daughter.

Oct. 12—Matilda Burge, col......Mrs. Sarah Wells, Lafayette Weaver.

Oct. 15—Tommy Weaver, Rob't Tate. Wm. Nichols......Oct. 20—Albert Cole's child, col......Oct. 21—Stella Burge, Miss Nettie Burge......Oct. 22—Richard Burge.

Dr. F. E. Daniel was assigned to duty at Lake by the Howard Association at Jackson. The following is an extract from one of his letters:

One physician and four nurses arrived from Vicksburg. More needed. We want mattresses and blankets, also a druggist and a cook for the soup house. Every household is broken up and not a family has escaped the fever.

After the storm many new graves sunk and emitted extremely offensive odors which attracted the buzzards. Of course it was remedied, but seems to have strongly impressed the prevailing fever—which heretofore, although malignant in many cases, was amenable to treatment. It is now unmanageable, and treatment heretofore successful beyond the average results, appears to make no impression whatever. Many cases have black vomit in the first stage, (during the fever,) and sometimes in a few hours after being attacked. The wind was from the north after the storm, and the graveyard is north of and near the town; and an excellent family living nearest the graveyard were all attacked at once, and most violently—seven in number. They are Mrs. Hugh McFarland, whose husband died recently, her three children, (two now dying,) her sister, Miss Fanny Sanders, her mother and father, Mr. and Mrs. P. Sanders. Dr. Gresham, of Forest, is in the same house, now convalescent. Amongst the recent cases in addition to those above mentioned are Capt. W. M. Thornton, President of the Citizens' Aid Association. He is doing well. His wife is convalescent, also Col. D. S. Holmes, and wife. Their son very sick. The last deaths are Miss Lulu Lowry—her father, G. F. Lowry, Col. Yarborough, Mayor of Lake, and his wife—several of the Lowry children are now down. You can form no idea of the suffering and distress here. The houses are generally small and several patients in one small room frequently. Many die probably who could be cured under more favorable circumstances; frequently the shock of seeing a child or husband or brother die and be carried out instantly prostrates a patient previously doing well. This fever was extinguished here at one time, but the people, deceived by the appearance of safety opened up the infected houses and aired the bedding and next day we had some twenty new cases. Meridian has been and is still supplying us with everything.

The facts with regard to the gasses arising from the graves, and the airing of the infected bedding, are significant and important, and emphasize the necessity of the utmost caution and the most stringent measures to prevent the spread of the deadly plague. In haste.

Your friend, F. E. DANIEL.

MERIDIAN.

From Meridian Homestead.

It will be seen from the list of deaths from yellow fever, that there were in all from Sept. 24th to Nov. 7th, 86 deaths. The whole number of cases was 382, so that it appears that the mortality, great as it was, was less than at other places visited by this dreadful scourge. The first death from the fever is supposed to be Lewis Carter, a negro who carried the mails from the Postoffice to the trains, and who died on the 24th of September. The next fatal case was that of John Etheridge, who died on the 28th of September. Up to this time the town had been remarkably healthy. There had been a few weeks previous some suspicious cases of fever. Brown Sprawling, a young man, whom it has since been learned was taken sick five days after leaving Vicksburg, had fever, and some other parties living near him also had fever, one of whom died. It is believed by many that these were the first cases of the fever here, and its origin. The night before Etheridge's death, Mrs. Taggert and Messrs. Terry, Preston and one or two others were attacked with chills followed by fever, and on the first of October Terry and Preston died. The same day Mr. Moesley was taken sick, and on the following day Messrs. Sadler, Tarver, Mr. and Mrs. Brookshire and two or three negroes. The Doctors hesitated about pronouncing the cases yellow fever, but the Board of Health refused to issue certificates of health, and the quarantine guards were discharged. The people of the town now became panic stricken and a general stampede took place. All the business houses but two were closed and almost every one that could leave town did so. It is difficult to say how many were left here, but the number did not exceed seven or eight hundred and of these more than half were colored. There were already 12 to 15 cases and the disease spread rapidly. With few exceptions the first cases were fatal. Some of the physicians denied that the disease was yellow fever, but after the night of October 3d, when Willie Tarver died with black vomit, there was no longer any doubt but that the same disease was here that had desolated Grenada, Holly Springs, Memphis, Vicksburg and other cities. The remaining citizens re-organized the Aid Society, and did everything in their power to see that the sick and destitute were provided for. Mayor Taylor and Messrs. W. A. Brown, W. T. McLean and A. A. Currie, of the Boards of Mayor and Aldermen, and Mr. Thos. Sullivan, City Marshal, Capt. R. L. Henderson, Sheriff, and A. R. Wilson, Jailor, all remained and rendered valuable services to the afflicted. Messrs. McLean and Currie fell at the post of duty, and Mayor Taylor was prostrated by a severe attack of the disease, but we are happy to state has now fully recovered. Drs. Redwood, Griffin, Philips and Smith, remained and did all that medical skill could do for the sick, and were finally aided by Dr. George H. Fowler, of Mobile.

Many of our most useful and promising citizens have fallen, and sorrow and desolation visited hitherto happy families, but we have no space in this hastily prepared paper to do more than mention their decease

LIST OF DEATHS.

Sept. 24—Lewis Carter, col......Sept. 28—John Etheridge......From Sept. 28th to Oct. 7th—T. J. Terry, Wm. A. Preston, Mrs. Jno. Taggert, McLister, W. S. Tarver, W. L. Sadler, Lem Hobson, col., J. Washington, col., Peter Brooks, col., B. Thompson, col., Nancy Marshall, col., McArthur'e child, col., Augusta Wilson.

Oct. 7—Jas. Terrell, Calvin Peoples, col......Oct. 8—Bettie Meads, col......Oct. 9—R. J. Moseley, Mrs. Lipscomb, Mrs. Owens......Oct. 10—Miss Taft......Oct. 11 Wm. T. McLean, Chas. T. McLean, John Ward......Oct. 12—Miss Mattie Phillips Mary Riley, Nellie Childs, Mary Perry, col...... Oct. 14—Willie Owens, —— Owens, Sallie Echols, col......Oct. 15—Ben Vail, Edward Tucker, Henry Harris, col., Mat Gallis, col.

Oct. 16—Mrs. Ellen Bragg, Adaline Moore, col......From Oct. 17th to 21st—Ellen Rainey, Ed. Habercorn, Willie Driver, col., Mr. Lawrence, W. V. Rainey, Mrs. Lawrence, Pierce Nelson, col., Andrew Carr, col., Nelson's child, col., Peter Johnson, col......Rob Harrington, col., Peter Johnson's child, col., Mollie Patton's child, col.

From Oct. 21st to Oct. 24th—Mrs. S. J. Tarver, Henry White, col., Mrs. Dr. Gould, Dick White, col., Jno. White, col......Oct. 24—E. H. Tallicher, D. Pullham, col., B. F. Moseley, Emma Robinson, col., Josiah Jones, Nancy Marshall, col., Thos. hodgers.

Oct. 25—Mrs. Holmes, col......Oct. 26—E. V. Early, A. A. Currie......Oct. 27— S. C. Thielgard, J. Bell, col......Oct. 28—Violet Williams, col., Rebecca Morris, col......Oct. 29—John Henderson, Richard Goodin, col., Diana Lee, col.

Oct. 30—Chas. Link, Mrs. Ben Williams, Wm. Hoffer......Oct. 31—T. R. Williams......Nov. 2—Lulie Sinclair......Nov. 3—Geo. White......Nov. 4—Mrs. W. P. Branch.

Nov. 5—Mrs. James Prestige, Jerry Jones, col......Nov. 6—Ritta Adkinson, col Nov. 7—T. C. Enslen's child.

Whole number of deaths 86.

HANDSBORO, MISS.

BY C. M. LIDDLE.—WRITTEN ABOUT DECEMBER 1ST, 1878.

Near the middle and latter part of August there occurred in Handsboro, Mississippi City and vicinity a number of cases of fever pronounced by the physicians as malarial, bilious and otherwise; no deaths, however, resulting therefrom.

At this time yellow fever was prevailing in New Orleans, Grenada and Memphis, spreading rapidly and becoming general throughout the Southern country.

Medical testimony regarding the disease was united, "that yellow fever features in initiatory cases were so absorbed by malarial elements as to render their presence almost impossible to detect," hence opinion was divided when the first genuine case of yellow fever appeared—September 2d.

The second case appeared Sept. 10th, almost in the center of town and the subject a negro woman. There were a few cases between this date and October 1, after which there was a rapid increase, the disease becoming general. The principal seat of locality during the epidemic may be termed central. It early extended eastward on Main street, from Church to Gulf thence north to Magnolia, thence west to Bridge, thence south near its origin to Main.

THE DEAD.

P. Mateo, native of Aus-ria, died Sept. 24; ill three days; 26 years.

Mary Ann Cleary, native of Ireland; died October 12; ill nine days; aged 39 years.

John Cullinan, native of Ireland; died Oct. 12; ill four days; aged 72 years.

Mrs. David McVay, native of Mississippi; died Oct. 15; ill seven days; aged 26 years.

Walter Cullinan, native of Ireland; died Oct. 16; ill four days; aged 34 years.

Mrs. John Murphy, native of Handsboro; died Oct. 12; ill thirteen days; aged 31 years.

Dr. John E. Lyon, native of South Carolina; died Oct. 18; ill ten days; aged 38 years.

Daniel Andrews, native of New York; died Oct. 20; ill four days; aged 69 years.

Joseph Zundt, native of Switzerland; died Oct. 21; ill thirteen days; aged 33 years.

Elizabeth McVay, native of Mississippi; died October 22; ill eleven days; aged 26 years.

Monica Waycott, native of Handsboro; died Oct. 26; ill three days; aged 3 years.

Georgiana Vierling; native of Handsboro; died October 27; ill three days; aged 16 years.

Matilda Bailey, native of Handsboro; died Nov. 1; ill five days; aged about 4 years.

Alexander McVay, native of Handsboro; died Nov. 1; aged 5 years; taken sick October 13, and relapsed after recovery.

Lewis Edward Hempstead, native of Mississippi; died Nov. 4; ill five days; aged 15 years.

John G. Blacklidge; native of Mississippi; died Nov. 15; ill four days; aged 51 years.

Last death—Mrs. Rutland, December 23, 1878; last case, January 10, 1879. Contributions $1,100.

SUMMARY.

Origin—Imported from New Orleans; first case, September 2; first death, September 24; last death, December 22; fever epidemic, October 12; epidemic ended, November 5; first general frost, November 1; lowest range of thermometer, 44 degrees; number of cases (to date)—Whites, 98; negroes, 28; total, 126. Number of deaths—Whites, 16; number made widows, 6; number made widowers, 2.

AT BARNES HOTEL.

J. D. Beany, died Sept. 9; Winston Hawkins, died Sept. 25; Mrs. John E. Row land, died September 27; A. B. Winston, died Sept. 28; M. A. Carter, died Oct. 1; Mrs. W. B. Brockett, died Oct. 1; John McEuery Brockett, died Oct. 4; Henry Chamberlain, died Oct. 4.

ON THE BEACH.

Chas. Walker, died Oct. 22; Pauline Clark, died Oct. 1; John C. Craig, died Oct. 19; Susie Latimer, died Oct. 23; Polly Jackson, died Oct. 28; C. L. Wells, died Nov. 15; Chas. Odom, died Oct. 27.

WATER VALLEY.

Total cases, about 250. Total deaths, 75, as follows: Adult males, white 44—females, 7; adult males, colored, 8—females, 5; 3 children, males, white—5 females; 5 children, females, colored.

From Water Valley Courier, Nov. 16.

On the 10th of August, the authorities here telegraphed to Grenada to know if it was true that there was yellow fever in that city, and received a negative answer, from the Mayor himself. The next day, however, the tenor of the telegrams from Grenada were changed, and then it was that our people begin to realize the danger that threatened us. To add to the anxiety and suspicion of our people, on the night of the 10th of August, Mr. J. E. Booker, who had been working in Grenada, returned to his family in this city, quite sick. Sunday, the 11th, physicians were called in and the case of Mr. Booker was pronounced suspicious at least. This proved to be the first case of yellow fever.

From the 5th of October to the 27th, was the period of greatest gloom, the number of cases for that time being from forty to sixty. Almost every day there were deaths from yellow fever, and some days three and four interments. The majorities of the cases for this period was among the colored people, very few families of that race having left town, while many other families came from the country, making the population of the colored people during the prevalence of the epidemic even greater than in was before the fever began.

It will be seen by the list, which we publish below, that while the colored people had more cases, the whites suffered by far the greater mortality.

DEATH ROLL.

Aug. 30—Kenny Lees, engineer......Sept. 7—Wm. Goodwin......Sept. 12—Mrs. A. G. Buford, at Ocean Springs......Sept. 14—C. E. Summers.

Sept. 18—Peter Williams, conductor......Sept. 19—J. H. Fly, attorney; Jennie Morrison, col......Sept. 23—Walter Reems, engineer, Harrisburg, Tenn; Mark E. Pate, merchant, at Philadelphia, Pa.

Sept. 24—Bill Brooks. col......Sept. 26—R. A. Long, Mrs. N. U. Gartine.
Sept. 27—J. O. Hendricks, City Treasurer and insurance agent.
Sept. 28—Miss Jane Miller. Sept. 30—J. E. Becton, Master Mechanic, N. U.
Gartine, Lige Miller.
Oct. 2—L. M. Pennington, Train Dispatcher; D. Donahue, at Nashville.
Oct. 5—G. W. Strong, Wm. White, B. W. Brewer, Bill Meeks, col.
Oct. 6—W. H. Jones, engineer, at Ways Bluff......Oct. 7—H. Reese's child.
Oct. 8—M. A. Gross, Draftsman and Time Keeper.
Oct. 9—A. V. Simmons......Oct. 11—Jeff. Miller, Jack Coachman, col.
Oct. 14—John McClure, Mrs. Edstrom......Oct. 15—W. L. Bartlett, Conductor;
Tom Walker, Baggage Master; E. Block, Hotel Keeper; Mrs. G. W. Reed.
Oct. 16—H. W. Freeman, Attorney......Oct. 19—Mrs. E. F. Smith, David An-
drews, col., found dead.
Oct. 20—Miss Mollie Smith, A. C. Thorne......Oct. 21—Rob't Townsend......
Tom Tr iner.
Oct. 22—Jas. M. Creps, Clay McMillen, John Mattson, P. W. Pennell, Time
Keeper.
Oct. 24—Thomas Reasons, child of Mrs, Edstrom......Oct. 26—Mrs. Robert
Prophit......Oct. 27—Jack Ledbetter......Nov. 1—Jas. Hall......Nov. 3—Gus.
Holmes.
Nov. 5—Mrs. J. B. Taylor, Ike Watson, col......Nov. 19—W. J. Mauldin, mer-
chant; Miss Nellie Baker.
We have been unable to ascertain the dates of the following deaths: Jack
Howard, child of Thomas Mauldin, Kate Conway, Lucretia Ware, and two un-
known colored women.

JACKSON.

Aug. 31—Joseph Sayle......Sept. 23—Wm. H. Swett......Sept. 27- William Mc-
Callum..... Oct. 2—Junius Granberry......Oct. 3—Mrs. Ann Williams, col., Geo.
C. Granberry......Oct. 5—J. H. Ledbetter, Lewis Reinheimer, William H. Taylor
Oct. 6—Alonzo L. Brunson, (in 5th year)......Oct. 7—C. Cosmani......Oct. 8—Creed
Wade, col., George Granberry......Oct. 9—Mrs. W. H. Johnson, Andrew Wilson,
Miss Ida Granberry.
Oct. 10—James McKay, col   Oct. 11—William Barrett, Mrs. Cosmani, Mrs.
McCallum......Oct. 12—Maria Haley, col., Johnnie Phillips, col......Oct. 13—Wil-
liam Muller, William Ewing......Oct. 14—Daniel Eschelman......Oct. 15—Fannie
McInnis, Henry Eschelman, Ophelia Newman, col.
Oct. 16—Pierce Bonner, col., Willie Douglas, col., child, Matt Clark......Oct.
17—William L. Parker, Gertrude Washington, col., Eli Hammond, col , Joshua
Wells, col., Robert Black......Oct. 18—Birdie Clint, col., child......Oct. 19—Daniel
Clancy, Fannie Crawford, col., Moses Devoty, col.
Oct. 20—P. M. Watterson......Oct. 21—Toney McDonald, child, Harvey Pierce,
Geo. Morton, col......Oct. 22—T. J. Jackson, col., Pinkey Beasley, col., Martha J.
Kellar, col.
Oct. 23—Wesley Burton, col., Mrs. Daniel Clancy......Oct. 24—Milly Dickson,
col., Edward Bailey......Oct. 25—Joseph Muller, Mrs. Thos, Marion, Bettie Div-
ine, Judy Redding, col.
Oct. 26—Allen Joseph, col., John F. Bayol......Oct. 27—Jane Harrington, col.
Oct. 28—Ann Harris. col., Minnie Barrett, Susan Johnson, col.
Oct. 29—Patrick O'Leary, about 12 years, Lafayette Simpson, col., Sally
Douglas, col......Oct. 31—Mrs. Thos. McInnis, col......Nov. 2—Henry E. Sizer,
Annie Harrison, col.
Nov. 3—Marcellus Langler, col., Malvina Wallace. col.. ...Nov. 5—C. Eva
Johnson, 4 years, Mrs. P. C. Daughtry......Nov. 8—P. J. Roach, Simon White,
col., Joseph Kolb, in country.
Nov. 11—Dan Crawford, col., Miss Louise Taylor......Nov. 12—Anna Hill, col
Nov. 13—P. Kolb......Nov. 14—Eliza Godfrey, col......Nov. 16—Ben. F. Glennon.
Nov. 20—Mrs. Margaret Ryan.
Nov. 21—Annie Oliver Comfort, aged 7 weeks.. ...Nov. 26—Willie Coats......
Nov. 28—Miss Annie Wallace.
Total cases yellow fever during epidemic, 490; whites, 173; colored, 317; total
deaths from yellow fever, 84; whites, 49; colored, 3ʰ; first death August 31st; last
death, November 28.
Total average cost per case, $27 00, including burial expenses.

From Clarion, Sept. 25.

Mr. Swett, an employee of the Vicksburg and Meridian railroad, died in this city, Monday night. His attending physician has said that the case presented decided yellow fever symptoms, and there are circumstances attending it strongly presumptive of that disease. It has not been two weeks since he was exposed to the fever at Smith's Station, and probably other infected places. Prompt measures were taken to prevent the spreading of the disease, and disinfectants are still freely used. The occurrence of this case warrants us in warning our absent citizens to remain away; and our authorities and won't-go-aways, to continue on the alert.

From Clarion, Oct. 2.

The yellow fever case of William McCallum, who had not been out of Jackson, naturally produced inquiry as to the probable cause. It has been ascertained that on the square on which his mother resides, a colored man man—Buck Patton—received into his family about five weeks ago, his step-son, from a badly infected place. A young daughter of Patton soon thereafter died with a disease which the attending physician said at the time had strongly marked yellow fever symptoms. About the same time Gregg Richards, another colored man, living in the same lot, secreted a refugee from another badly infected place, who, under cover of darkness, probably had eluded the vigilance of the quarantine officers. Richards died very soon thereafter with what was then supposed to be a chronic case of long standing, but recent inquiry has induced the belief that he may have contracted the yellow fever before his death, by contract with the person whom he was harboring. Residing in that immediate locality, it is more than probable that poor McCallum, totally unconscious of danger, owed his death to this cause. Fortunately for the rest of the community the sanitary measures enforced by the authorities delayed the progress of the disease, else our town would ere this this have been enshrouded in the same gloom that has darkened so many other places. We have no patience to comment upon the criminal violation of the ordinances which were established to protect the public health, and which, in addition to the punishment it has brought upon the parties who were accessory to it, has brought unspeakable sorrow upon at least one unfortunate family.

Clarion, Oct. 16.

The large number of colored cases over whites is attributable to the preponderance of the former population, very few of whom left the town on the approach of the disease. It will be seen that the death-roll of the week just ended has not increased over the week before, and that thus far, it has been unusually small compared to other places of equal population which have been visited by the epidemic—a fact attributable to various causes, chief among them, the excellent sanitary measures provided in advance by our thoughtful authorities. Besides, our superb corps of able physicians have been on the alert, and from the start have contested every inch of ground with the fell destroyer. Time at this season of the year is an important ally. Let us take courage. "The stars in their causes are fighting against Sisera."

Clarion, Oct. 23.

The deaths for the past week have averaged nearly 3 a day—a slight increase over the week before. On the nights of the 17th, 18th and 19th, there were light frosts without any perceptible effect upon the disease. The sick and death rates have somewhat decreased among the whites, and have largely increased among the colored during the past week. Last night there was another light frost, with what effect remains to be seen. Unless nature has reversed her ordinances, cool weather will extinguish the disease ere long. Our people who have borne their trials so calmly will not despair now. The darkest hour is just before daybreak.

BOLTON.

Peter Shield, Sept. —; M. Schwartz, Sr., Oct. —; Miss Annie Walton, Oct. 2; Geo. Walton, Oct. 9; Mrs. R. A. Myrick, Oct. 1; E. K. Myrick, Oct. 25; Mrs. Mrs. D. J. Alexander, Oct. 10; Mrs. Jennie Fitzgera d, Nov. 5; Mrs. Ida K. Peebles, and Clifton Peebles, Oct. 11; Mrs. Ida McKay, Oct. 9; W. E Shofner, Nov. 12; Henry M. Wells and Eddie Wells, Nov. 19. Total, 14. Colored deaths at Bolton and vicinity, 40. Total cases, 167. Nearly all the whites had refugeed.

McCOMB CITY.

Total cases, between 350 and 400. Total deaths 52—adult males, 24; females, 11; boys, 9; girls, 8. Colored males, 1; female, 1.

Oct. 4—G. A. Boyd......Oct. 8—Thomas Leddy, John Easley .....Oct. 10—Wm. Fleming......Oct. 11—Katie Doyle, B. F. Busby, John McNamara, John Fenger. Oct. 13—Dudley Atkinson......Oct. 14—Victor Bauer......Oct. 16—Willie Abbott......Oct. 18—Mrs. Geo. Butland......Oct. 19—T. H. Brady, W. B. Freshwater. Oct. 20—Miss Katie Abbott, Willie Easley......Gertie Uter. Dan. Felder, col., Preston Smothers, col......Oct. 22—Mrs. G. A. Boyd......Oct. 24—Dr. A. F. Strawn.

Oct. 26—Mrs. S. Nelson......Oct. 27—Miss Lena Bauer, L. B. Ford......Oct. 29—Katie Freshwater, A. Johnson......Oct. 30—Mrs. B. Foley......Oct. 31—B. N. Freshwater.

Nov. 1—Jas. Bowen, John Killian......Nov. 2—Sam. Williamson, Jr......Nov. 3—Paul Thalheim, Thomas Foley......Nov. 4—Fred. Thalheim......Nov. 6—George Bewley, Celia Connolly, col.

Nov. 7—Hiram Rester, Mary Smith......Nov. 8—Nettie Uter......Nov. 10—Otto Thalheim. Mrs. Sopiah Tankersly......Nov. 11—John Hay, Emma Thalheim.

Nov. 12—Mrs. John Hay......Nov. 15—Mrs. K. Strawn......Nov. 16—Maud Sullivan......Nov. 18—James McBrain......Nov. 19—Dr. B. F. Gatlin. Peter McNamara......Nov. 24—Mrs. Sarah Sullivan.......Nov. 21—Thomas Sullivan......Dec. Dec. 1—Mrs. M. E. Thalheim.

From THE CLARION, Nov. 13.

It was our privilege to visit McComb City yesterday on a relief mission. We were furnished a list of forty-five persons—all white but one—who have died there of yellow fever since the 4th of October, out of about three hundred cases treated; the average population of the town being about eleven hundred. Some thirty cases are now under treatment. The family of Mrs. Laura C. Divine, formerly of this city, have been greatly afflicted. All the children, but one, have had the fever, and Miss Lettie was very low when we called to see her. We had the pleasure of meeting the Messrs. Greener, Kennedy, Gibson, White, Beard, and others of the noble Howards, who have done good work, in a quiet way, with but little outside assistance. We were also pleased to have an interview at Summit Quarantine Station, with John H. McKenzie, Grand Master of Odd Fellows, who has been indefatigable in his ministrations to the people of McComb City.

DEATHS AT "VALLEY HOME," TALLAHATCHIE COUNTY.

Plantation of Dr. G. W. Payne, 27 miles west of Grenada, 12 miles north of Yalobusha river, and about 12 miles east of Tallahatchie river. Eighteen white population in the house—5 adult males, 8 adult females, 5 children. All had the fever.

DEATHS—Lena Montgomery, Humphrie Montgomery, Mrs. Blackwell, Mrs. John Thompson, Mr. John Thompson, A. J. Thompson, William Payne, Mrs.

Grose, Mrs. Russell, Battie Thompson, Dr. Geo. Payne, Mr. Smith Murphy, Dr. Turnipseed, Mr. Sam. Berry, white, Colored, unknown, Garett Mariwether.

A STRICKEN FAMILY.

From THE CLARION, Sept. 4.

Several weeks ago, a lady from New Orleans stayed at the house of Mr. Young F. Griffin, in Pike county, for several days, and then left. She was not sick herself, but carried the germs of the fever in her clothing and baggage. The following death-roll in the Summit Times tells the story :

GRIFFIN—At the "Wallace Place," four miles from Summit, on Wednesday morning, August 21, 1878, Young M. Griffin, eldest son of Young F. and P. J. Griffin, aged 19 years, 5 months and 21 days.

GRIFFIN—At same place, on Wednesday, August 21, at 12 o'clock P. M., Alexander Ware, third son of Young F. and P. J. Griffin, aged 13 years, 11 months and 21 days.

GRIFFIN—At the same place, on Thursday, August 22, 1878, at 12 o'clock M., Young F. Griffin, aged 65 years.

GRIFFIN—At the same place, on Saturday, August 24, 1878, at 10:25 A. M., Mary Elizabeth, only daughter of Mrs. P. J. and the late Young F. Griffin, aged 9 years, 1 month and 17 days.

GARNER STATION.

Thirteen miles north of Grenada, Miss., on Miss. and Tenn. R. R. Population, previous to epidemic, about 150 ; during epidemic, 40. First case of fever, Sept. 7. Total cases, 30 ; deaths, 12—6 adult females ; 2 adult males ; 3 young men ; 1 male child.

DEATHS—John Vanderwort, Miss Jesse Lee Robertson, Mrs. Dr. J. L. Combs, Mrs. H. Combs, Dr. J. H. Payne, Mrs. Dr. J. H. Payne, Harry Robertson, Mrs. Broom, Mrs. Scobey, Morris O'Neal.

TILLATOBA STATION.

Population before epidemic between 80 and 100 ; during fever, 30—11 whites and 19 colored. Total cases, in town and country, 41. Total deaths 8—names not reported.

THE McNAIR DEATH ROLL IN HINDS COUNTY.

Hinds County Gazette.

The following is a perfect list of the deaths from yellow fever in the family of Mr. L. D. McNair, 9 miles southwest of Raymond :

A. G. Gibbs, aged 31 years, Oct. 8; Miss M. E. McNair, aged 23 years, Oct. 11 ; L. D. McNair, Jr., aged 18 years, Oct. 19; R. A. McNair, aged 39 years, Oct. 19 ; W. E. G. McNair, aged 21 years, Oct. 21; Miss M. L. Russell, aged 29, Oct. 21 ; D. R. McNair, aged 33, Oct. 22; Mrs. L. G. McNair, aged 28, Oct. 22 ; L. D. McNair, Sr., aged 71, Oct. 23; Mrs. L. Allen, aged 73, Oct. 23 ; Mrs. S. Hamilton, aged 59, Nov. 12; Mrs. Allen and Mrs. Hamilton, were sisters of Mr. McNair, Sr.

Thus in about one month the father, four sons, a son-in-law, a daughter, a daughter-in-law, a niece, and two sisters, all passed to eternity.

WINONA.

WHITES—J. C. Kittrell, Wm. A. Campbell, J. H. McGuire, from Grand Junction; Mrs. Helen C. Reese, Bennie Blackston, George W. Oury, Lyles Oury. COLORED—Frances Harris, Dump Brown's child, Mingo Vincen.

DEATHS AT HERNANDO.

HERNANDO, MISS., June 11, 1879.

DEAR SIR: As requested, I enclose a complete list of deaths from yellow fever at Hernando and vicinity during the epidemic of 1878. This list is complete and correct as to names and dates. I have copied it from the daily register kept by our Relief Committee, and I know personally that it is accurate.

Truly yours,

D. McKENZIE.

Sept. 5—D. C. Campbell, of Memphis,
Sept. 8—Mrs. R. R. West, of Hernando. This case is disputed.
Sept. 9—Mrs. Peter Vorndran, of Memphis.
Sept. 12—Mrs. Butler P. Anderson, of Memphis,
Sept. 13—Mena Solfker, of Memphis.
Sept. 14—Mrs. Barbara Johnston, of Hernando,
Sept. 16—Mrs. Schwartz, of Hernando,
Sept. 16—Mrs. Hildebrand, of Hernando,
Sept. 17—John Feldstead, of Hernando,
Sept. 25—Dr. J. W. Powell, of Hernando.
Sept. 26—E. Denhard, of Hernando,
Sept. 26—Mary Washington, col., of Hernando,
Sept. 27—Mrs. S. B. McNees, of Memphis,
Sept. 27—J. C. Avora, of Hernando,
Sept. 27—J. B. Ford, of Memphis,
Sept. 28—Bob Wise, col., of Hernando,
Sept. 28—Mike Connelly, of Hernando,
Sept. 29—Mrs. E. J. Vorndran, of Hernando,
Sept. 29—Mrs. Henry Taylor, col., of Hernando,
Sept. 30—James Flaherty, of Memphis,
Oct. 1—Miss Mary Murray, of Memphis,
Oct. 4—Mrs. S. P. Reid, of Hernando,
Oct. 4—Mrs. Mike Connelly, of Hernando,
Oct. 4—Miss Ella Harder, of Memphis,
Oct. 5—Henry Taylor, col, of Hernando,
Oct. 6—Mrs. Denhard, of Hernando.
Oct. 6—Peter Vorndran, of Memphis,
Oct. 6—R. Hickling, of Hernando,
Oct. 6—A. D. Thompson, col., of Hernando,
Oct. 7—Mrs. R. Hickling, of Hernando,
Oct. 7—Miss Ruth Pullin, of Hernando,
Oct. 8—Miss Ella Pullin, of Hernando,
Oct. 8—Miss Annie Harder, of Memphis,
Oct. 12—Mise Maggie Flaherty, of Memphis,

Oct. 12—Julius Hanck, of Memphis.
Oct. 12—Robert Walker, col, of Memphis,
Oct. 13—Pat Ligon, col., of Hernando,
Oct. 14—Mrs. Niles, of Hernando,
Oct. 14—Jack Coghill, col., of Hernando,
Oct. 14—Robert Gore, of Hernando,
Oct. 14—David Gideon, of Hernando,
Oct. 15—Mrs. Waller, of Hernando,
Oct. 15—O. Kellogg, of Hernando,
Oct. 15—Mrs. P. O. Woods, of Memphis,
Oct. 15—Donald L. McKay, of Memphis,
Oct. 16—George Kapline, of Hernando,
Oct. 16—Mrs. D. Gideon, of Hernando,
Oct. 16—Eddie Gillespie, of Hernando,
Oct. 16—Capt. J. A. Monroe, of Hernando,
Oct. 16—Mrs. J. C. Gillespie, of Hernando,
Oct. 17—Kattie Gillespie, of Hernando,
Oct. 17—Mary Monroe, of Hernando,
Oct. 17—Johnnie Moore, of Memphis,
Oct. 18—Helen Bobo, col., of Hernando,
Oct. 18—Hope Johnston, of Hernando,
Oct. 18—Robert Jackson, of Hernando,
Oct. 18—W. W. Case, of Memphis,
Oct. 21—Frank Dockery, col., of Hernando,
Oct. 21—Nathan Rice, col., of Hernando,
Oct. 22—Tilda Allen, col., of Hernando,
Oct. 22—James H. Baker, of Hernando,
Oct. 24—Miss Laura Pullin, of Hernando,
Oct. 24—E. Bullington, of Hernando,
Oct. 24—G. C. Lewis, of Memphis,
Oct. 24—Henry Hanck, of Memphis,
Oct. 25—W. L. Jones, of Hernando,
Oct. 26—Jimmie Wilcox, of Hernando,
Oct. 31—J. P. M. Pullin, of Hernando,
Oct. 31—Ferdinand Hickling, of Hernando.
Oct. 31—E. wi Hickling, of Hernando,
Nov. 3—Sam Johnston, col., of Hernando,
Nov. 4—Louis Denhard, of Hernando,
Nov. 10—Oldman Nelson, col., of Hernando,

White refugees, 19; colored refugees, 1; total, 20; white residents, 39; colored residents, 15; total, 54; total deaths, 74.

EXTRACT FROM COMMITTEE'S REPORT.

The most difficult work of the committee to control was the burial of the dead. Burials, during the epidemic, were conducted entirely by the committee, except in one or two instances. The work was done through a burial corps, in charge of a responsible member of the committee, appointed specially for such duty. This burial committee procured the coffin, saw the body placed in it and buried without trouble or responsibility to the family afflicted. The dead were buried within from two to six hours after death, when possible, the graves were all 4½ feet deep, well filled, packed and rounded. This burial committee was conspicuous for its good work done, and I regret to say was equally so, for the futility among its members. As first appointed, it consisted of E. J. Vorndran, V. J. Philippi and J. H. Baker. Mr. Vorndran died Sept. 25th. Geo. Kapline who was appointed in his stead died Oct. 16th, and Mr. Baker Oct. 22d. The death list of the *working members* of our committee, shows the fearfully deadly character of the epidemic. No member who came in actual contact with the sick, except Drs. Saunders and Jones escaped the disease, and only two of the members taken recovered. I am the only working member taken with the fever that reported for duty afterwards. I was taken sick on the same day with Mr. Hickling on the 2d of October, and reported for duty on the 8th, Mr. Hickling died on the 7th. The President, Dr. Bullington, Vice-President E. J. Vordran, Secretary R. Hickling, J. H. Baker, superintendent of nurses, and Geo. Kapline of the committee on burials, all died at their posts, and each in his sphere had nobly borne his part, and should be held in grateful remembrance by the people in whose service they died.

Total receipts $3 872 00. Total disbursements $3,672 50.

D. McKenzie, for Committee.

FRIAR'S POINT.

First case, on wharf-boat, August 17th. Last case, November 1st. Total cases, 18 whites, 7 colored. Adults—male whites, 12; female, 6; colored DEATHS.—Geo. R. Alcorn, Mrs. Geo. R. Alcorn, J. W. Dwyer, Jas. T. Rucks, Jas. Maynard, —— Wood, col.

Population, during fever, about 275.

DEATHS AT LEBANON, HINDS COUNTY.

Joseph Jacobs,	Eddie McNair,	Miss Bettie McNair,
Mrs. J. Jacobs,	David McNair,	Miss Emma Roberts,
A. Harrison's child,	L. D. McNair, Sr.,	Joseph Jacobs, Jr.,
Ben Jacob's infant,	Mrs. Jas. Hamilton,	L. D. McNair, Jr.,
——Ward,	Mrs. Allen,	Mrs. Ben Jacobs,
Mrs Moses,	Mrs. E. Edmondson,	Miss Essie Russell,
Mrs. O'Brien,	Ben Jacobs,	Mrs. David McNair,
Emmet O'Brien,	A. Gibbes,	Pat McDermon,
Mrs. Monell,	——Ward,	Mrs. Fannie Noble.
Robert McNair,	J. M. Moses,	

DEATHS AT YAZOO CITY, MISS.

Rev. W. B. Littlejohn,	Sister Zenobia,	James Kelly,
Mrs. S. C. Harris,	Sister Corona,	Sister Mary Lawrence.
Capt. Hal. C. Harris,	Father J. Monton,	

Total number of colored deaths, 1.

DEATHS AT CANTON AND VICINITY.

Miss Rachael Henry,
Dr. Nath. W. McKie,
Miss Elizabeth Henry,
Miss Lizzie Henry,
Mrs. S. D. Garrett,
Mrs. D. M. Fulton,
Miss Annie Steele,
Col. D. M. Fulton,
Miss Sallie Benthall,
Miss Minnie Mann,
Ben. F. Mann,
Dedrick Feldman,
James Wickham,
Mary Vance,
Mrs. C. Conway,
Edwin Conway,
Peter Capurro,
Mike Harter,
Fred Demarchi,
Geo. Noe,
Louis Botto,
Mrs. D. H. Otto,
Wyly Otto,
David H. Shaw,
Col. M. B. McMicken,
Father P. Cogan,
Dr. M. J. McKie,
Miss Zoe McKie,
Josie Benthall,
St. Clair Jeffries,
Wm. Welsh,
John Reid,
Mrs. D. Wm. Reid,
B. C. Gough,
J. V. Fitchett's child,
Jennie Belle Scales,
Mrs. P. Peyton,
Louisa Demarchi,
Jake Harter's child,
Mary Monnohan,
O. A. Luckett, Jr.,
Barney McCoskey,
Mrs. A. S. Lee,
James Leonard,
Wm. Jones,
Daisey Benthall,
M. Kennedy and child,
J. B. Catlett's child,
Mrs. Billings,
Mrs. Scheifler's son,
C. T. Collins,
Monti Smith,
Perry S. Stone,
John Montgomery,
Mrs. John Montgomery,
Mrs. Jas. A. Smith,
Miss Mittie Smith,
Mrs. Mark Joseph,
Frank Paul,
George Van Buron,
Dr. J. T. Magruder,

Mrs. Leitch,
Pat Peyton,
Rob't Morris,
Frank Demarchi,
August Arnold,
Sister Johanna,
Miss Mattie Leonard,
Freddy Leonard,
Pinkev Scales,
Miss Mary Hill,
Mrs. P. Capurro,
Joe C. Richards,
C. Canalli,
Chas. Clavarri,
Jas. A. Coplin,
Dr. A. H. Cage,
Mr. Petty's child,
J. Boersig,
W. A. Langley,
Miss Bridget Kennedy,
Mrs. Linderman,
Eddie Smith,
Mrs. W. H. Benthall,
Mrs. Smith,
Joe Blanchard's child,
James Duffey,
R. W. Durfey,
Daisey Young,
——Ford,
Jno. Ernst, son.
——Campbell,
Guieseppe Chavivari,
Mrs. Ben Alswerth,
Mrs. E. L. Thompson,
Mrs. Schiefler,
Mrs. Wilcox,
Mrs. Rob't Leonard,
Chas. Green,
Two children of Tom Peyton,
Susie Shackelford,
John Gray,
H. R. C. Benwell,
John Gray's child,
Mrs. James Leonard,
Willie Cassell,
Mary Kelly,
H. R. C. Benwell's child,
Mrs. Lucy Strobecker,
Elward Logue,
Mrs. B. Barnes,
Wm. Chambers' child.
John M. Henry,
B. Logue,
D. Leitch,
David Fulton's son,
Mark Latimer,
Fitz Semmes,
Mrs. Minerva Benthall,
——Engle,
Mrs. M. A. Wilson.
Geo. Harter.

Total number of colored deaths, 57.

DEATHS AT ROCKY SPRINGS, CLAIBORNE COUNTY.

Love Cessna,
Tom Goosehorn,
Sallie Goosehorn,
Nannie Ely,
Mrs. Duvall,
Mahala Duvall,
Lilly Emerick,
Aleck Emerick,
Mollie Wallace,
George Goza,

George H. McLean,
Ellen Haring,
Emily Harper,
Ed. O. Lum,
Laman McLemore,
Susan Henderson,
Mrs. George Goza,
L. A. Thompson,
Mrs. Mary Boggs,
J. J. Harper,

W. W. Brock,
Rev. D. A. J. Parker,
Mrs. D. A. J. Parker,
Alice Foster,
Mattie Harper,
Mrs. O. B. Harper,
Dan Emerick,
James Wright,
Mrs. M. M. Wright,
A. E. Flowers.

Total number of colored deaths 12.

DEATHS AT AND NEAR CARDIFF LANDING.

Alice Thompson, 5 years, 6 months, 24 days; Miss Elizabeth Ross, 25 years, 2 months, 13 days; Jesse S. Ross, 65 years; Manerva Wiley, 21 years, 4 months, 20 days; Malissa Ross, 21 years, 9 months, 3 days; W. N. Ross, 29 years, 11 months, 18 days; Mrs. Amy Murchant, 54 years; Mrs. Nancy Mathews, 31 years, 11 months.

OSYKA.

List of deaths in Osyka, Miss., from yellow fever, from August the 15th to December 1st, 1878 :

Aug. 20—Anna Barmore......Sept. 8—Wm. Daunies......Sept. 12—Maggy Sipple......Sept. 13—Mrs. Courtney......Sept. 18—Mrs. Loeb, Mrs. W. L. Varnado, Baby Varnado.

Sept. 29—Isaac Heuman......Sept. 30—Mrs. Mary Hart, Miss Janney Berdalis Sept. 21—Chas. Wailes......Oct. 3—M. D. Bond......Oct. 4—R. G. Rowell......Sept. 6—Adolph Cohn..... Oct. 8—Isaac Cerf.

Oct. 11—Henry Wolf, Miss Caroline Snider, Miss Maggie Miller, Henry Keating......Oct. 15—Moses Eastman, Joseph Rehorst......Oct. 16—Wm. Ricks, Emanuel Cerf......Oct. 17—Baby Bulion, August Weis.

Oct. 18—Granville Cutrer......Oct. 19—Mrs. M. D. Bond......Oct. 21—Henry Rehorst......Oct. 23—Lehman Dryfus......Oct. 25—Myer Wolf......Oct. 26—Benney Weil......Oct. 27—Wm. Jones, Jr.

Oct. 20—Webster Ford, J. D. Ford, Jr.........Oct. 25—Simon Ford.........Oct. 26—Clinton Ford.........Nov. 2d—A. J. Ott.........Nov. 3—Chas. Redman, Eddy Borus.........Nov. 4—Frank Barnes, Jake Smithner.

Nov. 5—Mrs. John Addison.........Nov. 6—Frank Butcher, Thos. Snider......... Nov. 17—Mrs. Joseph Hart.........Dec. 1—Jules Moyse.

Whites, 46; colored, 7; total deaths. 53; total number of cases treated, 257; widows left, 6; ophans left, (white) 29.

Attending physicians—Dr. O. C. Thompson, Wm. Jones, Dr. Ellis, of Osyka and Dr. B. F. Taylor and Dr. Shuppard of New Orleans.

VICKSBURG.

Vicksburg Herald.

THE SAD RECORD.—We present to our readers this morning a long list of names that make a sad record for the South. In this beautiful country where the climate is unsurpassed on the globe, the plague made a record that will not be forgotten by this generation. From our busy thoroughfares the numbers are hardly missed, but a perusal of the list of the dead will cause one to shudder at the extent of our losses. The yellow fever was no respecter of persons. It mowed down the rich and the poor, the good and the bad alike. Whole families were swept away, and dear, familiar friends were taken in almost countless numbers. The names of useful, respected citizens, the loss of whom wrung the hearts of communities, are recorded with a few letters, and this is all that remains to us of them.

THE DEATH LIST.

July 23—Thomas Murphy, 24 y, first case, from steamer John Porter, died in the Hill City Infirmary..........July 24—Henry N. Bryan, 24 y, died on board the steamer John Porter, residence Freedom, Pa., 26 miles below Pittsburgh, Pa. July 25—James McCallum, 32 y.

Aug. 1—Franklin Townsend, 20 y, came from New Orleans on steamer City of Alton, placed in a private Ward in Hill City Infirmary, where he died, residence Englewood, near Chicago, Ills..........Aug. 9—Paul Stoltz, 26 y, died in the Hill City Infirmary..........Aug. 10—T. J. Thompson, 50 y.

Aug. 12—Francis Ratigan, 44 y, died in Hill City Infirmary. Jno. Levins, 15 y, died in the Hill City Infirmary. Fanny Jones, col., died on a dray while on her way to the Hill City Infirmary..........Aug. 17—Frank Baurdo, 18 y. Frank Sagona, 4 y. Mr. Arnold. Mrs. Bridget Conway, 25 y.

Aug. 18—Joseph Conway, 2 y, child........Aug 19—Dominico Giovannini, 41 y. Jas. Burns, 52 y. Unknown white woman. Howard Shelby, 27 y. Geo. Murphy, 38 y. Chas. Conlan, 38 y.

Aug. 20—Mamie Baurdo, 9 y, L. T. Schwink, 5 y, Jos. Stangel. 22 y. Ellis Gerard, 38 y, Mrs, Baurdo, 35 y, Maggie Gehbauer, 10 y, W. J. Ellis, 18 y, Louis Kuntz.

Aug. 21—Mary Lynch, 14 y, Peter Sagona, 38 y, Geo. Guy, col., 38 y, J. Marrian, col., 6 y, J. Conway, 8 m, Abe Kaufman, 6 y, Unknown man, Minnie Allen, G. Fowler, 9 y, Katie M. Pierce, 2 y, G. M. Burd, col., 21 y, Frank Stutz, 50 y, died in the Hill City Infirmary, Mike Delaney, 60 y, died in the Hill City Infirmary, Chas. Behring, 49 y, died in the Hill City Infirmary, Mrs. Giovannini, 35 y, C. H. Gibbs, 40 y, W. S. Fleming, 35 y, T. Honlehan, 45 y, died in the Hill City Infirmary, Lizzie Roeshe, 2 y.

Aug. 22—Mrs. Pelton, W. R. Russell, Chas. Baurdo, 18 y, Mattie Burrell, 24 y, died in the Hill City Infirmary, Amelia Francis, 19 y, Frank H. Klein, 13 y, Jas. Hayes, 38 y, John Smoker, 28 y, David Morrow, Jas. Golden, Morris Winfield, 25 y, Rose Downs, 11 y.

Aug. 23—A. A. Bertoni, 28 y, Annie Brown, col., 34 y, Jno. Weyer, 25 y, Felice Petro, 25 y, Louis Kellar, 39 y, Anderson Wright, col., 30 y, Mrs. E. A. Welsh, 22 y, Mary S. Bobb, 12 y, Frank T. Brooke, 30 y. Jake L. Schwink, 30 y, Chas. Savard, 43 y, died in the Hill City Infirmary, Mrs. J. E. Johnson, 50 y.

Aug. 24—C. E. Dohler, 8 y, Mrs. J. Russell, 72 y, Annie Johnson, 28 y, G. A. Russell, 22 y, Robt. R. Eggleston, 23 y, Margaret J. Foley, 2 y, Belle Cooper, 12 y, Mary Rivers, col., 36 y, Nick Mullen, 35 y, Mary Ryan, 11 y, Unknown Italian, 30 y, Frank C. Fisher, col., 28 y, Chas. Devlin, 28 y, Michael Kauth, 15 y, Geo. F. Brown, Jr., 21 y.

Aug. 25—Emma Duval, 28 y, Mrs. Fannie V. French. 29 y, died in Warren county, residence Vicksburg, Samuel Stevens, Jas. J. Walsh, 20 y, Thomas McNamara, 40 y, Alex E. King, col., 25 y, Henry Hirsh, 2 y, R. Marks, 60 y, Angelo Demarchi, Lillie Tucker, col., 3 y, John Walker, col., 45 y, Sallie L. Ryan, 11 y, Frank Johnson, col., 13 y, Phillip Fox, 2 y, Tim O'Brien, col., 28 y, Peter Guntz, 28 years, died in Hill City Infirmary, Cecilia Clary, 26 y, Adam Schmidt, 50 y, A. Black, 35 y, R. Williams, col., 32 y, Katie Travis, 13 y, Mike McCabe, 45 y, Sam Folz, 10 y, Mary Allen, 15 y, Mrs. M. A. Burell, 61 y.

Aug. 26—J. A. Robinson, 36 y, John Spillaine, 32 y, M. G. Parlen, 40 y, died in the Hill City Infirmary, Chas. Parker, 33 y, died in the Hill City Infirmary, C. E. Jones, 27 y, died in the Hill City Infirmary, —— Pieroin, 29 y, died in the Hill City Infirmary, Vito Ponito, 30 y, died in the Hill City Infirmary, J. N. McEver, 28 y, died at the Hill City Infirmary, Unknown man, died in the Hill City Infirmary, Lewis Bryant, col., 2 y, Stella Thomas, col., 14 y, C. Jones, col., 30 y, Geo. Elliot, 4 y, Dave Moore, col., 40 y, Geo. Dexter, 10 y, Mrs. Margaret Wolters, died in Warren county, residence Vicksburg, 26 y, Tom Owens. 20 y, Bruce Brown, col., 21 y, Albert King, 18 y, Mary E. Hayes, 24 y, Willie E. Little, 3 y, Mary Lamkin, 21 y.

Aug. 27—Rosa Neely, 24 y, W. H. Smith, 30 y, Kate Davis, 34 y, L. Schwartz, 38 y, Albert Parker, 32 y, E. H. Miller, A. Page, 29 y, James Semple, 48 y, Mary Conkley, 7 y, S. Thomas, col., 30 y.

Aug. 27—Mattie Williams, col., 18 y, Henry Tucker, col., 2 y, M. Gray, col., 11 y, J. Hardy, 50 y, died in Hill City Infirmary, Sallie Myers, 17 y, Ida Tatum, 19 y, died in Hill City Infirmary, Dr. D. W. Booth, 37 y, George W. Hutcheson, Jr., E. H. Searles, J. Cambridge, 10 y, M. Rylie, col., 59 y, G. Wehrman, 6 years.

Aug. 28—C. Curtis, 23 y., Jos. White, 36 y., Ben. Schumacher, C. Whitehead, 53 y., M. M. C. Hill, 42 y., Sallie Dickson, 16 y., Frank Dent, Jr., 6 y.

Aug. 28—M. A. Wilson, col. 12 y., Patrick Kinney, 38 y., H. Owen, col., 20 y., John Winston, col., 20 y., died in Hill City Infirmary, Geo. Carter, col., 21 y., died in the Hill City Infirmary, John Gleeson, 36 y., died in the Hill City Infirmary, G. Gorden, 27 y., died in the Hill City Infirmary, Thomas R. Quin, 35 y., W. F. Sneelan, 2 y.

Aug. 29—Wash. Strong, col., 17 y., S. Hassell, Leon Hirsch, Dr. L. E. Barber, 40 y., H. Myers, J. Jones, col., 11 y., Lizzie B. Freeman, col., 22 y., Mrs. Milley Wehrman, Thos. Noland, 31 y., L. Fisher, 20 y., Patrick Bradley, 48 y., S. Ross, 4 m., Hattie Moore, col., 29 y., Matt Reynolds, col., 26 y., C. P. Hennegan, 2 y., J. P. Allen, 45 years.

Aug. 30—Mollie McGuire, Albert Spengler, 21 y., Bridgett Doyle, 23 y., Annie L. Ryan, 9., Henry Perry, John stringer, col., 35 y., Alfred Simpson, col., 5 y., C. Wolters, 10 m., died in Warren county, M. Conners, 4 y., Henry E. King, 19 y., Jerry Murphy, 34 y., died in the Hospital, Fred Boettcher, 30 y., died in the Hospital, John F. Eggleston, 19 years.

Aug. 31—P. J. Touhey, 35 y., F. Keller, col., 70 y., Annie E. Fitzpatrick, 11 y., John Miller, 23 y., A. A. Bursely, 45 y., M. E. Netherland, 19 y., Mrs. R. H. Bowman, 19 y., W. H. Clements, 50 ys., Angelo Podesta, 31 y., Mollie Neville, 19 years.

Sept. 1—Helen Watt, 9 m., S. Ransom, col., 28 y., Julia Jenkins, col, 40 y., Wm. W. Huener, 4 ys., Pete Rouen, 36 ys., Lizzie Perry, 35 y., Rob't Mitchell, col., E. Gant, col., 38 y., Brown Winston, col., 30 y., David Crump, col., 30 y., Henry Nason, col., Lit Cash, col., Harry Rutley, Cecilia Flieller, y., Mary Johnson, 40 y., died in the Hill City Infirmary, Dr. Ferro, 62 y, died in the Hill City Infirmary, Martin O'Donnell, 20 y, died in the Hill City Infirmary, Jerry O'Brien, 46 y, Mrs. Ann Travis, Pat. Lamb, 18.

Sept. 2—Father J. H. McManus, 40 y, Louisa Haining, 35 y, Maggie White, 4 y. Charles Bradley, col, 11, John Parmer, col, 6 y, I. P. Box, 40 y, Mrs. Delia McKenna, 36 y, Hugh Gillan, 35 y, Delia Morrow, 24 y, C. H. Nathan, 26 y, Maggie Burt, J. W. Jolley, 28 y, Miss Jessie Alexander, 17 y, Jos. F. Doll, 86 y, Mrs. B. C. Camillo, 25 y. J. W. Woodruff, 42 y, Hospital, Ellen Clark, col., E. Jordon, col., 45 y, Milton Cooper, Lee Rice, 49 years.

Sept. 3—Henry James, col., 28 y, —— Record, 35 y, Farnatore Moltedo, 40 y, Maliso Cross, col., Harry Brown, col, 28 y, A. M. Stubble, 60 y, M. M. Schiller, 36 y. Thos. Trainor, 46 y, Warren county, Antonio Gomes, 14 y, —— Riddell, 20 y, Lizzie Dixon, 20 y, Hospital, Rob't Sims, col., Hospital, Lummie Gerard, 7 y, A. Simons, 45 y, Hospital, C. F. Duggan, 23 y, Hospital, Isaac Hanley, 43 y, M. McNamara, Clarence Enlow, col, 2 y, T. Haines, col., 35 y, Bettie Williams, col., 40 y. Jos. Fegilno, 30 y, Ike Fagans, col., 34 y, Hospital, Scott Tyler, col., J. S. Methua, Willie Spengler, 21 y, Luke Mason, col., 32 y, Warren county, Sam. Coleman, col., Warren county, Willie Haines, E. Thornton, col., Geo. Homan, 58 y., E. Kalmbach, 4 y, Maurice Meyer, 25 y, Joe Jones, col., 32 y, Hospital, P. A. Ware, col, 25 y, Daniel J. Marchant, 13 y, Warren county, J. A. Cooper, 26 y, Hospital.

Sept. 4—Fred. Hardwick, Ida S. Huener, 24 y, W. H. Rice, col., 40 y, A. H. Middleton, col, 24 y, Margaret Middleton, col., 41 y, Mrs. White, 28 y, Annie Davis, col., 23 y, J. T. Tinney, A. B. Manlove, 20 y, C. Salley, 24 y, Geo. Moore, col, 87 y, Phillip Roe, 48 y, Wm. Scott, col., 35 y, Wm. Jackson, col., 35 y, Bettie Roberson, col., 23 y, Miss Eliza Thrift, 23 y, Louisa Voeinkle, 3 y, Willie M. Auter, 19 y, Caroline Roost, 36 y, J. J. Bowen, 40 y, Dave P. Kennedy, 4 y, Thos. Allen, col., 21 y, Hospital, Geo. Berry, 27 y, Hospital, Thomas Kendall, 19 y, Alice V. Hundermark, 14 years.

Sept. 5—Mrs. West, 28 y, J. H. West, 1 y, M. C. West, 4 y, Pomp Green, col., 50 y, John Bodine, 48 y, W. V. North, M. McManus, 40 y, Annie Davis, 21 y, Wm. Porter, col., 40 y, Mollie McCoy, 25 y, Miss Addie Barnett, 22 y, M. Brown, col., 41 y, Annie McKenna, 14 y, Hospital, Hugh McKenna, 11 y, Hospital, Joe Marona, 40 y, Hospital.

Sept. 5—J. S. Blanchard, 30 y, Hospital, Gustave Harlan, 30 y, Hospital. Louisa Arther, col., 44 y, Maggie Mathias, col., 20 y, Calvin Fishback, 11 y, Henry Williams, col., 45 y, R. Walsh, 33 y, D. Davis, col., 24 y, Jake Zimmerman, 29 y, J. F. Ferguson, 48 y, Dr. P. F. Whitehead, 40 y, Wm. Miles, 23 y, Warren county, Martha Ward, col., 7 m, Frank Coleman, col, 21 y, John D. Roach, 22 y, John Karney, 4 y, Miss Mary E. Horn, 20 y, Hospital, Charles L. Carter, col., 21 y, Robt. A. Hundermark, 45 y, R. Anderson, col., 25 y, Hannah Graham, col., R.

Langford, 26 y, Mary Entel, 22 y, Miss Lena Duffner, 18 y, Louisa Schmidt, 10 years.

Sept. 6—Arthur Vincends, col., 6 y, Miss Mattie McClendon, 19 y, Maggie M. Leofold, 1 y, Chas. Hennesy, 4 y, Susie Wheat, col., 22 y, Fay Dunbar, col., 29 y, John Whitehead, col., 40 y, ——Moon, col., 6 y, Annie Parker, col., 8 y, Mrs. Margeret Crawford, 40 y, Miss Mary A. Fitzpatrick, 43 y, Miss Martha McElroy 18 y, Lucy Wilson, col., 8 y, Phillip Hubbard, 41 y, John Carr, col., 40 y, J. R. Levie, 30 y, C. Pellrin, 35 y, Hospital, W. McHenry, Hospital, Green Adams, col., Hospital, Sarah Williams, Hospital, Louisa McKenna, Hospital, Augusta Stewart, col., Hospital, Sarah Caldwell, col., 50 y, R. Tindal., 26 y, Sister Mary Regis Grant, 22 y, ——Burtz, Mrs. Ann Fends, Mrs. Edward Ryan, 22 y, Thos. Metzler, Jr., 22 y, Unknown colored man, Hospital, J. C. Fitzpatrick, 31 y, John Cullen, 74 y, Chas. M. Rose, 27 y, Louisa M. Guscio, 2 y, Fulton Carter, col., Emma Clark, 10 y, Geo. Burns. 35 y, W. L. McCrady, Bettie S. Hanes, 3 y, Thos Fitzpatrick, 7 y.

Sept. 7—C. Parvangher, R. C. Benson, 44 y, Mary Carroll, 23 y, Albert Edwards, Jacob Roost, 13 y, Jerry Murphy, 40 y, E. Melvaney, 37 y, Dolly Brown col., Francis P. Walmsley, M. Jacobson, Sister Mary Bernadine Murry, 30 y' Sam Fields, col., E. Mosyel, col., Mrs. S. C. Potts, Isaac Robinson, col., 40 y Child, col., Mrs. Gussie Zucker, J. B. P. Dardinnac, 49 y, W. S. Harrison, 43 y,' N. Camillo, 9 m, G. W. McGinty, Robt. Diggs. col., 24 y, Mary Wallace, col., 25 y, Rev. Calvin Brown, col., 56 y, Martha E. Perry, 13 y, E. Margueritz, 56 y, Hospital, Nancy Glass, col., 45 y, Hospital, Peter Burns, 40 y, Hospital, J. C. Wilson, 24 y, Hospital, Richard Mason. Hospital, Mary F. Owens. 13 y, Mrs. Minnie Larsell, 21 y, Peter W. Guecio, 7 y, E. F. Conners, 1 m.

Sept. 8—Walter C. Rose, 23 y, H. E. Brown, col., 10 y, D. Shorter, 8 m, Frank Davis. 41 y, D. A. Shields, 24 y, Royal Chambers, col., 85 y, Luke Thornton. col., 38 y, Oscar Jones, col., 38 y, Lizzie Atwood, 6 y, John McCann, 22 y, J. W. Smarr, 21 y, Emma Crayton, col., 6 y, Fred Miller, 36 y, Mary Mason, col., J. Moore, col., 22 y, died in the Hospital, J. McField, col.. died in Hospital, D. Coleman, col., 14 y, died in the Hospital, Wm. B. Lavins, 4 m, C. Sally, 26 y, Jas. Conway, 28 y, John Simpson, Warren county, Abe Lowenberg, 16 y, S. M. Haining, Hugh McCoy, 20 y, Justice Hudson, col., Rosa E. Schuler, 19 y, Jas. Warrington, 42 y, Mrs. C. Conklin, 26 y, Wm. Ferrell, col., 4 y, Robt. French, 4 y, Minty Brown, col., 21 y, Hospital, Jas. Moore. col., 22 y, Hospital, Antonio Hannelin, 38 y, Hospital, Henry Lawrence, 20 y, Hospital, Carrie Fousse, 19 y, Josie Auter, 16 y, Alfred Berg.

Sept. 9—Letitia Murphy, 14 y, Eddie Frank, 10 y, Ella Duffner, 16 y, Warren county, Mollie Dixie, col., 25 y, A. Burke, col., 40 y, Josephine Delaney, 24 y, H. Starks, col., Belle Lee Maloy, 13 y, Clarinda Scott, col., 45 y, Chas. Claver, 26 y, Sarah Gray, col., 40 y, J. W. Alvis, 25 y. Ral'h Rosenthal 30 y, Honora Cody, 3 w David Kyle, 41 y, A. K. Ellis, col., 13 y, Margaret D. Harris, 10 y, Wm. Butcher, col., 5 y, C. S. Boswell, 4 y, A. Methun, 18 y, ——Lafayette, col., A. B. Caskey. 30 y, ——Gibson, 29 y, Bettie Baum, 33 y, Mary E. Dougherty, 10 y, Calvin Russell, col., 14 y, ——Peacock, col., 40 y. Infant of Mrs. Box, Henry Meny, 49 y, Hospital, Caroline Roost, 12 y, Hospital, Jacob Lirgot, 23 y, Hospital, Jno Kelly, 32 y, Hospital, Rosaline Roost, 8 y, Hospital, Lewis Cass, 20 y, Martin Keary, 56 y, Emma Daymond, col., Francis Read, col., 17 y, Mamie Rooks, 7 y, Warren county, W. G. Moore, Jr., 16 y, Delia Tvargosky, 21 y, Warren county, H. Carrington, 50 y, Warren county.

Sept. 10—Albert Wheat, col., 52 y, Charlotte Mack, col., 30 y, Wm. Jackson, col., 60 y, Warren county, Wm. Cash, col., 22 y, Chas. Roeshe, 31 y, W. McDonald, 40 y, Jim Jones. col., 36 y, J. C. Brown, 33 y, S. Powder, 50 y, Jas. W. Geary, 23 y, C. Lewis, col., 21 y, Katie Butler, 3 y, Robert Mays, 12 y, John Thomas, col., 32 y, Burrell Reid, col., 24 y, James Goldou, 45 y, Dr. J. B. Norris, 32 y, volunteer physician from Chattanooga, Chas. Colovan, 27 y, Mrs. C. C. Knight, 26 y, Dr. Sappington, 40 y, E. Carter, col., 32 y, Jeff. Porterfield, 18 y, Sister Mary Columba McGrath, 22 y, Mathew Frank, 16 y, Thomas Johnson, col., 35 y, Katie Gallagher, 14 y, Dave Harmon, 25 y, R. Wilson, col., 4 y, John Dyke, 31 y, J. W. Hubbard, col., 3 y, Jas Mitchell, 29 y, Sam Donaldson, col.. 1 d, Jim Donaldson, col., 1 d, Antonio Johnson, col.. 41 y, Jas McKenna, 10 y, died in the Hospital, John Smitta, 30 y, aied in the Hospital. W. H. O'Rourke, 35 y, died in the Hospital, Maggie L. Arnold, 16 y, Joseph Mahin, 27 y, Lucy Johnson, col., 36 y, James Revnolds, 40 y.

Sept. 11—Chas. T. Kendall, 13 y, Virginia Dyke, 4 m, J. H. Graff, 35 y, Mrs. E. Rebay, 22 y, Sarah Maberry, 23 y, Ben Green, col., 4 w, Laura Coleman, col.

30 y, Hiram French, 40 y, Josephine Fishback, col., 13 y, Otto Wherman, 45 y, Lizzie Wherman, 16 y, George Bridge, 33 y, Chas. F. Taffe, 35 y, Miss Mary O'-Connyr. 28 y, William Grinstead, col., 17, Abe Stringer, col., 26 y, Edward Harrison, 28 y, Miss Mary Geary, 18 y, Dr. Potts, Dr. Blichfeldt 39 y, volunteer physician from Chattanooga, Primas Clowery, col., 24 y, Frankie Owens, 10 y, Albert Beling, 25 y, died in the Hospital, Julia Yerger, col, 23 y, died in the Hospital, Thos. B. Walker, 14 y, Miss Maggie McMellen, 20 y, D. A. Culley, 49 y.

Sept. 12—I Wagner, Mary Plump, col., 8 y, Mary Briscoe, col., 35 y, Mrs. Ella Grammer, 31 y, John Harris, 8 y, Phœbe Carter, col., 60 y, John Brown, col., 35 y. —— Rashell, col., 22 y, P, Ipolite, 20 y, died in the Hospital, Miss Minnie Haining, 20 y, Willie Holmes, 14 y, Florence Anna Dowart, 8 y, Charles P. Sharp, 4 y, Katie Saunders, col., 22 y.

Sept. 18—Eva B. Moody, Eddie Rothschild, 3 y, Miss Virginia Augusto, 20 y, Hattie Duffner, 12 y, Warren county, Harriet Scott, col., 27 y, Orelia Rankins, col., 22 y, Geo W. Arnold, 21 y, G. V. Wood, 36 y, C. M. Carr, 32 y, died in the Hospital. Matt McClendon, col., 46 y, died in Warren county, J. W. Graff, 7 m, Robert Wilson, 30 y, C. W. Kellogg, 31 y, J. D. Jamison, 47 y, died in the Hospital, E. E. McGuire, 8 y, Thos. H. Jones, 18 y, Oliver Dyer, col., 85, y, Thomas Edwards, col., 36 y, Chattanooga nurse, Margaret Davis, col., 37 y, died in the Hospital, Frank Morris, col., 26 y, died in the Hospital, Nellie Doyle, 18 y, Mrs. Haining, 55 y, Mrs. C. B. Harrison, 82 y, Warren county, F. B. James, col., 1 y, Nat. Engle, 26 y, W. Johnson, col., 18 y, LeRue C. Thompkins, 3 y, John Johnson, col., 26 y, Miss Bridget Mulvihil, 19 y, died in Warren county, Wm. Gannon, 17 y, LeGrand Swafford, 8 m, Miss Mattie Mullen, 18 y, Freeman Edwards, col., 52 y, Daisy Munroe, 4, y, died in Warren county, Julia A. Walmsley, 10 y, Sister Mary Gonzaga Dailey, 22 y.

Sept. 24—Sandy Sterling, col., 25 y, John McMorrow, 65 y, Katie Haining, 12 y, Hospital, Sanford Shelliday, col., Warren county, Clotilda West, 7 y, Eliza J. Morrison. 27 y, Hospital, Josephine M. Hossley, 1 y, D. O'Sullivan, 32 y, Florence A. Hanes, 15 y, Rev John Vitola, Conway Flowerce, 10 y, Geo. Gannon, 10 y. Robert Marble, col., Lelia Salley, 11 y, Miss Ella McCabe, 28 y, G. M. Thomas, 3 m, Geo. M. North, 4 y, H. E. Lewis, Jr., col., 9 d, Phillip Hoggatt, 32 y, Matilda Smith, col., 43 y; Mary E. Boswell, 7 y, Edward Ryan, 40, y, Anthony Blake, col., 21 y, Warren county.

Sept. 15—James Anderson, col., 40, —— Chapman, Thos. H. Rigby, 21 y, residence Vicksburg, died at Newman's Grove, Jim Green, col., 6 y, Calvin Porter, col., 42 y, Warren county. Jennie Brown, col., 22 y, John Augustine, 43 years, John Russell, col., 11 y, Henry Bolton, col., 9 y, Charlotte L. Green, 8 y, Gramilla Vincent, col., 56 y, Warren county.

Sept. 16—Lewis H. Haines, Carter Williams, col. 54 y, Mrs. Credon, 36 y, Miss Annie Bitterman, 19 y, Pierre Rivinac, 20 y, George Rebay, 45 y, John Snow, 26 y, Hospital, F. G. Shaw, 12 y, W. H. Edrington, 60 y, Ed. Massengale, 40 y, Chatanooga nurse. Mrs. M. A. Bridges, 27 y, E. V. Marble, col., 1 y, Geo. S. Walmsley, Jr., 2 y, A. Jingles, 30 y, James Beresford, 9 y, A. L. Bridges, 6 y, Mrs. M. A. Cully, Lelia Mann, 2 y, Phillip Drushell, 40 y, James Smith, col., 17 y, James B. Cox, 19 y, Poladore Austin, col., 19 y, Thomas Demarchi, 8 y.

Sept. 17—Annie M. Wood, 4 y, Chas Hasie, 35 y, Lena Duffner, 1 y, Warren county, Carminio Bonizio, 28 y, Rev. Jeff Thompson, col, 30 y, Mary Jingles, 35 y, Frank Mitchell, 40 y, Stephen Johnson, col., 30 y, Warren county, —— Geary, John W. Munroe, 11 y, Warren county, Violet Jackson, col., 24 y, Mike Golden, 5 y, Taylor Brady, col., 45 y, Mary A. Vanderburg, 13 y, Morris Geary, 45 y, Miss Mary J. F. Wolfe, 22 y, W. R. Jones, 37 y, Wm. Hammond, col., 32 ys, died in Warren county, George Heflinger, 30 y, Joseph Alerdice, 40 y, Mary E. Graff, 37 y, Mrs Fannie Brown, 30 y, Norman Hunt, 35 y, Warren county.

Sept. 18—Miss Sallie L. Tanner, 16 y, Miss Annie R. Tanner, 14 y, Cornelia Rivinac, 18 y, Bessie Owens, 5 y, died in Warren county, Robert Snow 69 y, died in the Hospital, Wm. Pintz, 48 y, died in the Hospital, Patrick Henegan, 42 y, James Martin, 25 y, Willie Golden, 2 v, Joseph Spengler, 17 y.

Sept. 19—James English, 34 y, Bernard Duffner, 3 y, died in Warren county, Mrs. Cyrille Lambert, 24 y, Rose Leonard, col., 22 y, Miss Rosanna Ragan, 36 y, died in Warren county, Mrs. F. J. Harris, 30 y, Mary Aiken, col., 50 y, Bill Rigley, col., 70 y, died in the Hospital, Henry Taylor, col., 1 y, L. Munroe, 8 y, died in Warren county, Lewis Williams, col., 75 y, Emeline Coleman, col., 40 y, Mattie Smith, col., 33 y, Angus Cameron, 7 y, Miss Clara Wadsworth, 25 y, F. W. Goodrich, 25 y, W. J. Shuler, 22 y, Miss Riddell.

Sept. 20—Annie McGinnis, 9 y, —— Watson. col., 2 y, died in Warren county.

13

Miss Annie McCabe, 19 y, Frank C. Lewis, 25 y, died in the Hospital, Chas. Sutherland, 4 y, died in the Hospital, Wm. A. Fairchild, 41 y, John A. Davidson, 18 y.

Sept. 21—Andrew Duffey, 32 y, Fanny Pierce, col., 30 y. Albert Rothschild, 10 y, Sandy Moorehead, col., 25, died in the Hospital, A, R. Kezer, 41 y, died in the Hospital, T. M. Baggett, 4 y, died in Warren county, Fannie Washington, col., 30 y, —— Clark, 8 m, died in Warren county.

Sept. 22—Mary C. Klein, 10 y, W. Mitchell, col., 6 m. Henry Jackson, col., died in Warren county, Mack Thomas, col., 25 y, —— Adams, 10 m, died in Warren county, Unknown colored man, died in Warren county.

Sept. 23—Mrs. Wertz, L. Fort, col., Lucinda Jenkins, col. 7 y, Mary Henessy, 2 y, died in Warren county, Patrick O'Neal, 10 y, died in Warren county, John Young, col., 30 y, Thomas Matox, col., 50 y, Henry W. Cook, 20 y.

Sept. 25—Fred L. Flowers. 6 y, died at Bovina, A. W. Hedrick, 25 y, Annie M. Klien, 19 y, Willie M. King, 6 y.

Sept. 25—Malisa Onsley, col., 13 y, died in Warren county, Rosa Frank, 6 y, Maggie Hennesy, 4 y, died in Warren county, Thos. C. Russell, 3 y, Rosalie Collins, col., 33 y, Mary Toohey, 5 y, Annie L. Morgan, col., 20 y, Albert Ross, col., 35 y, died in Warren county, Louis Turner, col., 23 y, died in Warren county, Minnie L. Vanderberg, 2 y, James J. Boswell, 2 y.

Sept. 26—Isadore Meyer, 33 y, died at Bovina, Wm. M. Rockwood, 40 y, Chas. Reede, Lucy W. Cook, 8 y, H. Potts, col., 75 y, Mrs. Cameron, Dr. J. S Roach, 26 y, ——Bennett, died in the Hospital, Albert Dugan, col., 12 y, died in Warren county, Chas. B. Shottman, 5 y, Mrs Augustine, Milton Harris, 5 y, Mattie McClenon, 1 m, John Marcus, died in Warren county, Hanna Marcus, died in Warren county.

Sept. 26—Benny O'Brien, 6 y, Minnie Green, col., 6 w, Sister Agnes Weaver, ——Kingspight, 1 y, Phillip Drushell, 4 y, died in Warren county, Bettie Taylor, col., 30 y, Stephen R. Mount, 83 y, Lou Williams, col, John Kluch, J. A Neal, 51 y, died in the Hospital, G. C. Washington, col., 24 y, died in the Hospital, Mrs Schendal, John Sagona, 3 m, died in Warren county, Minnie Schendal, 6 y, Kate Hennesy 1 y, died in Warren county, John Golden, 6 y.

Sept. 28—Richard M. Dohler, Jr., 2 m.

Sept. 28—D. R. Black, 40 y, died in Warren county, Elisha Clark, 22 y, L. Sadler, col, 34 y, died in Warren county, Wm. J. Feelan, 5 y, died in Warren county, Willie Geary, 12 y, Thos. Fultz, col, 32 y, died in the Hospital, Oscar N. Stith, 32 y, died in Warren county, Matt. Willingham, 84 y, died in Warren county, C. F. Davenport, col, 3 y, Valentine Zollinger, 45 y, died in Warren county, Chas. M. Reynolds, 1 y.

Sept. 29—Marks Brown, 20 y, Zack Taylor, col, 43 y, died in Warren county, Rob't Jingles, 5 y, Julius Susman, 21 y, Miss Laura Ford, 22 y, Mrs. Mary M. Puncky. 22 y.

Sept. 30—Isadore Mayer, 22 y, Carrie Williams, col, 1 y, James J. Fox, 23 y, died in Warren county, James McGinnis, died in Warren county, Alex. M. Butler, 3 y, Mrs. M. L. Jordan, 56 y, Ignatius O'Leary, 1 y, Israel Mendle, 9 y., W. J. McGinty, 26 y, John M. Scannell, 19 y, Albert A. Flowers, 8 y, died in Warren county, Willie Weatherly, 5 y, C. W. Dwight, Mary A. Smith, 18 y, Daniel Schiller, 35 y.

Oct. 1—Robert Jones, col, 47 y, Bertha Schendal, 9 m, Mrs. R. C. Adams, 30 y, N. O'Neal, 54 y. Warren county, Maggie Moore, col, 5 y, Warren county, Herman Wesche, 24 y, died in the Hospital, Miss M. A. R. Evans, 13 y, died in Warren county.

Oct. 2—Mrs. Carrie T. Russell, 29 y, Henry A. Miller, 24 y, Oscar F. Genella, 18 y, W. H. Peoples, 40 y, died in the Hospital, A. Alexander, 57 y, Wolf Sokolosky, 28 y, Joe Holmes, col, Warren county, Antoine Sutbrocker, 24 y, John Bowen, 5 y, John Latcher, 16 y.

Oct. 3—Terrance Laughlin, 10 y, John Chatam, 20 y, W. Russell, col, 9 m, Mary Allen, 20 y.

Oct. 4—Violet Marcus, 5 y, A. W. Dennett, 22 y, died in the Hospital, Sam. Scott, col, 50 y, Eliza Sheppard, 24 y, Warren county, Ida W. Huner, 9 m, Catherine Lucett, 37 y, Herman Mendel, 34 y.

Oct. 5—Marcus Schendal, 4 y, Chas. Bingham, col, 40 y, Warren county, Susan Cox, col, 50 y, Warren county, Kate Harris, col, 19 y, Maurice Schendal, 37 y, James Anderson, Warren county.

Oct. 6—Mrs. Mattie E. Bacon, 35 y, Minnie Drushell 13 y, Warren county.

Oct. 7—Dr. M. Blackman, Warren county, E. H. Hammett, 1 y, Warren county, Arthur N. Bacon, 2 y, Sam Williams, col, 5 weeks, Henrietta Terrell, col 27 y, Warren county, William Q. Arnold, 18 y.

Oct. 8—Fred Walker, col, 3 y, R. Kalmbach, 45 y, Bessie K. Powell, 3 y, Henry Powell, col, 25 y, died in the Hospital, Irwin Dixon, col, 32 y, Warren county, Charles C. Spengler, 9 y.

Oct. 9—Lizzie Grey, col, 32 y. Barney Bog'e, 45 y, verdict of the jury: came to his death from yellow fever. Gus. E. Marks, 27 y, Mrs. Sophia W. Woods, 66 y.

Oct. 10—Minnie Mendel, 5 y, James Lewis, col, 30 y, Isham Davenport, col, 40 y, Warren county, James R. Jackson, 1 y, Warren county, Houston Fate, 39 y, died in the Hospital, Patrick Collins, 31 y, died in the Hospital.

Oct. 11—E B. Davison, Jr., 4 y, John King, 4 y. Warren county, Lafayette King, 2 y, Warren county, Joseph Weyer, 22 y, Warren county, Julia Crecey, col, 8 y, Warren county, Alois Zollinger, Warren county, Dr. Hapholdt, 52 y, died in the Hospital, B. Worthey, col, 5 y, Warren county, Betsy Minor, col, 50 y, Warren county, Annie Floyd, 13 y., died at Delta, Louisiana.

Oct. 12—Augusta Raum, 11 m, Warren county, B. N. Jordan, 32 y, Warren county, Charles Owens, col, 18 y, Warren county, Ellen Willingham, 1 m, died in the Hospital.

Oct. 13—Willis J. Bacon, 4 y, Mrs. E. L. Gray, 42 y, died in Warren county, Samuel J. Hassell 2 m.

Oct. 14—Lucelia Winbush, 6 m, John W. Brackett, 30 y, Sophia Haven, 6 y, Warren county, Joseph Feibleman, 21 y, died at Delta, Louisiana, Barbara E. Latcher, 13 y, Louis Schaffer, 9 days, Geo. S. Yerger, 35 y.

Oct. 15—Jeney, col, 6 y, Floyd Porterfield, 6 y, died at Delta, Louisiana, Horace H. Snead, 1 m. George C. Cox, col, 1 m.

Oct. 16—Levie Cook, col, 25 y, Mrs. C. Goldberg, died at Delta, Louisiana, Frank E. Love, 21 y......Oct. 17—Lieut. H. H. Benner, U. S. A., interred in National Cemetery, Helen Tilitz, 6 y, Warren county, Antonio G. Bobb, 8 y, Warren county, John Griffin, 45 y, died in the Hospital.

Oct 18—Miss Carrie Lacroix, 13 y, died in Warren county, J. M. Dalton, 52 y, died in the Hospital, Mike Laughlin, 30 y.....Oct. 19—Percy Smith, 13 y, Warren county, Louisa Graves. col, 72 y, Will H. Hall, 24 y.

Oct. 20—Julia Curran, 18 y, Freddie B. Miles, 17 y, Clayton Augustus, 67 y. .....Oct. 21—Sam Steele, 28 y, Delia Dorsey, col, 29 y.....Oct. 22—R. J. Hill, col, 1 m, Edwin B. Hill, 30 y, died in Warren county, Virginia Kidd, 28 y, Warren county.

Oct. 22—Mitchell Cox, col, 7 y, Stacey A. Hoggatt, died at Mounds, Louisiana Jacob L. Katzmier, 18 y. died in Warren county......Oct. 23——Ransom, col, 9 days, Ida Smith, 16 y, Warren county, Dr. Lewis Gilland, died in Delta, Louisiana, Mary Belle Peale, 9 y, died in Warren county, Capt. E. B. Willis, 52 y, G. W. Edwards. 61 y.

Oct. 24—N. V. Jane, Jr., 7 y......Oct. 25—Edward O'Neal, 40 y, Mary E. Meyer, 2 m, Alex. V. Brown, 45 y, died in Delta, Louisiana, Mamie L. Katzenmier, 3 y, E. Jacobs, col, 1 m, Bessie S. Hammett, Warren county, Unknown white man, 45 years, Warren county.

Oct. 26—Maj. J. B. Corkern, died in Delta, Louisiana. Ada A. Smith, 11 days, Warren county, John Lahen, 50 y, died in the Hospital......Oct. 27--Charles Sanguinetti, 17 y.

Oct. 28—John M. Wall, 3 y, Clara J. O'Hara, 1 y, Andrew Richards, Marshall Smith. 4 y. Warren county......Oct. 29—Moses Conway, 5 y, died in Delta, Mrs. J. B. Corkern, died in Delta, Mrs. Mary E. Lawrence, 21 y, died in Delta...... Oct. 30—Mead Hylliard, 38 y.

Oct. 31—B. O. Tucker, col, 1 y ......Nov. 1—Miss Henrietta Jones, 53 y......Nov. 2—Halsie Howard, col, 70 y, Warren county, James Cunningham, 78 y, Mrs. Jennie N. Fitzgerald, 29 y, died at Bolton, Miss......Nov. 3—Infant child of M. O'Neal, 1 week.

Nov. 4 -James P. Raney, 35 y, died in the Hospital, Sandy Buckley, col, 2 m, Martin Kanard, 20 y, Warren county......Nov. 5—C. Alexson, 43 y, Warren county.

Nov. 7—Tom Smith, col, 50 y, Frank Lewis, col, 86 y......Nov. 9—William Armstead, 15 y, died at Ditchly, La......Nov. 11—Miss Messinger, 12 days......Nov. 15 —Nora Carson, col, 20 y.

Nov. 16—Samuel Kahn, 30 y, died at Delta......Nov. 17—Belle Thomas, col. Mary Hughes, colored, 25 y, Remains of Mrs. Cooley and two children ; removed from Louisiana.

Nov. 20—Clifton Fitzgerald, 8 y..... Nov. 22—John Mannell, 36 y, died in the Hospital.

DEATHS IN WARREN COUNTY, FROM YELLOW FEVER.
From Vicksburg Herald.

There may possibly be some few errors in this list, as there has been no regular record kept of the deaths, and we were, therefore, compelled to depend upon the memory of persons living in the different portions of the county, from whom we obtained the lists.

Miss Bettie Collier, 18 y,
James Collier, 64 y,
Miss Alice Collier, 15 y,
Eola Maud Trindle, 1 y.
Wm. George Trindle, 8 y,
Margaret Belle Trindle, 4 y,
Miss Agnes Axelson, 16 y,
Cornelius Axelson, 44 y,
Henry P. Axelson, 18 y,
Mrs. Mary Standard, 68 y,
Mrs. Millie Standard, 23 y,
S. W. McHam, 39 y,
G. B. McHam, 1 y,
Mrs. S. H. McHam, 33 y,
Miss H. G. McHam, 6 y,
Mrs. Ryan,
—— Ryan,
Merris Solomon, 4 y,
Wm. Loyd, 52 y,
Sophie Loyd, 46 y,
Freddie Loyd, 12 y,
Miss Annie Loyd, 16 y,
Albert Loyd, Jr., infant,
C. A. Warnaph, 25 y,
Miss Bettie Beall, 16 y,
Miss Katie Gibson, 15 y,
Miss Emmie Gibson, 13 y,
—— Westerberg, 55 y.
Mrs. Patience Kline, 60 y,
Mrs. D. B. Nailor, 60 y,
Ninion F. Kline, Jr., 21 y,
Larson Vickstron, 24 y,
Lewis Holt, 55 y,
A. Oberg, 20 y,
Mrs. Sallie Monette, 44 y,
Miss Annie Kline Monette, 18 y,
Gibson Monette, 12 y,
C. A. Larson, 30 y,
Mrs. Sophia Pettit, 16 y.
Dr. Wm. E. Monette, 44 y,
Mrs. Mary E. Featherstun, 43 y,
Wesley Featherstun, 10 y,
Miss Laura Featherstun, 10 y.
Abbie Featherstun, 15 y,
Willie Featherstun, 12 y,
Miss A. A. Rundell, 30 y,
W. B. Cleland, 26 y,
Bobie Cleland, 4 weeks,
Mrs. Sarah Billingslea, 67 y,
Wm. Bullock, 20 y,
Jones Wilkins, 34 y,
Joe. Johnston, 32 y,
Mrs. Joe. Johnston, 29 y,
Miss Annie Johnston,
Dick Taylor, 45 y,
Eddie Taylor, 13 y,
George A. Tribble, 25 y,
Mrs. George A. Tribble, 22 y,
Dr. B. H. Gotthelf, 60 y,

Isadore Meyer, 20 y,
A. C. Cameron, 55 y,
Benny Cameron, 23 y,
L. Cameron Fox, 25 y,
Mrs. Roberts, 28 y,
J. A. McInnis. 30 y,
Mrs. Lau a McInnis, 26 y,
Mary Belle McInnis, 1 y,
Aleck B. Powell, 32 y,
Clarence Powell, 4 y.
Augustus Newman, 54 y,
Mrs. Sallie Newman, 48 y,
Mrs. Dr. J. C. Newman, 54 y,
Mrs. Chesley Newman Brabston, 26 y,
Dr. Geo. T. Birdsong, 30 y,
Mrs. Ben. Dart, 27 y,
Julius Dart, 1 y,
Maj. J. Reese Cook, 63 y,
Capt. E. Bryant Willis, 52 y,
Louis N. Shannon, 33 y,
—— Marvin, 55 y,
Dr. W. J. Nesmith, 35 y,
Miss Matilda Edwards, 20 y,
S. B. Wall, 64 y,
Willie Spears, 16 y,
Mrs. Weaver, 60 y,
Lawrence Lanier, 24 y,
Aaron C. Brooks, 34 y,
Child of Mrs. Holt,
Adolph Lorch, 27 y,
M. Baker,
L. King,
John King,
W. R. Cushman,
W. A. Cushman,
C. B. Cushman,
Mrs. M. Cushman and two children,
Mrs. M. E. Kendall and child,
Mrs. W. R. Cushman and child,
Mrs. D. W. Clark,
Four children of Mrs. Jas. Higgins,
Mrs. J. C. Jones,
J. L. Ketzenmier,
Mr. Martz,
Mrs. Martz,
Mr. Wertz and two children,
B. T. Edwards.
Miss Matilda Edwards,
S. W. Wahl,
Mrs. Jessie Standard,
Henry Jones,
—— Wilson.
Mrs.—— Wilson,
Mrs. Margaret Johnson, 75 y.
Henderson Hall, 68 y,
Thomas Hall, 22 y,
Mrs. M. A. Hall, 27 y,
Mrs. A. Brown, 30 y,
Dr. Ferriss, 40 y,

Morris H. Gotthelf, 21 y,
Miss Strealy, 6 y,
Jerry Streely, 4 y,
Ben. Davis. 48 y,
Mrs. Ben. Davis, 40 y.
Judge Davis, 6 y,
Sally Keller, 24 y,
Jaurdie Oates, 14 y,
Addison Oatis, 60 y,
Lesly Oatis, 32 y,
Warren Oatis, 25 y,
Laura Otis, 27 y,
Amanda Oatis, 16 y,
Fannie Oatis, 14 y,
Willis Oatis, 11 y,
Laura Ferguson, 5 y,
Mr. O'Brien, 55 y,
Son of Mr. O'Brien, 12 y,
Mr. J. W. Finch, 38 y,
Milton H. Biglow, 40 y.
Robert W. Chapel, 50 y,
Wm. Bullock,
Mrs. Biblingstone,
Dr. Brodsing,
E. Flowers,
Mrs. L. Fox,
D. A. Cameron,
Mrs. J. W. Gray,
J. W. Powell,
S. W. Shannon,
Aaron Brooks,
Mrs. Jewell.

Mrs. Dr. Ferris, 30 y,
Son of Dr. Ferris, 4 y,
Charles V. D. Riddle,
Lottie Tuley Riddle,
Thomas Riddle,
Charles Hollman,
Mrs. J. C. Jemerson,
Alex. McCarty,
Mrs. McCarty's infant,
James C. Watts, Sr.,
German Gardner,
James Dye.
Miss Ada Brown,
Miss Lillie Snyder,
Miss Sallie Snyder,
Mrs. Wilson.
Miss Cora Wilson,
Mollie Wilson,
Willie Wilson,
Mrs. Dr. Ferry,
Douglas Ferry.
H. T. Jones.
Wm. Mac Ever,
Mrs. Holt,
H. Leach,
J. N. McEnnis,
Mrs. L. McEnnis,
Mrs. W. H. Bigelow,
Mrs. Joseph J. Fox,
John McInnis,
Mary E. Smith,
Dr. Wuyman,

THE SITUATION IN VICKSBURG.
Herald, Saturday, Aug. 24.

The shadow of a great woe hangs over our devoted city. The number suffering from the pestilence is fearful, as accurate reports published elsewhere will prove, and every hour swells the list. The medical fraternity of Vicksburg are worn out, and many of them are on the sick list. Let immediate application be made for competent medical assistance. Vicksburg and Grenada are twin sisters in sorrow, and we have not the heart to dwell upon the heart-rending subject. All that humanity and self-abnegation can accomplish is being done, but aid must come from sections not stricken. Yesterday we saw corpses hurried to the grave without attendant, and God only knows the ghastly sights and scenes of pain transpiring in Vicksburg to-night. We have seen the horrors of the battlefield, and have tasted the sorrows and deprivations of prison life, have buried comrades, and friends on lonely, far-off battle-fields, but we have never, in a varied and eventful life, witnessed anything which so awakened the sensibilities of our nature. May God have mercy on us all.   *   *   *   *

All of the physicians in the city have had to refuse applications on account of sheer physicial inability to give them proper attention. They are overworked, and if the progress of the disease is not arrested they will soon be *hors du combat*. There are at least one hundred new cases in the city, and the whole number sick—not including those under treatment—swells into the hundreds. This is not a statement published to excite apprehensions, but to lay the facts before those who are able to lend their assistance in this hour of our bitter need.

LEBANON DISTRICT, HINDS COUNTY.

Joseph Jacobs, Mrs. J. Jacobs, child of A. Harrison, infant of Ben Jacobs, —— Ward, Mrs. Moses, Mrs. O'Brien, Emmett O'Brien, Mrs. Monell, Robert McNair, Eddie McNair, David McNair, L. D. McNair, Sr., Mrs. Jas. Hamilton, Mrs. Allen,

Mrs. E. Edmondson, Ben. Jacobs, A. Gibbs, —— Ward, J. M. Moses, Miss Bettie McNair, Miss Emma Roberts, Joseph Jacobs, Jr., L. D. McNair, Jr., Mrs. Ben Jacobs, Miss Essie Russell, Mrs. David McNair, Pat McDermon, Mrs. Fannie Noble.

BAY ST. LOUIS.

Alice Arnold, Julian Adams, C. Breath, Henry Barthe, Frazier Barnard, child of — Campe, Wilfre Combel, Hubbard Cameron, Mrs. Doyle, daughter of Mrs. Doyle Miss DeWolf, Eliza Davis, Mrs. Dore and daughter, Alphonsine Estapa, Francis Estapa, Josephine Estapa, Sister Etiena (St. Joseph Convent) Lena Fischer, Bernedina Frederick, Barbara Frederic, Mary Foster, Susie Foster, Harry B. Fairchild, Ella Fairchild, Stephen Franklin, Joseph Gonzales, Malcomb Henderson, Henry Howell, John Henderson, col., Sallie Johnston, James Johnston, Mrs. E. Krost, Mr. Klein, W. B. List, Ellen Lawler, Emma Lawler, Dan. Lawler, Lissa (adopted daughter of Simon) Philman Lamourant, Victor Lassabe, Delphine Lassabe, Bertrand Lassabe, Miss Lawlor, Geo. Mayo, Ephraim C. Mudge, child of —— Muller, Helen G. Mayfield, G. S. May, Antoine Maggiore, Mittenberger, Odile, Abel Nicaise, Rebecca Nicaise, Carolina Prestel, Nicholas Prestel, Antonio Pierre, Mrs. Helen Suarez, Regina M. Suarez, Walter Sylvester, John J. Saucier, Capt. L. L. Taylor, Alfred Taconi, Jules Taconi, Salvador Tarrant, Steffano Terzia, P. Vassali, Francois Valconar, —— Vicelli, —— Vicelli, —— Vicelli, Mrs. White, Stella Walters, Geo. Williams, col., Annie S. D. Wolff, and 9 unknown.

BILOXI.

Miss Dunn.

STONEVILLE, WASHINGTON COUNTY.

(Several of these names are included in the list at bottom of Greenville list, on page 168.)
Ida Brown, Jno. Byrne, Walsh Burdett, Miss Burdett, Nathan Burdett, Sam Crockett, Geo. Dawkens, three children of —— Davis, J. E. Evenitz, B. F. Foley, Dr. A. S. Gerdine, Dr, Thos. Gaddis, Dr. Griffin, J. W. Hill, M. Hartman, Henry Jones, Dr. Kirby, Jacob Kleiber, Jr., Jacob Kleiber, Sr., Adolph Kausler, Henry Lemler, Mrs. Nancy Lamkin, Henry Monk, M. J. Morzinski, child of —— Morzinski, C. K. McAlister, Mrs. A. W. McAlister, Mrs. Wm. Montgomery, Dr. Wm. Montgomery, Phil McLean, Mrs. Rebecca Mellvin, Pat. McKeon, Andy McDonald, Dr. Oden, Thos. O'Brien, Dan. Olson, —— Priest, Sr., —— Priest, Jr., Pat. Quinn, James Steverson, D. L. Stone, Blanche Snowberger, —— Spears, Dan. Shaunchau, son of J. B. Walker, Eddie Winters, child of, —— Winters, Jack Winters, Mrs. C. A. Winters, Willie Wingfield, Walter Winfield.

OCEAN SPRINGS.

Father Charles, Joseph Ryan, Col. Strout.

SENATOBIA.

C. W. Creager, Mrs. Mira Davis, Mrs. D. L. Dean, Dabney Dickey, Mattie Dickey, George Dickey, Margarett, McGehee, Mrs. Cora Parker, Mrs. A. V. Saunders.

HORN LAKE.

Wm. Collins.

TERRY AND VICINITY.

Lisa Grayson, col., Jane Grayson, Dr. H. R. Godman, Joe Samson, col., one unknown.

CAYUGA, HINDS COUNTY.

Gen. Thos. M. Griffin, Mrs. Griffin, Mr. Hack, one colored.

MASONS WHO DIED OF YELLOW FEVER.

WASHINGTON LODGE, No. 3, Port Gibson—H nry S. Wheeless, Aug. 26; Claude H. Barrot, P. M., Sept. 11.

PEARL, No. 23, Jackson—Edward Steinberg, P. M., at Greenville, Sept. 13; Wm. M. Compton, near Holly Springs, Oct. 23; Geo. C. Granberry, Oct. 3.

HAZLEHURST, No. 25—M. W. Trawick, at New Orleans, Oct. 8.

VICKSBURG, No. 26—Wm. A. Fairchild, P. M., Past Grand Commander Knights Templar, Sept. 20; Chas. H. Taffe, Sept. 11; James Warrington, Sept. 8.

WM. H. STEVERS, No 121, Vicksburg—Chas. H. Nathan, Sept. 2; R. Kalmbach, Oct. 8; J. W. Conklin, Oct. 13; C. V. D. Riddle; Benj. C. Bookout, Oct. 17.

WALNUT HILLS, No. 191, Vicksburg—Thurston J. Thompson, P M, Aug. 10; Geo. H. Heffinger, Sept. 17.

Other Masons who died in Vicksburg and Vicinity—Dr. J. B. Norris, of a Lodge in Chattanooga Tenn., Sept. 10; B. H. Gotthelf, (Jewish Rabbi,) of Louisville, Ky., Sept. 7; G. W. Edwards, of a Lodge in New York City; J. F. Tenny, of a Lodge in Boston, Sept. 2; J. P. Allen, non-affiliate, Aug. 29; Dr. P. F. Whitehead, non-affiliate, Sept. 5; Geo. S. Yerger, of Mississippi Commandery, No. 1, Jackson, Oct. 14.

GRENADA, No. 31—R. Coffman, P. M., August 21; A. P. Saunders, P. M., Aug. 28; O. B. Rollins, P. M., Sept. 9; C. M. Coffman, Aug. 21; R. A. Collins, Aug. 26; W. M. Hankins; Dr. E. W. Hughes, Aug. 31; Dr. W. W. Hall, Aug. 30; Dr. W. B. May, Sept. 7; Dr. J. L. Milton, Aug, 15; R. A. Irwin, Sept. 4; J. M. Knox, Sept. 7; John T. Moore, Aug. 24; T. E. Peacock, Aug. 12; Jacob Poitevent, Aug. 27; Henry Rafalsky, Aug. 20; M. Wile, Aug. 27; Wm. Willis, Sup't. So. Ex. Co., at Memphis; S. S. Angevine, Aug. 28; John S. Paine, Oct. 27; W. A. Dejarnett, En. Ap., Aug. 22.

Other Masons who died at Grenada and Vicinity—W. C. Eskridge, Commandery No. 15, Aug. 15; W. T. Cole, P. M., Ebenezer Lodge, Senatobia, Sept. 2; Dr. P. F. Fitzgerald, P. M., Wm. Cothran Lodge, No. 361, Oct. 13; W. A. McMillian, Lexington Lodge, No. 24, Aug. 11; Thos. Powell, of Garner Lodge No. 376, Aug. 16; Butler P. Anderson, of DeSoto, No. 299, Tenn., Sept. 1; John Morrow, non-affiliate, Aug. 15; R. S. Bowles, non-affiliate, Aug. 15; H. M. Jones, of Michigan.

Number of members of Grenada Lodge, sick of the fever, 25; died, 18; members of brothers' families sick, 105; died, 42; widows surviving, 7; orphans, 47.

HOLLY SPRINGS LODGE, No. 35.—Harvey W. Walter, Past Grand Master, Sept. 19; William Clark,———; Thos. A. Falconer, Sept. 5; Howard Falconer, Sept. 20; Jas. Nutall, Sept. 5; B. P. Oliver, Sept. 5; Clem Reid, Sept. 10; Sam'l Abernathy, Sept. 6; W. O. McKinney,———; W. T. Long; Joseph Herr, Oct. 1; Chas Schneider, Sept. 10; R. W. McClain, Sept. 4; W. F. Megary,———; U. H. Ross, Sept. 9.

Other Masons, who died of fever, in Holly Springs and vicinity—E. W. Upshaw, non-affiliate, Aug. 13; Dr. W. M. Compton, of Pearl Lodge, No. 23; John Chenowith, of Tennessee, Sept. 6; R. L. Watson of late Geo. R. Freeman Lodge, Sept. 7; Wm. Crump, of late Geo. R. Freeman Lodge, Sept. 10; J. W. Brannon, of Cornersville Lodge No. 284, Sept. 13.

MISSISSIPPI No. 56.—Dr. H. C. Snodgrass, Oct. —.

WILSON, No. 72.—W. J. Adams, at Lake, Sept. 18.

EBENEZER, No. 76, SENATOBIA.—W. T. Cole, P. M., at Grenada, Sept. 2; R. L. Wait, Sept. 2.

PONTOTOC, No. 81.—W. R. Todd, Sept. —.

COAHOMA, No. 104, FRIARS POINT.—George R. Alcorn, Oct. 17.

CLAIBORNE, No. 101, ROCKY SPRINGS.—J. J. Harper, Oct. 28; Rev. D. A. J. Parker, Oct. 28.

BOVINA, No. 112.—D. A. Cameron, P M., 62 years. Oct. 13; R. W. Chappel, Oct 17; S. B. Wall, Oct. 21; Jones S. Wilkins, Oct. 15; J. B. Johnson, Oct. 5; J. W. Finch, Oct. 17; F. H. Featherston, Nov. 20.

HYLAND, No. 113—Dr. W. E. Monette, P. M., Nov. 7; John W. Hullum, Oct. 8.

UNITY, No. 117, EDWARDS.—Dr. W. B. Williamson, P. M., Sept. 27.

PATTON, No. 129, LAUDERDALE SPRINGS—A. A. Currie, at Meridian, Oct. 26; B. C. Estus, Oct. 26.

LAUDERDALE, No. 308, MERIDIAN.—W. T. McLean, P. M., Oct. 11; John Etheridge, Sept. 8.

Non-affiliates who died at Meridian and vicinity.—W. V. Raney, between

Oct —; Dr. J. H. Lyles, at Lauderdale Springs, Oct. 25; J. C. Peters, Nov. —; John Ward, Oct. 11; E. V. Early, Oct. 26; R. J. Moseley, Oct. 9.

WATER VALLEY, No. 182—John E. Becton, Sept. 30; L. M. Pennington, Oct. 2; and J. O. Hendricks, of St. Cyr Commandery, No. 6, Sept. 27.

BAY ST. LOUIS, No. 147.—John J. Saucier, Oct. 15.

JEREMIAH, No. 158.—John Fennell, at Holly Springs, ——.

AUBURN, No. 166.—Joseph Jacobs, Sept. 5; J. M. Moses, Oct. 11.

MADISON STATION, No. 192.—John A. Gould.

PASCAGOULA, No. 202.—R. G. Davis, at Scranton, Oct. 20.

GREENVILLE, No. 206.—W. A. Haycraft, P. M., Sept. 5; Edward P. Byrne, P. M., Sept. 6; Newman J. Nelson, Sept. 18; Lyman Stowell, Sept. 5; Wm. J. Manley, Sept. 18; Geo. W. Elliott, Oct. 5; John Manifold, Sept. 25.

Other Masons who died at Greenville.—Edward Steinberg, Pearl Lodge, No. 23; John H. Nelson, Tillman Page, Duncan C. Green, A. B. Trigg, M. J. Morzinski.

RISING GLORY LODGE, No. 215, OSYKA.—M. D. Bond, Oct. 4; Isaac Corf, Oct. 8; J. A. Ott, non-affiliate, Nov. 2.

TUNICA, No. 257.—Dr. J. F. Sample, at Memphis.

CORNERSVILLE, No. 284.—J. W. Brannon, Sept. 13.

LAKE, No. 298—Dr. G. C. McCallum, Wor. Master, Sept. 8; W. H. Evers, Sen. War., Sept. 9; J. H. Crossly, Treas., Sept. 26; Lee C. Scott, Sen. Dea., Sept. 7; J. N. Couch, Sept. 25; Robert Davidson, Sept. 13; Geo. F. Lowry, Sept. 22.

TUPELO, No. 318.—M. L. Leake, at Louisville, Ky., Sept. 13.

ABBEVILLE, No. 320.—S. C. Arnold, at Memphis.

DRY GROVE, No. 321.—E. Coker, Aug. 8; J. C. Stubbs, Sept. 7; W. D. Kyle, Oct. 25; J. C. Williams, Oct. 30.

BOLTON, No. 326.—A. Alexander, at Vicksburg, Oct. 2.

JOHN A. GALBREATH, No. 334, Brandywine Springs, Claiborne county—James I. Brumley, Sept. 1; J. D. Fairley, Aug. 23; T. E. Jones, Oct. 7.

WM. COTHRAN. No. 361, near Grenada.—Dr. P. F. Fitgerald, Wor. M., Oct. 13.

NEWTON, No. 372.—W. D. Maguirk, at Lake, Sept. 24.

GARNER, No. 376.—Thos. Powell, Aug. 16.

H. C. ROBINSON, No. 379, Arcola, Washington county.—Dr. A. S. Gerdine, Sept. 23: Dr. Thos. A. Gaddis, Sept. 30.

McCOMB CITY, No. 382—G. A. Boyd, Oct. 4; Dr. B. F. Gatlin, Nov. 19.

PHYSICIANS WHO DIED OF YELLOW FEVER.

List of Physicians who died of yellow fever, in Mississippi, during the epidemic of 1878:

GRENADA.—E. W. Hughes, Wm. Fielder, W. W. Hall, R. S. Ringgold, Henry Gillespie, P. F. Fitzgerald, Dr. Wolfork.

VICKSBURG.—P. F. Whitehead, D. W. Booth, L. E. Barber.

Volunteer.—Dr. Sappington, J. B. Norris, Dr. Blickfeldt, J. S. Roach, Dr. Happoldt, Dr. Blackman, Dr. Potts, Dr. Glass.

WARREN COUNTY.—W. J. Nesmith, Wm. E. Mornette, Geo. T. Birdsong, Dr. Leatch.

CANTON.—N. W. McKie, M. J. McKie, A. H. Cage.

LIVINGSTON.—J. T. Magruder.

HOLLY SPRINGS.—W. M. Compton, J. W. Fennell, F. M. Fennell, Chas. W. Bonner.

Volunteer from Austin, Texas.—T. D. Manning.

Volunteer from Albion, Ill.—J. C. Lewis.

LAKE.—G. C. McCallum, J. J. Tate.

DRY GROVE—Geo. Dickson.

McCOMB CITY—B. F. Gatlin, Frank Straun.

EDWARDS.—W. B. Williamson.

HERNANDO.—J. W. Powell.

DESOTO COUNTY.—D. L. Bridgeforth.

GREENVILLE.—J. V. Alexander.

Volunteer from Pt. Coupee, La.—W. E. Archer.

VICINITY OF GREENVILLE.—A. S. Gerdine, Thos. Gaddis, J. L. Griffin, J. H. Oden, Dr. Kirby.

PORT GIBSON.—J. G. Strowbridge, H. C. Snodgrass. Dr. Brumley.

HANDSBORO.—John C. Lyon.

A PEN PICTURE

OF THE SITUATION IN THE HEART OF THE YELLOW FEVER DISTRICT.

From the Lockport, (N. Y.) Daily Union.

JACKSON, MISS., Sept. 18th, 1878.

John Hodge Esq., Lockport, N. Y.:

MY DEAR SIR AND BRO.—I am in receipt of the Daily Union of the 10th, containing the appeal of our Grand Master to our Lodges in Mississippi for help for our afflicted communities, and the kind editorial reference to myself. I suppose that I am indebted to you for this fraternal and personal courtesy; and I suspend for a moment the busy work in which I am engaged to express to you my thanks, and to acquaint you with the sad condition of affairs in our section at this time.

The telegraphic reports give you the number of deaths daily in New Orleans, Memphis, Vicksburg, Grenada, Holly Springs, Port Gibson, Canton, Greenville, and other places where the yellow fever is prevailing, but no one but an eye-witness can realize the confusion and desolation, and destitution, consequent upon the present scourge. In New Orleans, the deaths to date number about 2,000; Memphis, now over 100 per day; Vicksburg about 500, thus far; Grenada, about 200 whites out of a population of about 2,500; at Holly Springs, one hundred of the best citizens have died within the last two weeks: at Canton, about 60 deaths to date; at Port Gibson, about 100; from Greenville, on the Mississippi river, we can learn nothing definite, as telegraphic communication has been interrupted.

The fever has also broken out at Bolton, on the Vicksburg railroad, 18 miles west of here; at Dry Grove, in the lower part of this county; at Lake Station, 45 miles east of here, and at several other places in the State.

When the fever became epidemic in New Orleans, this city and Vicksburg quarantined against New Orleans; when it appeared in Vicksburg, this place and many other points quarantined against Vicksburg; and against each successive place where the fever appeared, the health and municipal authorities of all the surrounding counties and towns issued their quarantine ordinances, and established their quarantine stations, with officers and guards to enforce them. All who could conveniently do so, fled from the infected towns on the first approach of the fever. Of course many have felt it their duty to remain, such as physicians, druggists, ministers, journalists, and some public officers, and some not occupying public positions, who were anxious to serve their afflicted fellow-citizens in every way possible. But the majority of the white population of all the places named, and many others, have gone to distant States, or are living in the country adjacent to their homes—some in log cabins and others in tents, many without sufficient food, or good water, and beyond the reach of medical attention in case of sickness. In this city, for instance, where we have been wonderfully spared, in having had only one case of fever—on the 31st of August—there are not more than four hundred white persons who remain. Of my own household, of eleven white persons, I am solitary and alone, and have been for five weeks. My family are eighty miles south of here, in a section of country supposed to be safe, but even in their vicinity, the fever has been scattered by refugees from Port Gibson. Our colored servants have remained, and they take very good care of me, and I of them. There is only one other white man on the square. In scores of houses there is not an occupant; in others, the old servants are in charge, and all, I am happy to say, have been faithful to their trust. So far as I have learned, the property of absentees has not been disturbed. It is true, our police force has been greatly increased, and constant vigilance is exercised. The public bell rings at ten o'clock at night as a signal for all to retire from the streets.

When the stampede first took place from here and other places, the colored people generally remained. Heretofore they have been comparatively exempt from the fever, but they are equally subject with the whites to the present type of the disease. When they began to realize this fact, many were quite willing to leave, but the quarantine regulations against infected points are enforced without regard to "race, color, or previous condition." Hence the five thousand or more colored people in Vicksburg, and the two thousand or more here, had to stay and take their chances. Their subsistence became a matter of immediate concern. Those who gave them employment and paid them wages had gone, and all opportunities of providing for themselves and families were abruptly closed against them. Hence the applications that have been made to the Government for rations, and its prompt and timely furnishing of the same.

As before remarked, this place has wonderfully escaped. Vicksburg is only 45 miles west and Bolton still closer on the same line of railroad. Canton is only 23 miles north, Dry Grove 18 miles south. Freight and passenger trains to and from New Orleans and Vicksburg passing through here daily and yet we have been spared. We are duly grateful, we trust, to a kind Providence, and we feel that the precautionary means used have been blessed to our preservation. In the first place the city has been thoroughly cleansed and disinfected. Carbolic acid is daily sprinkled on all the streets, and car loads of lime have been scattered about on all the highways and private premises. The invoices of carbolic acid will amount to about one hundred barrels, thus far, and we think it the best investment the city has ever made. Its now delightful odor is inhaled not only by the citizens, but by the people in the surrounding country, for miles. In addition to this, we allow no one to come here *from* or *through* any infected locality. The train from the North, for instance, has to stop at the quarantine station seven miles above here, and discharge its mail and express matter, and then go through the city at the usual rate of speed. The train from New Orleans proceeds to said quarantine station, without stopping in Jackson. We have to send our paper (THE CLARION) to that point to be mailed. The train from Vicksburg has to stop a respectable distance from town also. Freight trains from the North, and supplies for Vicksburg, are passing from one road to the other without hindrance. The Mayor and health officers have been inexorable in the enforcement of the quarantine and sanitary regulations, and every citizen is co-operating. If a stranger would appear on our streets now he would have to show "his papers" about as often as he met a citizen. All the public and private roads leading to the city are picketed, and the Mayor's permit, countersigned by the City Clerk, and stamped with the seal of the city, is now necessary in order to obtain admission within the corporate limits of Jackson; and the same document is necessary in order to get out. A colored woman was heard to remark the other day, that she thought the city was too closely *canteened*, and another expressed the hope that the *pontoon* would be raised. "Quarantine" is a new phrase in their vocabulary, to which they will in due time become accustomed.

Well, I find that I am writing you a long letter; but I cannot close without a reference to the particular work in which I am engaged in connection with our present troubles—a work that has grown upon me until my strength for further duty is almost exhausted. When the plague first attacked Grenada and then Vicksburg and Port Gibson, I called our Grand Master's attention to the propriety of affording such relief as we could from our Grand Lodge Treasury. In my suggestions, he most heartily acquiesced. Just then, on the 21st of August, I received a telegram from the Masons of New Orleans, that they had sent me two hundred dollars for the relief of their distressed brethren in Mississippi. In a dispatch to the Associated Press, this fact was stated, and also that I would be glad to receive and distribute such relief as might be sent me by the craft wheresoever dispersed. As Grand Secretary of Masons, and as Grand Treasurer of Odd Fellows, I have been kept very busy receiving dispatches and money packages, acknowledging relief and distributing it to the Masonic, I. O. O. F. and other recognized Relief Committees at the various afflicted points in our State. For this purpose, the telegraph companies gave the free use of the wires, the express companies mark every package, large and small, " D. H.," the banks charge no discount or exchange, and the railroads carry supplies, nurses and doctors all free of charge. I supposed, when contributions first began to reach me that the aggregate might amount to five thousand dollars. My entries up to to-night show nearly thirty-five thousand dollars!—and all this, (save about $2,500,) from the Masons and Odd Fellows of the Union,—contributed, not for members of the Orders only, and their families, but for all in distress. The general instruction to me is, put it where it will do the most good. As far as possible I have placed it in the hands of the Masonic and I. O. O. F Committees, but they have been zealously co-operating with the Howards, and helping all, regardless of race, color or class. I am now, for instance, buying up a car-load of beef-cattle, and a car-load of sheep for shipment to Vicksburg this week. To-day I sent a thousand dollars to Rev. Dr. C. K. Marshall, who has been laboring like a hero among the poor people of Vicksburg since the first of the fever. I telegraphed him notice that a good Samaritan like him ought to have the means of dispensing relief at discretion. He has just replied: "A thousand thanks. I will give a good report of it." In several instances, those remitting the funds have charged me to see to it that those who are made widows and orphans by the plague, and who have peculiar claims upon the fraternities for whom I am acting, shall not be forgotten. How many there may be, cannot be ascertained until the close of the epidemic; but I feel so solemnly the obligation thus imposed upon me, that I shall discharge it as judiciously as possible, to the extent of means that may be sent me. A letter from the Grand Master of the Grand Lodge of West Virginia has called my attention to the Hufflington family, who went from Wheeling to Grenada. Six out of the family of eight died within a few days. I am trying to get into communication with the surviving two, but although I have written to them, and to the relief committee, I can learn nothing. To show you how difficult it has been to distribute systematic relief to that point, I will give my own experience. My first remittances were to Dr. Hughes, a zealous Mason. After his death, I remitted to the Relief Committee; on their death, I remitted to the Howard Association, and on the very day that the only surviving member of that Association acknowledged the receipt of a package of one thousand dollars, he was himself attacked with the fever. I then noticed in a Memphis paper, that Bro. Ayer, the Noble Grand of the Odd Fellows' Lodge, was among the survivors, and so sent him five hundred dollars, but the package reached there a few hours after his death; and the express agent, Mr. Armistead, notified me that he had it in his care. In a few days, the express agent was prostrate, and the report to-day is that he may possibly recover. Of course terrible suffering, destitution and death must be the rule, when those who were willing to administer relief have themselves been hurried to the grave. God help the people of Grenada! Until several decided frosts shall come, and until the entire town shall be thoroughly disinfected, it will be unsafe for any person to breathe its atmosphere, and therefore but few will venture to their relief.

Among the brightest and best of our Masonic lights that have been extinguished by the plague, I may mention Past Grand Master A. J. Wheeler, editor of the Masonic Jewel, Memphis. He was a chairman of the Masonic Relief Committee, and had won the name of a hero in former trials to which the people of Memphis were subjected. But he went down in this. At Vicksburg, our Grand Commander, Sir W. G. Paxton, has been down for several days, and to-day word comes that his co-laborer, Past Grand Commander W. A. Fairchild, has been attacked.

In the matter of contributions, the Empire State has done nobly. In due time I will send you as complete a report as I can prepare of this terrible ordeal through which we are passing, and will place on enduring record the loving words and material aid that comes to us from every quarter. May the good people of Lockport never feel the shadow of a yellow fever plague settling down upon their fair city.

Fraternally and sincerely yours,   J. L. POWER.

The following passport to Mr. Hodge, which illustrates the method of passing quarantine, was enclosed with Col. Power's communication:

MAYOR'S OFFICE, CITY HALL,)
JACKSON, Miss., Sept. 18th, 1878.)

[L. S.] John Hodge has permission to pass the Quarantine on the Livingston road until further orders.   JOHN McGILL, Mayor.
By the Mayor:
HARRIS BARKSDALE, City Clerk.

THE MASONIC PROTEGE.

Sacramento Daily Bee, Oct. 28.

For some time past a committee of the Masonic fraternity of Sacramento, consisting of N. Greene Curtis, Past Grand Master; William M. Petrie, Past Master, and J. A. Fillmore, have been looking anxiously for the arrival of Master Walter Wilcox, a little five year-old orphan boy, whose parents died of yellow fever in New Orleans, who was put on the cars at the latter city, ticketed for Oakland, where he has a grandmother named Mrs H. Carey, who agreed to raise him if he was sent to her. The little fellow has been heard from at various times through the Eastern States, where he was received and taken in charge by the Masonic fraternity, his every want looked after, and he was seen safely on his journey.

The little fellow left New Orleans on the second of October, having a letter indorsed by the Deputy Grand Master of the Masonic fraternity of the State of Louisiana, bespeaking for him all the kindness and attention possible from the conductors and members of the fraternity wherever he should arrive, also setting forth the circumstances of the death of his parents, a copy of which appears below:

NEW ORLEANS, October 3, 1878.

The bearer of this is Walter Wilcox, who has been orphaned by the epidemic which has prevailed in this city. He is five or six years of age, and he is now enroute to San Francisco, via Louisville and Chicago. He has been forwarded from this point by the Masonic Relief Lodge, and is the holder of a through ticket, No. 356, and funds have been placed in the hands of the conductors to defray the necessary expenses which may be incurred on his account. He will be received at Chicago by parties representing the Masonic Relief Lodge in that city. I bespeak for him on the part of railroad men between New Orleans and Chicago every possible attention looking to his comfort and protection.

(Seal,)   F. CHANDLER,
General Passenger Agent, Chicago, St. Louis and New Orleans Railroad.

The conductors of the Sacramento division were requested to keep a sharp look-out for the boy and telegraph to this city when he was on the train coming West. Accordingly a dispatch was yesterday received from M. J. Goodrich, the conductor of the express train which reached here late last evening, saying the boy was on board, and the result was that when the train arrived here last evening a large delegation of Masons and the committee were at the depot to receive him.

When the cars had stopped N. Greene Curtis, Past Grand Master of the Order in California, went into the sleeping car, found the little fellow, and soon appeared on the platform carrying him in his arms. The scene was a most affecting one, and drew tears from eyes long unused to such exhibitions of weakness. The head of the little boy reclined on the shoulder of Judge Curtis, whose silvered locks and beard showed more strongly with the contrast of the wealth of golden hair worn by the boy. The little arms were lovingly entwined about the Judge's neck, and an air of confidence and perfect happiness was apparent on the child's face, as if he felt that every one of those men drawn up in line were his friends whom he could call upon for aid. About the little fellow's neck was a ribbon, to which was attached a shipping tag, on which the following was written :

CHICAGO, Oct. 22, 1878.

The bearer of this is Master Walter Wilcox, an orphan son of a brother Mason. He was orphaned by the yellow fever in New Orleans, and is en route to Oakland, Cal., to join his grandmother, Mrs. H. Carey, who will meet him at the depot. He has been forwarded by the Masonic fraternity and is the holder of through tickets, and funds have been placed in the hands of conductors for incidental expenses.

(Signed) H. HOLCOMB,
Garden City Lodge.

As soon as those present had seen the little traveler he was taken in a carriage to the residence of W. M. Petrie, on J street, between Eight and Ninth, where Mrs. Petrie took him in charge and where he still remains, full of life and happiness and evidently well satisfied with his new home.

This morning the little boy was furnished with a full outfit of underclothing and a new suit by E. Lyon and W. M. Petrie, and to-day he has been visited by a large number of ladies and gentlemen, many of whom left some token of their feelings for the little orphan.

The boy will be kept here until it can be learned who are the proper parties to send him to in San Francisco or Oakland, and will be sent forward from here with a tag from the Masonic fraternity of this city to their brethren at the Bay.

When he was taken from the cars yesterday, a lady passenger, en route to San Francisco, stated she was abundantly able to provide for the boy, and expressed a wish to be allowed to adopt him, but he will be sent to his relatives before any steps are taken regarding his future.

He also carries credentials from the Grand Lodge of Free and Accepted Masons of the State of Louisiana, signed by Edwin Marks, Deputy Grand Master of Masons of the State of Louisiana. This letter recites the circumstances of the death of the boy's parents from the yellow fever and the sending of him to California, and concludes thus:

"To a child of his tender years the journey is one fraught with difficulties, privations and dangers, and he will need the kind offices and protection of all humane people he may meet, and to all such I commend him with the hope that for the time being he may be regarded as their own."

The seal of the Grand Lodge of Louisiana is attached to the above.

He also had with him a letter from D. N. Welch, General Superintendent of the Pullman Palace Car Company, instructing all Pullman car conductors to look after the boy and give him every attention in their power.

Also, a card from Charles Hubener, stenographer of the L. and N. and Great Southern Railroad, at Louisville, Kentucky, on which was written:

"Master Walter Wilcox—May Heaven guard and speed him on his journey, is the wish of his friend, Charles Hubener."

HEROISM OF THE SOUTHERN PEOPLE IN WAR AND IN PESTILENCE.

London Standard.

The younger among us cannot perhaps remember the keen, warm sympathy with which the English of '61–65 witnessed the heroic struggle maintained by their Southern kinsmen against six-fold odds of position, resources, vantage ground simply incalculable. Even those who from sympathy with the Northern States were unfavorable to the cause of a great nation revolting against tyranny, could not but feel proud of our near kinship with the incomparable soldier—so designated by the enemies—which on fifty battle-fields, maintained, and at last, when all hope was gone, hold for six months, with 45,000 men against 150,000, a slender line of earthworks thirty miles in length; who marched out 28,000 strong, and after six days retreat in face of a countless cavalry and overwhelming artillery and infantry pressing them on all sides, surrendered at last but 8,000 bayonets and sabres. It is this people, the flower and pride of the great English race, on whom a more terrible, more merciless enemy has now fallen. There can be now no division of sympathy, as there is no passion to excite and keep up the courage needed for the occasion. Yet the men and women of the South are true to the old tradition. Her youth volunteer to serve and die in the plague-stricken cities as readily as they went forth, boys and gray haired men, to meet the threatened surprise of Petersburg—as they volunteered to charge again and again the cannon crowned hills of Gettysburg, and to enrich their blood and honor with a name of a new victory, every field around Richmond. Their sisters, and wives, mothers and daughters, are doing and suffering now as they suffered from famine, disease, incessant anxiety and alarm throughout the four years of the civil war. There may be among the various nations of Ayran family one or two who would claim that they could have furnished troops like those which followed Lee and Johnston, Stewart and Stonewall Jackson; but we doubt whether there be one race beside our own that could send forth its children in hundreds to face in towns desolated by the yellow fever the horror of a nurse's life and the eminent terror of a martyr's death.

The Howards—From Whom and Why they Took the Name.

John Howard, F. R. S., was born in 1729, at Hockbury, near London, the son of a tradesman, and inherited an independent fortune. It was not used for any low ends, not even for that higher of low ends mentioned by the poet who advised the acquisition of wealth:

> "Not for to hide it in a ditch,
> Not for a train attendant,
> But for the glorious privilege
> Of being independent."

Far from seeking independence, he used it in making himself the slave of humanity in a physical sense, but thereby secured that noble independence of a man whose moral nature lifts him above all trammels of sense and low desire. He visited most of the prisons of England, and induced the Commons to begin a system of prison reform. From that, 1784, he spent his life traveling over Europe, visiting prisons and hospitals, nursing and relieving the sick, sharing the prison fare with the worst criminals and exhibiting the most heroic devotion. He was temperate, self-denying, simple in habits, and in diet, rigidly abstemious. In 1860, after a life-time spent in a good work, he died on the field of honor at his post. His last act was one of a piece with his life. A terrible pestilence of fever had broken out on the Black Sea, and he hastened to labor for the relief of the suffering and study the causes of pestilence in the interest of coming generations, when he was stricken down at Cherson, and died away from country, home and friends, but died at his post, walking the dreary round on his beat, guarding others against death. Such a life is fitly perpetuated in the name of Howards in our cities, where hundreds and thousands of heroes, imbued with the same humanity, enlisted in the same cause, with the same bright crown, either in an honorable death nobly won, or an approving conscience.

THE HOWARDS OF THE SOUTH.

From the New Haven Journal and Courier.

"Cover with the shield of thy protection such as are exposed to danger."

The gloom is in our cites, and the darkness everywhere,
For the hot breath of the fever fills the hot September air;
From the city and the village comes the weary cry, "how long!"
Oh! bravest hearts in all the South, be tender and be strong.

Brave hearts that cheer the dying, brave hearts that watch the dead,
Brave hearts that bear up nobly the stricken fever head,
God will reward your ministry of tenderness and love,
And write your name in glory on the honor roll above.

The North will send her treasure—her silver and her gold,
You give your time, your courage and sympathy untold;
Brave hands that fight the fever with many toils and cares,
We send you love and sympathy and keep you in our prayers.

All through the days of fever and weary nights of pain,
For you our tears are falling, as falls the silent rain;
Brave, patient, tender nurses, whose hearts have proved so true,
As you remembered others, may Christ remember you.

From hospital and sick room goes up the bitter cry,
From the little helpless orphans who fold their hands and die;
God give you faith and patience to endure the fever's breath,
And shield with his protection from danger and from death.

Watch by the sick, dear Saviour, in all their pain and loss,
To all the sick and dying send the comfort of the Cross;
Take Thou this dreadful fever from our stricken land away,
And hold these patient nurses in Thy dear love to-day.

DR. MITCHELL ON YELLOW FEVER.

PUBLISHED FOR THE BENEFIT OF COUNTRY PHYSICIANS.

MEMPHIS, October 10, 1878.

Dr. N. C. Knox, Courtland, Miss:

DEAR DOCTOR—In relation to my mode of treating a yellow fever patient, I submit the following: Empty the stomach of the patient, if a meal has been taken within the four hours before before the invasion of the disease. Commence treatment by giving ten or twelve grains of calomel, followed in six hours afterward by a dose of oil; reaction is established by a mustard foot-bath; perspiration is to be kept up for twelve or sixteen hours. If the temperature ranges above one hundred and two, sponge with cold water and whisky (equal parts) from head to foot for forty minutes. This should be kept up until the temperature is brought down to one hundred and one, and if the patient is restless, keep up the sponging with tepid water and whisky after the fever has entirely subsided. This, in my opinion, is the only measure to secure quiet, rest and sleep. Give two ten-grain doses of quinine within the first twenty-four hours. As a diaphoretic and diuretic use bicarbonate of potash, chlorate of potash and sweet spirits of nitre.

For the first forty-eight hours use tincture of gelseminum. If after the subsidence of the fever there should be a rise of temperature at night give quinine freely the day following. Repeat this each day as long as the temperature rises a night.

After the first twenty-four hours of illness there must be absolute quiet of body and mind for the next five days, I do not permit any one to go in the sick-room but myself and nurse; in fact, the world closes on the patient until I turn him loose; he sees nothing, hears nothing, and remains perfectly quiet in bed.

The use of the bed-pan is essential to recovery. When the fever subsides give the blandest articles of diet, such as milk and lime-water, and rice-water, followed by chicken broth; no solid food to be taken for ten days.

I do not permit my patient to sit up in bed until the ninth or tenth day.

Give small quantities of ice and draughts of ice water or any cold teas at short intervals and in small quantities.

Irritability of stomach that comes on with the invasion of the disease will usually subside within twelve or eighteen hours, without any treatment addressed to that particular symptom. If it appears later, I use sinapisms or blistering ointment to slight vesication. Creosote, in small doses, I use sometimes with decided advantage.

After the subsidence of the fever, and during the stage of prostration, I use stimulants very cautiously, and prefer milk punch in small quantities. During the sixth, seventh and eighth days, or during convalescence, I prefer the malt liquors, such as ale and porter.

Champagne I never use. My experience is that that it is decidedly injurious to the patient. Very truly yours,

R. W. MITCHELL, M. D.

DISINFECTANTS.

(CIRCULAR OF MISSISSIPPI STATE BOARD OF HEALTH.)

The following resolution was adopted by the Board of Health:

Resolved, That while we do not advise the disuse of the popular disinfectants in purifying the exhalations from cess-pools, privies and other foul accumulations, we desire to announce the fact that observation and experience in the late terrible epidemic, do not demonstrate their efficacy and reliability in destroying the germs or cause of yellow fever.

The object of disinfection is to prevent disease. It is known that certain diseases are the result of an infective poison; and it is also known that this infective poison has a close connection with the decomposition of animal and vegetable matter.

Cleanliness, pure air, pure water, good food and proper clothing are great safeguards against infectious disease. Artificial disinfectants cannot be made to supply the place of these essential conditions of personal and public health.

Hence the first rules against infection, are:

1. That no house refuse, filth, exeremental matter or foul dirt, producing noxious gasses, should be allowed to remain about inhabited premises.
2. That all occupied dwellings should have an abundant and uninterrupted supply of pure fresh air.
3. That all water used for cooking and drinking shall come from uncontaminated sources.

Some diseases are capable of rapid increase and multiplication in filthy, foul and damp places, hence all unclean and damp places about dwellings, places of business and places of public gatherings, should be cleansed and dried.

Disinfectants are naturally divided into three classes:
1. *Those which chemically destroy or effectually restrain the contagious and infectious virus.*

The principal of these are *heat, nitrous acid gas, sulphurous acid gas, bromine, sulphate of iron, sulphate of zinc, chlorine and ozone.*

2. *Agents that arrest chemical change and check the fermentive process—antiseptics.*

They embrace most of those enumerated in the first class, the most important of which are *nitrous and sulphurous acid gases, carbolic and salicylic acids, chloride of zinc, chloralum, bromo chloralum, sulphate of iron and perhaps thymol.*

3. *Deodorants and absorbents—agents that destroy putrid exhalations and physically restrain noxious compounds.*

The principal of these agents are *dry earth, charcoal, quick lime and chlorine.*

From the long list of disinfectants the following have been selected, as it is believed they will meet all ordinary demands.

1.—FRESH STONE LIME.

Application.—To absorb moisture and putrid fluids.
How Used.—Pulverized and scattered over places to be dried. In damp-rooms, it should be placed in pans in liberal quantities. Mixed with water it is used to lime-wash walls and ceilings. It is useful when spread over heaps of fresh manure as a preservative.

2.—CHLORINATED LIME.

Application.—To destroy putrid gases and check putrefaction.
How Used.—A solution of *chlorinated lime* made by straining and decanting a gallon of water into which a pound of lime has been dissolved is a a good disinfectant fluid to use in washing the bodies of those who have died of small-pox, cholera, scarlet fever and other diseases. It is a good solution to use in the sick room for cleansing the hands of the nurse, and into which small articles can be immersed which are awaiting an opportunity to be boiled.

To generate *chlorine gas,* pour 'strong vinegar or dilute sulphuric acid upon chlorinated lime placed in pans in the room. Or, place in an earthen vessel four ounces of peroxide of manganese and pour upon it one pound of muriatic acid.

Chlorine gas is regarded as an efficient disinfectant, but it must be *efficiently applied.* It is very efficient in disinfecting confined or infected atmosphere and porous substances. Its rapid diffusion and power of penetration are great. It destroys sulphuretted hydrogen, ammonia, and all fetid organic compounds. Its odor penetrates far beyond its power as a disinfectant, hence its real degree of influence may be deceptive. It can appropriately be used in disinfecting foul cellars and rooms unoccupied.

3.—DRY EARTH.

Application.—To absorb effluvia from decaying animal and vegatable matter, and appropriately human excreta.

14

Dry Earth is nearly a complete disinfectant if used in sufficient quantities to absorb all moisture. It is especially applicable to the deodorizing of privy contents, where the basin is shallow, with a limited quantity of fluid. It should he abundantly applied.

4.--SULPHUROUS ACID GAS.

Application.—To disinfect rooms and infected clothing. Applied only in case of unoccupied rooms. To be effectual in destroying disease germs, the fumes must be so strong that they would destroy human life.

Can be used in disinfecting rooms and clothing after cases of *yellow fever, small-pox, scarlet fever, cholera and typhoid fever.*

Sulphurous acid has long been esteemed as a powerful disinfectant. It is to be preferred to *nitrous acid or chlorine gases,* because of the great irritation these latter produce upon the mucous membrane of the air passages when inhaled.

These gases should only be used under the direction of a competent physician.

How Used.—Place in an earthen vessel or iron kettle containing a small quantity of ashes, a few live coals, upon which place from one to four pounds of sulphur, in powder or fragments, according to the size of the room. One and one-half ounces is the proper quantity to each 100 cubic feet of space.

To guard against accident by fire, it is well to place the vessel on some fire-proof article or suspend it over a tub of water. As soon as the sulphur is ignited, the room having previously been rendered tight, should be closed and remain closed for twelve or twenty-four hours.

Ventilation, and painting the wood-work, white-washing and re-papering the walls, will complete the process, and fit the room for re-habitation.

5.—SULPHATE OF IRON (copperas.)

Application.—To disinfect privies, cess-pools, drains, sewers, and all vessels and places receiving the discharges of the sick. It decomposes the sulphuretted hydrogen and the ammonical compounds so poisonous and offensive in privy vaults.

How Used.—Dissolve eight or ten pounds of the copperas in eight or ten gallons of water. Add to this solution, one pint of the impure carbolic acid. The solution will be rendered more complete if hot water is used. A privy which accommodates an ordinary sized household will require at least one-eighth of this quantity twice every week during the hot summer months. Masses of filth in privies, sewers or drains should be thorougly saturated with it, at brief intervals, until all offensive odors are gone.

6.—CARBOLIC ACID.

Application.—Mixed in the proportion of one part of acid to from forty to one hundred parts of water.

How Used.—In solution in water of varying strength, according to the purposes to which it is to be applied. It is especially adapted to disinfect *sewage, foul grounds, drains, sinks, foul heaps of manure or, garbage, stables, privies,* and the air of foul places. On account of the offensive odor of the impure it would be better to use the pure acid.

7.—HEAT.

This may be applied as *dry air, or boiling water, or heated steam.*

Dry Air.—Hot dry air is the most powerful and complete disinfectant. It chemically disorganizes noxious substances, and by producing thorough desiccation, prevents putrefactive change.

It also sets in motion atmospheric currents which mechanically dissipate morbic agents. It has been proved that a temperature of 212 degrees Fahr., destroys the virus of small-pox; one of 200 degrees that of scarlet fever, and that vaccine virus being subject to a temperature of 140 degrees becomes speedily inert.

In the use of *dry heat* two things are to be observed :

1. That the heat shall be equally distributed throughout the fabric so as to secure safety in all its parts.

2. That the temperature shall not be raised so high, or continued so long, as to destroy the fabric.

A temperature of 240 degrees or 250 degrees should be employed. This degree of heat can be applied to white woolen fabrics, linen, cotton, silk and paper, for two or three hours without danger. A longer time produces discoloration. An oven cautiously heated may be used to disinfect small articles.

Such articles or infected garments as will admit of being *boiled*, should be subjected to this process for at least two hours. Until such a process is commenced, all infected articles should remain immersed in some of the disinfecting fluids already mentioned.

For infected substances and garments that may be destroyed, *heat to destruction* should always be used.

8.—FRESH AIR, PURE WATER, AND SUNLIGHT.

These are God's free gifts to all. These benign and conserving agents are always at command. They have no substitutes. Accompanied by an even temperature, they promise all that is needed in most cases in the sick room.

There are a number of other disinfectants. Among them may be mentioned, *pulverized charcoal, nitrous acid fumes, permanganate of potassium, chloralum, bromo chloralum, chloride of zinc, sulphide of zinc, sulphate of zinc, iodine and ozone.*

It is suggested that the graves of those who died of yellow fever, be covered with fresh stone lime and re-mounded.

NOTE.—Most of the foregoing has been gathered from an article on disinfectants by Dr. E. L. Griffin, President of the Wisconsin State Board of Health, and published in the Second Annual Report of that Board.

RELIEF DISBURSEMENTS.

(CONTINUED FROM PAGE 64.)

1878.

Date	Description	Voucher No.	Amount
Nov. 21.	Burial expenses of H. P.	Voucher No. 1	$ 20 00
Dec. 29.	Dr. R. M. D., Crystal Springs	2	50 00
Jan. 29.	Holly Springs Commandery, No. 3	3	300 00
Jan. 2.	Holly Springs Chapter, No. 5	4	200 00
Jan. 13.	Masonic Relief Committee, Vicksburg	5	1,000 00
Jan. 17.	Mrs. M. P., Okolona	6	30 00
Jan. 20.	Family of a Knight Templar, Jackson	7	25 00
Jan. 20.	Expenses of messengers to Tchula during epidemic	8	10 00
Jan. 20.	Misses M., Okolona	9	25 00
Jan. 20.	Mrs. L., fare to New Orleans	10	7 35
Jan. 20.	Widow and children of Bro. C., Paulding	11	100 00
Jan. 25.	Daughters of Bro. A., (who died at Vicksburg,) Atlanta, Ga.	12	100 00
Jan. 27.	Mrs. E. D., Jackson	13	25 00
Jan. 27.	Mrs. E. J. C., Jackson	14	10 00
Jan. 27.	Dr. T. G. Birchett, Vicksburg, for needy families	15	150 00
Jan. 29.	Children of Bro. J. A. R., Ashland	16	75 00
Jan. 29.	Mrs. W. and children, Edwards	17	75 00

Jan. 29.	Children of Bro. Butler P. A., Memphis..........18	150 00
Jan. 29.	Mrs. A. P. S. and children, Grenada..........19	150 00
Jan. 29.	Mrs. L. and children, Handsboro..........20	100 00
Jan. 29.	Mrs. B. and children, Scranton..........21	50 00
Jan. 30.	Mrs. R. L. W. and children, Senatobia..........22	150 00
Jan. 30.	Mrs. G. E. D., Senatobia..........23	50 00
Jan. 30.	Mrs. J. E. W. and children, Senatobia..........24	75 00
Feb. 3.	Miss A. S., Senatobia..........25	25 00
Feb. 3.	Orphan children of Bro. C. H. M., Brandon..........26	25 00
Feb. 3.	Mrs. V. H. F. and children, Yazoo County..........27	150 00
Feb. 3.	Widow and children of P. J. R., Jackson..........28	50 00
Feb. 4.	Widows and orphans, through Bro. W. D. Christmas, Eulogy Lodge, No. 248, Holmes county..........29	40 00
Feb. 4.	Protestant Orphan Asylum, Natchez..........30	1,000 00
Feb. 4.	Children of Mrs. J. J., Jackson..........31	50 00
Feb. 5.	Widow and children of Dr. St. C., Vaiden..........32	100 00
Feb. 6.	J. W. H., Edwards, for supplies to sick in Lebanon neighborhood..........33	50 00
Feb. 6.	Mrs. Laura A. J., Port Gibson..........34	60 00
Feb. 6.	Mrs. B., Port Gibson..........35	40 00
Feb. 10.	Orphan son of Bro. M. L. L., Tupelo..........36	100 00
Feb. 10.	Mrs. H. R. G., Terry..........37	50 00
Feb. 11.	J. J. W., Grenada..........38	50 00
Feb. 11.	Mrs. F. A., New Orleans..........39	50 00
Feb. 12.	Mrs. R. V., Newton..........40	50 00
Feb. 12.	Orphan child of Bro. A. S. G., West Point..........41	200 00
Feb. 14.	Children of Mrs. S., Canton..........42	50 00
Feb. 14.	Mrs. W., Chicago..........43	25 00
Feb. 15.	Mrs. W. D. McG., Lawrence Station..........44	50 00
Feb. 15.	Fred. Meyer, nurse, ticket to Memphis..........45	9 50
Feb. 15.	Catholic Orphan Asylum, Natchez..........46	200 00
Feb. 15.	Miss Ophelia H., Pontotoc, Miss..........47	160 00
Feb. 17.	Young Men's Christian Association, Greenville, for widows and orphans..........48	100 00
Feb. 17.	Family of Bro. J. W. W., Greenville..........49	100 00
Feb. 17.	Orphans of Jonesborough Lodge, No. 249..........50	75 00
Feb. 19.	Widows and Orphans of Dry Grove Lodge, No. 321..........51	100 00
Feb. 20.	Orphan son of Frank Parish, late of Chulahoma Lodge, No. 55..........52	50 00
Feb. 22.	Widows and orphans of Newton and vicinity..........53	100 00
Feb. 22.	Mrs. O. D. W., Holly Springs..........54	50 00
Feb. 22.	Mrs. E. D., Jackson..........55	10 00
Feb. 24.	Family of Bro. A. H. K., Natchez..........56	100 00
Feb. 24.	Family of Bro. J. C. Hollinsworth, Tabernacle Lodge, No. 340..........57	10 00
Feb. 27.	Needy families in Episcopal congregation, Holly Springs..........58	100 00
Feb. 27.	Water Valley Lodge, No. 82, I. O. O. F..........59	100 00
Feb. 27.	Miss M. A. P., Jackson..........60	25 00
Feb. 27.	Sir Kt. J. H. L., Canton..........61	25 00
Feb. 27.	Mrs. L. and children, Canton..........62	50 00
Feb. 27.	Canton Lodge, No. 28, widows and orphans..........63	75 00
Feb. 27.	Bros. W. H. C. and J. W. B., Canton..........64	125 00
Feb. 27.	Family of Bro. A. K., Canton..........65	100 00
Feb. 27.	Widow and children of Bro. B., Canton..........66	75 00
Feb. 27.	Mrs. L. and family, Canton..........67	50 00
Feb. 27.	Mrs. J., for caring for S's. children, Canton..........68	25 00

Feb. 27.	Widow and child of Bro. A. McC., Canton..........69		25	00
M'ch 12.	Widows and orphans of Bovina Lodge, No. 112.....70		50	00
Feb. 25.	Widows and orphans and of Bovina vicinity.........71		300	00
M'ch 1.	Widows and orphans in Methodist congregation, Holly Springs...71		150	00
M'ch 3.	Mrs. N. S., Byram...73		25	00
M'ch 3.	Mrs. G., Jackson..74		36	16
M'ch 3.	Strohecker children, Canton, transportation and cash..75		48	30
M'ch 4.	McCallum orphans, clothing, transportation and cash...76		118	96
M'ch 4.	Mrs. C., Dry Grove..76½		25	00
M'ch 4.	Gen. A. M. West, for afflicted and needy colored families in Holly Springs...............................77		100	00
M'ch 4.	Rev. E. D. Miller, Holly Springs, afflicted and needy families in his congregation...............78		100	00
M'ch 4.	Mrs. A. M. B., Brookhaven.................................79		50	00
M'ch 7.	Mrs. Mary G., Wayne county.............................80		25	00
M'ch 7.	Mrs. B., Jackson, boarding orphans...................81		25	00
M'ch 8.	Park Bank, New York, refunding duplicate remittance to Holly Springs...........................82		398	90
M'ch 8.	Mrs. B., boarding orphans..................................83		50	00
M'ch 7.	Bro. A. M. G., Canton.......................................84		25	00
M'ch 7.	Bro. A. M. G., Canton.......................................85		25	00
M'ch 7.	Mrs. J. H. N., Oxford..86		50	00
M'ch 7.	Mrs. A. McC., Oxford..87		50	00
M'ch 11.	Family of Bro. W. F. E. Jackson........................88		32	50
M'ch 12.	Mrs. S. F., Holly Springs...................................89		100	00
M'ch 14.	Mrs. Y., Jackson...90		25	00
M'ch 19.	Mrs. D., Holly Springs......................................91		50	00
M'ch 19.	Mrs. D. and children, Jefferson county...............92		50	00
M'ch 20.	Mrs. Mary R. S, Lawrence county......................93		25	00
M'ch 26.	Five orphan children of Bro. J. J. H., Claiborne Lodge, No. 110..94		150	00
April 1.	Mrs. L., Holly Springs.......................................95		50	00
April 1.	Mrs. J. C. K., Canton..96		30	00
April 1.	Mrs. R. C., Brandon..97		75	00
April 5.	Mrs. G., Wayne county......................................98		54	00
April 7.	Mrs. G., Osyka...99		10	00
April 10.	Orphan children of Bro. J. A. C., Dry Grove.......100		50	00
April 19.	St. Mary's Orphan Asylum, Natchez..................101		50	00
April 20.	Mrs. M. and family, Jefferson county.................101½		33	00
May 1.	Stockman Lodge, No. 19, I. O. O. F., Macon........102		100	00
May 15.	Miss O. R. H., at Surgical Institute, Atlanta........103		50	00
May 22.	Jas. L. Ridgely, Grand Secretary Grand Lodge U. S., surplus I. O. O. F. relief fund............104		1000	00
May 31.	Mrs. G., Jackson..105		20	00
June 4.	Family of Bro. H..106		53	90
June 17.	Mrs. L., Jackson, whose house was destroyed by fire..107		100	00
June 20.	Bro. H. E. C., Oakland......................................107½		5	00
June 27.	Bro. D., Jackson...108		50	00
June 30.	Widow and eight children of Bro. G., Smithville Lodge, No. 165, Monroe county...................109		105	00

Total...$10,902	57
Disbursements, pages 56 to 64.............................. 62,786	66
Total to July 20, 1879..$73,689	23

INDEX.

CORRECTIONS AND FINAL REPORT.

Page 24—Total from Iowa should read.................. .... $ 2,238.05
Page 26—Total from Minnesota should read.......................... 1,050.00
    ($300.00 received Sept. 10 being omitted.)
Page 33—Total from Pennsylvania should read.................... 1,482.05
    (the total from Sir Chas. E. Meyer being $475.00)
Page 37—The total Masonic receipts should read.................... 48,357.44
Page 48—The total I. O. O. F. receipts should read................ 16,160.66
Page 55—Total Miscellaneous receipts should read.................. 12,751.24
    Grand total receipts should read......................... 77,269.34
Page 211—Cancel disbursement to Holly Springs Commandery
    $300.00, and Holly Springs Chapter, $200.00, and
    deduct same from total on page 213. These amounts
    being included in disbursements on page 57, and
    voucher inadvertently filed with the series on page
    211.

Extract from Final Report to Masonic Grand Lodge, February 4, 1880:

While on the subject of finance, I am happy to be able to submit to Grand Lodge a final report on the Relief Work, which has occupied so much of my time since August, 1878. The total receipts may thus be stated:

From Masonic sources.. $ 48,357.44
From Odd Fellows.. 16,160.66
Miscellaneous... 12,751.24

Total... $ 77,269.34
When the Grand Lodge met last January, I had disbursed, as
    per vouchers then submitted, the sum of........................... 62,786.51
From that date to June 30, 1879, voucher No. 1, to 109, as per
    detailed statement in Epidemic Report, pages 211 to 213...... 10,202.57
From July 1st, 1879, to January 29, 1880, vouchers 110 to 168   4,409.10

Total... $ 77,398.18

The story of this relief work was told at last Grand Communication, and has been detailed in a volume of 216 pages, two thousand copies of which have been distributed to the generous contributors in every State and Territory and to several foreign countries.

From every quarter, I have received gratifying, and often extravagant expressions of satisfaction, of the exhibit which has thus been made of the large sums of money which poured in upon us in the time of pestilence and death. I trust that I am truly grateful for the opportunity afforded me of dispensing the benefactions of the humane and generous everywhere, to our stricken and impoverished communities; and if, in the discharge of the duties and responsibilities which the emergency seemed to warrant me in assuming, I have acquitted myself so as to merit the approval of you, brethren, who best know me, it will be ample reward for the heavy labors and anxious cares attending the disbursement of so large a sum, with unlimited discretion as to how and to whom it should be distributed. In reviewing my work, I would not recall a single disbursement, and my only regret is that I could not give larger amounts in many instances. While I rejoice that this work has been brought to a close, it will be a matter of regret that I cannot respond to the occasional calls for assistance that I am sure will be made upon me.

The Committee to whom my books and correspondence have been referred will make their report during the session, and I flatter myself that they will find every disbursement sustained by a satisfactory voucher.

The disbursements of the past summer include $500.00 to Memphis, $400.00 to Concordia, $100.00 to General Hood's children, and $100.00 toward sending some orphan children to relatives in England, their father and mother having died of yellow fever at Concordia. It has been my privilege to send several children, orphaned by the plague, to their friends in other States. Two that I sent to Ohio were received and cared for in Chicago, and forwarded to their present home at Lima, by our Grand Representative, Past Grand Master DeWitt C. Creiger; and two that I sent to Charleston were tenderly cared for on the route, and at Atlanta, by friends to whom I had telegraphed. Mr. Clarke, General Manager of the Chicago, St. Louis and New Orleans Railroad, very kindly furnished free transportation for these children—two of them to Grand Junction, and two to Chicago. The Memphis and Charleston Railroad also made a generous reduction. Indeed all the Railroads, and the Express Company, honored the many demands which I made upon them in prosecuting the work of relief. It has been said that railroad corporations "have no souls;" but after many calls made upon railroad managers, during many years, in behalf of those destitute of means to travel, I can say that not one has been denied, and that, as a rule, railroad men have much of the "milk of human kindness" in their composition.

I had set apart, and invested in a Mississippi 8 per cent. bond, the sum of $500.00 toward the support of the infant daughter of Bro. M. D. Bond, the Senior Warden of Rising Glory Lodge, No. 215, the father and mother having died when the child was only four days old. When I visited Osyka on relief business, the child was six weeks old. I told the grandmother that the Masons and Odd Fellows of Mississippi would adopt the child; and Bro. John H. McKenzie, then Grand Master of Odd Fellows, who accompanied me on my visit, heartily ratified the proposition. I left $100.00 for the immediate care of the child, intending to send the interest of the $500.00 to be invested, semi-annually to its grandmother. During the epidemic I had received large contributions through Bro. John D. Caldwell, Grand Secretary of Ohio, and packages amounting to about $600.00 had marked on them instructions to this effect: "to be invested for some child or children orphaned by the plague." I concluded to concentrate these special contributions on this special object. I asked for and was granted the privilege of naming the child, and named it Mary Caldwell, after the wife of Grand Master Cunningham, of Ohio, and after the worthy Grand Secretary of that jurisdiction, both of whom expressed great satisfaction, and stated that the Grand Lodge of Ohio would see to it that Mary Caldwell should be provided for in the years to come. But this child, on whom so many had centered a substantial interest, died on the 25th of May last, and the expenses attending its sickness and burial constitute one of my vouchers. Of many affecting incidents in the relief work, this one touched me most, and although not permitted to carry out our good intentions, we have the satisfaction of knowing that the object thereof is secure forever against all want and care, and sorrow and sin. So mote it be!

REPORT OF COMMITTEE ON THE RELIEF WORK.

IN GRAND LODGE, February 5, 1880.

To the M∴ W∴ Grand Lodge of Mississippi :

The Special Committee appointed at the Sixty-first Annual Communication, to which was referred the R∴ W∴ Grand Secretary's "Report of Relief Work during the Epidemic of 1878," having completed the examination begun twelve months ago, beg leave to report that the receipts were as follows, to-wit:

Masonic sources	$ 48,357.44
Odd Fellows	16,160.66
Miscellaneous	12,751.24
Total from all sources	$ 77,269.34
That the total disbursements amount to the sum of	77,398.18
Showing an excess of disbursements over receipts of	$ 128.84

This excess of disbursements resulted from the Grand Secretary having charged himself twice with certain receipts aggregating that amount.

The Committee, acting upon the expressed wish of the Grand Secretary, and in view of the great responsibility devolving upon them, have made their examination thorough and critical, and are prepared to report that the extraordinary trust suddenly imposed upon R∴ W∴ Grand Secretary Power, as the almoner of the bounties of the generous and charitable of all classes, has been wisely and faithfully discharged, and that his report is supported by proper vouchers for every dollar disbursed.

The Committee therefore recommend:

1st. That said Report be approved and adopted, and that the same, together with the accompanying vouchers, be filed among the archives of this Grand Lodge.

2d. That R∴ W∴ Grand Secretary J. L. Power be reimbursed out of Grand Lodge funds for the sum shown by this report to have been disbursed by him, in excess of receipts, to-wit: the sum of one hundred and twenty-eight dollars and eighty-four cents.

Respectfully submitted,

ROBERT C. PATTY,
C. L. LINCOLN,
A. M. HICKS,
B. T. KIMBROUGH,
J. S. JONES,
Committee.

The report of Committee was adopted by Grand Lodge, by a rising vote; and on motion of Past Senior Grand Warden H. M. Street, the public press generally was requested to publish the same.

Extract from Report, as Grand Treasurer, to the Grand Lodge of Odd Fellows, July, 1879:

I beg leave, also, to submit a statement of my work, as your Grand Treasurer in the receipt and distribution of relief during the epidemic of last summer and fall.' As Grand Secretary of the Masonic Fraternity, I submitted to the Grand Lodge in January last, a detailed report of the Relief Work, including all funds, from all sources, that came into my hands As my labors were not yet completed, my vouchers were referred to a committee, who will hereafter give their report to that Grand Body and to the public. In the meantime, and within the next ten days, I will be able to send to all the generous contributors a detailed report of the disbursement of all funds entrusted to me; and I also submit to this Grand Lodge, a full exhibit of receipts and disbursements on account of yellow fever relief, and the distress resulting from the epidemic.

* * * * * * * * *

On the 15th of May last, I estimated that of the general fund then on hand the proportion contributed by Odd Fellows, amounted to about $1,000, and this amount, after consultation with Grand Master, I forwarded to R. W. James L. Ridgely, Grand Secretary Grand Lodge United States, to be invested as a surplus fund for relief, as the authorities of the Grand Lodge may find it necessary hereafter to dispense it.

Early in September, the Grand Master and Grand Patriarch of this jurisdiction received official inquiries from the Grand Sire of the Grand Lodge of the United States, as to whether this Grand Lodge had complied with the law of the Supreme Grand Lodge, enacted in 1875, which among other things, provides that "when any jurisdiction shall suffer under some great calamity, and a relief committee shall be duly authorized to receive and disburse money to the sufferers, it shall be the duty of the M. W. Grand Master of such jurisdiction to see that the Treasurer of such fund shall execute and deliver to him a bond to secure the money placed, or to be placed, in his hands, for the purposes of relief;" also, that one of the conditions of said bond shall be, that should there be any surplus left in his hands, after the purposes for which such fund is contributed have been completed and performed, then the same obligor shall pay the same to the Grand Treasurer of the Grand Lodge of the United States upon the order of the M. W. Grand Sire."

Our Grand Master, and Grand Patriarch, replied substantially, that although the above law had not been literally complied with, it was complied with in spirit, and that the Grand Treasurer was ready to receive and disburse all funds that might be sent him. There was no time then for making bonds. Most of our people, who would be considered as good bondsmen, were not then in the yellow fever district, and even were it convenient to make any required bond, I would not have executed it under the circumstances. It must be a matter of sacred trust, or not at all; and how that trust has been discharged, an examination of the work will fully show. Recognizing the propriety and wisdom of the law of the Grand Lodge of the United States, on the subject, I closed the account so far as I. O. O. F. funds were concerned, by sending the surplus to Bro. Ridgely, and his receipt, dated May 22d, is herewith filed.

To the credit of the generous contributors of our noble Order, be it said, whether the relief came from Grand Lodges, Subordinate Lodges, or individual brethren, I was not restricted in the disbursement of funds to afflicted Odd Fellows, or their families, but the general wish expressed was, that I would use the money where it would do the most good in relieving the sick and needy.

I respectfully suggest that the Grand Lodge adopt a suitable expression of gratitude to the generous contributors, and that our Grand Representatives be requested to present the same at the next session of the Grand Lodge of the United States.

Fraternally submitted,

J. L. POWER, Grand Treasurer.

Extract from Proceedings of Supreme Grand Lodge of Odd Fellows, pages 111, 112, 113, of 1879:

To the R. W. Sovereign Grand Lodge of the Independent Order Odd Fellows:

In accordance with instructions from the R. W. Grand Lodge of Mississippi, we hereby submit the report of a special committee appointed at the last session of that jurisdiction, to take into consideration the report of the R. W. Grand Treasurer, as relates to the yellow fever fund, which we tender as a tribute of our appreciation for the liberal responses to our calls for help in our time of trouble and tribulation, to our brothers of other jurisdictions, for their prompt and liberal responses to the call of our Grand Master.

Respectfully,

A. B. WAGNER, JOHN H. McKENZIE,

Grand Representatives of Mississippi.

REPORT OF THE SPECIAL COMMITTEE APPOINTED TO PASS UPON THAT PORTION OF THE GRAND TREASURER'S REPORT AS RELATES TO THE YELLOW FEVER FUND.

The Special Committee appointed to pass upon that portion of the R. W. Grand Treasurer's report as relates to the "Yellow Fever Fund," submitted the following report, which was adopted by a rising vote:

To the R. W. Grand Lodge I. O. O. F. of Mississippi:

Your Special Committee, to whom was referred that portion of the Grand Treasurer's report which relates to his management of the funds placed in his hands for the relief of the yellow fever sufferers during the epidemic of 1878, respectfully report: That we find said report so full and ample and at the same time so satisfactory that we cordially recommend its entire approval by the Grand Lodge. We further recommend the adoption of the following resolutions:

"The Grand Lodge of Mississippi, fully appreciating the eminent services rendered in the cause of suffering humanity by our M. W. Grand Master, JOHN H. McKENZIE, and R. W. Grand Treasurer, J. L. POWER, during the late terrible epidemic, and profoundly conscious that, in the administration of their sacred trust, they have not only won the highest honors that can be accorded to true manhood, but that their conduct has reflected credit upon Odd Fellowship itself. We desire to give expression to the deep and lasting affection and regard entertained by the brothers of this jurisdiction for these distinguished officers.

"We recognize the fact that they have fairly won the 'Golden spurs of Knighthood,' and that henceforth they must march in the van of our great brotherhood—leaders, indeed, in thought and action.

"Upon our records should be engraven, in letters of gold, a tribute to their unfaltering courage, tireless energy, and distinguished devotion to duty, that those who come after them may know how Odd Fellowship has stood the test of danger and of trial.

"And when the history of the epidemic of 1878 comes to be written, the faithful chronicler of the events of those troublous days will attest their devotion to truth and justice by dedicating a page in that sacred volume in commemoration of the noble work performed by JOHN H. McKENZIE and J. L. POWER; therefore be it

Resolved, That this Grand Lodge further evidences its admiration and love for our worthy brothers by adopting by a rising vote a resolution of thanks for the able and efficient manner in which they have discharged the other high and onerous duties of their respective stations.

"*Resolved,* That this Grand Lodge desires to make public and fitting acknowledgment of their heartfelt gratitude to our brothers of other jurisdictions for their prompt, cordial and liberal response to the call of our Grand Master for assistance in our days of trial and hour of need.

"The plague of 1878, coming upon our people with startling suddenness and unprecedented severity, our own resources for relief were soon exhausted, and but for the timely and liberal aid of our brothers in more favored localities, the distress and suffering in our own jurisdiction must have been vastly greater than they were.

"We would like our brothers to know and feel that we are not ungrateful for their kindness nor unmindful of the charitable and Christian spirit in which their aid was tendered.

"May their generous acts of practical charity, and active benevolence return to them as blessings, as angels of mercy and consolation, in any trial through which they may be called to pass, and ever plead for them before the throne of our Father and our God.

"*Resolved,* That our Representatives to the Grand Lodge, I. O. O. F., take proper steps to communicate to our brothers the gratitude and feelings of this Grand Lodge, either by communicating a copy of the foregoing resolutions or otherwise, as they may deem best."

(Ssgned)   JOSEPH HIRSH, D. N. BARROWS,
H. S. VAN EATON.

A true copy:
J. T. McCOWN, *Grand Secretary.*

APPRECIATIVE EXPRESSIONS FROM BRETHREN.

MILWAUKIE, WISCONSIN, August 11, 1879.

J. L. Power, Grand Secretary—

DEAR BRO.: Your "Report of the Epidemic of 1878" was received today. As you say, it is "a practical demonstration of the generosity and gratitude of the American people." I regret my inability to place it before all our people, for I feel it would annul the power of politicians to keep alive the damnable feelings of animosity which, I must acknowledge, pervades some portions of the Northern States. I have sometimes thought that the hand of an all-wise Providence was visible in the sufferings of your people, and the noble acts of our Northern friends in trying to relieve their sufferings and tide them through the terrible hurricane of death. It has no doubt brought the hearts of the suffering ones, and those who tried to relieve them, closer together; and the sentiment that we are brothers and citizens of one common country is gaining ground, and the efforts of political "hacks," to stir up strife and animosity are becoming more and more futile every hour.

My sentiments are: "Damned be he who first cries war!"

With love and respect, yours fraternally,

JOHN W. WOODHULL.

CINCINNATI, December 23, 1879.

* * * I am also obliged for the very interesting pamphlet, "The

Epidemic of 1878 in Mississippi." You have done your work well, and such a minute report, so unusual in such cases, and yet *always wanted,* does great credit to you personally, and is most honorable in your Grand Lodge. I do most sincerely trust that the time is remote when there shall be an occasion for preparing another such report. When it does come, it is to be hoped that it may be done by some one who will imitate your most excellent work. * * Truly and courteously yours,

E. T. CARSON.

OXFORD, Miss., October 16, 1879.

* * * Please accept my cordial thanks for the copy of your "Report of the Epidemic of 1878." I shall treasure it as a faithful record of the trying, the crucial ordeal to which our people were subjected ; of the noble courage and self-sacrifice with which it was borne ; of the work of heroic benevolence which you and some others performed ; of the useful and splendid lives that closed during those dark, historic days of the awful pestilence. * * * Yours very truly,

R. W. JONES.

CHICAGO, August 19, 1879.

* * * Please accept my thanks for this renewed evidence of your good will. I have read the Report, and while I tender you my sincere congratulations for your splendid and heroic work in behalf of suffering humanity, and commend the high sense of honor displayed in your labors and in framing your report, I do pray God that you may never again be called upon to undergo and suffer thus.

With assurances of profound regard, I am
Fraternally yours,
DeWITT C. CREIGER.

NATCHEZ, August 28, 1879.

* * * Many thanks for your very valuable work on the great Epidemic. It is a thrilling and wonderful record of human suffering, human sympathy, and of your own unparalleled energy and self-sacrificing labors. I can scarcely read it for my tears, but the more I read it the better I love our country and its noble charities. I shall have the volume bound in the highest style of art. Truly yours, J. F. H. CLAIBORNE.

CLINTON, Miss., September 9, 1879.

* * * Accept my thanks for the volume. I shall place it in the library of the College, that future generations of students may learn of the noble deeds and manly qualities displayed by our people during the fearful epidemic of 1878. Your truly, W. S. WEBB.

VICKSBURG, Miss., September 3, 1879.

COL. POWER—ESTEEMED FRIEND : I have read your interesting yellow fever financial report from end to end with profound satisfaction. You have built a lasting monument to hand down to the future. Your toil and painstaking, and ceaseless labor for the vast multitude that sweeps ro und you as its centre—forcibly illustrated in your report—will fix your n ame indelibly upon the marvelous history of this epoch. And having done so much, and done it so well, before you have felt the weariness of years, what may we not hope for coming years from the same zeal and philanthropy? May Heaven reward you—men cannot. I send you many thanks for the valuable present.

Ever and very truly yours,   C. K. MARSHALL.

———

JACKSONVILLE, FLA., August 13, 1879.

* * * Three copies of your Epidemic Report received. Thanks. It manifests a huge work in behalf of suffering humanity, for which you are entitled to great credit.   Fraternally,   D. C. DAWKINS,
Grand Secretary.

www.ingramcontent.com/pod-product-compliance
Lightning Source LLC
Chambersburg PA
CBHW030118030726
47498CB00007B/2449